THE BOOK OF BONES

THE BOOK OF BONES

NICK THACKER

JERONIMO

The apu rose high above the others, a mountain among mountains. Snow-capped this time of year and too high for trees to survive, the peak was a desolate, bare crag, wrapped in rock and nothingness. It gave the impression of an easy ascent, a simple conquest.

But Jeronimo Valera knew better. The forty-five-year-old man may have been more wiry, thin, and less agile than he'd been in his younger years, but with age came wisdom. He had heard the legends of this peak and its inhabitants since he was a boy, and while many of his men seemed to toss those myths aside as fairy tales, he knew the danger in letting his guard down.

The peak would be their final destination. It would allow them to see across the vast region of mountainous peaks and wide valleys, and it would allow them to set up a camp on the highest ground in sight.

First, though, they would need to cross the dangerous valley that lay in front of the massive mountain they were aiming toward. The danger didn't lie in the known factors — treacherous terrain, predatory jungle life, and a fast-moving river crossing. Instead, the danger

Jeronimo sensed was in the *unknown.* The fear he felt arose from what he couldn't see, yet knew lay waiting for their arrival.

The peak loomed above, beckoning. But the actual *goal* of their expedition was something that he sensed would be waiting for them somewhere between their location on the opposite side of the valley and on the steep slopes of the mountain. They hoped to use the peak as their lookout, but their true desire was to find what they were looking for, and he suspected that they would find it in the dense, dark jungle down below.

He took a breath, then let it out, not seeing condensation but feeling the sharpness of the cooling air. At this elevation and time of year they would be in danger of getting stranded in a snowstorm, but he knew they were running out of time.

His men — five Jesuit priests from his order, and five more Inca warriors he had hired for the three-month journey — stopped behind him, and he knew they were all wondering the same thing: *would he make them go through the valley?*

He would, and he sensed that they knew it. He had told them of the treachery of the expedition, of the danger and possibility that none of them would return, but he'd also explained to them the importance of it. The mission was simple: descend into the depths of the Chachapoyas, into the area that had never been explored, and find the wak'a — the 'sacred place.' From what Jeronimo had read, he believed that they would discover the wak'a 'beneath the great apu on the final zeq'e.'

There were 41 zeq'e, or lines, that pointed to the great round stone tablet in Cuzco, the Inca capital, and each of the lines radiated outward from the stone in different directions, each forming a 'sight-line' back to the homeland. According to his translations, Jeronimo assumed that on one of those invisible sight lines was where they would find the hidden Temple of Wiraqoca Pacayacaciq, or Vira-cocha, the creator and father of the Inca.

The god had come out of the sea to teach the scattered bands of Inca refined ways, agriculture, and science.

He had created *civilization*.

Then Viracocha had disappeared, by walking out into the ocean and returning west, promising that one day his followers would return.

The temple Jeronimo was looking for was all but a myth, but he had more of a reason to find it than simply hunting for long-lost sacred sites.

He turned to the man who'd stepped up next to him, Luis de Acosta, and waited for him to meet Jeronimo's eyes.

"It is down there, my friend," Jeronimo said.

Luis nodded, but didn't speak.

"We are within a day of the base of the apu, where we will find the temple."

"We hope."

"Have faith, brother," Jeronimo said. "It is there, just as the prophecy states. We will find it, and we will find him."

Jeronimo saw a quiver of hesitation in his friend's eye. He didn't fault him or his men for doubting — his brother, Blas Valera, had supposedly died in Spain four years earlier. His brother, the son of a Spanish conquistador and a Chachapoyas woman, had long been chastised for his mestizo blood, yet held in high regard by some Spanish courts for his deep knowledge of Quechuan. He had worked hard to marry the interests of the Inca with those of the Spanish, but that had ultimately ended in failure and his death.

But Jeronimo had heard rumors. Stirrings, really. There were whispers that a light-skinned Inca had returned from Spain and immediately headed to the Chachapoyas region, where he had disappeared.

Rumors spread, and Jeronimo discovered that there were a few people who believed the man had fled to the hidden temple to join the ancient race of giants created by Viracocha just before he had created the human race. It was a tall-tale, to be sure, but Jeronimo didn't care about any of that.

He wanted to find his brother.

JERONIMO

JERONIMO TOOK a deep breath and tried to relax. *We are here,* he told himself. *We will find him.*

He felt a conflict of emotions. He was excited to find his brother, but he also knew there was a reason no one had ventured into this area before. Or, if they had, they had never returned.

He thought about his brother, Blas Valera. A member of the Jesuit order, like him, Blas had always been a rash, risk-taking leader. He was a man of strong moral principle, and it had caused him no shortage of grief over the course of his life.

Blas had been born to a Spaniard father and a Chachapoyas mother, which had allowed the boy to gain an insight few people in the world had: he understood the Quechuan language of his mother's people as well as the rich history of his father's. He respected both and used it to his advantage. Blas had become one of the crown's trusted advisors, helping translate Quechuan manuscripts and interpreting some of the more challenging Inca texts.

He had then turned his eyes on religion, and that was where he had gotten himself into trouble. Blas felt that the religion of the Inca was as deep and profound as Catholicism, and that the language of his mother's people was so nuanced and complex that it held up to Latin.

The Spanish, of course, took issue with this theory, and Blas had eventually ended up in prison in Cadiz, where he lived out his final days.

But Jeronimo Valera did not believe that his strong-willed brother had allowed himself to be defeated so easily. He had spent what little he had to put together this expedition, hoping that it would prove fruitful.

Finding anything in the valley would be cause for celebration — his people had lived in this region for centuries, and the legends and stories of what existed in this part of the jungle had evolved into fantastic stories of treasure and gold. Jeronimo did not believe many of the stories, but he did believe one thing: *something* was out here, and it had never been found.

Had his own brother set out on this very expedition four years ago? Had Padre Blas Valera found the legends itself?

And if he had, had it consumed him?

Jeronimo shook off the weariness of the unknown shifting through his mind and stepped forward, now eager to continue his journey. His men and the Inca warriors behind him followed suit.

"We are close, Jeronimo," Luis said a few minutes later. "The air is different here."

Jeronimo smiled. His Jesuit brother had a keen sense of the jungle, which was a part of why he wanted him along for this journey. Luis had grown up in a small village that had nearly been destroyed when the Inca conquerors came to annex it, then again by the Spanish many years later. As such, Luis had learned to make the jungle his home, to move through the trees and stay off the well-trod paths. Before he had joined the Jesuits, he had been revered in his village as a great tracker and hunter.

Jeronimo hoped the man's experience would help on this journey, as well.

"How far?" Jeronimo asked.

"A day to the apu, like you said," Luis said. "But..." his voice trailed off.

"But we do not know what might be waiting for us down there."

Luis nodded gravely.

"We are no threat to them," he said. "We are simply looking for answers."

"Many have died in the quest for answers," Luis said. "But you are correct. It does no good to worry. Our Lord will protect us."

"Our Lord may not be able to." Jeronimo had not intended to blaspheme, but his fear had caused him to revert to his human instincts. This land was not theirs, and it had never been. To invoke the Lord's help, he feared, was to invoke a power that might be met with an opposite — and far more sinister — power.

There was a small rise in a clearing in front of him and walked along in silence until he had crested it. At that moment he noticed the volume of the rainforest drop.

From this spot he could see in every direction, though every direction looked remarkably similar. Dense brown and green jungle sat like a wall on all sides, a sentinel that silently guarded this clearing. The jungle itself had been silenced, the animals and insects seeming to have sensed their arrival.

He held his breath as he waited for the sounds to return. This phenomenon had been common as they had moved through the densely forested areas. The birds and animals knew that outsiders had arrived, and their silence served as a warning to others.

Luis and a few of the Inca joined him on the rise, each looking in a different direction.

After a few more seconds, Luis frowned and turned to Jeronimo.

"It is quiet," he said. "The sound of the jungle should have returned by now."

Jeronimo felt the hair on the back of his neck rise as his senses tuned to the forest. He saw nothing out of the ordinary, no movement behind the tree line, no activity or rustling of birds.

"What does it mean?" he asked.

"It means there is something else here."

One warrior nodded slowly, apparently able to understand enough of the Spanish to agree with Luis' assessment.

"We keep moving," Jeronimo said. "There is nothing for us here, and to stop could be more dangerous than to continue."

Again, the Inca man nodded. Jeronimo hoped that it meant he agreed with his assessment.

They trekked on for another three hours, the humidity and heat of the afternoon sun finally beating out the cooler weather, and Jeronimo began to sweat. He wiped his brow with the back of his hand, then stopped.

"Wait," he said, softly.

"You see something?" Luis asked.

"I think. I believe we are near a zeq'e post." He walked over to a section of trees that had grown together, their canopies now condensed into one great mass of leaves and vines. Their bases were spread apart, dotting the earth with twenty thin trunks. Jeronimo reached a section where two of the trunks were spaced about ten feet apart and their vines and branches reached all the way to the ground.

The effect was a natural wall, an impenetrable thicket of jungle growth. He reached a hand into the thick, twisted growth and grabbed a handful of vines. He yanked back, and the vines ripped apart, breaking their seal with one another and pulling down a mess of leaves and sticks.

When he had finished, Luis gasped from behind him.

Where there previously had been a wall of tree branches and vines, there was now a wall of stone. *Hand-carved* stone, built of interlocking bricks.

"We are here," Jeronimo whispered. "We have found it."

He couldn't read the glyphs on the stone, but he didn't need to. To find a zeq'e post this far in the jungle meant only one thing: they had found a lost temple.

JERONIMO

"MOVE SWIFTLY," Jeronimo said. "And quietly. We do not know what is out here."

"There is nothing here," one of the Jesuit men said from somewhere behind Jeronimo.

"Perhaps you are correct," he replied, "but we will take no unnecessary chances. If my brother is here, he may have been captured. We must not attract attention."

As he said the words, Jeronimo examined their surroundings. In front of him, three massive huicungo trees grew together into a tall collection of huge fronds, their foot-long, spindly green leaves dancing with one another as they moved in the wind. Behind the huicungo in that area Jeronimo could see another, smaller rock totem, this one likely a sacrificial stone from a long-lost civilization or a simple relic of a larger structure.

The rest of the area was just as densely packed. A Cashapana, the 'tree with many legs' as he knew it, loomed over the group, its many thin trunks winding around one another as they rose from the ground and combined into a larger form. It was larger than any he'd ever seen, and the 'legs' were thicker and more numerous, creating an impenetrable wall on that side of the clearing.

He took a few steps forward, toward the huicungo and the stone rectangle just beyond. As he grew closer, Jeronimo realized that the stone structure sat right at the end of a path, one that wound around a few more trees and disappeared out of sight.

He felt his heart quicken. *We are close,* he thought, echoing Luis' words. *We are very close.*

He could hear his brother's voice in his mind. They laughed together over two cups of Madeira shared between them. He missed his brother, but he truly had more important — and more pressing — reasons for finding him.

His brother had rushed off to Spain before Jeronimo could confront him about his expeditions with the Spanish. As a man versed and fluent in both Spanish and Quechuan, Blas Valera was a popular addition to many of the Spanish conquests in and around their homeland, and as such had traveled more than anyone else Jeronimo knew.

Further, Blas had written to Jeronimo that he needed to 'confront the King about the death of our Inca leader, Atahualpa.' Blas believed that Francisco Pizarro had executed the Inca king for reasons besides attaining gold and fortune.

He would not explain further in the letter, for fear of sabotage and espionage, but Blas hinted to Jeronimo that he believed the Spanish — and their largest benefactors, the Catholics — wanted something *else.* They had enough gold and treasure, and they would have an endless supply for the rest of all their lives.

What they wanted instead, Jeronimo had inferred, was something of far greater value.

Something much more powerful.

But after Blas had left for Spain, Jeronimo had read that his beloved brother had been executed in Cadiz. He did not want to believe the letters, but after waiting three years for his return, he began to think his brother may have been bested.

Then he began to hear rumors. A Jesuit priest had been found walking through the region of the Chachapoyas, one said. Another hinted that a light-skinned group of men and women had appeared in a village and traded a Catholic crucifix for supplies and food.

Finally, a letter had reached Jeronimo that a man had stumbled into the very same village only a few months later, claiming to be looking for healing from a terrible injury: he was missing a hand, his wrist nothing but a bloody stump.

Jeronimo had been quietly putting together a plan, and they had set out three months ago on the most perilous journey of his life. Unsure of what they might encounter here, he had opted for a split group of Jesuits and warriors, hoping it might prepare them for anything from indigenous peoples that needed conversion or tribal hunters that wished them harm.

Now they were here, wherever *here* was, and he felt all the fear and anxiety come rushing back in. This place may not be friendly, and even if it were, his brother may not be here at all.

"Jeronimo," Luis said, calling his attention to the path he'd seen earlier. "What do you make of this?"

Jeronimo looked over. Luis was pointing at a line of stones that had been set into the side of the path, as if forming a barrier between the path and the forest beyond it. Another line of stones sat on the other side of the path. It was the strangest sort of path Jeronimo had ever seen. The stones were huge, nearly boulders, and it puzzled Jeronimo about how or why they would be necessary here. It would have taken at least two men to lift each one and place it down.

"Why would they place stones near a path?" He asked. "What purpose can it serve?"

"It seems a waste," Luis said. "What people would construct a stone-lined path, especially stones of this size?"

Jeronimo had no answer, but he noticed that the warriors were in a crouch, watching the surrounding trees. Their arrows were nocked, their eyes steady and their breathing controlled.

"Are we to be attacked?" He asked.

"They are simply staying alert," another Jesuit man whispered. "For this is an unknown construction style to them."

"I understand," Jeronimo said. "But let us continue onward."

The men followed behind, and while Jeronimo pressed forward down the path, he wished two of the Inca men would have taken the lead. Still, he knew his warriors were some of the best money could buy, and they would do everything in their power to protect their group.

The warriors were trained from a young age to hunt, trap, and fight. They could move as swiftly and silently as any jungle beast, and Jeronimo felt confident that should they come across anyone wanting to do them harm, the warriors would be able to fend them off. Furthermore, his Jesuit brothers had been hand-picked for their hardiness. Many of them had grown up in dangerous lands, fought with or against the Spanish, and had earned their edge.

And yet Jeronimo couldn't help but feel the weight of the unknown pressing down on him. The forest seemed alive here, watching them. It seemed to have secrets of its own, and the farther they marched into it, the heavier those secrets seemed to become.

He needed to get out of his own head, but he was trying to prepare himself for meeting his brother once again. Eleven years his elder, Blas had always been a bit of an enigma to Jeronimo. He was a good older brother, but their age difference meant that Blas was more of an estranged uncle, returning from his adventures with hardly more than stories and tall tales.

Was his brother here? Was his brother one of the secrets kept by the forest?

After another two hours of walking, Jeronimo noticed that the path had become wider, the ground made up of small crushed pebbles. It was unlike anything he had ever seen, and the sheer audacity of its creation took him by surprise.

He was so fascinated with the strange path that he almost didn't notice where it led. He stepped out into a clearing once again, this one far larger than the one from which they had discovered the path in the first place. There were more stone structures, but they too were built in a style that he had never seen. The buildings were utilitarian, plain. There were stele standing tall in a wide open area in front of him, but they too were bare of advanced designs. A wide building sat behind the stele, and long steps stretched across the front of it. If it was a temple, it was the most empty-looking, plain temple he had ever seen.

Strangest of all, the structures were far larger than the temples and buildings he had seen the Inca create. These buildings seemed to be almost twice the height of normal stone houses, and the doorways leading into them were taller and wider than he would have expected.

The temple, if it was one, had a rounded front, the sides bending in toward the main open space while the entrance was pushed backward into the forest a bit, giving the impression that the building was a small chunk that had been cut from a huge circle and placed here.

It, too, was larger than any building needed to be. Where the Inca, and even the Chachapoyas, built massive temples when they intended to elaborate and accentuate them in honor of their gods, this temple was nothing but a semi-circular building that seemed disproportionately large.

What gods do these people serve? He wondered.

He stepped forward again, then stopped. He sensed movement to his right, but he hadn't heard a sound.

Luis was on his left, and must have sensed something similar, as he grabbed Jeronimo's left arm and squeezed. Jeronimo slowly turned his head and tried to find the source of the movement.

But there was nothing. Whatever movement he had sensed had vanished, or it had been a tree playing tricks on their minds.

"I am looking for a man," Jeronimo said, first in Quechuan, then in a dialect more similar to the Chachapoyas region. "His name is Blas Valera. Is he here?"

He raised his voice and then repeated the question. He waited a full minute.

"We are alone, my friend," Luis said, his voice barely above a whisper.

"No," Jeronimo said. "I know someone is here. Someone is listening to us."

Luis grabbed Jeronimo's arm once again. "No, my brother," he said, his voice still quiet but nearly frantic now. "I meant that we are *alone.*"

Jeronimo frowned, then caught his breath when he realized what Luis meant. He turned, slowly, taking in the strange world they had stumbled into.

As he turned, he tried to understand what he was seeing.

Nothing. He was seeing nothing. More specifically, Jeronimo was seeing *no one.*

His team — the four other Jesuits besides Luis and the five Inca warriors — had vanished.

They were gone.

Jeronimo felt his heart race. *Where could they have gone? And how did they leave so quietly?*

He kept his eyes steady, focusing on everything and nothing at once, studying the edge of the jungle for any sign of movement. He slowly stepped in a circle until he was turned fully around again, and he began to speak to Luis.

"We must leave, Luis. We must —"

Only then did he notice that Luis, too, was missing.

Jeronimo was standing a clearing, alone.

Worst of all, he knew that whatever had taken his team was still here, somewhere.

And it would take him next.

CHAPTER 1
BEN

THERE WASN'T much light left, and what little there was had been mostly consumed by the thick knots of forest that hung high above his head. Harvey Bennett was running in near pitch-black conditions.

He hadn't intended for it to end this way, but he hadn't had much of a say in it to begin with. His mind raced, trying to calculate, to extrapolate. *What do I have in my possession that's helpful?*

He'd run out of ammunition three hours ago, and he'd left his pack and survival gear back at camp. He'd only intended to take a minute to relieve himself, but he'd wandered about thirty paces into the thicker forest and found that while he'd been gone someone had snuck into his clearing.

He heard his feet thudding heavily over the packed-snow trail, feeling the intense bass rhythmic as it pounded throughout his body. *Left, right, left...* on and on and on until he wouldn't be able to push on any longer.

His breath poured out in front of him and swirled around his head, the warmth doing little to warm him. The condensation froze nearly immediately and the heavier drops fell back down, some of them landing on his face and stinging his eyes. Still, he powered through it. *Discomfort is a luxury we're lucky to get used to*, his old man used to say. Harvey Bennett's father, Johnson Bennett, was a Marine, a hard man on the outside, saying little and often letting his featureless expressions speak for him. But on the inside, Johnson had been a loving, caring father, a devoted husband, and the kind of man Harvey wanted to become.

His father had instilled in Harvey and his younger brother long ago values like that one — that getting used to a bit of discomfort was a great way to prepare for the inevitable discomfort that would eventually visit a man in life. Pain, suffering, sorrow, and loss were synonyms with 'discomfort,' and Harvey had tried to live up to his father's training.

Harvey stopped, both to assess his surroundings and catch his breath. He was still being chased, but he knew he couldn't afford to lose track of the trail and miss his destination. The trail had been shrinking over the last few hours, thanks to the massive amount of snow that was falling around them, somehow finding a route through the thick canopy where the light had failed to.

Cabin's back that way, he thought, silently analyzing the scenery. *Camp is behind me, a few hundred yards due east of here. That means —*

He turned, just as a dark shape lunged at him from behind a tree.

He grunted as the massive body heaved into his own, and both men went down. The fall would have been stifled by the soft fresh powder covering the trail, but somehow the two men had gotten twisted around and Harvey landed on top of his attacker. He momentarily lost his bearings, but quickly regained his composure and rolled off the man.

Can't... lose the...

He felt at his side, checking to ensure he hadn't lost the payload. It was still there, strapped to his belt loop through the end of a huge silver carabiner. The container was small, cylindrical, and a dark pewter color. It was heavy, but the weight had been an asset, allowing

Harvey to run and move around without needed to constantly check that it was still attached to his pants.

Harvey "Ben" Bennett was a bear of a man, hardened and thickened through years of service in national parks and later as the leader of the Civilian Special Operations, a team of civilian operators who worked with the US military on projects that had been deemed by the government to be too small, too insignificant, or too politically dangerous.

Together the team had scaled the ice cliffs of Antarctica, traipsed through the jungles of Brazil, and explored hidden tombs in Egypt. They had lost members, gained more, and become a close-knit group over the course of just over a year. Harvey had become the de facto leader after they had lost their previous commander in Philadelphia, but he liked to think their group was more of a democracy than a dictatorship.

Still, the others — including his soon-to-be wife, Juliette — looked to him for leadership. They followed him willingly, knowing that he had their best interests in mind. He had a knack for finding the clues that led to the answer to a puzzle or mystery, and he had a very hard time ignoring the unjust. He was quick to rush in and fight, even if it meant risking his own life.

He pushed the man back down before he could recover, and Ben took off again, this time ignoring the paths, heading in the direction of the checkpoint directly. He needed to get there first, before the rest of the —

"You're not going to win, Bennett," the voice called out from behind him.

Right behind him. The man had recovered and was chasing him down. Ben would lead him right back to the checkpoint where the others should be waiting. He was hoping someone at the checkpoint could help him, but if no one else had reached it yet...

PROFESSOR VICTORIA REYES looked around the small lecture hall, her eyes having trouble adjusting to the brilliant white spotlights shining down on her from the ceiling. She recognized the students in the front row, and most of the second, but beyond that her eyes couldn't make out anything but shadows.

Still, the room was full. All 80 seats occupied by members of the graduate-level course she had been teaching for a few years. She'd designed the course and written the curriculum herself, based on her own PhD dissertation, *Ancient Orders and Fraternal Development of Modern Religion.* It was a tome of work, but it was her life's work, and she had plans to write follow-ups. This course, Impact of Ancient Orders on Modern Religion, was a testing ground for those later works, and the discussions she had with her students helped push her research forward.

One of those students, a young Catholic minister who was working toward a PhD in Catholic Literature, raised his hand.

"Yes, Mr. Edwards?"

"Mrs. Reyes," the man began. She didn't correct him — she *had* been married, and she'd kept her ex-husband's name. While she would have preferred *Ms.*, she also liked to keep her personal life separate from her work life. "Since the Regius Poem is the first official mention of the Freemasons, and that was in 1390, how can you say that the birth of the Freemasons predates that of the Catholic Church?"

Victoria smiled. "A perfect question to lead into my next slide." She clicked the presentation remote's button and advanced the slideshow. The image now filling the wall-sized screen behind her was a picture of an ancient text, adorned with red drop caps at the beginning of a large, embossed title. Beneath that the Halliwell Manuscript, or the Regius Poem, continued in black inked lines. "This is the Regius Poem, in its original Middle English text. It was rediscovered and referenced in a paper in the 1800s by a James Halliwell, and from there it became one of the Mason's 'Old Charges,' and the first-ever written account of the Freemasons.

"But," she continued, "if you read the text carefully, you realize that it is not a *foundational* document — it is not a poem written to act as the *formation* of a new organization, but as a *description* of one. Take the opening stanza, for example:

"Hic incipit constituciones artis gemetriae secundum Eucyldem." She paused. "Anyone?"

A student near the center of the hall raised her hand and began. "Here begin the constitutions of the art of Geometry according to Euclid."

"Precisely," Victoria said. "The Regius is a poem describing the moral standards of 'the art of geometry,' which as we know is another term for 'masons,' but the poem assumes the existence of such an art long before Euclid came across it in Egypt."

She clicked the remote again, and another slide appeared, this time a picture of a similar document, though the text on the scrolls was nearly illegible.

Victoria read the translation she had memorized. *"Every chronicle, and history, and many other clerks, and the Bible in principle, witnesses of the making of the tower of Babel, and it is written in the Bible, Genesis Chapter... Noah's son begot Nimrod, and he waxed a mighty man upon the earth, and he waxed a strong man, like a giant, and he was a great king. And the beginning of his kingdom was a true kingdom of Babylon, and Arach, and Archad... And this same Nimrod began the tower of Babylon... and he taught to his workmen the craft of measures, and he had with him many masons, more than 40 thousand.*

"Elsewhere in the manuscript, during the history given that aligns with the pre-flood histories we read in the Bible, the Cooke Manuscript says this: *...these 3 brethren had knowledge that God would take vengeance for sin, either by fire, or water, and they had greater care how they might do to save the sciences that they had found, and they took their counsel together and, by all their wits, they said there were two stones of such virtue that one would never burn, and that stone is called marble, and that the other stone that will not sink in water and that stone is named latres, and so they devised to write all the sciences that they had found in these two stones, so that if that God would take vengeance, by fire, that the marble should not burn. And if God sent vengeance by water, that the other should not drown, and so they prayed their elder brother that he would make two pillars of these two stones, that is to say of marble and of latres, and that he would write in the two pillars all the science, and crafts, that all they had found, and so he did...*"

A student in the front row spoke up. "The two pillars — like the two pillars that are part of the Masons' rituals?"

"One and the same," Victoria said. "Meant as an homage to Solomons' temple, whom the Masons believe was built to house the Ark of the Covenant, they feature prominently in Freemason rituals to this day. Further, the history of the Cooke Manuscript and the Regius Poem both describe geometry — the science of the masons — as one of Biblical descent. A science that can trace its lineage to generations before Noah and the flood.

"So although the written texts we have today describe some of the ritualistic similarities and share some common ancestries, and the formal organization as we know wasn't founded until the 1700s, I believe that Freemasonry is, in fact, older — *much* older — than the Catholic Church."

She stepped aside and forward to bring herself out of the glare of the light, so she could see the auditorium more clearly. A few students in the back of the room were furiously scribbling notes, but one was staring directly at her. She waited, expecting a question or comment.

That question came in a few seconds. "Mrs. Reyes," the young woman said. "If the Catholic Church was founded *after* the Masons, is there reason to believe that there is a struggle for legitimacy between the two?"

Victoria shrugged. "Hard to say, exactly. I tend to believe there is — both have storied histories that coincide with one another and share many elements, and both are well-respected, and simultaneously highly suspect, organizations today. They both boast many members, and both claim significant support from advocates worldwide."

"And yet," the student continued. "There is animosity between the groups. The Catholic Church does not allow *any* of its members to be involved in Masonic rituals, correct?"

"It not only frowns upon the rituals, it downright prohibits any of its members from joining the Freemasons. That has been Papal policy since the 1700s, and it has never been overturned. If you ask me, I think the Catholic Church and the Freemasons have been fighting an epic battle for thousands of years, both trying to prove its own validity while disproving that of its main rival. The battle hasn't been public, nor has it been acknowledged in writing, but... I can't help but imagine there is one."

"But the Freemasons aren't a religion, are they?" A student asked.

"Why would the Catholic Church care if they exist or not, and vice versa?"

Victoria smiled again and looked up at the wall clock. She knew she could talk about this subject all day, but they were running out of time. "Well," she said. "I guess that depends on your definition of religion."

CHAPTER 3

BEN

THE MAN WAS GAINING on him. He was thinner than Ben and actually seemed to *enjoy* running. Running, to Ben, was something done only when being chased. And since he was being chased, Ben figured now was as good a time as any to run.

Still, the man was faster. He would catch up, and that meant Ben would have to fight him one-on-one, without the help of anyone back at the checkpoint. He wasn't afraid of his ability — he was brutally strong and had held his own in plenty of head-to-head engagements — but this was a different sort of battle.

This battle wasn't a kill-or-be-killed battle. He couldn't just blindly throw his weight around and hope for the best. He wouldn't be able to strike any lethal blows, and he wouldn't be able to resort to the scrappy, risky fighting style that he'd used in the past.

He needed to use his intelligence to win this one.

He stopped, turned around. The man came at him again, and Ben threw a punch that was meant more to destabilize his attacker and throw him off balance than to injure him.

Yet his attacker was even better trained than Ben, and even more agile. He ducked out of the way, allowing the blow to glance off his side while he shifted his feet slightly and changed direction. He slammed into Ben's chest with his head, once again knocking the wind out of him.

This time Ben went down hard, only a rock beneath him to break his fall, and the man piled on top. Ben felt his lungs compress and his breath disappear, and he wondered how the man could keep his hands and feet moving so fast, so effectively. He had almost wrapped Ben in a jujitsu hold three times in the three seconds they'd been on the ground, and it was only Ben's sheer size that kept the other man from succeeding.

"You're not going to get it," Ben said, breathlessly. He threw an elbow up at the man's head, taking advantage of the momentary lapse as the other man looked at his face as he spoke. The blow hit him in the chin, and it was enough to shake him off Ben's body.

Ben stood, hands up. He backed away, knees slightly bent. He was prepared for a third attack, but it never came.

"You think you've won?" the man asked.

Ben shook his head. "Neither one of us is back yet," Ben said. "Neither one of us has won."

"True," the man said, smiling. "But only one of us can *go* back to the checkpoint."

Ben frowned. He knew the rules — return to the checkpoint with your own payload, within 24 hours. Return with someone *else's* payload and you win immediately. Return with *no* payload and you lose immediately.

"What do you —" Ben stopped. He noticed it at that moment, feeling the pressure from the weight of his cylindrical payload no longer present. "How did —"

The man in front of him — Gareth Red, or Reggie, Ben's best friend — was laughing. "You were too focused on taking *me* out, you didn't even care about your payload."

"Where is it?" Ben asked.

Reggie grinned, then shrugged. "No idea, actually. I tossed it over my shoulder right after I pinned you to the ground."

"*Pinned* me to the — you didn't *pin* me, you schmuck. I *let* you attack me."

Reggie threw his head back and laughed. "Seriously, Ben, you have *quite* the imagination. If I hadn't let you land that elbow blow, you'd still be stuck to the snow, pleading for me to let you go."

Ben stared at him. "Still, no one's won yet. We have to —"

Reggie bolted, flying past Ben and launching himself in the direction of the checkpoint. Ben turned and watched him go, hoping that he would get lost in the woods and be unable to find his way back.

Ben found his payload — carabiner still attached — lying next to the root of a tree he'd felled the year before. It was dinged, the metal canister showing the wear and tear of a few rounds of their game, as well as the years of use it had already put in as a water bottle. He brushed the snow from its side and clipped it onto the other side of his pants. The belt loop he'd had it on had been ripped off on one seam by Reggie, and it was now flapping against Ben's left leg. He found another loop to clip the payload to and started out.

You owe me a pair of pants, he thought as he finished clipping the water bottle-turned-payload and headed deeper into the woods. Ben knew the area better than anyone — he owned the land — but in the dead of winter in Alaska, things got white, still, and homogenous *very* quickly. He sniffed, letting the sharp pain of the below-freezing temperature wake him up.

And I owe you a good right hook.

Reggie was going to find the checkpoint; Ben knew it was behind the woodcutting pile they'd erected not a year earlier, east of the cabin and about two-hundred yards to the north. It was in a natural clearing, marked by the pile to the south and a small frozen stream to the north where Ben and Julie had practiced their ice fishing technique last spring.

Ben hiked quickly, no longer worried about beating Reggie but still excited to get back to the checkpoint — it meant the end of the training game and a return to his nice, *warm* cabin.

And it also meant a free drink — whoever won the game had to buy the first round at the bar in town.

CHAPTER 4
JULIE

JULIE RAN FORWARD to intercept Ben as he marched into the clearing where they'd made camp. She embraced him, and they kissed. About three seconds later, she pushed him back.

"Yuck," she said. "You smell disgusting."

He laughed. "You're puttin' off a nice aroma yourself, dear."

She raised an arm and sniffed. *Crap*, she thought. *He's not kidding.*

The CSO group had only been out here for a day, but it seemed like their exertion had caused them a bit of extra strain, and their bodies were paying for it. Julie had groaned when Reggie announced the offsite camp and training games, and she groaned again now, knowing she was still one night away from her shower.

The worst part of it was that her shower was only half a mile away — the cabin she shared with Ben also served as the headquarters of the Civilian Special Operations group, a group in which her fiancé served as leader — and yet she couldn't hike the half-mile and use it until tomorrow.

Gareth "Reggie" Red was the team's unofficial training and development coordinator, as he had years of Army and Special Forces know-how and experience under his belt. In addition, he had spent years training corporate executives survival skills in a high-end training course he'd built in the Brazilian forests. He was more than qualified for training his civilian friends to hunt, track, fight, and survive, but at times like this Julie wished he wouldn't take things so seriously.

They'd spent the first half of the day learning from Reggie about tracking techniques, all of which they'd been tested and drilled on, and all of which had been part of a set of actual homework assignments he had prepared. The training camp they were now "enjoying" was the culmination of a semester-long curriculum Reggie had written himself.

And he was, apparently, quite proud of it. He stumbled into the circle of tents behind Ben and slapped him on the back.

"Well, we *almost* had a winner besides me," he announced.

The two other women that made up the CSO walked out of the woods on the other side of the fire pit. Mrs. E and Sarah Lindgren had been joking and laughing with one another, but stopped and stared at the animated Gareth Red as he kept moving toward the group.

"Ben would have *had* me," he said, keeping his voice loud enough to ensure that *everyone* heard — especially, Julie assumed, Sarah. "But he second-guessed himself."

"Bullshit," Ben said in a snicker. "You got lucky."

"Pfft. Lucky would've been getting back here without being spotted. I could have spotted you through a brick wall with my eyes closed."

"Good thing there isn't a brick wall in a hundred miles."

Reggie sniffed the air. "Ah, ain't that the truth. You got a nice place here, Ben. Too bad I keep beating you at your own game."

Ben scoffed, and Julie tried to hide her smile as the two men bantered. "My own game?" Ben asked. "How is running around like an idiot *my* own game?"

Reggie cocked an eyebrow and came up closer to Ben. The two

men were almost eye-to-eye, but Reggie had a couple inches on Ben. However, Ben was taller than most men and had the shoulders of a bear.

"Weren't you the kid who spent an eternity traipsing around a national park in order to 'find yourself?'" Reggie asked.

Julie laughed out loud. "You think he's found himself? I thought he was still looking."

Ben looked from his best friend to his fiancée, Julie, and feigned an expression of pain. "You *both* are against me, now? Come on, man. I almost won!"

"But you didn't!" Reggie sang, and Mrs. E and Sarah joined in the laughter.

Julie pulled up a camp chair and began lighting the fire in the dying light of the evening. She could see and feel her breath tumbling out of her mouth as she worked, both appreciating and respecting the fast-changing weather. Alaska was the most beautiful country she'd ever seen. Weather here could change from open skies and bright sun to dreary overcast and brutal cold in a matter of minutes. She'd seen it happen, and if it weren't for having a warm cabin stocked with a full pantry and plenty of firewood, she'd feel vulnerable out here tonight.

But she'd also seen the frozen hellscape of Antarctica in person, had fought for her life in a below-freezing dungeon beneath a mile-thick sheet of ice, and had come out the other side stronger for it. Reggie's training aside, she had become the type of woman she'd always looked up to — strong enough to do anything on her own, and confident enough to want to.

The team gathered around the growing embers of her lit kindling as she stoked and nursed it to life, and she heard Reggie cajoling Ben into a rematch.

"No," Ben said. "Game's rigged."

"What? How can it be rigged?" Reggie responded.

"You set up the rules, you won," Ben said. He shrugged. "I don't know. It's rigged, I just don't know how."

"You're a sore loser," Reggie said. "If these ladies hadn't run into each other first, one of them would have *easily* beat you."

"I seem to remember one of us sitting on top of the other one," Ben said. "And one of us not being able to do *anything* about it."

"And *I* seem to remember you losing. Period."

Ben grinned. "Doesn't matter. I get paid more than you."

Julie saw Reggie's tongue poking the inside of his mouth. "Well... that's just... I mean you're married. Well, almost. And Mr. E wants to make sure..."

Julie stood up and stuck her chin in Reggie's direction. "Make sure of what?"

"Just that... I mean Ben has to take care of you and all..."

Ben guffawed from his side, and Julie herself couldn't hide her laughter. "The day Ben thinks *he* needs to take care of *me* is the day I move out," she said.

"Well, maybe that's when you move in with me," Reggie said, cracking one of his massive, bright-white teeth-bearing grins.

Sarah stomped over and smacked his shoulder. "Really, now? Seriously?"

He and Sarah had been dating on and off for some time, and lately things had been obviously in the "on" phase. Sarah had been staying with Reggie in his apartment in Anchorage when they weren't working.

"What?" He said. "I was just joking."

"Damn right you were," Sarah said. She turned on a heel and walked back to her tent.

"Because I wouldn't be able to get any peace with *two* women in the house."

"I heard that," Sarah called out.

CHAPTER 5
GARZA

"I TOLD *you where to find the book,*" the man said on the other end of the phone.

Vicente Garza spat, then brought the phone back up to his ear. He was growing irritated, but he couldn't afford to upset a client. *Not again.* "I understand that. I am en route to the book now," he said. "But I can't even be sure that the book is what we need, nor can I be sure it is there."

"*The book is what you told me you needed to find the temple,*" the man said.

"I believe it is," Garza replied, forcing his voice to remain calm. "And yet I am not even sure what it is I am looking for. You realize there are *thousands* of temples in South America."

"*This temple holds the key to a remarkable break—*"

"—'Breakthrough in genetic technology,'" Garza said, interrupting. "I know. I read the brief, and you've said it a thousand times. But I don't expect there will be a sign hanging above it saying as much."

"*I expect not,*" the voice said, dropping a few notes. "*And yet you are the man I hired to find it. Shall I reconsider?*"

Garza felt his blood heating up. He gritted his teeth. He absolutely hated to feel inferior to anyone — especially those paying his bills. This client was just that — a *client*. He could break off the deal at any moment, tell the man to take a hike, and spend his time and considerable talents elsewhere, where it was appreciated.

But he needed a win. He *needed* to bring this one home.

"There also is the matter of your daughter."

His blood's temperature changed direction, and within seconds it ran cold. He felt his forehead beginning to sweat, his back now moist and sticking to his shirt. "What of my daughter? She is none of your concern."

"Your daughter is working against our interests. That is not a secret, Garza."

"She's not part of this investigation!" he said, nearly shouting.

"And yet she is a bargaining chip, played onto the table of fate."

Garza pulled the phone away from his ear. *What the hell does that even mean?* he thought.

"You will deliver the package, within the agreed upon boundaries, at the designated time, or we will remove your influence in the South American region."

"Remove my *interest?* You don't have the jurisdiction to —"

"If you fail to deliver, we will take further action. I know you love your business, Mr. Garza, but I also know how much you love your daughter."

Garza felt frantic for a moment, but he quickly regained his composure. *As it should be,* he thought. He had spent a lifetime — and a lifetime's salary — working to control his emotional state, seeking to perfect his emotional and physical grounding. It had helped in his quest to perfect himself in every way. Though he had some distance to go, he felt that he was on the correct path.

But he was human. There would always be certain things that caused his emotional state to waver. The list of those things was a short one, but his daughter topped it. When his client mentioned his daughter, he'd felt violated, vulnerable. Flipping the imaginary switch in his mind helped keep him in check, but instead of feeling trapped and scared, he began to feel angry.

The adrenaline began coursing through his veins, and he allowed it. The rush of anger filled him, and unlike anxiety, fear, or vulnerability, he knew how to use it to his advantage. Anger wasn't a hindrance — to Garza, it was a crutch.

He seethed, silently, as the client droned on.

"There is more at stake here than your money," the man said. *"If we do not secure the book, and what it leads too, there will be others."*

Garza frowned. "Others? I thought you were the only party who knew of the book?"

"Nonsense. You know all along that was not true. We are far from the only party interested in its whereabouts, though we may be in the best position to acquire the book. However, please do not make me question that statement."

"Understood," Garza said through gritted teeth. "I'm en route to the location of the book. If it is not there, I will at least have new information to point me in the right direction."

"Very well. I will await your next call."

Garza didn't respond other than by hanging up the cellphone and jamming it into his front pocket. He cursed, then turned to the driver. "Speed up," he said. "We're close."

The trees in this area had thickened to the point of being nearly a continuous wall of green and brown. Snow covered the ground, making the dirt road they were on nearly invisible, and the driver of the jeep they had rented pressed down on the gas pedal, using only the part between the solid rows of trees as a guide.

Garza hoped they would catch the team with their guard down. His information suggested that they were working on a state-of-the-art security and communications system, but that they were still a month away from going live. He hoped that was still the case, otherwise he would be in a situation he hated: having too few men to get a job done.

Besides the driver, Garza had brought along one of his best soldiers, who was napping in the jeep's backseat. If all went to plan, Garza and his team would be heading the opposite direction on this road before afternoon the next day.

If all goes to plan, he said silently to himself. He thought once more of his daughter and then looked out the window to his right, watching the trees blur into a never-ending line of green.

CHAPTER 6

JULIE

JULIE REACHED *up and took the weapon. She felt it in her hand. Glock, 9mm. They'd all trained on it at a range when...*

She couldn't remember.

But she knew she'd held this weapon before. It felt warm in her hand, yet cool at the same time.

It feels right.

She knew she was dreaming, but she couldn't wake up. She'd gone to sleep next to Ben in the tent, unaware that her mind had prepared the same dream for her. She wasn't sure why — she'd only had the dream a few times in the past, and each time it had been an out-of-body experience. She was looking down at herself, at the top of her head. She couldn't see much else in the "scene" that her mind had created. Just herself, and the gun.

"Ms. Richardson, you know how to handle this weapon, correct?"

She did. The standard-issue 9mm was found all over the world. Easy to use and clean, and easy to break down for storage and transport. Reggie had trained her on it himself.

Reggie was suddenly in the dream, a concerned look on his face. She couldn't quite *see* him, but she could *feel* him. Ben was there, too. As if she had just conjured his ghost. He stood — no, leaned — by her side. *Was he hurt?*

She nodded. "I do."

"Good."

She couldn't see the man talking, but she could hear the voice. She could remember the voice. Deep, menacing. Or was that just her imagination? Was her imagination allowed into this dream?

Footsteps, moving toward the wall.

"Ms. Richardson, please follow me."

Julie stood up and trailed behind the voice. When the man had reached the side of the gym — she was in a gym? — he stopped. He moved sideways over to the soldier standing in front of Joshua, then stopped again. Julie followed, now standing next to the man.

She could see him now, but not clearly. She tried to move her head around in the dream, but it was as though her subconscious brain was in control. Dark features, dark complexion. Nothing helpful. Nothing she recognized.

There was another form — a man? — sitting next to her.

"Ms. Richardson, who is this man?"

"Joshua Jefferson." She heard the words in the dream as though she'd spoken them aloud.

"And do you know him well?"

She mumbled, something, felt Ben stir next to her. *"Reasonably well. We're friends."*

"I see. And how long have you know Mr. Jefferson?"

"Probably six, seven months."

"And do you like this man?"

She nodded. "I like him. He's a good friend, and a good leader."

The man tapped her shoulder. She frowned.

"Julie?"

She tried looking around, but again her brain had her riveted, forcing her to look at the man sitting down. Joshua? She pulled at a memory, something hidden deep inside.

It couldn't be Joshua. He died. Back in Philadelphia. When —

"Ms. Richardson, please shoot Joshua Jefferson in the head."

She screamed in the dream. In her own head. No. But no sound came out, not in the dream, and not in real life. Whatever real life was.

The man tapped her shoulder again. She pulled away. No.

Again, a tap.

"Julie?"

"Julie!" The voice rang into her mind with the ferocity of a gunshot. She saw one more image in her mind, in the dream. Of a man, sitting down, then falling sideways. His head...

"No!" she screamed. She was awake now, breathing rapidly. She blinked a few times, but the darkness was total.

Where am I?

"Julie," a man's voice said, calmly. "Hey, Jules. You okay?"

Ben.

She shook, breathing slower now. *Calm down.*

"You must've been having a horrible dream. You all right?"

She looked over to Ben, seeing his silhouette masked out by the lighter moonlight that had found its way down to their tent. She reached a hand out and felt his shoulder. She nodded, but knew he couldn't see her.

"Yes," she whispered. "I'm okay."

He pulled her close to him, wrapping his arm around her back and pushing her head down and under his chin. He didn't talk, didn't ask questions.

She felt him breathing, the gentle rise and fall of his massive chest, and she finally felt relief.

She closed her eyes, but she knew she wouldn't be sleeping again that night.

CHAPTER 7

BEN

THEY BROKE camp and snuffed out the morning fire in record time, as if they'd all been camping together for years. They divvied up their gear and split it between them, tied their packs and strapped in the sleeping bags and tents, then headed the half-mile back to the cabin.

Reggie and Sarah had taken a longer loop around the northwest side of a small pond, so they could have some time together. Ben made sure to give them a decent ribbing, and even Mrs. E joined in.

When the pair left, Ben, Julie, and Mrs. E hiked in line with Mrs. E at the lead. After a few minutes of walking, Ben sidled up to Julie and waited until Mrs. E had curved around a bend up ahead.

"You okay?"

She frowned. "What do you mean?"

"Last night. The dream you had. Or nightmare — I'm not sure what it was."

She smiled. "Yeah, that was rough. It was crazy, almost like a memory."

"Of what?"

"Of... I don't know. Something deep down, like something that either didn't happen or didn't stick."

"Or something that you're repressing," Ben said. He wasn't sure how far he should push it. The team had decided early on that they would let Julie heal on her own terms, on her own time. They wouldn't urge her to do anything other than reach out to them for help, when and if she was ready.

"What do you mean?" Julie asked, turning to Ben. She stopped on the trail.

"I... don't mean anything, Jules," Ben said. "I was just saying that sometimes we repress certain memories. Sometimes they're traumatic, but sometimes they're just funny, stupid things that don't mean anything."

"I'm not sure this is one of those funny, stupid things, Ben."

"Yeah, I doubt it."

"Is there something you're not telling me?" she asked.

Ben sighed. The air was calm, but it had dropped about ten degrees since yesterday, and he felt it catch in the back of his throat. *Definitely winter*, he thought. He was glad to get back to the cabin where he'd have a fire lit and whiskey poured before he even had his boots off.

"Jules, can you tell me more about the dream? Who was in it?"

She thought for a second. "Me, obviously. Like I was floating over my own head though, like I wasn't really experiencing it in first-person. And you, I think. I'm not sure I really saw you, but I think your voice was in it."

"What was I saying?"

"I don't remember."

Ben nodded. He knew all too well how easy it was to wake up in the middle of a dream with the vivid recollection of every detail, every word spoken, and every emotion felt present in his mind, then feeling totally unable to recall it minutes later.

"And Joshua."

Ben turned his head. "Joshua... Jefferson?"

She nodded, then continued walking. "Yeah, he was sitting... or something. I don't really know. And there was someone else."

Ben felt his blood run cold. "Who else?"

"A man, judging by his voice. I remember a man. Dark skin, or at least his hair or face or something. Maybe it was just my mind's version of what I remember."

"What did he do?"

"I don't know," she said, shaking her head. "He said things to me, but I can't remember what. Or who he was, or why he was there."

Ben nodded along as if he was hearing this all for the first time, but the truth was that he knew *exactly* who the man was, and he knew *exactly* what he had wanted.

And he knew the man had gotten it.

"We're almost there," Julie said. Ben noticed a little excitement in her voice and decided to drop the subject for the time being.

"I've got a bottle of whiskey I've been wanting to break open," he said. "Just been waiting for a special occasion."

"And losing a training exercise is a special occasion to you?" Julie asked.

He laughed. "Ouch. Et tu, Brutus?"

"Wow," Julie said. "Where'd you learn that?"

"You think I've just been hanging out in the woods for two decades, but I've read a book or two since I graduated high school."

"*Maybe* two," Julie said. "But that's a stretch. Usually you don't want anything to do with them unless they're full of pictures."

He shrugged. "You're not wrong. Comic books are just a different type of literature, you know?"

"I really don't. Anyway, if you think you're going to disappear into the new wing and relax with Reggie, you've got another thing coming."

Ben's mouth dropped open in mock surprised. "What? You've got a bunch of chores for me now? And it's called the 'man cave,' by the way."

The 'man cave' was just an extra bedroom that sat off a new

section that had been added to the cabin. The CSO had invested heavily in Ben's property, and construction was still underway on a completely new, modernized meeting space and additional bedrooms for team members to stay in when they visited. The goal Mr. E shared with Ben was to have a self-sufficient, remote meeting and living space for all the team, year-round.

Ben enjoyed the company, but he also enjoyed the times in-between training and meetings when he and Julie shared the cabin alone. But since those opportunities were becoming more and more rare, he and Reggie had set up his bedroom with a super-sized curved television, a gaming console, and a high-end stereo system. They called it the man cave, even though Julie, Sarah, and Mrs. E often would hang out in there as well.

"I don't have 'chores' for you, Ben. I'm not your mom. But you did say you were making chili for everyone, right? And I know it takes the better part of a day for everything to cook."

"Aw, man. I forgot." He groaned. Even though he had a killer chili recipe and enjoyed cooking, sleeping on the ground and running through the woods while fighting off an ex-Army guy had caused him to reconsider his promise to the team. "Maybe we can just order pizza or something."

She knew it was a joke. The nearest pizza restaurant was fifty miles away, and they wouldn't even know how to find the cabin, much less deliver all the way to them.

Julie held up her hands. "Sorry. Rules are rules. You committed to chili, and now I want chili. I will settle for nothing less."

He was about to respond with some asinine-sounding teenager voice when he rounded the final bend and his cabin came into view. He saw the additional wing first, the construction equipment strewn about and disorderly, yet noticed nothing amiss.

But when his eye fell to the cabin itself, his jaw dropped again. Where there once had been a solid oak door, there was now nothing but a few splinters of wood hanging off the hinges.

CHAPTER 8

BEN

HE SAW a few pots and pans on the snow in front of the doorway, and a suitcase — Julie's "ready pack" — laying on its side nearby. Its contents, mostly clothes, had been tossed haphazardly around.

"A bear?" Julie asked.

"No," Ben said. "It wouldn't mess with clothes and pots and pans. A bear would go straight for the kitchen and stay there, not bothering with the rest of the place."

He walked up to the front door and peered inside. There were no sounds, no telltale rustlings or bumping of a large mammal.

Julie was at his side, and he noticed she had a camp shovel in her hand.

"Good thinking," he said, grabbing the best thing he could find at arm's reach — a rubber mallet. *Better than nothing,* he told himself, then stepped inside.

His eyes adjusted from the bright, late-morning snow to the darker, dimmer cabin interior, and then they naturally fell on the thing that was most out of place in his vision: the couch.

Nearly everything had been overturned or moved, and some things had even been completely broken. His mother's antique end table, for one, had been turned into a pile of broken boards. While his peripheral vision registered the shambles and disarray around the cabin, it was the couch he focused on.

Sitting nearest to him was Mrs. E, facing the door. She had a blank expression on her face, her jaw set in stern, hard lines.

Seated next to her, with a massive 50-caliber Desert Eagle held out and pointed at her temple, was Vicente Garza.

The man smiled at Ben as he walked in, but the pistol remained on Mrs. E. "Ben," Garza said. "Welcome. Please come in."

"What the hell are you doing here, asshole?" Ben growled.

"Quite a different climate than the last place we got to hang out in," he said.

While Ben and Garza had first crossed paths in Philadelphia, they had last seen each other off the coast of The Bahamas, at a science-based floating amusement park that had been — rightfully — reclaimed by the sea. Garza had escaped that time, but Ben had sworn to kill the man, at all costs.

Now he had that chance. He started shuffling sideways, toward the rifle he kept in a cabinet just at the end of the kitchen, just as Julie entered.

"I only have the one weapon, Harvey," Garza said. "So I will not threaten you by swinging it around and pointing it at you, but I will tell you this: your rifle is in two pieces, lying on the floor in the kitchen. I know there are other guns lying around, so if you so much as *breathe* in their direction, I remove this fine lady's head."

Ben stopped moving, and he saw Julie catch her breath as she saw Garza. He wasn't sure if she recognized him or not.

"What do you want?" Ben asked.

"I want a book."

"I'm not much of a reader," he said.

"And I'm not an idiot. I'd appreciate that we get through our business quickly, so we can both get on with our lives."

"I'd appreciate that too," Ben said. "Asshole," he added under his breath.

"This is a book I believe you brought home from Egypt."

Egypt. Ben swore under his breath as recalled their escapade in Egypt. They had traveled to Cairo and then Giza to visit the Sphinx and Great Pyramid, and more specifically to visit a woman whom they believed had been working toward a very unusual — and sinister — goal.

Their time there had been cut short, thanks to a man working for Interpol who was not terribly pleased about the CSO's interference in his own investigation, and they had narrowly escaped with their lives.

Ben also knew exactly what book Garza was referring to.

The problem was they didn't have it.

He told Garza as much. "Sorry, Garza. It's not here."

"I believe you," he said, flashing a glance around the room. "I do like the new addition, too. Had a little look around before you got back."

"Yeah," Ben said. "It's... different. But it'll be nice when it's done. I'm really looking forward to the hot tub."

"Cut the crap, Ben. Where's the book?"

"The Book of Bones?"

Garza nodded.

"I don't know. Honestly. I wish I did."

"I truly wish you did as well, Harvey. You see, I've got a client. They're a thorn in my side, but they pay the bills. And right now, they're breathing down my neck to find this little book."

"It's that valuable, huh?"

Garza didn't take the bait. Ben had been in situations like this more than a few times before, so he knew that if he could get at whatever it was Garza's client wanted *inside* the book — whatever information it held — he could figure out what Garza was truly after.

"It is," the man said. "And you're running out of time."

"That so?"

"Have I ever lied to you?"

"Nope. Murdered my friends, sure. But lied to me? No, you're a stand-up guy, Garza."

Garza half-smiled. "I'll make this easy. Tell me where to find the book, and your friends don't die."

Ben looked at Mrs. E, who was as stoic as ever, staring straight ahead, then at Julie. Julie's eyes seemed glazed over, as if she were in a trance. He couldn't tell if she was shocked by Garza's presence or just shocked that their home had been broken into.

Ben cleared his throat. "You're arrogant."

Garza raised an eyebrow.

"Maybe you pop off a shot, get Mrs. E." He glanced at her with an expression he hoped looked like '*sorry,*' but she wasn't looking. "But there's no way in hell you get that gun flicked around fast enough to get me and Julie as well.

"And if you *don't* get me and Julie, *one of us will murder you.* I will rip your eyes out of your head and —"

"Stop with the pleasantries, Harvey," Garza said. "First, I'm better trained than you and your girlfriend ever will be. I've *trained* men who are better trained than you'll ever be. Trust me, if I wanted — or want — you dead at any point in this discussion, your life is over."

Ben seethed, but didn't interrupt.

"But we're not talking about Juliette or Mrs. E," Garza said. He flicked the gun up and back down, readjusting his aim at Mrs. E's head. "I'm talking about your friends Gareth and Sarah."

CHAPTER 9
REGGIE

REGGIE PULLED AGAINST HIS RESTRAINTS. Zip ties, the thick, semi-opaque kind used for heavy-duty purposes. They cut into his wrists and ankles, but he barely felt the pain. He was in a rage, but his calm countenance and demeanor said otherwise.

He shifted, rolling to his side and leaning into Sarah. His girl-friend moaned, but the duct tape she had over her mouth muffled much of the sound. He tried to tell her it would be okay, but his mouth too had been taped over, and the best he could muster was a grunting sound as his eyes bulged out of their sockets.

They were in the back of a jeep, but the vehicle wasn't moving. He could see out the windows, and he could tell they were close to where they had been camping and training. He couldn't recall all the details, as he'd been unconscious until about five minutes ago.

He remembered walking through the woods with Sarah, opting to take the longer way around back to the cabin. The others — Ben and Julie, mostly — had made fun of them for it, but Reggie was feeling like a little alone time together would be perfect for both of them.

And then, that was it. He couldn't remember anything else. He'd woken up gagged, his head whirling and his vision spinning. He couldn't feel any specific throbs of pain, which told him that the way their captors had subdued them was related to some sort of chemical. They'd been knocked out, dragged back to the jeep, and then bound and tossed inside. Their seatbelts were on, and Reggie couldn't decide if it was just a cruel joke about ensuring their safety or just another layer of protection that would prevent their escape.

Either way, Reggie's hands hurt from the tight bonds and the fact that he was sitting on them, and his ankles didn't feel much better. He leaned over again and bumped Sarah.

"Where are we going?" he tried to ask, but the words came out as a mixture of grunts and mumbles. She looked at him blankly.

"Shit," he said. Again, it was just a mumble.

He squeezed his eyes shut, trying to push away the growing headache and remember what had happened. *There had been nothing out of the ordinary,* he thought. *Just me and Sarah. We were walking, and then...*

Nothing. He had no idea what had happened after that. There had been no signals, no flashes in his peripheral vision. Reggie was a trained tracker, and an experienced wilderness survivalist. He knew for a fact nothing had been in front of or around them as they'd walked through the woods.

Which means they're professional. Well-trained.

He opened his eyes.

Like special forces.

The driver's side door opened and Reggie saw a huge brute of a man get inside. He crushed the seat, his head scraping the ceiling of the jeep. The man wore a tight parka that did little to hide his massive arms. He had a close-shaved crop of brown hair on his head and a beard that was kept broad and tight. While he looked American or European, he had no other discernible features.

Special forces, Reggie thought again.

But he knew there was no reason for any Spec Ops team to be up here, much less looking for him. And certainly not for his girlfriend.

Reggie may have had a past that still had the US government's hackles raised, but he had done nothing remotely bad enough to warrant this sort of treatment.

And that could only mean one thing.

"You're a mercenary," Reggie said. The mush that actually came out of his mouth, however, wasn't understood by anyone in the car. The man looked into the rearview mirror with eyes that could have been on a dead fish, and shrugged.

"Whatever," Reggie said.

The passenger door opened. Reggie turned to see who the newcomer was, and he felt his blood heat up before the man had entered.

The man's features were unmistakable. Tall, chiseled, mid-forties to early fifties. Jet-black hair that was cut close to the sides but longer on top, even falling into a perfectly placed disarray in places. Reggie saw a few strands of gray, and if it weren't his hair, he would have thought the man could have been in his early thirties.

But he knew better — Reggie knew exactly who the man was.

"Vicente Garza," Reggie mumbled, knowing no one in the car would understand him. "The Hawk."

Reggie felt a flash of nostalgia, then a strong desire to vomit. He pushed the feeling aside, knowing it was a psychological response triggered by the memories of this man. Long before he'd been involved with the CSO, long before he'd been out on his own as a survivalist training expert, and long before he'd given it all up for a compound in Brazil, he'd been a soldier.

Sarah met his eyes, and he knew that *she* knew the truth: he knew this man.

He knew this man *very* well.

Employed by the US Army, Gareth Red had been a sharpshooter, a hotshot sniper who had been recruited for a mission by a bank that was not exactly "on the books." He'd made a few mistakes, barely escaping with his life, then getting wrapped up in vigilante justice in Puerto Rico and eventually landing in Brazil, where he'd started over.

Before all that, as a grunt in the Army and quickly rising through chaff as the best shot his superiors had trained in a long while, he'd had an opportunity.

An opportunity I'm still thankful I didn't take, he thought.

That opportunity had come in the form of Vicente "The Hawk" Garza, a once-captain who'd been slowly recruiting young men into a defense contracting company that specialized in security for foreign corporations. It paid well — *extremely* well — and it had a carte blanche attitude toward legality and ethics.

"Hello again, Reggie," The Hawk said, as the large man swung into the front seat. He turned and addressed Sarah. "And you must be Reggie's new little fling, is that it? Dr. Sarah Lindgren, I believe?"

Sarah glared at him.

"Has Reggie told you about the others? He has always been quite the charmer. That huge grin of his usually works wonders in a crowded bar."

Sarah looked at Reggie, but Reggie just shook his head.

"Oh, yes," The Hawk said as the driver began to back away down the driveway. "He's had several intense relationships, I believe. One, even, with a pregnancy?" The Hawk cocked his head sideways as he stared at Sarah.

Reggie wanted to scream. He tried lifting his hands to work them free, but the men who'd bound him — no doubt trained by Garza himself — were professionals. He wasn't going anywhere. Furthermore, Reggie saw that the driver had slowed once again, and two other men were now mounting the step rail on the opposite sides of the jeep. They grabbed at the roof rack and held on, and the driver picked up speed once again.

A team of four, Reggie thought. *Small, quick, efficient.* He knew it was a good tactical choice, made even more so by the exclusion of a second vehicle. They had the ability to get in, get the payload — Sarah and him — and get out. Simple.

"He didn't tell you?" Garza continued. "Yes, well, I can't remember her name. It was a long time ago, and our intelligence only dips so far. But she was gorgeous. Absolute stunner. Not unlike you, my dear. Anyway — he got her pregnant. A baby girl, I think?"

Reggie seethed. His mind raced, his heart was pumping out of his chest, and he felt scared. Truly, utterly, scared. He hadn't felt this — vulnerability — in a *very* long time.

But The Hawk's words brought him back. His apartment, empty, long after she'd left him. The television, on yet showing nothing. Hungry, yet not wanting to eat.

"How did that end again?" The Hawk asked. "You *really* should be more open with your lovers, Reggie. It's only polite."

He hadn't told Sarah about her — his ex-girlfriend *or* his daughter. The pregnancy had been terminated, and he still couldn't bear the thought of knowing that he'd had something to do with it.

Sarah looked from The Hawk to Reggie, incredulity in her eyes. He wanted to reach out, to grab her hand or her arm Something. He wanted to hold her.

I'm sorry, Sarah. He couldn't say anything, and he knew she wouldn't understand it anyway. He had to hope that the least she understood was that he had made mistakes. Those mistakes were in the past, and he was paying for them every day of his life.

If only I'd fought harder, he thought. *Then maybe I'd have —*

"We've got a bit of a drive ahead of us, you two," Garza said. "Might as well get as comfortable as possible. Once we're in the air, I'll take off the tape on your mouths. But I'd get used to those zip ties. They're not going anywhere."

Reggie calmed himself down and looked out the window, at Ben's woods passing by as the jeep accelerated onto the wider section of dirt road. They had a few miles to go before they hit the highway, and then another hour or so before they reached Anchorage. Assuming they were headed to Anchorage.

Reggie loved Alaska, but the part that he loved most about it was ironically now the thing he was most terrified of.

Alaska was massive, and it was easy to hide in.

CHAPTER 10
JULIE

"LET'S GO," Ben said. "Mrs. E is staying here to figure out how the *hell* they got past our communications."

Julie nodded absently as she reached for the weapons in the gun case. Since the CSO had set up a permanent headquarters at their cabin, Reggie had significantly upgraded the defense systems they'd had in place. And since there had been effectively none to begin with, those upgrades, to Julie, seemed over-the-top.

Now, however, she was grateful that he'd had the foresight to have the contractors put in a special "defense bunker," similar to the one Reggie had had in Brazil. The concrete basement was a room that had been built underground, right behind the cabin, with plans to connect it to both a staircase that would start in the cabin's kitchen and the rest of the CSO building that would be erected just above the bunker.

The bunker had been finished even though the building above it and the connecting staircases had not been, and it was into this bunker that Julie had rushed after Ben had snapped into action. She'd found what she was looking for, entered the combination, and the massive, titanium steel door popped open. To Julie, the weapons inside looked like those out of a sci-fi movie. Even though they'd all trained on each of them, she only felt comfortable with the AR-15 assault rifles at this point. She grabbed two of those, two clips of ammunition, and a few spare magazines. She'd hefted the door shut and waited for the latch of the lock, then run back up the ladder and out into the bright morning light.

Ben was waiting for her. "Ready?" he asked.

She nodded and tossed the weapons and ammunition into the front seat of Ben's SUV. He got into the driver's seat and before she could enter and close the rear seat door, he had floored it. She felt the force of the vehicle lurching forward onto the gravel driveway and the door close by itself. She had no time to put on a seatbelt, but she knew she wouldn't need one, anyway.

It was simple: Ben was a great driver, and she was a great shot. She'd be riding "shotgun," even though she was carrying a massively upgraded version of the Old West's description of a shotgun and she'd be riding in the backseat, but the term still fit. If they could catch up to The Hawk, there might be a chance at rescuing Reggie and Sarah before they got away.

The trouble was that once they hit the highway, they weren't sure where The Hawk was going. There was only one dirt road in and out of Ben's property, but the highway went in two directions: toward Anchorage to the northwest, or head south on Seward highway and end up anywhere on Turnagairn Arm or along the Chickaloon.

If they couldn't catch up to Garza by the time they hit the high-way, they were hosed. They had no idea what he was driving — Garza had run down the dirt road after leaving the cabin, and he'd parked his vehicle behind the tree line, so when Ben and Julie had finally emerged, armed, he was nowhere to be found. Only the sound of the car starting in the distance told them what they needed to know: Garza had gotten away, and the longer they waited, the longer the odds.

So they'd jumped into action and were now racing over the

bumps and troughs of the road as if they didn't exist. Julie knew Garza would be moving fast as well, but Ben was treating the road as if it were the smoothest highway on the planet. She saw the odometer and was stunned to see that he'd been able to hit 65 MPH on the rutted dirt road. The ice and snow-packed divots helped, but she also knew that it was risking their lives if they hit one wrong or if Ben didn't see a disguised patch of black ice.

But none of that mattered — they were moving fast, and that meant they had a chance at saving their friends. She loaded the rifle, rolled down the window, then grabbed the seatbelt. She wrapped it around her left arm and pulled the belt all the way out of its housing until it clicked, then released it. She felt it cinch up around her upper arm and shoulder and tested its resistance. Barring a head-on collision with Garza or a tree or rock, the belt should keep her in place and stable as they barreled onward.

She sat back down and held onto the edge of the door as they rode. Ben didn't speak, and Julie didn't need him to. They were a team, always had been, and they were good together. They didn't need to talk through things or discuss anything. All of that would happen later. Right now was about the closest thing to a simple smash-and-grab mission as she could think of.

Another few minutes passed and Ben spoke. "Coming up, dead ahead," he said through gritted teeth. The words jostled in the air as the SUV jostled over the bumps, but Julie could see the jet-black jeep in the distance, about two-hundred feet up.

"How long until we engage?" she asked.

Ben shook his head. "I don't care. You're the sharpshooter. Depends on how much ammo and how well you think you can hit the tires — and *not* hit the back seat."

She nodded. "I think a hundred feet or closer. Get me there and I might be able to pick off the guys holding onto the side."

"Either they're Mr. Universe-level strong, or Garza's driver will have to go slower so they can hold on. Should put us within range in a few seconds."

"Copy that." She checked her magazine again, she leaned forward and kissed Ben on the cheek. "Love you. Don't kill us."

"Love you, too. And *you* don't kill us, either."

She gritted her teeth, leaned out the window, and opened fire.

CHAPTER 11
GARZA

"TAKE A LEFT ON THE HIGHWAY," Garza told his driver. "Ignore what I say on the phone." Edgar Nunez, the young Mexican-American he'd recruited two years ago, nodded his affirmation. They had already discussed the plan, so nothing about what Garza had just said was news to him.

The kid was smart, thanks to a four-year degree paid for by the United States Army and a graduate degree in mechanical engineering paid for by Garza himself. He preferred to be in control of as much of the lives of his men as possible, including enforcing a no-marriage policy while they were under his employ. His soldiers were free to leave, but he also had a pay-what-they're-worth policy that made most young men's eyes water.

Vicente Garza paid his active-duty men salaries that started at $200,000 a year. Bonuses went up from there depending on the projects taken, the number of missions performed, and an overall quantitative assessment at the end of the year. From the beginning Garza had tried to build an organization that was based on merit, qualifications, and performance. He was the de facto head, and his word was law. But beneath him, the men jostled for power and recognition, and they voted in their own leadership. Many of his career soldiers were making upwards of a million dollars a year, an incredible amount in security and defense contracting.

Yet Garza's organization, Ravenshadow, accepted missions that were as incredible as the salaries he paid. They had fought in the favelas of Brazil, the deadly outback, and the open seas. They took jobs that no one else would touch, as Garza responded to one enticement: money.

He didn't want power, and he didn't care about who might be in power in whatever country they were operating in. He cared about getting paid, and he had turned on more than one client who'd refused to pay what his team was worth. His reputation had reached the corners of the globe, from companies interested in protecting their investments in energy in places they shouldn't have been in to governments interested in protecting their stranglehold on the local economy.

His men had taken down corrupt dictators in order for a more corrupt dictator to take their place, and they had killed anyone standing in the way of their clients' goals.

He pulled his phone out of his pocket just as the *ping* of a rifle round bounced into his ears.

"Boss, they're shooting at us," Edgar said.

"I hear it. Keep moving." He banged on the hardtop roof of the jeep, and within seconds he heard his men firing back. He knew it was unlikely they would be accurate while holding onto the top of the jeep with one hand and trying to fire backwards, but he would use any strategy available to him. He pulled the phone up to his face once again and dialed the number.

It took a few seconds, but connected with a clear signal.

"Listen, asshole," the voice began.

He cut him off. "Harvey," Garza said. "Shut up. Listen to me. You shoot your friends on accident and I'll finish the job for you. You shoot *my* friends, and I'll kill you and yours." He turned around to see Sarah and Reggie sitting forward in their seats, their eyes strained.

"The only way out of this with your friends alive is to let us get to the airport. Anchorage is only..." he stopped mid-sentence, hoping the ruse would reach Ben's ears. "We're going to leave without interference Ben, and I hope you understand what it means if you disobey me. After that, you have one week. Find the book."

He didn't wait for Ben to respond, disconnecting the call and turning once again to his driver. "Turn left at the highway."

Edgar nodded once again as the sounds of his soldiers outside the vehicle continued firing.

CHAPTER 12

BEN

BEN STRUGGLED to keep the SUV pointed straight on the dirt road. The ice and snow had crept in from the sides, and he hadn't plowed in a few days. The SUV kicked and swayed as he pressed the gas pedal down harder.

The call had come in just after Julie had fired her first shots. He pressed a button on the steering wheel to route the call through his car's Bluetooth speaker system, once again impressed with the new technologies onboard. He hadn't driven much of anything as an adult besides a beat-up '86 pickup he'd taken to Yellowstone, so when he'd met Julie and the rest of the CSO team, he'd also met the new era of driving technology.

After the call ended, he looked back at Julie, who had taken a brief break from shooting to hear what Vicente Garza had to say. "He said he's taking them to Anchorage," Ben said.

Three shots rang out, but they sailed wide of the SUV since the jeep was hurtling over a few bumps and a curve in the road put a stand of pines between the two vehicles. Furthermore, Ben knew bulletproof material had replaced the windshield glass shortly after the CSO had purchased it.

"It's a lie," she said.

"I think so. He's a professional soldier. He had this all planned out, and he knew we'd follow him out. But…"

"But where's he going, then?" Julie asked, finishing the sentence for him.

"Exactly."

"Could be anywhere," she said. "The Seward runs along the coast, but there aren't any towns until the reservation down that way."

"And for all we know, Garza's got an in with the rez, too." He banged a hand on the steering wheel. "Are you *sure* he's not going to Anchorage?"

"Of course. He wouldn't have slipped up. If he said it, it's because he wanted us to hear it."

"And he needs us for leverage, so he doesn't exactly want to kill us, or Reggie or Sarah. So that means he needs to *lose* us, but not *destroy* us."

"Yet."

"Right. Yet."

Julie sniffed and then pulled herself back up and out the window just as the last stretch of straightaway came into view. This 300-yard span of dirt road was the best-kept, cleanest patch of Ben's driveway, and he knew it would be their last chance to get the jeep before they were on the highway. And because of a few well-placed trees and a quick dip before meeting Highway 1, his driveway was all but impossible to see.

And it meant that if they *didn't* gain on the jeep before then, Garza could slip away easily and be completely lost to them.

He pressed the gas pedal to the floor, ignoring the signs of ice on the road in front of him. It would be a hell of a trick to get the SUV slowed down fast enough to merge onto the highway, and he was making a risky bet that there wouldn't be any oncoming traffic in either direction, but it was a risk he felt ready to take.

Garza was in the same position, and a collision at this speed would mean the death of two of his friends. He wasn't about to let that happen because he feared for his own safety, but knowing Julie was hanging out the window, aiming with an assault rifle with an arm twisted into the seatbelt, was almost enough to change his mind.

Almost.

He gently maneuvered the SUV over a patch of ice on the left side of the road just as the jeep hit the few hundred feet of dip and disappeared. They would come up on the other side, but Ben would be blinded to their location for a few seconds as his vehicle dipped down and out of sight. He intended to be at the other side of the dip and cresting the hill when Garza turned onto the highway — it was the only true way to know which direction he'd head.

He clenched his teeth. The SUV barreled forward, staying true to the road's layout as it flew over ice, snow, and patches of mud. He forced the wheel in gentle directions to correct course, and just as he began to crest the hill, the jeep appeared again.

"There!" Julie screamed.

"Got it," he said under his breath. The jeep was moving much faster now, and he could see it was preparing to merge across the highway and head to the left — southeast.

Just the opposite of what Garza had said.

Ben pulled the SUV to the side and told Julie to hang on, but the road was much smoother here and he was able to get the vehicle across the highway and into the right lane, about two-hundred feet from the jeep. There were no other cars on the road, and Ben said a silent prayer in thanks for that.

Julie peppered a round of shots toward the jeep and Ben saw one of the soldiers hanging onto the jeep's roof reach to his arm. As he did, the jeep hit a patch of ice and had to correct, causing the man to lose his balance and fall to the asphalt. Ben could almost hear the crunch and scraping as the man hit and began tumbling end-over-end down the road.

The SUV moved toward the man at a breakneck speed.

"Got him!" Julie yelled. "You think he's alive?"

Ben saw the man's tattered gear, his clothing shredded and his head a bloody mess. He came to a stop in the center of the road, perpendicular to the lane with his chest on the yellow lines. Still, the man moved slightly, pulling his head up and looking up at Ben.

"Yeah," Ben said. "I think he is."

He pulled the SUV to the left, ever so slightly, just as the man tried to push up with his hands, obviously anticipating what was about to happen. But Ben's vehicle was already there, and he felt the punch of the man's skull blasted into a crater as he made impact.

"Never mind," he said. "I don't think he made it."

Julie didn't hear him, or she ignored him, as she immediately began firing again.

Ben saw the second soldier on the right side of the vehicle ducking out of the way, trying to put the back of the jeep between himself and Julie's rifle, but not having much luck. As Ben pressed forward and gained on Garza, his engine much larger than the jeep's, the man's backside grew larger.

Julie placed two rounds right into the man, one in the buttocks and another through the spine. The man fell lifeless from the vehicle, bouncing off into the dirt and snowbanks on the side of the road.

"Great shot," Ben shouted.

"Thanks — one more should get their tire out of commission, and then we can —"

Before she could finish the sentence she yelped. Ben realized he hadn't been paying attention closely enough, and he'd missed what Garza had thrown out the window.

It was bouncing closer to them, and Ben wasn't sure what to do. A grenade, no doubt "cooked" to detonate at a particular time, and he knew Garza wouldn't need more than a few chances to get one to explode right in front — or beneath — them.

He swerved into the left lane, only then noticing that there was a massive eighteen-wheeler bearing down on them from that direction. He slammed on the brakes just as the grenade exploded.

THE GRENADE'S detonation lifted the SUV's right side off of its tires. It slid sideways and narrowly missed the eighteen wheeler. Ben saw the driver of the semi-truck yanking his steering wheel hard to the left while the truck's brakes pressed hard to slow it down. He saw the smoke from the wheels and tires and the snow and dirt kicked up in the air, but the wall of filth that rained down on them from the grenade's explosion blocked most of his vision.

Pebbles and larger rocks smacked against the bulletproof glass and the side of the frame, and he heard a few bounce into the interior of the vehicle through Julie's open window. He hoped the explosion hadn't harmed her. The rocks were followed by another blast of air, a sort of sucking feeling coming over him as the pressure wave pulled more air through the SUV.

The SUV righted itself and the shocks took the brunt of the impact, but Ben's head smacked against the window as the car rocked side to side. He wondered how Julie was faring, but he couldn't afford to look. His forearms locked the wheel in place and he applied pressure to the gas pedal as the trailer of the eighteen-wheeler slid sideways, directly in front of him.

He needed to get out of the way of the massive trailer before it slammed into him — and through him. He didn't want to get jack-knifed beneath the trailer, but he also didn't want to slam on the brakes and take the chance that the driver of the semi could right his truck in time. He guided the SUV to the left more, now completely off the left side of the road and bouncing over the rocks and debris on the shoulder. A few feet more and he was off the side of the road completely, and the trailer was only a few yards in front of him.

And it was moving quickly.

Ben panicked. He jerked the wheel to the left, not knowing or caring if there was a tree or rock that would be in his way, and simultaneously yanked the handbrake. The SUV jolted, and he felt himself propelled toward the windshield, held in place only by the strength of his seatbelt. The SUV seemed to groan against its own weight as the vehicle changed direction, and Ben held his breath as he watched the trailer bearing down on him.

Come on. He willed the vehicle to move faster, to move out of the way of the ongoing trailer.

It was no help. The trailer continued moving, Ben's SUV kept turning, and he knew it would be close.

There was a small gap between the two vehicles when Ben's car came to a stop on a log. He hadn't seen it, as it had been buried beneath snow, but now his front axle was bottomed-out on top of it, and as hard as he tried, it wouldn't move.

The remaining five feet between the two vehicles closed to nothing in an instant. He yelled something incoherent just as the trailer filled his vision, still moving brutally fast. It rose up, looming over him, then smashed through the SUV as if it weren't there.

The body of the front-right corner of the SUV was completely destroyed, but a piece of the metal frame caught on the edge of the trailer and was pulled along with it as the trailer moved back onto the highway. The SUV spun around, now being pulled the opposite direction.

Ben's head whipped around again, once again smashing into the window, and he cried out in pain. His body felt like a rag doll, and he expected the seatbelt to rip free of its enclosure at any moment. He tried to brace himself for whatever impact may come or whichever direction he might find himself pulled in, but he had no control, and his body and the hard surfaces inside the SUV reminded him of that.

He ping-ponged off the console, his hip cracking against the seatbelt clasp, then his shoulder crushing against the seatbelt clasp on the opposite side. Somehow the airbags didn't deploy, but he wasn't sure it would have been more or less helpful if they had.

The SUV bounced and hiccuped a few more times before it detached from the trailer. It had dragged them back onto the highway, but the SUV was leaning precariously to the right side, and he knew that a tie rod and probably two or three wheels had been completely snapped. The vehicle seemed to slouch, to dip into the ground on the right side, and as it came to a complete stop, he could smell antifreeze and gasoline, and wondered if there were any open flames nearby.

Then, as if his mind were on autopilot, he felt the sense of impending doom.

Get Julie.

He forced himself into action, fighting against the unbelievable pain in his side. He must have broken or significantly bruised a rib or two, but it was hardly the only pain he was feeling. His neck felt stiff, as if it was one good crack from falling apart completely, and his shoulder felt like it had had a nail driven through it.

He knew there was no way Julie would have been able to hold on throughout the madness. He unbuckled his seatbelt, forcing himself to breathe slowly, purposefully. He turned and looked into the back seat.

Julie was gone.

No...

He shouted her name. "Julie!"

He threw the door open and fell out, coughing as he hit the hard, rock-strewn asphalt beneath the snow. It felt cold, in a satisfying and terrifying way, as if he wanted to lie down there forever and just die. He knew it wouldn't be hard to do, the way he was feeling, but he also knew that he needed to just get up and shake it off. He wasn't any more injured than he'd been in the past, and his friends were still gone — they needed him to be okay.

"Julie," he said again.

"Ben?"

It was a whisper, or it was a shout, he wasn't sure. His ears were ringing. *Probably from when I smacked my head,* he thought. *Am I even thinking clearly?*

"Ben," she said again, this time louder. *No. She's here.* He opened his eyes, not realizing they had been closed, and looked up. The sting of the sunny morning hit him first, burning through his retinas. He closed them again, took a deep breath — as deep as his side would allow — and opened his eyes again.

"Julie," he said. "That you?"

"Yeah," she said. "Bruised my arm pretty bad, and I feel like I've got a punctured lung, but since I'm talking, I must be okay."

"Yeah, well, I'm not sure I fared as well."

She frowned. "Really? You look fine to me."

He groaned. "Why can't you just leave me alone to die? Start throwing snow on top of me and just leave me be?"

"Because," she said. "You do most of the cooking. And I like to eat."

He smiled, against his better judgement. Somehow, that hurt too. "Fine," he said. "Help me up."

REGGIE FELT the crushing pain of his own bodyweight against the zip ties. His hands were numb, long since having lost the circulation from the rest of his body, and he felt like he'd rather cut them off.

Sarah seemed fine. *Well,* he thought, *as "fine" as you can be while being kidnapped.*

The jeep hadn't deviated from its course. They were heading south on Seward Highway, the open ocean on the right side of the vehicle. Garza and his driver hadn't spoken a word to each other after their encounter with Ben and Julie, and that encounter had ended with their vehicle being blown to bits and then run over by an eighteen-wheeler.

Reggie had seen Ben and Julie survive against narrow odds, but he'd never seen anything like that. Ben's black SUV had disappeared behind the larger semi truck as it swerved out of the way, but he saw the explosion launch the SUV sideways and into the ditch on the side of the road — right in line with where the semi's trailer was about to be.

He had turned away just before the collision, but he'd heard it. The grinding, twisting rip of metal-on-metal told him everything he needed to know.

If they weren't dead, they'd be close to it, unless Ben had performed some miracle behind the wheel.

Sarah hadn't watched. Her eyes had remained riveted onto the back of the driver's head as they traveled on, and Reggie wondered what she was thinking. *Was she trying to decide how to escape? Did she even care about escaping? Was she waiting for me to act?*

He couldn't tell. Everything he knew about her told him that the *last* thing she'd do was wait to be rescued. She was terrible at playing the "damsel in distress" role, and he didn't blame her. He liked to keep things in control as much as possible, and he absolutely *hated* being out of control. The problem was that he had nothing to work with here. He had been completely taken out of commission, even his trusty switchblade pocketknife removed from his person when he'd been moved to the car.

But this car ride wouldn't last forever. Garza was taking them somewhere, and unless he had a way to knock them out again, he'd have a moment — a brief instant — to act. For an over-six-foot frame like his, getting in and out of a jeep was a feat in and of itself, not considering trying to do it while his hands were tied.

He'd have a few seconds, he guessed, when his kidnappers would try to yank him out of the car. A few seconds to smack his hands against his lower back as hard as he could, snapping the zip tie apart. He'd taught that very lesson for years in Brazil. "Urban escape," he called it. Zip ties were effective at resisting indirect force — twisting, rubbing, and tearing were almost entirely ineffective at breaking the ties. But direct force, such as that caused by snapping the wrists apart from one another, often did the trick.

He'd have to cause a distraction to pull it off — and then he'd have to figure out what to do once he'd broken free of his ties. Sarah would still need help, and Vicente Garza was a formidable opponent.

He spent the rest of the car ride considering these obstacles, trying to decide on a course of action.

The drive ended fifteen minutes later, and as the jeep pulled off the side of the highway and began heading inland, he tried to find any markers or signs that would identify their location. The road was bare, but it was a road — not a dirt path like the driveway to Ben's cabin and the CSO headquarters — and it was in good shape, which meant there was a chance they'd come across a town, or at least another human.

He wasn't sure there'd be anything he could do in that case, but it might help him get his bearings.

Unfortunately, the jeep turned off this road and turned north, less than a mile after they'd exited the highway. They drove along a beaten, worn path, only as far as it took to get out of sight from the access road. The pines quickly grew inward toward one another and covered their tracks, eventually creating a thick wall of green, impenetrable and invisible.

Reggie began to think they would be brought to a secure location near Ben's cabin — after all, they were only an hour's drive south of his land. But as close as they may have been, it would be impossible for Ben and Julie to find them out here. The backcountry of Alaska, Reggie had learned, was as impossible as it was beautiful. The trees could hide just about anything, and when he considered how remote most of the state was, as well as its sheer size, he realized it wouldn't matter if they were one mile or a thousand miles away from Ben — out here, they were as good as gone.

But they *would n*ot be kept here. As they rounded a final corner and the trees gave way to a small clearing, Reggie saw a helicopter, its rotors already beginning to spin up. The driver of the jeep pulled in tight to the chopper's line, parallel to the aircraft's fuselage, and Garza immediately jump out.

"Get out," he barked.

CHAPTER 15

BEN

"OKAY," Ben said, grimacing, "let me have it."

He rolled his shoulder backwards and forwards a bit to ease out some pain. It did nothing but excite the injury and cause more strain than it was worth. He tried the same with his face, hip, ribs, and arms, and found that nothing he could do would alleviate the pain of the car crash.

He and Julie had managed to walk halfway back to the cabin, but Mrs. E had picked them up before they'd journeyed far. She told them she had contacted her husband, who was reviewing the security feeds from the solar-powered cameras that were mounted along the road to the cabin. He would fill her in, then she could tell Ben and Julie what he'd found.

That was an hour ago, and Ben and Julie had showered and changed clothes, and Julie had dressed Ben's rib and hip wounds with a pad of gauze and given him an icepack for his shoulder. None of their injuries were serious, though Julie had sprained her elbow and bruised a few ribs in the wreck.

And Garza had gotten away. She'd killed two of his men, but they both knew all too well how easy it would be for the mercenary to replace them.

Now, Mrs. E was sitting calmly on the edge of his couch, and Ben wished he could borrow her stoicism. While she was preparing to explain how Garza had gotten into his home unseen, while his team had brought down Sarah and Reggie without issue, all he could think about was how he would get them back. He wanted the man dead, and he knew Julie felt the same.

"First," Mrs. E began, "he could get into your home because, well, it's not protected."

Ben frowned. "I thought your husband said we could lock the entire facility down, even automatically?"

She nodded. "He did. And that is true. But the facility is not finished yet. We have not yet installed the CCTV systems or the automatic triggers — there would be no point with all the workers running around." She took a breath, then looked at Ben. "And you specifically asked that we excluded your cabin from much of the renovations. To keep it 'quaint,' as you put it."

Ben shot her a glance, then realized she wasn't trying to rile him up. *I did say that,* he realized. He now wished he'd been a little less adamant about keeping his cabin 'rustic.'

"Second," she continued, "Garza did not *go* into the facility, or the attached wing. None of his men did. He came right to the house, to the cabin, where they looked around and destroyed everything. He would have certainly set off alarms if he had ventured into the headquarters building, but he did not."

Julie frowned, and Ben watched her expression changed as she realized something. "He *knew* not to go in there," she said. "He knew he'd have a hard time getting away without being caught."

"Perhaps," Mrs. E said. "But he came here looking for something, correct?"

Both Ben and Julie nodded. "The Book of Bones," Ben said.

"But if he did not find it in the cabin, why would he not then assume to check the other building?"

Ben thought about it for a moment, but Julie answered. "Because he knew it wasn't there?"

"Exactly."

"He knew we didn't have it," Ben said. "So why did he come?"

"He told us that," Mrs. E said. "He wanted Reggie and Sarah. To use as leverage. That's why he came."

Ben thought again, then shook his head. Julie and Mrs. E watched him, waiting for his response, but he was already deep in thought. He stood, walked over to the small kitchen, stepping over broken furniture and picture frames and stopping in front of a small table he used as a liquor cabinet.

He examined the bottles — none of which had been smashed in the break-in — and chose a scotch. He had always been a rum and coke guy, the 'easy drinker' that made bartenders happy, and he hadn't ever drank much, anyway. He and Julie shared a bottle of wine every now and then, and he and Reggie enjoyed tasting new whiskeys when Reggie found them in Anchorage, but left to his own devices and desires, Harvey Bennett would just as soon enjoy a simple glass of water as he would a Cuba Libre.

However, he felt he needed a little extra help finding a way out of their dilemma. He poured a couple fingers of the amber liquid, then sprinkled a drop of water from the kitchen sink over the top of it, and finally turned back around walked into the living room once again.

"He's afraid," he said.

Julie and Mrs. E looked confused.

"He fears something. His employer — whoever's paying him? I'm not sure. But he's scared to fail."

"How so?"

"Well, he needs *us*. He said that. He told us he expects us to find this book for him. He didn't say why, but there's one thing that's more important to him than anything: money."

"Right," Julie said. "He'll do anything for money, and he'll do even more to not lose it."

Mrs. E jumped in. "So he will not get paid if he does not find the book. And we know he will kill for what he wants…"

She trailed off, and Ben watched Julie's face. To him, her expression spoke volumes. He thought he could see her considering what Mrs. E had said, thinking about what it truly meant. *We know he will kill for what he wants…* Ben knew that was true, but he was afraid of another truth.

We know he will kill out of convenience.

He and Julie had nearly been killed on the highway, both from the rifle fire and grenade, as well as the near-death interaction with the massive semi truck later. He'd seen Garza and his men kill others just because they were in the wrong place at the wrong time, and he'd seen Garza himself order Julie, drugged and under his influence, kill their friend and leader in cold blood at point-blank range.

This was what Ben was searching Julie's face to find. He couldn't find it — either Julie was still struggling to resurface the memory, or she wasn't entirely sure it was real. He knew that her dream from the night before had actually happened, but he wasn't sure she was ready to fully process it.

If it were him, he might even choose *not* to process it. He'd always been good at hiding his emotions, keeping them hidden deep down inside. He'd been a park ranger for years before meeting Juliette and getting involved with the CSO, and his natural inclination was to stuff things down inside and not deal with them. Eventually, he knew, those things would simply not matter as much anymore.

This belief had consistently been the biggest thing he and Julie fought about. It was their first fight, sitting across from one another in a hotel restaurant back when they were trying to save the United States from a catastrophic volcanic eruption and subsequent bacterial infection, and it had been the thing they talked about most. Because of his past, Ben wanted to ignore what he'd gone through until it no longer bothered him, but Julie wanted to talk about those same things for the same reasons.

Now, the tables had turned. He looked at the woman he loved, knowing something about her past that she herself didn't fully understand. She knew it, but she didn't *know* she knew it. And when that memory finally crystallized in her mind, Ben wasn't sure how she would react.

"So it's life or death for Reggie and Sarah," Julie said.

"Probably. What we know for sure is that we *are* the people most likely to find the Book of Bones. We got closest to it, and if it weren't for Sharpe and Interpol, we'd still have that journal."

"But the journal is not the book," Mrs. E reminded him. "It was Rachel Rascher's great-grandfather's, and it only references the book."

Ben started pacing as he sipped his drink. "What we know is that the Book of Bones is a lost dialogue of Plato. Somewhere around the time he wrote his *Timaeus and Critias,* he wrote the Book of Bones, which chronicles Atlantis and its rise to power over Athens and the Greek mainland."

Julie picked up the thread. "And when Rascher's great-grandfather got his hands on it, he used whatever Plato wrote of the Atlantean race to justify Nazi experiments. Eugenics, genetic alteration, that stuff."

"You think this is about that?" Ben asked.

Julie shrugged. "No way to know until we find the book. But it's clear to me now that we *need* to find this book. To get Reggie and Sarah back, but also to see what the big deal is. So I'm thinking we pick up where we left off."

Ben nodded. He knew what she meant. Where they'd "left off" was trying to discover who Rachel Rascher had been working with. The CSO team knew that she must have had outside investment, but they weren't sure if it was governmental or private. All they had was what they could piece together from her subterranean research facility, and what they could remember from her great-grandfather's journal before Agent Etienne Sharpe with Interpol had confiscated it.

They knew it would be impossible to convince Sharpe to hand over the journal, but they'd decided it wasn't necessary. Rachel Rascher had, according to a comment she'd made, been working both from her great-grandfather's journal that referenced Plato's lost work... as well as from a copy of the original text, in full, of Plato's lost work itself.

They had seen no evidence to support this, but Ben's theory had been that Rascher had been working with an organization much larger, and much more powerful than any of them had imagined. If she truly had *access* to the Book of Bones, without actually having it *in her possession*, it meant they trusted her, but she was only on a short leash.

And it meant that the organization pulling the strings, whoever they were, were in a position of power over her. It meant *she* had been working for *them*.

Ben's theory, and his idea, was to track down this organization and somehow gain access to the Book of Bones itself. The original, full text.

The problem was that his theory of the organization who controlled the Book of Bones wasn't an organization any of them wanted to mess with. It was an organization known for its ability to control situations from afar, using a massive, wide network of operators working completely off the radar, able to move unilaterally to achieve its greater purpose.

It was not an organization Ben and the rest of the CSO wanted to upset, and their discussions on the matter after the events in Egypt confirmed that. But now, after Reggie and Sarah's abduction and Garza's rude awakening, their hand had been forced.

They were about to head into a literal hell.

"He said it couldn't be done," Ben said.

"Of course he did," Julie said. "He knows them better than any of us. But he's also *never* tried."

Ben sighed, then took a deep sip of his drink. *Time to decide,* he thought. They'd come close to making plans to track down Rascher's benefactors before, but they had reached the conclusion that it would take more than what they alone were capable of — and that was when Reggie and Sarah were involved. Now, with the two of them out of commission, it would be an impossible task.

But the answer was as clear to him as it was to Julie and Mrs. E, who was nodding along and watching Ben for his decision.

"Okay," he said. "Fine. You're right. We don't have a choice. We break in to the Vatican Archives. We go up against the Catholic Church, on their turf."

CHAPTER 16

REGGIE

REGGIE WATCHED HIM FOR A SECOND, waiting to see what else the man wanted. But Garza didn't hesitate. He turned on a heel and jogged over to the opening door of the chopper.

The driver stayed back, exiting the jeep slowly after turning off the engine, then stepping out and away from the vehicle. He pulled up a pistol from his side holster, aimed it at Sarah, and looked at Reggie. "Get out," he repeated. He had to raise his voice to be heard above the rotor wash.

One armed man. Single pistol. Vehicle between me and him. Reggie counted off the situational variables like it was a bulleted list. He flicked his left and right as he struggled to get out of the jeep, Sarah doing the same to his left.

Sarah's also *between me and gunman. Can't use her as collateral. Garza will be at the chopper in three. Could be more bogies inside.*

He stared down at the ground, but he allowed his peripheral vision to fill in the details. The treeline shimmered and moved, nothing out of the ordinary. The ground, hard-packed ice and snow, dark and gritty with the addition of pine needles and dirt that had blown over the coating of white, seemed just like any other ground he'd seen here.

Still, something felt off. Something told him he'd be making a mistake by trying to get away, by trying to fight back. *Garza doesn't make mistakes*, he reminded himself. *Garza doesn't leave things to chance.*

But out of the corner of his eye he saw Sarah. Head held high, she was out of the vehicle and staring at the man pointing a gun at her. She was slightly taller than the man, her curly brown hair poking up even higher.

And there was a tear in her eye.

He hadn't noticed it before, or it was new. Or it was nothing, just a remnant of her eyes trying to adjust to the sudden drop in temperature as they exited the vehicle.

But it was there, and he decided to act. He whirled around to his left, keeping the gunman — the only known threat to him at that moment — in his frontal vision, ensuring he could see and counteract the man's motions before he could fire a shot.

He ducked beneath the top of the jeep, knowing that a straight shot would easily travel through both sides of the vinyl and fiberglass frame, and called Sarah's name. "Get to the back of the jeep!" he yelled.

Sarah didn't need to be told twice. She ducked and backpedaled, just as the man swiveled to shoot at Reggie. Reggie heard the *crack* of the pistol ring out through the air, twice. Both shots hit the jeep, but only one made it through.

Reggie saw that shot hit the dirt and ice, mere inches in front of him. But he knew Garza's man wouldn't shoot again. It was a blind shot now, and he could easily regain the high ground by moving toward the back of the jeep.

And that's where Reggie would meet him. He pulled his wrists up and slammed them down again, hitting his waist hard and fast and immediately feeling the ties yank apart.

His hands were free.

He pulled Sarah toward him and down, skipping in front of her as he threw her toward the earth. It was a hard toss, and she let out a yelp in surprise as she fell. He jumped over her legs and crouched near the bumper of the jeep, waiting.

It only took a half-second for the man to appear. Reggie wasn't surprised by the man's distance from the jeep — Garza had trained him and he wasn't about to let himself get too close. But that meant Reggie's next action would have to be perfectly in sync with the man's reaction time, if not slightly faster. Any missteps and he'd have a large-diameter hole in the center of his chest.

The man came fully into view, and Reggie was already in motion. He had calculated the man's distance intuitively, allowing his training to take over, and he launched his body headfirst into the man's legs.

He wanted to stay low, to prevent an accidental discharge — or a purposeful one — from catching him. The man would react in kind, lowering his aim and eventually getting a shot off, but Reggie hoped he'd make an impact and take out the guy's shins before that happened.

He did. Reggie's head landed on the man's right shin, but he had his fists wrapped around both his legs before he'd even finished falling. The man went down, crumpling on top of Reggie's long, lanky body, and by the time he realized he'd been felled, Reggie was rolling sideways and preparing his second blow.

This hit he aimed toward the back of the man's neck — the closest thing to Reggie's fist. It wasn't a great spot to aim a punch, but Reggie also knew the man wasn't going to give him a second chance. *Come on, asshole, make this easy.*

He threw his fist down on the man's neck, feeling a small pop, but knowing it wasn't nearly enough. The man grunted, but then rolled sideways quickly, trying to surprise Reggie and get away from his reach. Reggie was prepared, however. He caught the man's shirt and pulled him toward him, then landed a quick two-hit punch to his face and jaw.

The man's face slackened, and Reggie finished with two more

shots to the man's eyes. The driver looked up at him and snickered, then threw a leg around Reggie's waist. They were both already on the ground, the awkward fight taking place in a near-sitting position, so Reggie wasn't tripped.

He was, however, caught off guard. The man's trip felt like a Mack truck had slammed into his back, and he lurched forward a few inches. It was enough for the man to get an arm free and he wound up, then threw it forward, catching Reggie in the teeth.

Reggie groaned and tried ducking sideways, but his head felt heavy. He was seeing double, and the two jeep drivers were now squatting above him, preparing a barrage of blows. Reggie watched the man's four eyes, trying to calculate just when the attack would come so he could try to dart away, when two Sarahs entered his vision.

They were standing — no, running — and he blinked. At that moment Sarah hit the driver, launching him forward and down, back on top of Reggie. Sarah kept moving, now running toward the line of trees just behind him. He silently said her name, excited for the support, then realized he still had the driver — a massively built man, he now realized — to contend with.

And then, as if his subconscious had a realization it hadn't told him about, he stopped. His fist was ready, the man's face was directly in front of his, and he had the upper hand. But he stopped.

Pushed his head up and around to get a better view of Sarah's escape attempt.

She, too, had stopped.

Something isn't right.

He threw the man's torso off of him and the driver scrambled away, trying to recover in case Reggie attacked once again. But Reggie had the felt the turn in the fight. He knew he wasn't going to be attacking.

He got to his knees, then slowly turned around fully, facing Sarah.

She was staring straight ahead, away from him.
Staring at the trees.

CHAPTER 17

BEN

MRS. E HAD GONE to the CSO facility headquarters to converse with her husband. The team was preparing a plan, and though that plan was far from solidified, they were beginning to understand what they needed to.

Ben and Julie were still in the cabin, on a conference call with Archibald Quinones. The Jesuit priest lived in Brazil, five time zones ahead of them in Alaska, and answered the phone on the second ring. They had met in Brazil, when Reggie introduced them, and the professor's help in tracking down the history of a strange genetic trait in an ancient Amazonian tribe had been crucial.

They remained friends, checking in with one another as often as they could, but none of them had seen the man in person in over a year. He assured them he was well, still living in Brazil, and still teaching history part-time at the local university.

He was ecstatic to hear from them once again, but his attitude quickly turned when he'd heard about Sarah and Reggie.

"So, where do you think Garza will take them?" Quinones asked.

"It's impossible to say," Julie replied. "They headed south on the highway, but..."

"But you're in Alaska. So that means literally anywhere in the United States," Quinones said, chuckling.

"Right," Ben said. "But this is Vicente Garza we're talking about. He's well-connected and well-funded. We're assuming he's got a chopper or plane lifting them off and taking them farther away. So they could be anywhere by tomorrow."

"I see. And if they do take a flight — can you somehow track it?"

"Mrs. E is working on that," Julie said. "She will check with her husband to see if he can tap into the flight path data. Everything's private, but it's all there. The question is if he can gain access."

"Of course. And you said he wants the Book of Bones? This is the same book you were tracking down in Egypt, no?"

"It is. But we weren't looking for it as much as we were just curious about it. We wanted to know what the big deal was — a lost book of Plato would carry some weight in the antiquities and history crowds, but it seems there's more to the book that what any of us thought. Apparently it's important enough to Garza — or whoever's paying him — that he's willing to kidnap and kill for it."

"Any idea what is in the book?" Quinones asked, his voice nearly a whisper, the weariness of his years sneaking through the phone line.

"Not really," Ben said. "Rachel Rascher was doing Nazi-era experiments in Giza, with Die Glocke. Her great-grandfather's journal said they were trying to work out problems with the human physique, but that's too vague to go off of."

"But last time we called you," Julie said, "we had the theory that it involved the Catholic Church somehow. Either a benefactor, or a silent partner, or both."

"You think they are now involved with Garza?"

"We can't know for sure yet, but yes. There just isn't any information about the Book of Bones, so the fact that Garza now knows about what Rachel Rascher was working on makes us think there's a common thread."

"But we were not sure the Catholic Church was involved with Rascher before," Quinones pointed out.

"Right," Ben said. "But I think there are enough signs that point to it being possible. The car that took Sarah in Santorini was registered to a local priest. Might mean nothing, but then consider that they — whoever was helping Rascher — had the funding to support a massive extraction effort, her research, *and* stay out of the way of the entire Egyptian government, who we know is not very keen on outside interaction and has entire ministries to prevent snooping and sneaking around.

"Whoever was helping her, and whoever might be helping Garza now, has the assets to pull it off. It's a carte blanche operation — they don't know how much it will cost, or how much time it will take. It could be a fruitless endeavor, too. Who's to say the Book of Bones is even out there?"

"Which brings me to my question," Quinones said through the bluetooth speaker on the coffee table. *"Why try to access the archives? If the Church is, in fact, involved, don't you think they would waste time and money telling Garza to find the Book of Bones if they knew it was already in their possession?"*

Ben nodded, knowing Quinones couldn't see him. This was something he and Julie had already discussed. "Well, for one, we're still not entirely sure it involves the Church. And if it is, we're not sure it's the *whole* church. There have been factions of the Church throughout history, operating on their own terms, away from Papal governance."

"Absolutely."

"And second, we're not sure they know they have it. From what we've read the Vatican Archives gives such limited access to even its own hierarchy, it could be that whatever faction within the Church that's trying to find it either can't or won't try to access the Archives. Or they don't know it's there. *We* don't know it's there, but..."

"But we need to start somewhere," Julie said.

"And breaking into the Vatican Archives to find a lost document that may or may not exist, and may or may not exist there *is your best plan."*

"Well, when you put it like that, I guess we should clarify that we *are* still entertaining other ideas."

CHAPTER 18

REGGIE

NO. *Not at the trees.*

She was staring at a *man*. Or, at least, that's what Reggie thought it was.

But it was no *normal* man. This man was nearly twice the size of Reggie, who was tall to begin with.

My eyes are playing tricks on me, he thought. *But then why did she stop, too?*

He knew that what he was seeing *had* to be real. *Somehow.*

The "man" was holding a rifle, the object nearly miniature in his massive hands. His arms were tree trunks, his legs spindles of rock, the sheer musculature on him unlike anything Reggie had ever seen.

What the —

"Red," he heard a voice say. *Garza.* "Please do not waste my time. I have a lot of work to do, and as I'm sure you can see, our research is not quite ready for mainstream release."

Garza had walked up to him while he and the driver had been fighting and was now standing directly behind him.

"We've been here before, haven't we, Red?" Garza asked. "You, appalled and amazed that I am *continually* one step ahead of you?"

"I'm not —"

"Save it, Red. I'm not interested in games. And I'm not interested in whatever witty banter you've been able to cook up over the last hour. We have an appointment, and I expect to keep it."

As he spoke, Reggie watched the tree line in front of him. The shimmering sensation he'd noticed before wasn't a hallucination. There *was* something in the trees, waiting just out of sight behind the pine trees and boulders.

They stepped out from behind their hiding spots, two of them to his right, and one to his and Sarah's left, and walked forward. He thought he could feel their steps as they reverberated through the earth.

Before, as he'd been observing and analyzing his surroundings upon exiting the jeep, his eyes had expected to see normal-sized men, soldiers, enemies. He'd expected, as he'd been trained to expect, to see *humans*.

But what he was seeing now defied all reality. Never in his life had he known such a thing could exist.

And that was when he noticed their faces. These "men" were not men at all, or if they were, they were the most deformed, disfigured faces he could ever imagine. Literal monsters. Their skin hung off limp cartilage that clung to a rock-solid bone structure that somehow kept it all from melting to the ground. Eyes, drifting in hollowed-out sockets, seemed darker than normal. Their mouths were a twisted cacophony of evil, lips unable to pull together to hide hideous teeth that seemed more random than purposeful.

They looked down on him, both staring and noticing and seeing right through him, and he wondered if they were thinking anything at all. Could they talk? Imagine? Articulate emotion?

He shook his head. *No, there's no way this can be real.* He twisted around and faced Garza, but instead of seeing the man — his long-time enemy — he saw more creatures.

Three more of the beasts.

Brutes in every sense of the word, three more of them, stood over

Garza and behind the jeep. The driver was cackling, blood pouring out of a wound near his eye, but he too was just watching Reggie.

"This — this isn't real," Reggie said.

Garza smiled. "I'm afraid it is, Red. This is *very* real, and it has been the culmination of research that began shortly after you and I last saw one another. There's more I would love to tell you, but I need your cooperation."

Reggie shook his head. "I — I can't... there's no..." he took a breath and looked Garza directly. "There's no way *in hell* I'm cooperating with you. This is madness."

"This is *science*, Gareth," Garza said. "And I'm almost out of time."

He snapped his finger, and three of the giants walked toward him. He turned to Sarah, who was watching the exchange between him and Garza, her eyes wide. She, too, was taking it in, and Reggie could see on her face that she was not handling it well.

"What do you need us for?" Reggie asked.

Garza walked up beside him, facing the tree line and Sarah once again. "I don't, Gareth," he said, his voice low. "I need *you*."

As he said the words, the giant who had tumbled out of the forest in front of Sarah aimed his rifle downward, directly at the space between her shoulder blades.

"Do it," Garza said.

The giant pulled the trigger.

BEN

"THAT'S MRS. E," Julie said, looking at the front door of the cabin. They were still on the call with Archibald Quinones, and they had been discussing some of the research Archie had been doing lately.

"Go ahead," Ben told her. "Archie, Julie's going to grab Mrs. E. She's got information from her husband that might help us out."

"Very good," Quinones said.

"Hello, Archibald," Mrs. E said. She rarely used their shortened names, a formality her husband shared with her. Her Russian accent was still only barely concealed by the years she'd spent in the States. "I trust you have been well."

"I have, thank you," he said. *"I am sorry to hear about Reggie and Sarah. I want you to know I will do whatever it takes to help you get them back."*

"Thank you," Mrs. E said. She turned to Ben and Julie before speaking again, but she kept her voice loud enough so that Quinones could hear. "My husband just got off the phone with a man who can access the flight registry data."

"Anything useful?" Ben asked.

"Yes, perhaps," she said. "He did, it seems, have a helicopter waiting. And as you might have suspected, Garza did not log his entire plan with the authorities. It is not required unless the aircraft is flying under Instrument Flight Rules, or IFR. And IFR is only necessary for commercial flights or when expecting to fly through cloud coverage, storms, that sort of thing."

"You said he didn't log his *entire* plan?"

"Yes," Mrs. E said. "He most likely decided that flying manually, without the use of IFR, would be a better way to stay out of sight. But he also decided not to invoke the wrath of the government. Anchorage has the only Class C controlled airspace in the state, *and* there is a storm picking up south of there, likely right where they were flying from. The man my husband contacted was able to confirm that there was a small flight logged — most likely just a first leg — in a helicopter, lifting off from a field in unmarked territory and landing 45 minutes later southeast of there, outside Whittier."

"That's great news," Julie said. "Can we get there —"

"We cannot get there in time," Mrs. E said, cutting her off. "Unfortunately, it would take that long just to get a flight ready in time."

"And you think this is just the first leg of their journey?" Quinones asked.

"We do. They are heading south, and we now have an identifier that will hopefully turn up again, but other than that we do not know where to look. You can imagine how hard it is to find a single aircraft, out of tens of thousands, flying somewhere over the continental United States, not to mention Canada."

"Right," Ben said. "So we're hosed?"

"Unless the identifier turns up again. But there is a good chance it will. The problem then is that we cannot be certain Garza did not change aircraft somewhere, as a way to stay ahead of us."

"Great," Julie said.

"It is what we have to work with," Quinones said. *"So that is what we will work with. We will watch the skies and see where this chopper ends up, and we will go there."*

Ben was more than happy to have Quinones' support, but he didn't share the man's optimism. He'd been in far too many scrapes like this to think they'd have such luck. "Can we get a head start?" Ben asked.

"We can move south," Mrs. E said. "But we cannot know for sure they will keep going that direction forever. Best case, we move down the coast to the Pacific Northwest and then see where they are."

"Best case," Julie said, "is that we figure out where the Book of Bones might be. Or where *he* thinks it might be."

"This is true," Quinones said. *"He will still focus on his priority — finding the book. Taking Reggie and Sarah was collateral to get you involved, but it is secondary to his larger goal."*

Ben nodded. *It's all too much to process,* he thought. *So, take things one step at a time.* He knew their first — and therefore, only — priority was to rescue Reggie and Sarah. That meant tracking Garza and his men, and if the only way to track them was to find the Book of Bones and bring it to him, that was what they'd do.

"We have to find the book," Ben said. "Julie and I can travel south. Mrs. E, it's probably best if you stay here and keep a watch on things."

She nodded. "Of course."

"And that means you'll be able to keep us abreast of any changes, or any new information."

Again she nodded.

"We'll head to Seattle. At least we'll be in the continental United States, and from there we can catch a plane to anywhere. Can your husband —"

"He will have a private jet ready in Seattle for you," Mrs. E said.

"Perfect." Ben looked at Julie. "Does that work?"

She forced a smile. "It has to. Archie can work on how we're going to get into the Vatican, and then how we might access the Archives. It might be that we can 'borrow' some clearance from someone he knows."

"*Yes,*" Quinones said. "*I will get started immediately. Expect an update by the time you reach Seattle. It is the middle of the night in Italy, but I have a few contacts who are closer to home, and even more only a phone call away. And there is still plenty of research I will need to do to understand fully what we are up against.*"

Ben looked around at the team — the *remaining* team — of the Civilian Special Operations. Since they had formed the group, they had sought answers to questions their own government couldn't, wouldn't, or shouldn't ask, and they had mostly succeeded. They'd found trouble after just about every turn, but they were better for it.

This time, however, the trouble had found them.

CHAPTER 20

JULIE

THE FLIGHT to Seattle-Tacoma International Airport had gone smoothly, and both she and Ben had gotten a little rest. Julie knew Ben hated flying, but whatever phobia he had about it had been mostly quelled, thanks the to sheer amount of flying the CSO team was expected to do.

She watched him wake up from her window seat on the small commercial airliner. He had chosen an aisle seat, but then switched with a passenger when he'd found out that they had booked the seat between his and Julie's. Now the bear of a man was crushed between two smaller women — Julie on one side, and a tiny old lady on the other.

He snorted, then sat up. "We almost there?" he asked.

"We already landed, Ben," Julie said, laughing. "How many of those rum and cokes did you drink?"

Ben looked like he'd just been caught stealing. "What? They give you these tiny little bottles and like a half-pour of soda in a flimsy plastic cup, and I'm supposed to be satisfied with that?"

"Each one is like eight bucks, too."

Ben shrugged. "It's on the company dime," he said. "Besides, they were weak."

"You were passed out from about half an hour into the flight until now."

"Short flight."

Julie laughed again. "Whatever. We need to get to the cargo and shipping terminal on the other side of the airport where Mr. E's plane will be."

"And maybe Quinones will have news for us then."

"Maybe," she mumbled. She knew Archie would call, but she wasn't optimistic he would have anything much to say. Gaining access to the Vatican Archives — legally or not — was no small feat. They had already discussed as much after they'd returned from Egypt, and in their brief discussions about it since then, they'd written it off as an impossibility.

Still, there was hope. If the Catholic Church was involved, in any capacity, with whatever Rachel Rascher had been working on, there was a possibility that they might find a clue in the Archives.

If not... she didn't know what to think. She hoped Ben had a plan he was still working on, something that might still allow them to find the Book of Bones and get their friends back.

"There," Ben said, pointing.

Julie followed his finger. A man stood outside the plane's window, directly on the tarmac, holding a sign that said *Bennett.*

"Looks like Mr. E saved us the hassle of having to go through the terminal," Ben said.

"Us? That sign only has your *name* on it."

"Guess Mr. E's trying to tell us he wants the wedding to happen sooner rather than later," Ben said.

Their wedding had been planned — and postponed — three times now. No matter when they attempted to put something together it seemed that life got in the way. And more often than not, their version of "life" getting in the way was really someone, somewhere, trying to kill them.

"Well, I'm ready when you are."

Ben frowned. "What's that supposed to mean? We're going to get married here? At an airport?"

"I'm ready to *get off the plane*, Bennett," Julie said. "That's what I meant."

He nodded, blinking a few times, and Julie wondered again just how many of the rum and cokes he'd enjoyed.

The flight attendant came directly to their seats before the plane had reached the terminal, and she escorted Julie and Ben to the front of the plane. "We had a request for you two to disembark before our other passengers. There's another plane waiting for you, and you both have clearance to head directly there."

"Thank you," Julie said.

The woman took them to the front of the plane just as the door opened. They were led to a set of stairs at the end of the jetway, and they took these down and onto the tarmac. The man holding a sign was there, introduced himself, and asked them to follow him.

They walked a few hundred feet to a hangar where there was a Learjet idling nearby, and Julie and Ben climbed the stairs into this smaller jet. Inside, the fuselage was painted white, faux leather and wood trim decorating everything in sight. Ben immediately crashed into a seat on the aisle side and pulled out his phone.

"Message from Archie," he said.

"Yeah?" Julie asked. "Go for it." She sat in the seat across the aisle from him, buckled her seatbelt, then waited for Ben to press play.

"*Ben, Julie,*" Archie's message began. "*I hope your flight went well. I am on my way to the university, where I can spread out and have access to the library there. I will call again when you arrive at your next destination, wherever that may be.*"

Julie saw Ben looking at her. She shook her head, as if to say, *nothing to report.* She hadn't heard from Mrs. E or her husband about where they were headed next. Chances are they didn't know either, and the plane would begin flying south until they'd had a chance to track down Garza's helicopter once again.

"Anyway, I wanted to let you know about something. I have been thinking about our 'plan,' or at least our goal. It — it remains a long shot, but I think I may have a way to achieve it."

Again, Ben looked over at Julie. She smiled.

"I can explain more, but I need to research the layout of the city. Please allow me a few hours, and I will fill you in then."

The message ended, and Julie spoke first. "Sounds like we're getting somewhere."

"Hope so," Ben said. "But if not, we're going to have to hope Mr. E can track that chopper."

CHAPTER 21
VICTORIA

VICTORIA REYES ZIPPED through the campus quad and back to her office. Her lunch had been cut short because of a cryptic, vague voicemail that she'd gotten on her phone.

Professor Reyes, the message began. *We need to talk. Please call me at this number and do not mention this call to anyone.*

She might have put it off, ignored the message until later, but there was something intriguing about the man's voice — deep, careful, articulate. A hint of a South American accent, but impeccable English. Somewhere between 50 and 70 years old.

She ran the phone number through a spam-filtering app on her phone, just to see if the number was publicly registered to anyone. She was surprised to find that it was, and even more surprised to discover who that caller was.

Archibald Quinones.

She knew the name — Quinones was an esteemed historian living in Brazil, and he had published papers on the Jesuit fraternity and their relations with the Spanish Crown and Incan populations during the years of the conquests. She had read them with interest, filing them away in her mind as the sort of thing that might prove useful someday, yet not critical to her current projects.

Victoria had always been what her father called 'book smart.' Studious, engaged, and interested in everything. She'd excelled in school, where reading and memorization abilities were strengths, and she had both in spades. Somewhat of an autodidact, she had a near-perfect memory for historical facts, and an uncanny ability to build a tapestry of history based on seemingly disconnected pieces and threads.

In her work, she often referred to the wealth of human history as a 'never-ending quilt,' an ongoing collection of stories and characters and settings that was constantly being reworked, patched up, fixed. It was her dream to finish this quilt, to piece together the entire web of human history, connecting all the dots and patches together in a perfect, linear story.

This, of course, was impossible. But that had never stopped Victoria. She'd been married, divorced, completed three undergraduate degrees and two graduate-level degrees, finished with honors each time, been recognized as one of the nation's top history talents under the age of 50, and she was still only in her mid-thirties.

Her success was nothing short of meteoric, and she'd been offered jobs and speaking engagements more often than she could count.

But her passion, and her goal, was simple: *understand the story of our lives.* Her mission in life was larger than a position at a prestigious university or having her face on the cover of a bestselling book. She intended to solve humanity's greatest mysteries, and to do it in a single lifetime.

She didn't have time for dating, though there were plenty of suitors. She didn't have time for writing books, though she wrote more words per week than most of her graduate students. She didn't have time for many things, including maintaining a social life.

But she had time to talk to historians like Archibald Quinones. The Jesuits had always been an enigma to her — a group of men within the Catholic Church who had originally existed as the strongmen of the Pope during the Spanish conquest. The men tasked with protecting and securing the myriad secrets of the Vatican. The order had evolved over the centuries, but her interest in the order was as strong as ever.

She reached her office and pulled out her phone once again, dialing the number Quinones had given her. She sat behind her desk, shook her computer's mouse to wake it, and waited for the man to answer.

"Hello?"

"Ar — Mr. Quinones," she began.

"Please, call me Archie. Ms. Reyes, I presume?"

"Yes. Thank you. I —" she realized she had no idea what to say. "I love your work."

There was a chuckle. *"Well, thank you for that. But it is because of your incredible work that I reached out to you."*

"My work?"

"Yes, indeed. Your paper on the similarities between fraternal orders among world religions was very well-researched."

"Thank you, Mr. — Archie. I'm flattered you took the time to read it. And thank you for reaching out. I have always wanted to have a discussion with you."

"Well, that discussion certainly must happen. But today, I unfortunately have little time for that — instead, I need to ask for your help."

"Of course," Victoria said. "Anything."

Archie paused on the other end of the line. *"Ms. Reyes, I need your help to make sense of a... set of events that have transpired."*

"Events."

"I have four friends in the United States that are under attack. Two have been kidnapped. I believe the two others are being hunted and are in significant danger."

"My God, Archie," Victoria said. "You need — you have to call —"

"Please, there is more. Trust me, if there were anyone I could call

whom I believe could help there, I would. But my hands are tied, and I believe the only way to find them — where they've been taken, or where the others need to go — is to find more information."

Victoria waited, listening to the sound of the older man breathing. He was pausing, thinking. *Trying to decide if he trusts me?*

"Victoria, if I may. I believe the kidnapping has something to do with the Catholic Church."

Victoria sat up straighter in her office chair. If she'd been drinking tea, she would have spat it out across her desk. "*The* Catholic Church."

"Yes," Archie said. *"As you know, I am a member of the fraternal Society of Jesus — a Jesuit Catholic. If the case were any different, I would never accuse the Church of such a thing. But... I strongly believe they are working against my friends, and — I cannot stress this enough — I have no reason to believe my friends have done anything wrong."*

"I see," Victoria said. She was twirling a strand of her light-brown hair between her thumb and forefinger. An old habit that she fell into in times of stress or deep thought. "You are part of a fraternal order — one of many within the Church. Could these people — the ones after your friends — be part of a different sect? One that might... *want* something within the church to change?"

"Almost without a doubt, yes. The Church is far too large and dispersed to be able to coordinate a singular attack such as this. Besides, I believe that if the Vatican somehow could come together in this way, united on one front against my friends, they... would not really stand a chance."

"True," Victoria said. "So tell me — what is it the Church wants? And why kidnap your friends because of it?"

Another pause, this one longer. Victoria sensed she was about to be told something Archie wished to keep to himself. She was about to check her phone's screen to see if the call had been disconnected when Archie spoke again, his voice nearly a whisper.

"Ms. Reyes, have you ever heard of the Book of Bones?"

She gripped the phone tighter in her hand, fingers white. Her mouth fell open.

THE BOOK OF BONES.

Victoria hadn't heard that name in over five years. She had heard it mentioned in the same breath as other lost works of antiquity, like the *Ab Urbe Condita Libri,* the Quixotic homage by Shakespeare, *Cardenio,* and plenty of individual works by Aristotle. *The Book of Bones,* or the *Hermocrates,* was a lost work of Plato, but many believed it had never even been written. In her professional career, her research required references that were *real,* thus she had spent little time on it.

"I thought Plato never started *Hermocrates,*" she said.

"That is what I believed as well," Archie said. *"Hermocrates, as you know, was to be the third dialogue in his series of discussions that included* Timaeus *and* Critias. *Since* Critias *ended mid sentence, we believe that Plato died before he could even start* Hermocrates. *"*

Victoria waited, knowing it was better to allow a professor and professional thinker time to talk, to allow their ideas time to emerge on their own.

"But we always assumed that he died before finishing Critias. What I believe — what my friends believe — is that he stopped

working *on Critias because the message of* Hermocrates *was far more important."*

"Can you explain that?"

"Yes. There is a longer story, but my friends were involved in an incident in Egypt about a month ago that led me to study this 'Book of Bones.'"

"A name given to it by conspiracy theorists and fringe scientists," she scoffed. *Hermocrates,* like *Timaeus* and *Critias,* was the name of an actual historical figure, a Syracusan politician who no doubt would have been featured prominently in Plato's dialogue.

"True, but in Egypt, my team found what they believed to be a journal that referenced the original manuscript."

"So he wrote *The Book of Bones* — the *Hermocrates* — instead of finishing *Critias?*"

"We think so. Further, he never allowed it to be copied and recorded as he had done with his other works. The Book of Bones contained powerful enough information — information that Plato would have wanted kept close to him — that he never allowed it out of his sight."

"Then how did your team in Egypt get their hands on it?"

"That — that is a long story," Archie said. *"For another time. But they intercepted a journal that contained pieces of the manuscript — copied, of course —"*

"Then how do they know it's accurate? Or genuine? Anyone could have faked a —"

"I am sorry, Victoria. I know how intrigued you are surrounding the details, but we may not have much time to get my friends back. If you can suspend your disbelief for a brief few moments, I promise you we can discuss the intricacies of what I am telling you at a later date."

Victoria smiled. She would indeed enjoy some face-to-face time with an esteemed colleague. Perhaps she could even get the department to cover the cost of traveling to Brazil. "Deal," she said. "From now on, what you say is truth."

"Thank you. The journal, unfortunately ended up in the hands of

an Interpol agent, and we believe it is essentially gone — lost in an unorganized vault of evidence. But the information contained within that journal... the referenced pieces of the original manuscript of Plato's Hermocrates... *Victoria, they were experiments."*

"Experiments?"

"Yes — Die Glocke, the Nazi bell, was apparently a weapon of some sort, originally described in Hermocrates. *The woman who originally owned the journal was a descendant of Sigmund Rascher, the Nazi scientist who —"*

"That's... gruesome."

"Yes, it is. Worse, we believe this woman was planning a larger... experiment. Something similar to the bell, but on a much larger scale."

Victoria enabled the phone's speaker mode and placed it on her desk, face-up. She opened a note-taking app on her computer and began typing.

"But this call is not about that woman. Her experiments, thankfully, are over. Instead, I would like your help finding this Book of Bones. *Plato's 'lost' dialogue,* Hermocrates.*"*

"Okay," Victoria said, "I would be happy to help. But tell me, Archie — why now? Why is it crucial that the Catholic Church find the *Book of Bones*? How does that help find your friends?"

"The man who took them explained it thus: his client, whom we believe to be some organization embedded within the Catholic Church, was told to find the book. He knew that my friends were the best option they had at finding it."

"Okay," she said. "Makes sense. But... *why*? What's in the Book of Bones that —"

She stopped. Blinked twice. Stared at something she'd just written on the screen.

> Book of Bones (Hermocrates) — 'unfinished' book by Plato

> Trilogy:

> > Timaeus: Speculation about the human world; introduces Atlantis

> > *Critias: Details fall of Atlantis; hubris. Description of Atlantic island*

>> *Hermocrates (Book of Bones): Details...*

"Oh my God," she whispered.

"Sorry? What was that?"

"I just... I think I may know what they want."

"The... Church?"

"Well, whoever's after your friends. I believe there's another piece to the saga of Atlantis, and Plato stopped his work on Critias because he *needed* to tell us something. Needed to *warn* us."

"And you know what that is?"

"I — I think I do." She looked again at her notes, then picked up the phone, turning off the speaker mode. "I believe the Book of Bones is about the *people* of Atlantis. Specifically, their *capabilities.* Each book of Plato's gets more and more granular, more specific. *Timaeus* describes Atlantis and the ideal state, *Critias* deals with the island, the geography itself, and therefore *Hermocrates* will describe what the Atlantean *people* were like. You said the book describes their experiments?"

"Yes, it does. At least the section my friends saw."

"Well, I believe there *is* more in the book similar to that. But above all, and why Plato was terrified enough to cut *Critias* short and finish *Hermocrates*, is that the book not only describes what the race of Atlantis *was* like, it described what that race *is* like."

"Are you saying —"

"I am. I believe that Plato wrote *The Book of Bones* not because he wished to detail a race of humans that had *fallen,* but to detail a population that was *still there.*

"And," she added. "I believe that the Church thinks they're out there somewhere, and they wish to find them."

CHAPTER 23
REGGIE

REGGIE'S ARMS and legs were tightly pressed against a hard surface. He pulled and bucked with his legs, but nothing moved.

He couldn't see.

He didn't know if his eyes were open and registering darkness or if they had been injured. He couldn't feel anything.

He tried to scream, pulling against the ties as hard as he could, but he was shocked to hear his voice reverberate quickly through the tight space he was in. It sounded as though the ceiling was directly above him, mere inches away. He pulled his head up, reaching with the only movable appendage he had available.

He was right — the ceiling was hard, and it was barely an inch above his head. He suddenly felt the urge to vomit. He began breathing more heavily, his lungs straining against the thin air.

Where the hell am I?

The box pressed in on him. He felt it growing smaller. *Is all of this part of my imagination?*

He suddenly realized what the box reminded him of, and the feeling of nausea returned.

A coffin.

No, that couldn't be right. He wasn't dead. And why would Garza go through all the trouble to kill me like this? Why not just shoot me in the back, like...

He tried to remember what had happened. *And how long ago?*

He saw Sarah, saw himself, standing with Garza in the woods of Alaska. They were scared. Terrified. He remembered looking around, seeing...

Them.

The... giants. *Is that what they really are?*

He wondered if Garza had been playing tricks on their minds, somehow forcing them to see something that wasn't really there. He'd done that thing before; the man had plenty of tricks up his sleeve and Reggie didn't for a minute think he wouldn't have the capabilities — some new drug, perhaps — to pull it off.

He'd seen what Garza had done to Julie. To their friend Joshua. It had torn them all apart, and it was only because Julie seemed to have no recollection of the event that they all could move on.

He focused back on his current predicament. He was in a box, judging by the hollow, dead sound of the walls and ceiling around him. It was cold, but not miserable. The air did, in fact, feel thin, but it was breathable.

He focused on the facts, of the objective truth about his environment around him.

Just like I've been taught.

They had trained him to handle these situations, but he'd never in his life thought he'd find himself face-to-face with literal giants — men who stood nearly twice his height. They had to be at least nine feet tall. He tried to picture the tallest person he'd ever seen. *A basketball player? How tall are they? Eight feet?*

As if he'd been struck over the head, he remembered Garza's words. *Do it.* Sarah had fallen, hit by the round the giant had blasted into her back.

Sarah.

He struggled again, fought again, and fell still again.

There was no way to know if she were dead. No way to do anything about it if she weren't. He wondered if she was being kept in a small box like this one.

And why?

He couldn't figure out what Garza was planning for them. He had giants — at least, the beginnings of them. Reggie recalled vividly the disgusting, twisted faces of the huge men. *Is that the problem? The soldiers aren't 'finished' yet?* Garza might want them for his army, to bolster his troops.

It certainly would be a deadly force, if Garza could pull it off.

But no — Garza *didn't* need Reggie for that. Why would he? He already had the giants, and Reggie knew the man had nearly unlimited resources through his network, so he wouldn't need Reggie's help with anything.

Garza had taken him — was taking him — somewhere. He'd told them he needed them to find the Book of Bones, Plato's lost dialogue on Atlantis and the city's ancient secrets. It was the same book Rachel Rascher had referenced in Egypt, and...

That was it.

Reggie tried to sit up, but he slammed his head against the top of the box. Pain shot through his forehead and down, but he shook it away. *Rachel was working for someone.* Rascher, the late Ministry of Antiquities in Egypt, had been working to perfect a Nazi-era science experiment called *Die Glocke*, which she believed would allow her to 'test' the purity of living subjects — essentially discovering if they were of the 'master race' or not.

According to Reggie, she was a whack job who'd deserved what she got. Her science experiment had killed many people, and might have killed thousands more if she'd been able to enact the next phase of it.

But even at the end of their mission in Egypt, Reggie's team had realized the sinister truth:

No one person could have pulled this off.

Garza, Reggie now knew, was working for the same person Rascher had been. Her resources, like Garza's, seemed endless, and that meant there was likely a group or organization on the other side of the checkbook that didn't mind draining a bank account to achieve their goal.

He didn't know what that goal was, but he didn't need to.

He needed to stop Garza, find Sarah, and get out this box.

Not necessarily in that order.

He almost smiled. He felt better. He'd trained himself over the years to react to situations with logic and rational thinking rather than emotion. He'd learned from years spent working through his own past that the tools he already had available to him — tools he would *always* have available to him, no matter what — were all he needed to cope.

He now had a goal — it wasn't a plan, but it was enough to create one. He knew the antagonist, their desire, their strengths. He knew himself, his own weaknesses.

Garza wasn't invincible, nor was his army of giants. Garza was a man, and so were the huge soldiers. He didn't understand them completely, nor did he know what it was Garza was *truly* after, but he knew enough.

Garza wanted Reggie as collateral. He *needed* him as collateral, because he needed Ben and Julie and Mrs. E to find the Book of Bones.

But he didn't need the book himself. Garza needed it for his client. He needed to get *paid*.

Reggie almost wondered if the giants — the mutated men — were part of this payment. That the client might allow Garza to keep them, to perfect them, if he delivered his end of the bargain. Or that they would give him enough money to continue researching them.

So if Garza hadn't killed him yet, it was because he needed him alive, either to entice Ben and Julie to find the Book of Bones, or because Garza wasn't sure if Reggie would be helpful in some other way.

But for now, he was alive. And he had a feeling he would stay that way.

CHAPTER 24

VICTORIA

VICTORIA'S EYES pored over the text in front of her, half-reading, half-rehearsing the words she'd seen so many times.

"For many generations, as long as the divine nature lasted in them, they were obedient to the laws, and well-affectioned towards the god, whose seed they were..."

The text was from Plato's dialogue *Critias*, and it described who the ancient Atlanteans were and how they fell from the grace of their 'god,' Poseidon. About 9,000 years prior to Plato's writings, the race of Atlantis attacked and conquered countries and states including Libya and areas within Egypt, and only Athens could 'stay the course of a mighty host.'

Victoria had read the dialogues plenty of times; for her, reading anything more than once meant it was essentially committed to memory. She'd been able to regurgitate long strings of the texts to her classes and having immediate access to Plato's writings had proven useful more than once in her career.

Today, however, she was reading with a purpose: she had a new piece of her puzzle. Her 'never-ending quilt' had a new patch, and she now just needed a place to put it. She wanted to find *where* to put it as well — what other pieces of history linked up to Plato's accounts of Atlantis? What other portions of history described these people? She had found, over the course of her career, that human history never exists within a vacuum. Everything was connected to everything else. Everything was *related* to everything else.

She continued reading, this time with a purpose, with a question posed toward Plato himself: *What are you trying to tell me? What are you warning me of?*

Victoria skipped to the end of the *Critias* text, reading the final known written account of Atlantis:

"By such reflections and by the continuance in them of a divine nature, the qualities which we have described grew and increased among them; but when the divine portion began to fade away, and became diluted too often and too much with the mortal admixture, and the human nature got the upper hand, they then, being unable to bear their fortune, behaved unseemly, and to him who had an eye to see grew visibly debased, for they were losing the fairest of their precious gifts; but to those who had no eye to see the true happiness, they appeared glorious and blessed at the very time when they were full of avarice and unrighteous power."

When the divine portion began to fade away... Victoria had read the words before, but this time she closed her eyes and tried meditating on the line that jumped out at her the most. *Divine portion. Became diluted too often.*

She knew that the mythology of Atlantis claims the god, Poseidon, as its deity. Poseidon bore children with a human woman, Cleito, and together they had five sets of twins.

Sons of god, daughters of men.

They named the eldest of these demigods Atlas, the son who was given the island Atlantis, and for whom the ocean was named after.

Sons of god, daughters of men...

That phrase played itself repeatedly in her mind, but its meaning was still subconscious. She wasn't sure where it had come from, where she had read it. She allowed it to exist in tandem with her active thoughts about Plato's text, trusting her instinct and intuition that her subconscious would provide her with the details when she needed them.

When the divine portion began to fade away. She pondered this line once again, knowing that the tugging feeling in the back of her mind was a sign that she was close to some breakthrough, some new understanding of the text. She had always assumed that this 'divine portion' was the lineage that linked the Atlanteans to their deity, Poseidon. Lineage had always been a powerful tool in ancient times, a tool that chose kings and monarchs and created an oligarchical society based on familial ties.

The stronger the ties, the more powerful the person.

But then what about becoming 'diluted too often?' Could Plato be describing something other than the dilution of a lineage because of extra-familial relations? Could Plato be talking about a physical, literal dilution?

Victoria considered what Archibald Quinones had told her, of the woman in Egypt who had been experimenting with information she'd claimed she had found in the *Book of Bones.* The woman had been working with... some chemical? Some sort of change agent? The Nazi bell experiment, Die Glocke, was also said to have been some sort of weapon of chemical warfare, but the Allies had never uncovered it after the war.

Could the 'divine portion' and 'dilution' have something to do with a reduced dosage of some chemical? In that sense, the Atlantean race — the source of their power — would have been 'diluted' enough that they eventually lost their power. Their fall would have been inevitable.

She focused once again on the text in front of her.

"Zeus, the god of gods, who rules according to law, and is able to see into such things, perceiving that an honorable race was in a woeful plight, and wanting to inflict punishment on them, that they might be chastened and improve, collected all the gods into their most holy habi-

tation, which, being placed in the center of the world, beholds all created things. And when he had called them together, he spake as follows-"

And that was it. Plato's work, *Critias*, ended mid-sentence. Either the rest had been lost to time, or Plato had never finished it.

Archibald Quinones had claimed that it was the latter — that Plato had simply moved on to a different, more pressing, dialogue. The *Hermocrates*, the final book of Plato's Atlantis trilogy, was also lost to time.

The final paragraph of *Critias* held no new answers for her, though there were some intriguing phrases. *'Collected all the gods into their most holy habitation, which, being placed in the center of the world...'*

Was the 'center of the world' Atlantis? To the Atlanteans, sure. Possibly. But from Plato's perspective? Where would *he* place the 'center of the world?'

These were the questions she was wrestling with when the office phone sitting on her desk began to ring.

VICENTE GARZA LEANED toward the pilot as he spoke into his headset. "ETA?"

The pilot, leaving one hand on the stick, checked his watch. "About seventeen hours. We have four refueling stops scheduled, but they should take less than an hour each."

"Very good," Garza said. He turned to his phone, which had a connection to the onboard satellite link, allowing his phone internet and cellular access. He opened his encrypted messaging app and typed out a question.

> *Status?*

He only had to wait a few seconds for a reply after the message had been sent.

>> *As scheduled. Beginning phase four-trials this afternoon.*
> *Fine. Alert me to any anomalies.*
>> *Affirmative.*

A pause, and then:

>> *How did the phase-five trial specimens hold up?*

Garza thought a moment, trying to decide how to answer the question. There was no need to get into details; the man on the other end of the line was a scientist. He would want details, but only those pertaining to the specimens' adrenaline, heart rate, muscle wear, and so on. Garza didn't have any of that information. This test had been a real-world, live-fire test, and while there hadn't *been* any live fire, he had a good sense for the giants' abilities.

> *Difficult to assess. No casualties, but also no direct engagement. I expect significant exhaustion, possible damage to bone structure.*

He didn't need to wait for his scientist's response to know that the man still thought it was a bad idea to bring the giants into the field this early. The flights alone — packing the massive humans into the back of a cargo plane and flying them across the world — had been an ordeal for everyone involved, not the least of which the giant soldiers themselves.

The scientists and researchers Garza had employed had warned him about the issues he could expect if he took the science experiments into the field: long-term loss of bone density, muscle failure, even death. The subjects were not ready, they'd told him. They would likely begin to physically break down, figuratively and perhaps literally. They weren't ready — they weren't yet strong enough.

But he wanted to know for sure. His team had done an incredible job building these soldiers. For years they had worked in laboratories around the world, each completing a small piece of a puzzle that none but Garza could see in its entirety. They had performed their duties, studied their problems, issued solutions... and he had his best scientists put it all together for him.

That process began years ago. Today, he was close. He wanted to turn over his research and receive his final payment. But he needed *proof* that what he was after was legitimate. He needed to know that it was *real*.

Seeing the soldiers earlier in the forest was *real*. He had to force himself to remain unmoved by the display, unfazed by the monsters walking out of the woods. He'd seen them in the lab, seen their images and files and reports, but seeing in real life — seeing them actually *operate* — that was what had convinced him.

He had been working toward this goal for most of his career. He hadn't realized it at the time, but this was his ultimate prize. He had spent his entire career building an army. A group of men so well-trained and disconnected from their own desires that he could fully control every one of them. They were autonomous in the sense that he could point them in a direction and they would march, not stopping until they received further orders. They would destroy — and had destroyed — anything and anyone in their way.

Best of all, his army, Ravenshadow, was for sale. He worked for money. Nothing else could break down language barriers, cross continents and oceans, and silence even most dissenting opinion like money.

And now, he had the opportunity to build and sell the next generation of super soldier. These men were the future, and now he had the proof of concept. They hadn't actively engaged an enemy, but they had achieved his goal perfectly.

He thought back to Reggie's face when he'd seen them. Slack-jawed, for once in his life completely dumbstruck. Garza had felt the same — most of the men were over nine feet tall, and their sinewy musculature rippled across their massive frames like vines around a tree trunk. He had watched Reggie's face register disbelief, then awe, then sheer terror.

And *that* was his brand. That was his product. Garza needed Ravenshadow to invoke fear and awe in his enemies and his supporters — that was how he would achieve his goals.

But there was a final piece to the puzzle, one that he had been tasked with finding. His latest client needed the soldiers as much as he did, and they were willing to pay an incredible amount to obtain them. But they, like he, needed a finished product, not a half-baked schematic. They needed the complete soldier, and to Garza and his team of scientists, the complete soldier was still just a dream.

His client had informed him that there was an answer to his dilemma, and he was close. They had instructed him to track the final resting place of a mystery they had been after for centuries. That place would offer the final piece to his puzzle, and then his mission would be complete.

CHAPTER 26

BEN

THE CAPTAIN HAD LOGGED their flight plan and had taken off —
to Rome, Italy — over an hour ago, while they waited for Archibald
Quinones to get back to them.

Which was why Ben was upset to hear Archie's first sentence
when the call connected.

"What you are attempting to do is impossible," Archie's voice said
through the phone's small speaker.

Ben looked up at Julie across the aisle, a concerned look on his
face. No matter what he thought his face looked like, he knew that
what he was feeling was even deeper.

"So, we're heading to Rome. To Vatican City. Should we have the
pilot turn around?" he asked.

"No," Archie said. *"But let me fill you in on where I am with the
research. The Vatican Archives are the private archives of the Pope,"*
Archie said. *"Passed from one Pope to the other, they are literally the
notes, collections, and scrolls of countless generations, saved and
protected by those who work inside the Archives."*

Ben waited for Archibald Quinones to get to his point.

*"I have been researching a few options here at the university
library. There are maps, books, and a few scholarly papers describing*

the Archives. I had a few ideas, but it seems... at least if these publications are to be believed, there is nothing we can do to get inside."

"How well-protected is it?" Julie asked.

"It's not just how well-protected it is," Archie said. "It's where it's protected."

Ben frowned.

"There are guards — the Vatican Swiss Guards — like there are guards everywhere else in the Vatican. And there are secret police who work for the Catholic Church hovering about. But it is not the guards that worry me."

"You said there was a way," Ben said. Julie nodded.

There was a pause, then the sound of coughing. "I said I was thinking of a solution. But let me start at the beginning — it will all make more sense that way.

"First, what many people believe the Vatican Secret Archives to be is wrong. The original plan for the Archives, established by Pope Paul the V, called the 'Archivum Secretum Apostolicum Vaticanum,' was simply a 'private' or 'personal' — hence the word 'secretum' — archive for the papal letters. It was meant as a repository for the sensitive yet crucial collections of decrees and papers the Pope was involved in, either as an author or recipient.

"Over time, it became the perfect place to maintain a living history of the papal seat, as well as the histories of the world itself. It became more broad, accepting anything and everything, and then it became a library of information — anything related to the Vatican, of course, had a place. But eventually anything related to the world at large, deemed to be important by the Pope and his council, had a home in the Archives.

"So anything that the early church deemed 'important' ended up in the Archives."

"Exactly. Some people theorize that copies of ancient manuscripts, long since lost, may be in the Archives."

"Like books written by Plato."

"That is my thought. Of course, if there were anything inside of that nature, it almost certainly would be under far more scrutiny than the rest of the Archives. Some people even postulate that there are documents — correspondence — between Mussolini and the Pope. Documents that could corroborate a famous rumor that the Vatican was complicit in certain war crimes against the Jewish populace during World War II."

"Wow," Julie said. Ben whistled. "That's some serious stuff."

"It is. And that is precisely why I believe it is impossible to gain access to the Archives if the Pope does not wish it."

"Can't we just get access to a 'less secure' area?" Ben asked. "Then sneak around and see if there's anything they're not telling us? Mr. E would have the technology to ensure we're running silent, and any cameras —"

"It is not the cameras, nor the guards, that I am truly worried about."

Ben stopped.

"I assure you both, I have analyzed the potential security flaws in the design of the Archives, at least the building that exists now. But it is more complicated than that. First, the Vatican only grants access to 'legitimate' scholars. Those they deem worthy. It is explicitly and without question off-limits to journalists, students, and anyone else.

"And if they grant access, that access takes place by walking through the Cortile del Belvedere, surrounded by guards and police. One entrance, one exit."

"Could you gain access?" Julie asked. "You are, after all, neither a student nor a journalist. You're still publicly listed on your university's website."

"Yes, that is true. And perhaps I could. But that is the true reason I called. I do not believe that in-person access is possible."

"We can't overcome the security issues?" Ben asked.

"We may be able to. But there is one major problem with that plan,

and that problem is one I am not sure we can overcome: I am not sure exactly where the Archives are."

"Wait," Ben said. "What? You just said it's accessible through the... Corteel del Belva-something, right? In Rome?"

"That is correct. That is the publicly listed location of the Archives. But I am not entirely convinced the Archives are in any one location."

Ben's jaw dropped. *Of course,* he thought. *If the pope wanted to hide some documents, why have them all in the same place?*

"Since 1881, the Pope has allowed access to his private archives, if you meet the credentials I mentioned before. But why should we believe that those people have access to all the Archives? Why should we expect that the Pope would not hide a few thousand documents — or more — in another location?"

"You think there's more than one Archive?" Julie asked.

"I do not. However, I believe there is not only one location for the Archives. It is all one network, but I believe there are many access points across the Vatican, depending on the level of clearance."

"Okay, so we need to find out how to gain access to the most secret one?"

"No. The problem with that is the Archives do not operate like a traditional library. One does not access the Archives, then freely browse. There is no centralized database that can access the Archives — computer or otherwise.

"To find a text, the scholar may request up to three items per day, and only three. If they request something that does not exist, or nothing at all, they are asked to leave, and must start again the next day."

"Sounds rude."

"And to request a document, they must choose from a catalog written in Latin. If the title they desire is not exactly what it lists on the catalog, they may never find what they are after."

"So if Plato's original title, translated to Latin, was not *The Book of Bones,* we may be out of luck?"

"Precisely."

"Okay," Ben said. "So what are you proposing? You said you had thought of something."

"*I did,*" Archibald said. *"And while it is a risk, I think it is the best opportunity we have. Furthermore, it keeps our names and faces out of the system."*

"I'm a fan of that," Julie said. "All we need is for another country to permanently revoke our visitation rights."

"And we won't have to break in to the Archives?" Ben asked.

"*No,*" Archie said. *"Not the Archives."*

Ben sensed this mission was about to get more difficult.

"Instead, you will need to gain access to the Papal Chambers."

"I'm sorry — what?" Julie asked.

"The Papal Chambers. The private quarters of the Pope."

CHAPTER 27

BEN

"SOUNDS IMPOSSIBLE," Ben snorted. He took a sip from his rum and Coke, then flashed a glance out the window. There was nothing but white — clouds for miles. They were thirty-thousand feet above the ocean, flying 450 miles per hour. The pilot had given them the update a half-hour ago — still ten hours to Rome — and as much as he tried to ignore the truth, he couldn't help but think of the fact that they were defying the laws of physics, hurtling through the air in a huge, heavy metal tube.

Ben had always had an aversion to flying. He wasn't when it had started. Or why. But for as long as he could remember, he'd hated being totally, utterly out of control. It wasn't a trust issue; he knew pilots were well-trained, and that flying was, statistically, one of the safest modes of transportation.

But there was still something *unnerving* about it. Over the years he'd known Julie, he'd had to travel cross-country, as well as inter-continentally, and he had gotten better at it all. He no longer felt the need to throw back a shot of whiskey and a Dramamine or Xanax, but that didn't mean he wasn't constantly checking the windows for any sign of catastrophic engine failure. Any turbulence they experienced caused him to grip the arms of his chair with all the strength he had.

Julie helped. Having a relationship with a woman who was, in just about every way, his equal, yet still somehow all the good things he was not, was one of the most miraculous things he'd ever experienced. How they had fallen in love was still a mystery to him, but he wasn't about to question a good thing, especially when he needed that good thing to keep his mind off the day-long flight.

Julie had moved over from across the aisle to the seat next to Ben's and ordered a glass of white wine from the flight attendant. After their conversation with Archibald Quinones, Ben had checked in with Mrs. E., who had received an update from her husband.

The helicopter, registered as N942FY, had stopped in Juneau, Alaska, where it had refueled and continued southward to Portland, Oregon. From there, it had flown to Sacramento, California, refueled, then taken off again and was headed south, destination unknown. Mr. E had informed his wife that he had an MLAT, or multilateration, track on the chopper, but that because of the extended time of the last refueling, as well as the fact that the helicopter was far slower than a plane, he believed it was possible that Garza and his captives had been moved into a faster jet. The chopper hadn't yet left the airport in Sacramento.

Mrs. E was still under the impression that Garza was heading south, and there was, in fact, a single aircraft, tracked with the newer ADS-B system, had logged a direct flight to Lima, Peru. There was no public information about the flight, nor was there any logged records of the flight, which led Mr. and Mrs. E to believe that the flight was a private charter. Mr. E was still working on retrieving that data, if it existed.

The key was that Mrs. E believed the flight to Peru was Garza, on a private charter, and he was making up for lost time. Further, she believed — and Ben had to agree, based on the information they had at the moment — that Garza *wanted* them to know where they were.

He hadn't come out and told them, but Ben knew all too well that the man, if he chose to, could completely disappear.

The fact that he had flown through three airports, kept his transponders working, abided by all flight regulations, and hadn't tried to conceal his steps, essentially meant that he *wanted* to be found.

It was almost a mystery to Ben why he hadn't just told them outright that he was heading to Peru. Maybe Garza wasn't sure, either. Peru could be a piece to the puzzle, or it just as likely could be nothing more than a base of operations. Or a place far enough away to keep Reggie and Sarah safely out of reach.

But where in Peru? What was his goal?

As far as Ben knew, Ravenshadow's headquarters was in Philadelphia — or at least it had been. *Had they moved?* Having an international office could benefit Garza, but Ben wasn't sure if he would have chosen South America as his base of operations.

So was there something else there? Was there a reason they were heading to Peru?

And after thinking about it for a few minutes, Ben had to wonder: *Are they actually going there?* Mrs. E, after all, wasn't at all certain — their data wasn't complete, and their analysis was, at best, preliminary. There was really no way to know where Reggie and Sarah would end up, but they had to decide.

Archibald Quinones was on the screen in front of him and Julie, who had opened Julie's laptop and connected to the in-flight WIFI. The picture and video was crisp, and Ben knew that the same feat would be impossible on a 300-passenger commercial flight. He couldn't help but feel pampered. Free drinks, unlimited in-flight food, and no one else jostling through the aisles.

Fifteen years ago I was scraping poop from privies in a national park, he told himself. *Fifteen years ago, I was alone. Fifteen years ago, I was scared. Fifteen years ago...*

He looked at Julie. For a moment he was drawn back to the past, back to when he was by himself at Yellowstone, then Rocky Mountain National Park as an exchange ranger, then back at Yellowstone. The years of solitude, barely interacting with his fellow staff and rangers.

Then... *her.* She had descended into his life like a tornado, nonstop and incessant, forcing him to accompany her through the twists and turns of her life. He was pulled in, consumed, infatuated by her. But if there were such a thing as love at first sight... what they'd experienced was not it.

He smiled when he remembered their first month together. Driving around the United States together, staying in hotels and bed and breakfasts, arguing about the best way to save the nation. And yet, through the harrowing experience of losing his mother and countless other souls, he and Julie had been drawn closer together. They had somehow pushed aside their differences and stuck it out, and when the dust had settled, they'd realized that their differences weren't as drastic as they'd thought.

In fact, they'd realized that their differences were precisely the things that drew them toward one another. Julie's outgoing, extroverted nature was a perfect complement to Ben's more withdrawn, introverted nature. She pulled him to a world he never thought he'd be a part of, and through it all he was her rock, a solid, unmoving structure on which they could build their future.

And while the picture of that future was constantly changing, sometimes a bit out of focus and other times opaque, Ben knew Julie was the center of it for him. No matter what happened, they were in this together.

CHAPTER 28

REGGIE

THE BOX above Reggie's head cracked open, as if split from above. He gasped as new, fresh air rushed inside, and he felt the cool, dry air pushing the sticky wetness off of his face.

His eyes adjusted, but it was difficult to make out where they were now. It was dark, but they were inside. A building — but not a modern-looking structure. Reggie rolled his head side to side and saw a low ceiling, cracked and uneven. Stone. The light hitting it was coming from somewhere else.

A shadow appeared over Reggie's casket. A man, not a giant.

"Mr. Red," the man's voice said. *Garza.*

He rolled his tongue around in his mouth, trying to generate some saliva. "Wh — where the hell am I?"

"This is a secure location my team established late last year," Garza said. "It's remote, so I don't need to maintain a full staff."

"Remote where?"

Garza smiled as he leaned down to unbuckle Reggie's arms and legs from the bindings. "Well, I could give you the coordinates, but I believe you would come to the same conclusion I have — we are in the middle of nowhere. A *vast* nowhere."

"What do you want with me?"

Before his left leg and arm were free, Reggie saw two soldiers — normal sized — step up behind Garza. They were both holding rifles, and Reggie didn't need to feel the weight of them to know they were fully loaded.

"I want to know everything you know about the Book of Bones."

Reggie sat up and tried to get a look at his surroundings. He wanted to keep Garza talking, to buy time. He needed to escape, to find a way out of... wherever he was.

"Okay," Reggie said. He shrugged. "Fine. It's a book, written by Plato. Long time ago."

Garza's face betrayed no emotion. The two men near him stepped closer as Reggie's left leg was finally freed. Garza stepped back, joining his men.

The room they were in was dark, the only light provided by a single construction lamp that had been set up on the far wall, and it cast a yellowish glow to the space in front of Reggie. That space was filled with the three men in front of him, and behind them a long, empty wall. The ceiling wasn't as low as he'd initially thought, or it was sloping upward.

The entire space felt subterranean, as if they were in a stone-walled structure that had been sunken into the ground.

"So... can I go now?"

Garza smiled again. "Mr. Red, the more you tell us, the less pain you cause yourself."

It was Reggie's turn to smile. "Ah, got it. Torture. You think you're going to get some information from me by causing physical pain. Well, that's fine. Wouldn't be my first bout with that sort of intimate touching."

Garza raised an eyebrow.

"Plus, I think you and I are on the same page — everything I know about the Book of Bones you know as well."

He was sitting on the edge of the casket now, and he pushed

himself forward and stood up. The two soldiers watching him tensed, but he had no intentions of escape.

Yet.

He cracked his neck, taking another chance to look around. The space behind him stretched back about twenty feet, and the lamp was standing in the center of the opposite wall. He couldn't see anything beyond it.

Other than the men, the casket, and the light, it seemed like the room was empty.

"Tell us about your girlfriend, Red."

Reggie flicked his eyes back to Garza.

"Sarah? What about her? I thought you guys had like special technology and stuff. Like Facebook. You guys have Facebook?"

"I don't want to know what she ate for breakfast, Red. I want to know what she *knows*."

"About the Book of Bones? Same as me. Nothing useful."

"I don't believe that."

"Believe whatever the hell you want," Reggie shot back. "I don't know a damn thing about that stupid book, and I don't want to. Rachel Rascher killed a lot of people because of it, and if I ever find it, I'll burn it."

"That would be an unfortunate choice, Red."

"Why's that?"

"Because I need it."

"In that case I'll burn *both* of you."

Garza stared at Red for a moment, then turned on a heel and started walking toward the side of the room. His soldiers followed, both men tracking Reggie as they left. He followed Garza as he neared the corner of the darkest of the space, then was surprised as he suddenly seemed to levitate.

Stairs.

He hadn't noticed it before because of the light, but there appeared to be a set of stairs in the room's corner. But they weren't normal-sized stairs. Each was about two feet tall, maybe two-and-a-half deep. He watched as Garza and the men slowly made their way up the six stairs and waited against the wall. One man tapped the butt of his rifle against the wall and it immediately shifted. Cracked open.

It was a door, also nearly invisible, also large. Standing about ten feet from floor to ceiling, he guessed. Wood or stone, Reggie couldn't tell from here. *But it was a door. So that's the way out,* he thought. He watched as the door slid open on hidden hinges, trying to see into the darker space beyond.

He didn't dare move, as he knew the men wouldn't hesitate to fight him back with their weapons. All he could do was stand and wait.

And observe.

He watched everything as they left the room — tried to see out the door, into whatever space was up and beyond. He tried to see if the men were armed in any other ways, but couldn't.

And he tried to recognize patterns in the way they moved. How they held their heads as they walked — did they drag their feet at all or look down as they took steps?

All of it was information. Not all of it would be helpful or useful, but it was information nonetheless.

"Mr. Red," Garza said, just before exiting the room. "You are free to move around in here. There is only one exit, and they will guard it every minute of every day. Even if you were to escape, your freedom means Dr. Lindgren's immediate death."

So she is still alive, Reggie thought. He grinned. "You think you'll wait me out? That it? That I'll get tired of pacing around down here, hungry, thirsty?"

"No," Garza said. "I don't expect you to last nearly that long."

Reggie frowned.

"When I had my soldier shoot your girlfriend, Red, he did it with a rubber bullet from close range. That wound is still open in her back, and we intend to keep it that way."

Reggie stiffened.

"The benefit of having a clean, open wound such as hers is that we can introduce *new* agents into it, without fear of immediate infection."

Reggie stifled a breath. His throat caught, and he nearly stumbled.

"It would *amaze you* at how resilient the human body is, Mr. Red. Homeostasis is a wonderful thing. We are experimenting with just such a thing here and in my Philadelphia labs. The ability of the mammalian body to completely regulate its temperature, reverse foreign intrusion, and heal wounds is unlike many other things found in nature.

"But that work comes at a cost, Reggie. The human body doesn't *like* foreign intrusion. As I'm sure you know, an open gunshot wound is a remarkably painful thing."

Reggie tried to swallow, but found that his mouth was once again dry. He tried to speak.

"And I believe you will find that this chamber, while very effective at keeping outside noise to a minimum, is not *entirely* soundproof."

No.

He balled his fists. Tried to force his legs to move. Nothing worked, nothing functioned. *Come on, man*, he told himself. *You're trained for this. You're* better *than this.*

But he knew it was pointless. The Hawk had captured him and brought him back to his nest, and there was nothing he could do to change that.

Nothing, of course, but tell the truth.

CHAPTER 29

VICTORIA

"HELLO?" she answered. Victoria sniffed and blinked a few times. She realized she hadn't lifted her eyes from her computer screen for over an hour, and her contact lenses were itching.

"We know what you are working on, Ms. Reyes."

Her hands immediately felt clammy. *What the hell?* "Who is this?"

"We politely ask that you cease your research into the subject and turn it over to us. We seek your help, and we will be requesting your in-person assistance soon."

"Turn over my... cease *what* research?"

"You are treading water, Ms. Reyes. In a sea of sharks. And all it takes is one, tiny cut. The sharks will turn on you in an instant. Consider this the only warning you will receive."

"What the f —"

The phone disconnected. Victoria held the earpiece on her hand for a few more seconds, then slammed it back onto the receiver. A piece of the cheap plastic broke and sailed across her desk.

"Was I just threatened?" she asked aloud. She sat up in her chair, pushing it backwards a bit, then looked around. She felt suddenly vulnerable, as if she were on display in a museum, and crowds were now gathering around and pointing at her.

But... her office door was closed, and the tiny window behind her desk had its shades drawn. No one could see her, and there was no one in the hallway walking around. She was alone.

She stood up, shaking her head. "This is bullshit. I won't be threatened at work, by..." she had no idea who'd called, and she decided then that this would be her first order of business. She poked around on the school's phone, straining to see the tiny LED letters, and tried to navigate the recent calls dialog. She'd never had to really use the phone for much besides answering calls — most professors, Victoria included, simply gave out their cell phone numbers to their students. She didn't care about people having her number. Most graduate students were above late-night prank calls and if there was any information one could gather from her phone number alone, there were plenty of easier ways to get that same information.

So she'd never had to click through the archaic three-button system built into her office phone, and it took her a full five minutes to find the most recent caller. When she dialed the number, she was surprised to hear a familiar voice pick up on the other end.

"This is Patty, Department of History."

"Patty?" Victoria asked.

"Yes — Victoria? How are you?"

"I — I'm good. I just... got a call from this number, I think."

Patty laughed. *"Well, I didn't call, and I don't think I know how to butt-dial on these dinosaurs we have for phones."*

Victoria smiled. "No, that's fine. Is there... any way to check to see if someone routed a call through your phone somehow?"

"A way? Sure, I bet there is. A way for me to do it? Victoria, I'm 67 years old and just figured out how to use an iPad, and that's got one button. This old thing has three."

"I understand — no worries. I doubt we'd find anything, anyway."

"Well, I'm sorry I can't help more. You sound a bit shaken up, are you okay?"

"It — it's just... I don't know. I thought I may have missed a call or something and saw this number on my phone. Could just be an IT glitch."

Using the 'IT glitch' line worked on any of the school faculty and administration that had been born before 1975, and Victoria used it whenever she needed a quick out. It had proven useful to explain her tardiness to meetings, why her biography had never been updated on the university's website, and why her 'required' email blasts about the latest and greatest in religious history rarely were sent.

"Okay, Victoria. Sorry again."

She hung up and frowned. Whoever had called had definitely routed their number through her administrative assistant's phone, knowing that she'd never be able to find the original caller.

But they hadn't disguised their voice, either. And the caller, a male, had used the pronoun 'we.' Was he working for a group? Or was he just trying to scare her into thinking so?

Should she call the cops? What could they do — start digging around her campus IT lab for the phone records? And she had little to go off of. She truly didn't know what 'research' they were referring to. Her entire *job,* besides teaching, was research, and most of it was tangential and unrelated to her classwork.

Still, she couldn't shake the feeling that something was wrong. It hadn't been an idle threat. The caller had assumed she knew what 'they' were talking about, and after Archie's call...

It was all too much. She hated to do it, but she needed to make a call of her own. To a man she knew could at least point her in the right direction. She hadn't seen him, or heard his voice, in over eight years. But now was the time. If he'd answer her call, she knew he could help.

She pulled out her cellphone once again and scrolled down to the 'Rs,' to his name.

Her name.

She hesitated for only a second before pressing 'call.' The phone immediately beeped and the connection began. She heard the ringing, and the screen lit up with her ex-husband's name.

Calling: Mark Reyes.

CHAPTER 30

JULIE

ARCHIE QUINONE'S voice rang through the video chat on the computer in front of Julie, awakening her. Both she and Ben had mostly slept through the last eight hours, until their pilot had landed in Barcelona, Spain.

From there, they had been shuttled to another, smaller plane waiting for them on the tarmac. When Ben had asked why they'd stopped in Barcelona for a plane change rather than a refuel, the pilot had shrugged. 'I got orders to change planes,' is all he'd said.

Ben and Julie had then crammed themselves into the back of a small prop plane and headed out over the vast expanse of the Mediterranean toward Rome. The in-flight WIFI had been replaced by a spotty cellular connection that the pilot had assured them was backed up by satellite, and that they should have no problem continuing their discussion with their team — he'd even tossed them a couple microphone-enabled soundproofed headsets and a splitter that could link directly to Julie's computer.

Julie knew Ben would be on edge; he hated flying, and the smaller the plane, the more the fear grew. But he was here, and he — so far — seemed calm.

She turned her attention back to the computer and Archie's face on it. She turned up her headphone's volume slider and adjusted her microphone so Archie could hear her over the sound of the plane's engine.

"There is a secret network of underground and elevated tunnels in and around The Vatican. The most notable one is called the Passetto di Borgo, and it extends about half a mile from The Vatican to the Castel Sant'Angelo. It was the escape route used by Pope Alexander VI, as well as Pope Clement VII during the Sack of Rome.

"The network has been used for clandestine intelligence gathering and trading, as well," Quinones continued. *"Runners bring news from outside the city's walls into the Pope's inner sanctum. Different groups over the centuries have used the tunnels for different purposes, but there is one constant that has always existed: those tunnels were created for, and are still used, for secret intelligence sharing, to and from the Pope himself.*

"I will send you a map of The Vatican's tunnel system to you. I need to find a copy in my library when we get off the phone, but please be aware that it is likely out of date. It was compiled thirty years ago by a Jesuit who worked there. Much of it is guesswork, and all of it is a patchwork of most likely locations."

"Sounds promising," Julie said, after a deep sigh.

"It is the best we have."

"What exactly are we looking for once we're in?" Ben asked.

"To answer that question, please see an image I have just sent you. It is a slide from one of the presentations I give in my Catholic Symbology course, and it is a collection of images depicting some of the symbols found in and on Papal bulls."

"Bulls?"

"Correspondence," Quinones answered. *"Yes. From the Latin word 'bulla,' which means 'seal.' Each pope throughout history had a collection of wax seals they would use for their public and private letters, to authenticate their contents. Some of these seals were adopted by later popes, but each pope had a personal seal created exclusively for their*

private and secret use — very much like a pope's personal logo or brand image.

"Usually the pope would adopt their own private seal that was based upon their public one — the same elements, perhaps, arranged in a different way. Some popes, like Pope Clement IV, we know adopted a completely different private seal, called the Piscatory Ring, or Ring of the Fisherman.

"There has been conjecture over the design of other popes' private seals. It is believed that Pope Benedict XVI used a form of the Piscatory Ring that had been altered to stamp his private correspondence, but of course, we cannot know for sure."

Ben and Julie leaned in toward the computer, and Julie opened a new window to find the image Quinones had sent.

Julie saw on the screen a collection of circular images, each labeled with the name of the symbol and a translation, or the name of the pope who had adopted the seal as his own. She recognized a few of the symbols found within the seals — the Christian cross, what looked like another version of the cross, and symbol of The Vatican itself.

"Right," Ben said. "So the pope could dispatch a letter through the Vatican tunnel system and the recipient could verify its authenticity because of the wax seal on it."

"Precisely," Quinones said. *"And considering that only people in the pope's closest circle would be entrusted with the knowledge of the design of their private seal, they could be satisfied that their secret communication was safe."*

"Very interesting," Ben said.

"It is," Julie added. "So this is what we're after? The pope's private seal?"

"Yes," Quinones said. *"If we have the seal, we can forge a letter from the Pope to the Archbishop who is the head archivist at the Archives. From there, we should be able to get the information we need."*

"Meaning the Archbishop will send the Book of Bones back through the Vatican tunnels? What if the Pope and the head archivist have *already* been in communication about the Book of Bones? In that case, another request for the same thing would be suspicious."

There was a pause. *"It seems like a long shot, but if we craft the message correctly, we may be able to have the archivists themselves, through multiple requests, send us blocks of information. If we can spread it out and get the Book of Bones in pieces, we may be able to get enough of it to understand what it is Garza is truly after."*

Julie thought for a moment. *Long shot, indeed.* But it was all they had. At the very least, they would have the Papal Seal, the secret symbol that unlocked the Archives, in their hands. With that alone they could access a wealth of information.

If they could get the seal...

On screen, Quinones continued. *"But as you have probably guessed, you will need to know which seal is the correct one. Many of the public seals have been converted to stamps, but I have it on good authority that the Pope still uses a true wax seal for his secret correspondence."*

"Do you know what it will look like?" Julie asked. "There could be more than one."

"Indeed, there will be," Quinones replied. *"Besides the public, offi-*

cial seals and stamps of the office of the pope, there is said to be more than one secret seal. But there are a few clues that might lead us in the right direction."

"Clues that will be obvious enough for us to find the right one?" Ben asked.

"I believe so. First, the private seal will be one with no writing. Every public seal has the pope's name scrawled somewhere around or in the image. Being a public seal of approval, the pope is not trying to hide his involvement in these letters.

"Second, the current sitting pope is the first-ever Jesuit pope."

"VIC, *what you're asking me to do is... well, it could get me fired. Immediately.*"

Victoria Reyes sighed and pulled the phone away from her ear. "I know. I'm sorry. I didn't — I would *never* put you and your family at risk if it weren't serious."

Her ex-husband, Mark Reyes, the man with whom she'd shared five years of her life, was employed by the university as well. That's how they'd met; her ongoing technical issues leading to her calling Mark's office and requesting an in-person meeting. That meeting had gone from explaining POP and IMAP email servers to discussing variants on spam emails to sharing email addresses with each other.

And after a few of these emails, the pair met at an off-campus restaurant to share a beer and discuss their future together.

At the time Victoria had been working as a teacher's assistant, working toward her undergraduate degree, and she had quickly become smitten with Mark.

They'd loved each other, but when Victoria grew up a bit and they realized that her career would always come before family, she reluctantly called off their marriage. Mark had been devastated, but he understood — he'd always wanted children, and to hear his wife finally admit that she wasn't 'that type of person' seemed to cause him grief as well as provide some much-needed closure.

I had surprised her to hear that he'd remarried fewer than two years later, and now he and his new wife had a one-year-old daughter, and there was another on the way. A small piece of Victoria's heart caused her a pang of regret when she'd heard the news, but she still knew that her ultimate goal was something far different from settling down and starting a family.

"Mark," she said. "I'm scared."

Mark sighed this time. She heard shuffling — he was moving into a different room, likely his home office. *"Hold on,"* he said. *"I need to remote in, but I'm going to use a VPN. It's not foolproof, but it will at least keep anyone looking in off my back."*

Victoria was far from unintelligent, but networking and IT stuff was like a foreign language to her. "Uh, sure. Yeah, VPN."

She heard Mark laugh. *"It's a — never mind. Sorry. Anyway, give me a minute to connect, and then it'll pull right up."*

She'd asked Mark if he could figure out who had called her. Assuming the man had somehow hacked into the university's phone system, there might be a chance he'd still used a hard-coded phone number to do it, which meant it might be traceable. At least, that's what Mark had told her. She didn't understand a bit of it, but he'd explained how it all might work, and then told her to call the police — they would be able to decide if and when a 'technical takeover' of the university's phone lines was necessary.

But she didn't want to wait — for one, Archie's friends' lives were at stake. Second, she feared that hers might be as well. She needed an answer, and she needed one far sooner than what the campus police could provide.

"Ok, I'm in. Hold on — there are... okay, I think this is it. You said the call came when?"

She had the time memorized, and she told him. He confirmed the timestamp, then read aloud a number to her.

She typed it into her computer, seeing that the area code was based in Washington, D.C. Mark told her he had an app on his phone that would allow him to search a call registry to perform a reverse lookup. It took a few seconds, and Mark said the name when it completed.

"Phone number's registered to a guy named 'Dieter Luthig,'" He said.

"Dieter? What kind of name is that?"

"German, maybe? The kind of dude who's serious enough to threaten innocent professors. You recognize him?"

"Not at all, but I'm searching now. Seems like —"

She stopped, clicking through a few articles on her computer while they spoke.

No, she thought. *It couldn't be.*

She came to a page that appeared to be a blog, written by a Dieter Luthig. It was written in English, but she could see that it was broken, as if it had been automatically translated, and poorly. Most of it seemed to be gibberish, nonsensical ramblings.

"This could be his site," she said, forwarding Mark a link. "He's a whacko, that's for sure."

"What's it about?"

"Can't tell, honestly. It's just called 'A Website for Erudite Light,' and it wasn't even on the first page for the guy's name. The first line of the first post just starts with, 'Smiling Guy Uttered..."

"Hmm," Mark said. *"Interesting."*

"What?"

"Well, I ran it through a traffic analyzer — just wanted to see if anyone ever visited it."

"And?"

"It... definitely a popular site."

"Wait, really?"

"Judging by these results, yeah," Mark said. *"Seems like the site had*

somewhere in the ballpark of 200,000 hits — not unique, but still impressive."

"200,000? That's incredible. This year?"

"No, Vic. This month."

Victoria put a hand over her mouth. Something about this website didn't work. There was *no way* it would have generated nearly a quarter-million hits in a single month — a month they weren't even halfway through — and still be sitting somewhere on the second page of Google. She knew Google's algorithm relied on easily parsable language, as well as an obvious topic, for it to display results, but she also knew that traffic played a significant role in web listings.

This man — Dieter Luthig — had somehow created a nonsensical blog full of illegible text, and yet there were people reading it. Further, his cryptic message to Victoria had used the plural pronoun 'we,' rather than 'I.' Whether it was just Dieter's posturing or he meant it, it seemed there was more than one person behind the phone call.

She continued scrolling down. More nonsense posts, followed by a gallery of images that contained broken links, and then, at the bottom of the page, a logo.

"Mark," she whispered.

"Yeah, I can hear you. You find something?"

She leaned closer to her screen, examining the image.

An egg-shaped crest, filled with swirls and other indecipherable symbols, boasted two angelic wings, stretching from the bottom of the egg to the top. A triangle sat beneath the egg, pointing up. And inside the triangle, as if looking upward at the crested wings, was an all-seeing eye.

"It's... upside down."

"What is?"

"This image — their logo, I guess. It's exactly like... I'd have to look it up, but it's exactly like the logo of an ancient organization, but upside-down."

"What organization? Are they in DC?"

"No," she said, shaking her head. "This organization hasn't been around for hundreds of years, and even then it's got a spotty history. But... like I said, I'm not sure this is the same one. The logo seems right, but it's like an upside-down version of the old group."

"What old group, Vic?"

"It was a group formed in Naples, Italy, in the late 1800s, but they based it on a *much* older one, one that was created in Egypt, or at least based on Egyptian beliefs and systems. It's called the Ancient and Primitive Rite of Memphis-Misraim. I found a picture of their logo." She clicked on the image result and enlarged it onto a second window, to compare with the other.

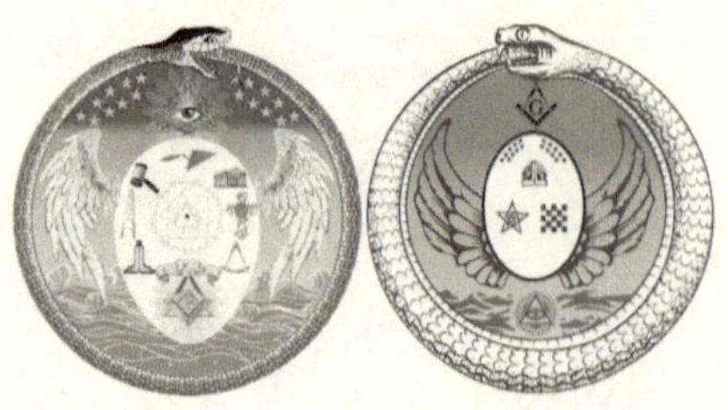

"*Never heard of it.*"

"Yeah, it's obscure."

"*You're a genius, which is why you know that.*"

"No," she said, smiling. "Though I appreciate you finally admitting it. I know about the Rite of Memphis-Misraim because it was an old order within a much newer, much more well-known group."

"*And that is?*"

"The Freemasons. The Ancient and Primitive Rite of Memphis-Misraim is a Rite within Freemasonry, based on Egypt's history and known for its irregular number of 99 degrees."

As she said the words, she realized a shadow had fallen over her open door. It was dark now, and she realized that she was mostly alone in the office building. *Maybe Patti came down to check on me?* she thought.

The shadow moved, and she felt her skin crawl.

"Mark," she said.

"*Still here.*"

"Mark, I think someone's here. They're — they're outside my office, and I don't know —"

The phone line disconnected, and the shadow hiding behind her door turned into the shape of a human being.

Victoria screamed, but it was too late.

CHAPTER 32

BEN

"WAIT A MINUTE," Ben said. "Jesuit, like you?"

"Yes, Ben. The Jesuits are members of the Society of Jesus, a fraternal order of Catholics founded by Ignatius of Loyola in 1534. It is just a fraternity, like the Freemasons, but it is one that exists within the Catholic Church. Men of faith who have taken on the additional burden of missional work for the Church."

Ben had grown up attending a church only on Easter and Christmas, but that church had been a Catholic church. He'd heard some of the words and phrases Quinones was using, but he didn't have a solid grasp on what exactly it all meant. "So, the pope we have now is a Jesuit?"

"He is. The first one. And I know he is still close with many Jesuits in and around the Vatican, as well as around the world. My guess is that he will have some version of the Jesuit symbol — our IHS, if you will — as part of his seal."

Ben looked at Julie's computer and the image of papal seals and symbols on it. The Jesuit seal was labeled, and he could see the IHS lettered within what looked like a sun.

"Iota, eta, and sigma. The greek letters for I, H, and S. They are

the letters that begin the words, Iesous Hominem Salvator, or 'Jesus, Savior of man.'"

"And what about security? Aren't the Papal Chambers going to be difficult to enter?"

"Not if you are the pope," Archie said, a grin on his face.

Ben rolled his eyes. "Wow, Archie," he said. "You're about as good with jokes as you are with plans."

Archie lifted his hands, palms up, and shrugged. *"I apologize. Yes, it will be difficult, but it is not impossible. The Apostolic Palace located in the center of the Vatican between the Sistine Chapel and St. Peter's Basilica is locked down with the force you might expect. Nearly the entire security force of the Swiss Guard patrols and hovers there, as it is the traditional home of the pope, as well as the home of countless works of art.*

"There are 135 men in the Pontifical Swiss Guard, and most of them are in locations surrounding the most foot traffic in and out of the

Vatican: the Piazza San Pietro, the Basilica, and the museums surrounding them to the north."

"I thought you said it wasn't impossible," Ben said.

Archibald laughed. *"It will not be impossible. The Apostolic Palace was the home of the pope, but the current sitting pope actually lives in a different building altogether. He moved his residence to the Domus Sanctae Marthae, or Saint Martha's Hotel, which is like a guest house for the Vatican. It is where the members of the Papal Conclave stay when they are electing a new pope."*

"The pope is living in a hotel?" Julie asked.

"Yes, that is exactly what it is," Archie said. *"Best of all, notice where the hotel is. It resides right along the southern side of the city, along the Stazione Vaticana. But it is not the location of the hotel above ground I want to draw your attention to. What I want you to notice is the hotel just on the other side of the wall from the Domus Sanctae Marthae. This hotel has changed hands over the years, but it has remained true to its first purpose: to serve as a permanent location for the entrance into the Vatican tunnel system."*

"An entrance?"

"Yes. Somewhere in that hotel, in the basement, is an entrance to the tunnel system that stretches into the depths of the Vatican."

"Have you seen it?" Ben asked.

"Personally, no. But I have friends who have spoken of it. They say it is easily accessible, if you are looking for it."

Ben smiled. "Well, that's assuming the guy looking for it is smarter than a park ranger from Yellowstone."

"It has been a long time since you have been at Yellowstone, Harvey," Archie said. Ben didn't need him to explain the meaning behind his words, but he did anyway. *"You are smarter than you think you are, and that is why you are here now. No one else in the world is in the position you are in, to bring back your friends and find out what Garza truly wants."*

"No pressure," Ben said. He wasn't sure Quinones had heard

him over the sound of the roaring engines, but on the screen, after a few seconds for the delay, Quinones smiled.

The plane dropped a few feet in the air, and Ben's stomach lurched.

"We must be getting ready to land," Julie said. "Archie, thank you. We're going to get ready to get on the ground, then we'll start right away. Get into the Vatican, find the Papal chambers in the hotel, get his private seal."

"I wish you luck, dear friends," Archie said. *"I have a meeting with another old friend here in an hour. My hope is that he can help locate Garza and where he might be taking Reggie and Sarah. I will send you an update after that meeting, and please let me know how Mr. and Mrs. E are getting on with their own research."*

"We will," Ben said. "And thank you, Archie, Anything else we need to know?"

The plane lurched again, and Ben felt himself involuntarily gripping the seat's armrest even tighter. *The sooner we're on the ground, the sooner I can relax,* Ben thought.

But his hands clenched even tighter when the plane dropped another dozen feet or so straight down. Ben's eyes went wide, and Julie switched the headphone's connection to the pilot's channel.

"Are we okay?" Julie asked.

Ben heard Julie's voice and the man's response through his own headset. "Trying — idled, but — make... to land."

What?

Ben's mind raced, and his heart beat faster to catch up. *We can't make it to land? We don't know if we can? What did he say?*

He looked over at Julie, trying to borrow the calm he saw in her eyes. It didn't work.

The plane jostled again, then Ben's entire body was launched forward into the back of the copilot's seat in front of him.

THE SEATBELT BEN was wearing cut into his waist like a hot knife, but it did its job. Ben felt his body pulled backward and down into his seat, but not before his face smacked against the hard, carpeted copilot's chair in front of him.

Julie had fared better, her seatbelt apparently having been a little tighter around her waist, but Ben hardly had a chance to check on her. The plane dodged right and Ben's arm and shoulder slammed against the armrest and folding tray table they'd had the laptop sitting on.

The laptop sailed across the cabin and exploded into pieces when it came into contact with the plane's window. Julie screamed, but Ben was preoccupied with his own injuries. His face was bleeding, but he wasn't sure where exactly the blood had come from. He lifted his left arm to grab at his nose, but before his hand could reach it his shoulder burst out a flare of pain and he, too, yelled.

"What's going on?" he screamed toward the pilot.

No answer save for the rocking of the plane.

Only then did Ben look out the window.

His stomach seemed to fall away into his intestines. He tried to swallow but found only dry, raspy sandpaper inside his mouth. The

Mediterranean was there, outside the window, greeting him by approaching *far* faster than he felt comfortable with.

Worse, it was spinning. Rather, the *entire world* was spinning. Ben's eyes tried to adjust, to hold on to something he could make sense out of, but it was a chore. Finally he saw a building in the distance.

Rome?

There was no way to know, but having a view of the horizon at least helped him gain his bearings. The problem was that the horizon, too, was spinning. It rocked up and down, then flipped nearly vertical, then came back down again.

Ben wanted to vomit, but he grabbed Julie's arm and squeezed. That helped a little, but the tiny plane only bucked against his efforts and threw them both sideways.

Air. There was air somewhere, escaping fast. The cabin had been breached somehow, and he could hear the faint warning signals from the pilot's controls and alerts ringing back to him.

He finally registered just what was happening, but it was too late.

"Brace — impact," he heard the pilot yell. He heard it from the pilot's mouth, not from his headphones.

Brace? Brace onto what?

Ben's breathing pace increased until he felt totally and utterly out of control.

This is it, he thought. *My nightmare.*

The plane seemed to right itself, but then it took a steep dive. Ben didn't need to — didn't *want* to — but he looked out the window, and it confirmed his worst suspicions.

They were flying straight toward the surface of the Mediterranean Sea.

He saw things then, things he never thought he'd have to see again. He couldn't be sure, but it seemed like he was dreaming, even though he could still fully see the pilot's head, the rocking and swaying of Julie in his peripheral vision, the plane's dials and lights singing and chirping and alarming.

He saw his father, Johnson Bennett. Young, near the age Ben was now. Standing and yelling, smiling, calling him and Zachary back to camp for dinner.

Zach.

Ben felt a ping in his heart as the plane bounced through some invisible gate. *Why didn't I ever call him?* he thought. *It was as easy as a phone call. Now he'll never know...*

Then he saw his mother. Diana Torres. The woman Julie had met while they had been running from a spreading disease. The woman who had succumbed to that disease. He saw her face as he told her what he'd been thinking all of those years.

He saw her tears.

Then he saw his own eyes. Right in front of him, staring down at him, beckoning. Also crying.

He reached a hand up, barely had to move a muscle thanks to the acceleration of their fall, wiped away a wet spot from his eye.

This is it.

He watched the Mediterranean approach, faster and faster. The pilot began to scream, not a word but a sound, just a scream.

The horizon tilted, the pilot pulled hard the opposite way, and Ben felt a tearing from his side, as if he were part of the plane itself. The plane, and Ben, groaned under the weight. The pressure of it all made him close his eyes.

The screaming — from the pilot, from Julie, from the plane, from himself — it all gathered together into a mess of fury and noise. It rose again and again, louder than Ben thought possible. He would die of an earache before the plane even crashed.

Then... nothing.

The world around Ben ended in blackness, darkness. Silence.

"WHERE ARE YOU TAKING ME?" Victoria asked. Her hands were tied, and her feet duct-taped together. Still, the man who'd thrown her into the van had been careful to buckle her first.

"Are you Dieter Luthig?" she shouted. "I know who you are. Who you're working for."

The man stopped, then smiled as he looked down at her. "No," he said. "I am not. And you know nothing."

Victoria felt the phone in her pocket, the number she'd pressed to redial still connected. *Hopefully.* She'd barely had enough time to jam the cellphone into her back pocket before the intruder had pulled up a silenced pistol, aimed it at her, and forced her out of the room.

She had gotten the man to speak, but she hoped it would be loud enough for Archie to hear it. *If he had even answered.*

"Where are you taking me?" she asked again. "Your headquarters? Washington, D.C.?"

He laughed, then slammed the door in her face. The man was alone, and he walked around the car slowly before entering the vehicle, likely checking to see if anyone had seen the kidnapping. There was a blue glow entering through the back window, and she found it ironic that they were parked almost directly next to one of the campus emergency call stations.

She hadn't heard a voice on the phone, but she hoped it only meant that Archie understood the situation, staying silent and hoping to keep her captor unaware that he was listening in.

"You've known about me for a while now, haven't you?" she asked.

The man put the car in reverse and eyed her in the rearview mirror. "Your work and reputation have far-reaching implications."

"What the hell does that mean?"

"It means yes, Ms. Reyes, we have known about you for a while."

"Who? The Ancient and Primitive Rite?"

The man's eyebrow raised, and Victoria was pleased to see that she'd surprised him.

"You truly *are* a gifted academic, Ms. Reyes. But you are only close to the truth. And as with the ultimate Truth, getting close is far worse than missing completely."

She frowned. *That means I'm close, but not quite right. Does he want me to guess? And what are the ramifications of 'getting it wrong?'*

"So it's not the Ancient and Primitive Rite, I presume? The Memphis-Misraim cult of Freemasonry? And where *the hell* are you taking me?" she asked for the third time.

The car sped onto the highway, and she noticed then where they were — about three blocks from the university was a regional airport that provided access to a handful of larger international airports. The man guided the car off the highway and onto the access road, toward the airport.

"Got a private jet fueled up?" she asked. She wanted to keep him talking, to keep Archie — if he was still there — in the fight. "You and your Mason friends have some secret bunker somewhere?"

"We are no more Freemason than we are American, Ms. Reyes. Yes, we live in America, and yes, we have borrowed many of the tradi-

tions and conventions of the Freemasons, but that is where the similarities stop."

His voice was deep, slow and articulate, and over the course of
the sentences he allowed it to lilt into a cadence, a slight accent that
she tried to place. *Italian? Spanish?* She also realized that this man
was not the same man who had called to threaten her. *But were they
working together? Both part of the same Mason-esque faction?*

"Our operations have taken us all over the world, but we have
one, singular mission: to bring about the change that this world
desperately needs. To be the catalyst for a *new* America. A *new*
world."

"Yeah," Victoria said. "That whole *New World Order* thing was
tried before. Remember how that ended?"

"We are not a *New World Order*."

"Good to know," she said. "But this, uh, kidnapping and
subterfuge thing really doesn't play well with your stated goal."

"Actually, it does. This is not a 'kidnapping' but more of a
'protection.'"

"Protection from what?"

"Protection from our enemies. From the group that *really* wants
to bring you down. From the group that you have sworn to reveal."

"Sworn to — what are you talking about?"

"You are a phenomenal researcher, Ms. Reyes, with a brilliant
mind that can overcome nearly any problem you can throw it. Your
assumptions and inferences, while impressive, have only gotten close
enough to the truth to anger those hoping to suppress it."

Victoria shook her head. "But I don't know what you're *talking*
about. *What* research?"

"Your paper, *The Spanish in South America: Conquest... or
Inquest?*"

She was about to protest, argue against the man's cryptic
communication style, when she felt a jolt of recognition. *No... That
was related?* She remembered the paper, remembered nearly every

word of the article that had been published in a quarterly journal. She hadn't heard anyone praise or argue her points, and since the topic was a relatively obscure subject with an equally obscure point of view, she hadn't been surprised.

The premise was simple: She postulated that the Spanish had come to South America for a much more nuanced reason. Something besides simple conquest and a hunt for gold and treasure. She'd written that the Spanish crown, interested in furthering their religious beliefs, had sent soldiers and missionaries to the New World to uncover the truth of a specific group of people. Based on her research of the history of a group of people in South America called the Chachapoyas, she believed the people had migrated to the region from somewhere in Europe hundreds or even thousands of years prior.

The Spanish, she thought, were interested in these people for reasons unknown to her or the pre-modern world. The Chachapoyas were brutally efficient fighters and warriors, staving off previous conquerors like the Inca numerous times, and opting to live a relatively quiet and peaceful life hidden somewhere in a valley that shared their name.

It was all fantastical from a historian's perspective: she'd had little to go off, and therefore her paper was filled with more questions than answers. She posed an interesting thesis, but she had known that she'd had little hard evidence to provide an academic reasoning behind it, so she'd written it as more of an interest piece than a peer-reviewed theory.

"The... Chachapoyas," she said. "The light-skinned tribe, thought to be of a European descent."

The man nodded, and she continued. "And the Spanish — they were trying to find them. I was right?"

Again, a nod.

"So that means the Spanish — the crown *and* the church — wanted something from them? Why send half their armies and navy to an unknown spot halfway around the world? Even if there was gold, it would take an incredible amount of investment and dedication just to set foot on the coast, much less conquer the nation."

"Why, indeed? Again, a perfect question that begs an answer."

"An answer I'm assuming you won't give me?"

"An answer," the man said, "that you already have."

THE SCREAMS AWOKE HIM.

Bloodcurdling, nasty things. Louder than he would have thought, especially since The Hawk had been correct. The basement space Reggie was in was not *entirely* soundproof, but it was close. The chamber felt like being deep inside a cave, which wasn't too far from the truth, considering the floor, walls, and ceiling had been carved from rock.

But he could still hear the screams, and they haunted him even as he was fully awake.

Sarah.

He knew the voice, the soft-yet-fiery timbre of the woman he'd fallen in love with, even though that voice was now masked behind a wall of misery.

Her screams rose in volume until Reggie thought she'd lose her voice, then died down to a mere whimper.

He was pacing, just like Garza said he would.

He was frantic, his mind working overtime. He *had* to get out.

Where are Julie and Ben?

He wondered if they'd somehow figured out where Garza had taken them and were perhaps on their way here.

But no. That wouldn't be the mission. He knew Ben well enough to know that they'd go after the Book of Bones. The reason Garza had taken them — without the book, there was little hope they'd get their friends back.

But where was the Book of Bones? Perhaps it was close to where he was now? Perhaps it was in the next room over, waiting for them to find it and deliver it to Garza.

Waiting to end all of this. To free Sarah.

Wishful thinking.

Gareth Red knew Vicente Garza better than most people. He'd trained with him in the military, as The Hawk had tried to recruit Red — a young, talented hotshot Army sniper — for his private paramilitary force, Ravenshadow.

He knew that Garza was motivated by one thing: greed. The lust for power had completely consumed the man, and his reach for funding and resources had created a monstrous force of young men willing to do anything for their boss.

And they *had* done anything. Murder, rape, torture — Reggie had heard stories of all of it. Garza's men weren't just well-trained and intelligent, they were ruthless.

Reggie had been one of the most talented of them all; what he'd lacked in experience he'd made up for with raw talent. But he'd had one glaring flaw that had gotten him washed out of Ravenshadow's ranks very quickly.

He wouldn't do just *anything*.

He wouldn't follow anyone blindly.

He'd made that mistake before, and he'd made it unknowingly since, but if Gareth Red was anything it was a decent human being. He fought for what was right — and he shut down and turned away when he felt the fight was anything but just.

He *hated* Garza, Ravenshadow, and all they stood for. Their corporate clients never asked about The Hawk's methods, so they kept him in the black. He'd made a fortune selling contracts on international hits, moving against corrupt governments, even usurping the power from a banana republic that held too tightly to the reigns of a cash crop that a rival manufacturing company wanted control over.

But after the events in Philadelphia that had left his good friend and fellow soldier dead, and with his and Sarah's capture, Reggie had made up his mind.

This was personal.

There was *nothing* that would stop him from destroying The Hawk and his crack team of mercenaries.

Another scream stopped him in his tracks. He heard Sarah's voice, but he felt another pang of sadness that had nothing to do with her.

He remembered another moment of helplessness. Standing in a doctor's office inside an abortion clinic.

A girl, a scared girl, but a girl he'd loved. A girl carrying *his* girl inside her.

It had been her decision, the doctor had told them.

Her decision *alone*.

They weren't married, and even then... Reggie had known all along that he couldn't fight it.

But he'd tried.

And failed.

Sarah screamed again, and Reggie fell to his knees.

He cried, large, warm tears he hadn't felt on his face in a long time.

The baby had never had a name; she'd not wanted it. But after she'd left, gone out of his life like their child, Reggie had begun calling her Clair in his mind. *Little Clair,* he'd thought. The nightmares had jolted him awake every night for years afterward, and still sometimes haunted him.

Little Clair.

And now Sarah.

His head fell, the tears collecting on the floor in front of him.

It seemed he was two people now, two different personas wrapped into one.

One of those personas wanted to cry, to sit here and weep for the moments he'd never had. To live in the past, as he'd tried to train himself not to do.

But the other persona won. He stood up, his fists clenched tight enough to crush a human skull, and he walked forward.

Toward the stairs.

The other persona only had one thing on its mind, and he allowed it to fill his thoughts, to fill his conscious brain and push out the rest of the emotions.

He stood at the bottom of the stairs, waited for Sarah's screaming to die down.

The other persona wanted something, and it was becoming his sole focus.

"Garza!" he shouted. "I'm ready to talk!"

The other persona wanted to kill.

CHAPTER 36

BEN

"BEN!"

Ben tried opening his eyes, but the surrounding pressure forced them to remain closed. He tried again.

Warmth.

It was warm here, satisfying.

He tried his eyes again, nothing. *Fine. They stay closed.*

He felt a tickle on his face, something brushing against it. It was wet. But warm.

"Ben!"

He cracked an eye open. Something came inside his head — no, just his eye. *What the hell?*

He saw streaks of light, azure shapes dancing across his one-eyed vision. *What's wrong with the other eye?* he thought.

He felt another brushing, another poke, this time harder. Then a grip. It pulled him — *yanked* him.

He opened his mouth to scream, finding that his mouth still worked, but then he was immediately choking. Coughing.

Panic set in, and finally his eyes adjusted.

The world around him was blue. Dark and getting darker.

Where am I?

It all came rushing back then. The plane, the pilot's last message, the rocking back and forth and the...

The crash.

We crashed into the Mediterranean Sea.

Only then did he notice Julie. Her face, nothing but a silhouette, but he knew her shape. Her hair floated around her head, an angel.

He reached for her, then found out he was too far away.

"Ben, you need —"

He didn't hear the rest. He realized he was slipping away, falling. *Falling.*

He was sinking.

He felt around for his seatbelt. He'd forgotten about it, but it was holding him in, the thing that had likely saved his life now taking it away just as easily.

Where the hell is the release button?

He found it, tried clicking it open. It wouldn't budge, but he tried again. And again. Finally, he felt the click, the sound of it dulled by the immense pressure of the water all around him.

As soon as he'd clicked the lap belt, he felt himself rising, his own buoyancy pushing against the gravity of the ocean. His right arm aimed upward toward the open, broken window, while his left dangled uselessly at his side. He could feel the pain there, the dull, slow throbbing, but the cold water helped. The warmth he'd felt was completely gone now, replaced by a blanket of sheer terror that felt like cold needles hitting him from every side.

His arm floated up through the window as the plane floated downward, and then his hand found Julie's.

He grabbed it and held on, allowing her to pull him up.

His body reeled, but his hand stayed fastened around Julie's. He realized she was floating on something, but he couldn't tell what. Her silhouette stayed motionless even as he fought, kicking against the pull of the small window around his waist. Thankfully, it was just large enough for his torso to fit through, and by pulling his legs together it slipped past him and sailed down into the murky depths.

His head blasted from the water, his mouth barely waiting to breach the surface before sucking in a huge gasp of air.

"Ben, are you okay?" Julie asked. Her voice was frantic. "I — I tried, but I couldn't get there. The belt. I thought — I thought..."

He tried to speak, but he had to breathe. Another breath, then another, then finally he fell face-first on the thing Julie was floating on. A wing, broken off the plane.

"Ben..."

"It's okay," he said, gasping. "You — you're okay."

She laughed, a bit of frantic deliriousness in her voice. "Yeah — yeah, I'm okay. But you were —"

"I made it," he said. "But I'm *never* flying again."

She dipped her head, looking down at the water around her. Ben did as well. There was detritus everywhere. Objects he couldn't identify, some he could. A seat cushion — perhaps the floatation device he'd heard flight attendants talking about? A can of something, apparently full of enough air that it floated. A bag, some sort of pack.

"Our stuff," he whispered.

She nodded. "It's gone, Ben. All of it. Our phone's, my computer. And the pilot..."

She didn't finish, but Ben looked down. The water was clear to about fifteen feet, then it disappeared into inky blackness. The plane — and the pilot, apparently — were long gone.

"It's okay," he said. "We're going to be okay."

"Ben, we can't keep —"

"Julie, we'll be fine. We just need to get to Rome. Okay?" he sniffed. He couldn't tell the temperature of the water, but it didn't matter. He hadn't died in a fiery plane crash. "We're close to something, see?"

He pointed to the building he'd seen off in the distance. It sat on a hill, raised from the land around it but nestled in amongst many other buildings. Small, as if they were part of a tiny town. The land extended around to the edges of his vision.

Good, he thought. *That means we're close to whatever* it *is*.

The land was less than a mile away. Swimmable, but they'd be tired. If the town was on a beach, there was a chance the depth of the Mediterranean here worked its way up to a long, shallow sandbar that reached the shore. They might be able to walk part of it.

"Is it Rome?" Julie asked.

"I don't think so," Ben said. "Not sure, but I'd guess the coast of Italy is a lot more densely packed and urban than this. I also hadn't seen any land for quite a while during the flight, so I'd guess this is one of the large islands in the north Mediterranean, between Spain and Italy."

"Corsica, probably," Julie said. "That's really the only one that's on the way."

They were on opposite sides of the wing, and it didn't appear to be sinking, so Ben took a deep breath and tried to get more comfortable. He reached his hand out and placed it on Julie's, whose arms were stretched across one of the plane's flaps.

"Good," Ben said. "Someone will be here soon, then. We should just —"

"Ben," Julie said, her voice nearly a whisper. "I saw the pilot, before he... died."

"What do you mean?" Ben asked. "Are you okay?"

"Yeah, I'm fine. I'm talking about the pilot's... reaction. He didn't seem to care."

"About... dying?"

"Yes."

"What are you saying?"

She paused, then looked around them as if searching for something. Ben did the same, and aside from the shoreline, he couldn't see anything. No planes, no boats, not even a bird in the sky.

"I'm saying he didn't care about going down with the plane. He was *alive*, Ben. I saw it. I was thrown out the side of the plane — it got a huge hole in it when we hit the water. But I swam back to find you, and I saw the pilot, through the cockpit window. He was... looking at me."

"Looking at you?"

"Like he knew what was happening, and he was okay with it. I can't — I can't say for sure, Ben, but I think he did it on purpose."

Ben scoffed. "What? He *crashed* the plane on purpose?"

She shrugged, then wiped her eyes of the sea spray. "Ben, I saw the plane. Both engines. The tail, all of it."

"Yeah?"

"It was *fine,* Ben. Totally fine."

"Could have been an instrument malfunction, an issue with communications, you know Reggie says that —"

"Ben," Julie held up a hand. "There was nothing wrong with the communications or instruments. And if there had been, it's a perfectly clear day outside, and we weren't exactly flying high above the clouds. He had near-perfect visibility. He probably wasn't even using any computer navigation."

"Julie, what are you trying to say?"

"The engines were *fine,* Ben. There was no visible damage to the plane, and I would have seen any other aircraft in the area. Doesn't it seem strange to you that we came down right off the coast, but there just *happened* to be no other planes or choppers in the sky at the time?"

"I guess. I don't know."

"And then the pilot. His face. Like he knew. About all of it. Did it on purpose."

"You think he killed himself on purpose? A suicide mission."

"Ben, we were *diverted* here. We switched planes in Barcelona. Why? Why not just refuel and keep going, same plane and everything? *Nothing* about that makes sense, unless the pilot wanted us on *that* plane."

In a flash, it all clicked for Ben. She was right. The plane change, the same pilot, the fact that he'd waited until they'd almost reached Corsica, until there was no one else around — no planes, boats, choppers. He'd done it on purpose, but that wasn't the worst part.

He looked at Julie, looked directly into her eyes. "It means he wasn't operating alone. This wasn't bad luck. It means he was working for someone."

She nodded. "Someone who wants us dead."

THEY SWAM TO SHORE. The swim was cold, but easy — they were only a few feet away from a long, wide, shallow sandbar that carried them to shore. They arrived on an empty beach within a gentle cove, the idyllic village sprawling out on the hill above them. They'd decided the island was, in fact, Corsica, and Julie wondered if anyone in any of the tiny houses and buildings on this stretch of coast had seen the plane hit the water.

Julie knew the crash wouldn't have been from this distance, nor was there any smoke or fire or debris. By the time they'd hit the sandbar, the wing they'd left behind had also sunk out of sight.

When she stood on the beach and looked out to the water, there was absolutely no trace of the plane. No one waited on the beach for them, and no one drove down to meet them when they reached the road.

"Is Corsica part of Italy?" Ben asked. "Sounds Italian to me."

She shrugged. "France, I think? But I'm not sure. I think Napoleon was either born here, or he died here. Either way, it's a detour, and I don't want to make this trip any longer than it needs to be."

"Agreed," Ben said. "Let's get up and over that hill — looks like that's close to the center of the island."

Ben was wrong.

Even before they'd reached the top of the small hill, Julie could see a mountainous region, spanning the entire width of her vision, towering up in front of her. She tried to recall on a map how large this island country was, but couldn't. They needed a way off this island, and more specifically, a way *to* Rome.

"Uber?" Ben asked, seeing a car drive by that had the ubiquitous logo emblazoned in the vehicle's front windshield.

"We don't have phones. Don't you have to use an app for that?"

"Ah," Ben said. "Well, guess I'm glad I'm going old school." Julie saw him reach into his back pocket and pull out a sopping-wet wallet. He let it drip off for a few seconds, then opened it. "Credit cards are waterproof, right?"

"Any cash?"

Ben shook his head. "Nope, nothing."

Julie snatched the card, then started walking. "I'd guess there's a town one way or another. Let's hope it's this way."

Ben followed behind her, and within fifteen minutes they came to a small corner store and service station with a sign in French, then smaller text in Italian.

"Guess we were both right," Julie said. "Now let's hope they take MasterCard."

The service station did, in fact, accept credit cards, and they had absolutely no issues purchasing a cheap, internationally unlocked flip phone and some snacks. Ben also purchased a cheap t-shirt that said *'I visited Corsica and only bought this shirt,'* but Julie's clothes had mostly dried already and she opted to keep them on.

The total purchase seemed reasonable — the cashier rung it up in Euros — though it was impossible to know for sure without knowing the current exchange rate, but Julie didn't care. The credit card was their lifeline, their access to the outside world. It would allow them, once they found a hotel or Internet cafe with access to the outside world, to eventually get a call out to Mrs. E and Archie.

It took another fifteen minutes to find such a hotel, and since they were mostly dry and seemed to look like every other tourist they'd seen, the hotel staff had no problem pointing them toward a pay-per-minute internet-enabled computer.

There, Julie fired off an email to Mrs. E and the rest of the team, using a secured webmail server they'd set up just for that reason. They'd discovered that they'd gone ashore near a town called Campomoro, so they scheduled a drive to the opposite side of Corsica, to a city called Porto Vecchio. Finally, Julie found a local ferry company that had scheduled boat tours available every hour, and one stop on the tour was a city on the Italian coast called Civitavecchia, which was only an hour drive from the Vatican. The ferry ride totaled just over 133 miles, and the crossing would take about five and a half hours.

In all — if all went to plan — they'd be in Rome in under eight hours.

A wasted eight hours, Julie thought. *But it's better than nothing.*

They booked the ferry and taxi, and within minutes an Italian man wearing a French beret and smoking the biggest cigar Julie had ever seen pulled up in a beat-up Toyota pickup truck. He puffed out a huge lungful of smoke, rolled his window down, then honked the horn.

Julie and Ben watched this all from inside the hotel lobby. None of the hotel front desk staff seemed to mind, and they were heading out the front door by the time the man honked a second time.

The ride was, surprisingly, informative and pleasant. The man's name was Ricard, born in Lyon, moved to Corsica many years ago, and supported his family of three on taxi fares. He pointed out a few tourist locations on their tour around the southern side of the island.

Julie would have preferred that the trip was silent, with some noise-canceling headphones, in the cabin of a plane, but Ricard's wasn't the worst she'd heard. Ben, for his part, somehow found it soothing enough to nap while crunched into the extended cab's backseat.

She was exhausted but alive. By the time they reached the city of Porto-Vecchio, Julie wished they could get away with simply booking a hotel for the evening, ordering a glass of wine, and watching the sunset over the mountains of Corsica.

But Reggie and Sarah were still out there somewhere. Garza was still alive. The Book of Bones was about to be in the wrong hands, unless they could get to it first.

They needed to press on.

Julie took a breath after they paid their fare, then exited the vehicle and began walking toward the ferry port. The taxi truck squealed as it peeled away from the building and launched itself full-speed back onto the highway. Ahead of her and close to the water-line, there were cars and people waiting to enter the massive double-decker ferry, and she could see steam rising from the surface of the water in front of the ferry.

Ben grabbed her arm.

"What's up?" she asked.

"Over there," he whispered, pulling her into an alleyway. He pointed with a nod of his head at a car that had parked on the opposite side of the lot. Three men, all wearing sunglasses and black jeans, stood beside the car. Their shirts were all different, likely an attempt at blending in with the rest of the tourists and Corsican population, but they were all tucked in tightly, and Julie — even from across the lot — could see muscles bulging beneath their sleeves. They were tanned, with well-kept hair, and they seemed to be from Europe or America.

Worst of all, she saw the flash of a rifle as it passed from the hands of a fourth man, still in the vehicle, to one of the men nearest her.

"You think they're here for us?" Julie asked.

"You want to stick around and find out?" Ben asked in return.

She grunted, then pointed next to the ferry. "There. A smaller boat. Something faster."

"I like your style, Jules," Ben said. They both began walking, heads down, alongside the edge of the parking lot near the buildings that descended toward the water. The ferry had begun allowing people onboard, and the people milling about to their left began forming a line. "They're going to be watching the line," Ben said. "Assuming that we're going to Italy by way of the ferry."

"Well, that's a good assumption," Julie said. "Since that's *exactly* what we were planning to do."

"You think they followed us?"

"No," she said. "Otherwise they'd have already spotted us. I think it was your credit card. They can see our temporary authorizations, and they knew where to look for them — they're probably the same people that the pilot was involved with. They brought the plane down, or convinced the pilot to do it."

"Okay," Ben said. "Then we're definitely taking that boat. See the owner anywhere?"

She shook her head and tried to keep up as Ben's longer legs began stretching as he sped up. He reached the watercraft first, turned to help her into it, and once in she looked around.

It relieved her to see a full canister of gasoline near the outboard motor, but she had no idea how much gas was in the tank. It would have to be enough.

Ben reached down to pull the ripcord on the motor, and two things happened in that moment. First, the man who apparently owned the boat came flying around the corner of one of the buildings, screaming at them in Italian.

Second, the four men who'd exited the vehicle were running on the opposite side of the parking lot, near the line of vehicles waiting their turn to enter the belly of the ferry. Julie saw them easily, their black clothing and sunglasses in stark contrast to the rest of the shiny, lighter vehicles around them. They weren't running full-out, but she knew they'd be well within shooting distance before they launched from the dock.

"Ben," she said, her voice frantic. "Time to go."

"Got it," he said. Finally, the cord pulled the engine over fully and the motor began sputtering, then came to life. "Let's go!"

Before she could hold on to anything, the boat shot out from its mooring and into the open harbor.

"Ben," she said. "I don't know if this boat will make it!"

"What do you mean?"

"The engine, the gas tank — I have no idea if it's big enough to push us all the way there."

Ben looked at her, and she tried to think. There had to be a solution. There had to be a way out. She let her eyes wander around the area. The ferry loomed over them to the left, but that wasn't what Julie was focusing on.

Directly behind the small boat, lined up on the shore and close enough that she thought she could see her own reflection in their sunglasses, the four men lifted brutal looking assault rifles and pointed them toward their boat.

And then they opened fire.

CHAPTER 38
BEN

APPARENTLY THEIR ESCAPE attempt had not gone unnoticed. Bullets pinged off the metal stern of the tiny boat, some hitting the water with a hiss and a small splash. Julie and Ben ducked into the center of the boat, but there was nothing there to block them from the gunfire. Nothing, in fact, at all.

Ben felt a sudden pang of regret — they were being shot at by a group of trained killers wielding high-powered rifles in a minuscule boat with nothing to protect them, but possible worse than that was the fact that there was nothing but a five-gallon jug of gasoline inside the boat.

No medical equipment, no communication gear, not even a fishing pole or life jacket.

They needed to get away from these men, and to Rome, safely — or they wouldn't get there at all.

Ben navigated the smaller, sleeker boat around the massive ferry and got out in front of it, still crouching in front of the engine. He poked his head up a bit and saw that the four men were now three. One man had disappeared, but instead of reducing his stress, Ben had a sinking feeling in his stomach.

Where is he?

"Ben!" Julie shouted. "There!" she pointed in the direction opposite the ferry, off the starboard side of their boat, and Ben followed her gaze.

No.

The man — Ben recognized his sunglasses and t-shirt from featuring a well-known cartoon character — was piloting a boat toward the edge of the dock where his team was waiting.

And the boat was *much* larger than Ben's. It looked like a small yacht, and Ben could see the twin engines' wake jetting out from the rear of the boat as it slowed near the dock. It didn't stop, however, and the three men were onboard and speeding up toward Ben and Julie within seconds.

Their guns were still drawn, and they had Ben and Julie's boat in their sights.

"Crap," he said.

"Can we go any faster?"

"Not unless there's another engine hiding under one of the seats."

The 'seats' were nothing but planks of wood that had been screwed down across the width of the boat. Three of them, and none had anything underneath.

"Nothing here," Julie said. "Not even a rope. What's the plan?"

"Hope that we can get to Rome before them?"

Julie's eyes met Ben's, and he knew she was thinking the same thing he was. *We're not going to outrun them. We're not going to get to Rome before they reach us.*

Ben knew they needed another plan. *Think, Ben.* He'd once used a boat's flare gun as a weapon, but that had been on land, and they didn't have a flare gun here. He considered using one of the seats in the boat as a weapon — the slats of wood would be heavy enough to do some damage — but it would be a death sentence to wait for all four gunmen to come into close enough range to do anything useful.

Julie was right in front of him now. "They're not going to stop."

Ben frowned.

"They're not going to leave us alone until we — or they — are dead."

"Yeah, I picked up on that," Ben said. "But we're low on resources here. Who are they, anyway? I can't imagine Garza would send out mercenaries to kill us if he wanted us to find the Book of Bones."

"He tried to kill us in Alaska."

"Fair point. But maybe that was just a warning, so we knew he was serious."

Julie made a face. "Still, I think you're right. This doesn't seem like Garza's men. For one, his guys are always wearing black. These guys are wearing street clothes, and those terrible sunglasses."

"So hired guns?"

"Maybe. But hired by who?"

Ben didn't answer, but he moved the boat out into the more open waters of the harbor's edge.

"I have an idea."

He cocked an eyebrow, waiting for her explanation. "Turn to the left. Head back toward the ferry."

Ben gently swung the boat around, pointing it north and following the shoreline of Corsica. The ferry was about three hundred yards away, but it had begun moving in their direction. The other boat saw their maneuver and turned, cutting off their angle.

"They're gaining on us," he said. His voice was no louder than a whisper, but Julie heard him.

"I know," she said. Her eyes were focused on the ferry.

"We can't just hide behind the ferry, Jules."

She smiled, then looked down at Ben. Then she explained their plan.

"It won't work," Ben said. "It's too risky."

"It's the only plan we have. Besides, you've always wanted to try a James Bond-style boat chased."

"I didn't think it would be like this. Bond always has some sweet technology or secret weapon."

She winked at him. "You've got me."

He sniffed and then looked back at their pursuers. The boat was gaining on them, but their own craft was moving faster than Ben thought. They didn't have a lot of time, but he kept their vessel pointed toward the rear-end of the ferry.

Julie sat down in front of him, and he looked directly into her eyes. "You know why I've been waiting to get married? Why I've been so reluctant?"

Julie's eyes widened. "We — we have to talk about this now?"

He shrugged. "We've got just enough time."

"We don't, Ben. Getting cold feet is normal, but it's going to take over fifteen seconds to get down to —"

"It won't," Ben said. "It'll take ten."

She looked at him, but didn't speak.

"I love you, Jules. More than anything. More than I ever thought I could love someone. But it's true, and I always have."

"Ben, I love you, too. But we don't —"

"Hold on," he said. "At least let me finish."

She nodded. She wiped her eye, but Ben couldn't tell if she was tearing up from the conversation or the wind.

"When I met you, I hated people. I told myself that because I wanted to think it was true, and I even started to believe it. I hated the idea that someone could become so involved with someone else that when they lost them their heart would be ripped out.

"I've been through that, Jules, and I wanted to protect myself from it."

She nodded again.

"But I learned — you taught me — that we're humans for a reason. Or that humans were *made* to be together. *We* were, and it saved our lives. I decided I'd stick it out, see what it looked like to be together for a while. I kept waiting for the other shoe to drop, you know? To eventually realize I was right all along and that being alone was really what I was made to be.

"But then the CSO happened, and there wasn't much time to figure that stuff out. I put in in the back of my mind, and just kept pushing forward. I didn't think it mattered, but I realized that I was constantly still thinking about it. Still considering it."

"Ben... are you suggesting that you *don't* want to get married?"

"What? No — I didn't mean that. I'm trying to say that it's *because* of the CSO — *because* we're together all the time... work, home, personal life, professional life — it's *because* of all that, that's *why* I want to marry you."

"Uh, sorry — I'm not sure I follow you."

Ben reached forward with his free hand and grabbed Julie's in his. "Jules," he said. "I thought I needed time to 'figure things out.' I thought I needed it in the woods, at Yellowstone, after I'd met you. I thought I needed it now, too. Time away from CSO, from you, too 'figure things out.' To know for *sure* whether I wanted this for the rest of my life."

"And?"

"Well, I realized I didn't need any time at all. I already knew, I just needed to actually admit it to myself. Jules, you're the one. You've always been it, and I've just been an idiot trying to 'find myself.' You knew me all along, you signed up for this, and you've just been waiting around for me to realize it."

"Well, it's about damn time you realized it, hotshot."

He laughed.

"But we have a problem."

"What's that?"

She pointed. "That took *way* longer than ten seconds."

Ben groaned, then looked behind him. The other boat had gained on them, and three of the men were standing on the bow, aiming their rifles at them.

"Ready?" Ben asked.

"Ready as I'll ever —"

The men opened fire, and Ben ducked. Shots rang out along the hull of the boat, and he saw one round had penetrated the side, leaving a small hole just above the waterline. He tried to hold the engine steady — they were only a few yards out from their destination — but it was difficult to stay low and drive at the same time.

He looked up to get his bearings, just as Julie slipped over the side of the boat and into the water.

CHAPTER 39

REGGIE

"WE FOUND a piece of the Book of Bones," Reggie said. "In Egypt, in a vault beneath the Sphinx."

Garza sat back in his chair, the front two legs lifting off the ground. He sat across from Reggie, who was seated in the basement cavern in a similar chair, five feet from The Hawk. His bodyguards stood behind him and to the side. Far enough away that Reggie would have a tough shot at running toward them, close enough that their shot wouldn't miss.

It had taken all of his nerve not to rush the stairs when the three men had returned. He'd stood in the center of the floor, near the table on which his casket had been placed, and waited for them to arrive. One man was carrying two chairs, and he placed these facing each other in the center of the room.

Reggie wanted to kill them. He figured he might even have a chance at it, but he knew they were expecting a right. *Prepared* for a fight.

He had to fight back feelings of fear. Of what had become of Sarah. When he'd called up to Garza through the door, the screaming had stopped.

But was that a good thing or a bad thing?

He decided to play along, to at least give her a chance.

"It was a journal, something Rachel Rascher's great-grandfather had been working on during the Nazi regime."

"Sigmund Rascher," Garza said.

Reggie nodded. "Yeah. Sadistic son-of-a —"

"I know who he is, thank you."

Reggie sniffed. He'd wanted to finish the sentence. *Just like you, asshole.* He stared at Garza, wondering how long he'd have to play along to win Sarah's freedom.

He knew it was far too much to ask to expect that *both* of them would be freed, but he had to play the game for Sarah's sake.

"Anyway, she was continuing experiments he'd started back in the '30s. Drowning people in ice-cold water, suffocating them to study the effects of high-altitude flying in low-oxygen conditions. Stuff like that."

"And Die Glocke."

"Yeah," Reggie said. "'The Bell.' A Nazi experiment that they believed would allow them to 'test' people for some kind of purity."

"The Aryan race, I presume."

"Yeah, I guess. Blond hair, blue eyes. Guess those traits weren't enough for the SS. They wanted more proof that their people were perfect, so they created a machine to prove it." He chuckled. "But it didn't work."

"It didn't?"

"Well, we think it *killed* people just fine. But it operated on some electrically charged chemical, one that would disperse a poison into the air and infect anyone close by. Some people survived, most didn't."

"And that was a failure?" Garza asked.

Reggie shrugged. "Arsenic kills people in high enough dosages. But people have different immune responses — they're more resilient, more capable of fighting against pathogens."

"True," Garza said. "So maybe it had nothing to do with race, but more to do with finding the strongest of the population."

"Right," Reggie said. "Too bad they didn't have giants." He cocked an eyebrow at his ex-boss and smiled.

"What else was in the journal, Red?"

"When are you going to let Sarah go?"

"When I feel you've told me everything I need to know."

Reggie sighed. *That's never going to happen.* "Look," he said. "I never read the journal. An Interpol guy took it right after we *barely* escaped the temple. And besides, it wasn't the full Book of Bones, just snippets that Rascher's grandaddy copied down."

"What else was she working on?"

"How the hell am I supposed to know that?"

"Would you like to hear about Sarah?" Garza asked. "Do you know what battery acid does to an open wound, Red?"

Red shot out of the chair but stopped himself after only a few inches. The soldiers near Garza didn't budge.

They're as well-trained as I suspected, he thought. *They expected a reaction, but didn't flinch.*

He sat back down. "We thought she was trying to use the serum — whatever that junk was inside The Bell — to test the entire population. A giant version of Die Glocke, if you will."

"But she didn't have the equipment?"

"The machine? That's easy. She was in position to do it, too." *The Great Pyramid of Giza. The ultimate chemical weapon.* "No, she ran out of juice. She had a team of scientists trying to work on a synthetic version of that serum, since the original stuff — stuff she found in that temple — was running low."

"Ah," Garza said. "But she never finished it."

"No, thank God. But she thought there was more of the original stuff — *lots* more of it — hidden in the Hall of Records."

"*The* Hall of Records?"

"Yeah, the hidden wealth of knowledge that the Atlantean race had collected until their demise. No one ever found it, of course, but people say the Library of Alexandria was a branch of this ancient Hall, or that it had original scrolls from the Hall of Records inside."

"And the Book of Bones describes where this Hall is?" Garza asked.

"Who knows? Never read it. But that's what Rachel Rascher believed, and — I suspect — your client."

Garza gave him a strange look. "That's correct."

"What do they want with it? What's the Hall of Records to them?"

"Nothing," Garza said.

"Nothing?"

"They want nothing to do with the Hall of Records. To them, it's a dead-end."

Reggie frowned. "What's that supposed to mean? They don't want the Hall of Records? The treasure that's inside it? The knowledge?"

"There's nothing inside the Hall of Records, Red. It's a farce, a fiction. One created by Plato to send explorers on a wild goose chase around the world."

"But how do you know that? The Book of Bones is supposed to —"

"The Book of Bones has plenty of other secrets in it. Stories of the greatest antediluvian civilization on the planet, one that rivals the civilizations of today. It holds within it the power to unlock the greatest scientific discoveries of mankind. But it does *not* tell anyone what's inside the Hall of Records."

"Why not?" Reggie asked.

"Because the Great Hall of Records is just a myth. An allegory. Plato was fond of those, as you well know. He created the Hall of Records legend as a way of explaining the collected wisdom of the ancients. It's their body of work, their knowledge. But it's *not* a physical place, Red. And what he *describes*; where he says the Hall of

Records lives is nothing but an empty shell of a temple. Just an old structure, cast aside for millennia. There's nothing there."

Reggie was confused. "I don't... understand. How can you know all this?"

"Because my client has the Book of Bones. *Most* of it, anyway, aside from a few key chapters that they're very intent on finding. But what they have tells us exactly where the Hall of Records — or at least what Plato calls the Hall of Records — lies."

"And?"

"And?" Garza asked. "What do you mean, 'and?' That's it — there's nothing there. As I said, an empty shell of a temple. Forgotten to the modern world, but never more than just a blank canvas."

"But how can you be —"

"I can be sure, Reggie, because you're sitting in it."

Reggie's eyes focused on Garza, then on the walls around them. The ceiling, the floor, it was all made of stone. Whitish gray stone with an almost blue hue under direct light. Smooth, as if carved by hand and sanded down over centuries.

No, he thought. *There's no way.*

But it had to be true. He recognized the space. It wasn't the same space, but it was modeled after and designed by the same hands as the space beneath the Sphinx at Giza.

Carved not by the ancient Egyptians, but by a race far more ancient still.

You're sitting in it, Garza had said.

"Gareth Red," Garza said, smiling while holding his arms open to his sides. "Welcome to the Great Hall of Records."

CHAPTER 40

JULIE

THE WATER WAS COLDER than she'd expected, but Julie was able to hold her breath and keep her eyes closed for the initial submersion. When she felt her head sink beneath the waves, she kicked — aiming her head straight down. She needed to get deep enough.

She heard the roaring of the boat's engine above her, and she swam downward, waiting for the second. She hoped their enemy's boat remained focused on Ben, assuming that they'd hit her and caused her to fall overboard. But if they stopped to check...

She heard the motor only fifteen seconds later — *were they too close to him already?* — as she began swimming toward the shoreline.

She couldn't hold her breath long enough to make the swim underwater, but she figured she could make it at least halfway. She'd come up for air quickly, then resume her underwater journey.

She also hoped Ben could fend off the attackers long enough for her to get into position. Their rifles were accurate, and Julie knew the mercenaries were trained well enough to use them effectively, but she hoped that Ben was a difficult enough target to hit on the open waters. Still, their boat was faster than Ben's, and they didn't even know if this plan would work...

Stop. She came up for air, took a massive breath, both to refill her lungs and to let out a deep sigh to help relax her, then she dared a look around.

She saw the four attackers first. The three men were still standing on the front of the boat — that was good. The driver was aiming for the smaller boat in front of them, and Julie could barely see Ben, crouched low in the back of their fishing boat and heading for the spot they'd agreed upon.

She went down for the second leg of her trip, then came up seven seconds later to see the boats just beneath the horizon line.

She reached the first buoy at the same time as Ben rounded the corner behind the ferry and disappeared onto its port side, but she didn't have time to celebrate. The second buoy was still a good twenty feet away, and she figured Ben would reach the stern of the ferry on its port side just as she was ready.

The buoy was a three-foot-tall metal statue in the shape of a miniature lighthouse, and it had a 'no fishing' graphic on a sign on two of its sides, as well as a second sign on one side that had a 'no wake' logo. She recognized the signs and the buoy — they were ubiquitous on the lake where she'd grown up — a way to delineate the border around a swimming spot or a slow zone.

She swam underwater once more, then beneath the buoy itself, reaching out with her palms open. Her left hand felt the rope holding the buoy to its anchor, and she pulled it up. There was a small amount of slack in the line, and she panicked when it went taut and she felt the anchor catch.

Come on.

She yanked again, this time resting her feet against the side of the buoy, and she felt the rope and anchor give. The anchor was a simple pyramid-shaped weight, probably no more than ten pounds, and she hauled in the line as fast as she was able.

She came up for air again and continued to drag the line with her, ignoring the beating of her heart and the gentle sear beginning to build in her lungs. She focused on her mission and reached the second buoy just as she heard the telltale sound of Ben's tiny boat rounding the corner of the ferry's bow.

But that wasn't the only thing she heard.

The gunfire was nearly constant now, the men obviously realizing that Ben was taking them on a scenic tour of the Corsican port. She saw out of the corner of her eye the boats, weaving back and forth as they dodged in and around the other buoys dotting the harbor's surface, and the gunmen traded positions on the front of their boat as they took potshots at Ben.

For what it was worth, Julie saw that the rear boat hadn't gotten much closer to Ben's, but it was now easily within what she would have called 'close range.' The fact that they hadn't hit Ben yet was nothing short of a miracle, but she also saw that Ben stayed very low in the back of the boat.

She saw that his engine was smoking — a long line of black smoke trailed off and behind him, dissipating into the air behind the boat. She knew that was bad news, but it seemed to also have the added effect of creating a difficult barrier for the men to aim through.

Just get here, she thought. *Just get here without blowing up.*

He did.

She hid behind the second buoy and peeked out to see Ben pointing the boat between the two buoys she'd just swam between. The boat was coughing, and she imagined it was leaking precious fuel.

The second boat had, in fact, slowed a little. It was keeping pace with Ben's, but it appeared to be far enough away that it could at least follow the trail of smoke safely, without getting lost in it. Still, it was traveling fast.

But Julie no longer needed to time out her attack. The smoke would conceal her machinations, and she only hoped the buoys and their lines would hold.

She crawled up higher onto the buoy's side, wrapped the *first* buoy's rope around the little lighthouse on the *second* one, then back over itself, then dropped the anchor.

The line went tight, and she saw the buoys, twenty feet apart, leaning toward one another. They held that way for a few seconds, then the anchor began to sink.

The line stretching between them rose out of the water about three feet, to the top of the lighthouse, and the first buoy began to move toward the second one, to ease the tension on the rope.

But the boat full of gunmen shot underneath the line as it was still hanging in the air, and it hit one man standing in the center of the boat first.

Julie watched the rope grow tight again, hold, and clothesline the man as the boat continued moving. It launched forward, but the man was still wrapped in the line, and he was quickly joined by his teammates.

The three men were smacked — hard — off the back of the boat. They piled into the water, one on top of the other two, and disappeared into the harbor. Their weapons landed nearby but sunk beneath the surface before any of them could recover.

She looked at the two boats. The driver of the second boat had slowed and was beginning to turn around, but Ben was already facing her direction and steaming toward her.

She made her move.

CHAPTER 41

REGGIE

AFTER GARZA and his men left the room, Reggie continued pacing. This time, however, he had a purpose.

Get out, get Sarah, kill Garza.

It was clear now what Garza was after. He needed his client's payment, the money for finding the Book of Bones. But the icing on the cake for him would be information in the book itself — information that would help him finish the monstrous giants he'd somehow created.

Reggie didn't know if they were some science experiment-gone-wrong, or if they were purpose-built based on some new technology. And they were incomplete somehow — weaker than they should have been, or fragile in some way. Reggie saw a bit of it in Alaska, when they'd stumbled into the clearing and he caught a glimpse of their seemingly melted faces.

But Garza believed that whatever was wrong with them could be fixed, perfected. And whatever it would take to perfect them he believed he would find inside the Book of Bones. Whatever Garza had done to 'grow' the giants was an incomplete answer. He needed something, and he believed the missing portion of the Book of Bones would have the answer. Something akin to the chemical that Rachel

Rascher had found? Something with near-mystical properties, a new element? Whatever it was, Garza wanted to get his hands on it.

And the Hall of Records.

Reggie spun around, taking in the space illuminated by the single work lamp. *This is the Hall of Records?* he thought. *The 'Great' Hall of Records?*

It seemed difficult to believe — there was nothing here. No markings on the walls, no telltale artifacts. And Garza had implied that they'd found it like this. Totally empty. Did that mean Plato was simply telling a story? A lesson, disguised as history? He'd done it before, and many historians believed that his stories of Atlantis were merely fabricated as an argument against hubris.

But... Reggie had seen Atlantis with his own eyes. Sure, it was nothing more than an ancient, collapsed civilization that had long battled with its Mediterranean rivals, but it was real nonetheless. They'd found proof of it, and he'd found proof of their technological prowess beneath the Great Sphinx.

He tried to put it together, but he knew there weren't enough pieces yet. Garza wanted the Book of Bones for his client, who wanted it... for what? And who was the client?

He was skeptical that it was the Catholic Church, but it wasn't impossible. More likely, he thought, it was a branch within the Church, a smaller organization operating as rogues to attain more power.

But how would the Book of Bones bring them that power? What was in it for them?

He shook his head. *Think about that later. For now: get out.*

The stairs leading to the heavy door was the only out of the room. He was sure of that, but he'd scoured every inch of the stone room, anyway. He could climb the stairs, but it was likely locked.

About an hour ago, a man had entered and dropped a bucket of water onto the top stair. Half of it had spilled out, but Reggie was never one to be picky. He'd slurped from the bucket the cool, refreshing water and continued his examination of the room.

A bucket, one-quarter full of water. A casket made of wood, nailed together with long, thin deck nails. It sat on a metal table, something he might find in a chemistry lab or veterinarian's hospital. A work light, 16,000 lumens split between the two square-shaped bulb housings. It plugged into a cable that ran through a tiny hole that had been drilled through the wall.

That was it. He had no tools, no gear, no phone. The clothes he was wearing were the same ones he'd put on their last day in the forest: a flannel long-sleeved shirt, wool 'jeans,' and two pairs of merino wool socks beneath his army boots.

He wasn't even wearing a watch.

Think, Reggie.

He wondered why Garza had left him alone in this room, without being bound or handcuffed. Completely free to move around. There weren't even any cameras inside, so he wasn't being watched.

Then it hit him. *He knows I can't escape.*

And if he *could* escape, where would he go? Garza would have the place crawling with enough grunts — or giants — to prevent him from getting far.

And, even *then*, Garza would have brought him somewhere so far off the beaten path — the 'middle of nowhere,' he'd said — that if he *could* somehow get out of this place alive, with Sarah, that they'd still be in the middle of nowhere. He might not have considered Reggie's survival skill set, but with an extra person in tow, it was a long shot that they'd survive.

So he was 'free' in the sense that Garza wasn't keeping a close eye on him. That didn't give him much leverage, but what little leverage it did provide, he intended to take.

A plan began to form in his mind, and Gareth Red got to work.

THE MEN WERE STILL, lying on the top of the water. She could see two of them, but both looked unconscious. She swam toward one of them, hoping they had a knife or sidearm attached to their belts.

She found the third man as she swam. He had been wrapped in the rope somehow and held underwater, and her foot kicked him as she passed. He struggled against the line for a moment, reaching out for Julie, but she moved to the side and swam on.

The two other men were unconscious, one face-up on the water's surface and one face-down. She reached the closest one to her, the face-up man, and found his pocket. There was nothing inside them.

She started to swim toward the second man but the water around her exploded into a fury. She heard the gunshots, ducking instinctively, then pulled herself underwater. She slid over, just beneath the face-down man, and pulled him toward herself, using him as a human shield.

She opened her eyes again and saw through the surface of the water, at the man shooting.

The driver.

The boat had been driven by the fourth man, and he was now

standing on the edge of his boat, aiming down at Julie with his own assault rifle.

Shit.

She would not be able to hide forever. The man didn't seem to care about his downed teammates, nor did he seem to be in any hurry to retrieve them. He aimed, pulled off a few shots, then Julie saw something amazing.

The man *launched* forward, dropping the rifle, and sailed through the air. He landed with a splash about five feet away from her, just as she was coming up for a breath of air. In the man's place on the edge of the boat stood Ben, recovering from the perfect tackle he'd administered to the driver. He caught his balance and peered through the water, trying to find Julie.

When she came up to wave and shout his name, the driver resurfaced, splashing around as he came for her.

She began to backpedal, throwing water to the sides as she tried to get away.

Then she heard the *crack* of the assault rifle. She winced, closing her eyes for a moment, but when she opened them, the man lay on the water, still.

"Jules!"

Ben's voice.

"Julie, are you okay?"

She nodded, then found her own voice. "Y — yeah, I'm good."

She met his eyes, saw their relief, and swam over, where he fished her out of the Mediterranean harbor and into the boat. She lay on the deck of the watercraft, panting. Ben stood over her, grasping her hand in his bear-like grip while holding his new assault rifle at his side.

"That was... different."

She laughed. "Not exactly what I expected to happen on our way to Rome."

"But it worked," he said. "It worked perfectly. Good call."

"Yeah, I guess," she answered. "But let's maybe... never do that again?"

"Agreed. I think I'll play my CSO leader card and ask Mr. E to supply us with a better outfit of firearms."

He paused.

"And I'm never flying anything but first class ever again."

She laughed again. "Technically, we *were* in first class in that Cessna. We just —"

"First class in a private jet. With a lot of whiskey. And a lot of guns. Waterproof guns."

"Fair," Julie said. She tossed her hair back — she kept it relatively short these days, nothing but a simple tuck behind her ear would be enough to keep it in line — and walked over to the wheel. "Best of all, we've not a new ride. Twin-engine, too. Looks like it's fueled up and has an extra couple of full tanks. That should be more than enough to get us to Rome and back."

"Hope so," Ben said. "And this one's way faster. You driving the first leg?"

"Sure. Why don't you look around for a map or a radio? There should be at least something. Oh, and let me know what those engines' horsepower is."

Ben gave her a funny look.

"What?" she asked, pushing the throttle down and nudging the boat forward. "My dad and his brother had a fishing boat growing up. He made us all learn how to drive. And a good estimate for gallons burned per mile is one-tenth of the horsepower."

"Good to know," Ben said. "Looks like Yamaha 350-HP something or other. That enough?"

She nodded. "That's perfect. Assuming we've got a full tank, we can expect to run those at about 35 gallons per hour, and for a fishing boat like this, I'd guess the tank holds somewhere between 250-300 gallons. The extra tank mounted on the back will add another 100 to that."

"So..." Ben said. "Is that enough?"

"Easily. We've got to burn 133 miles, assuming we can keep it pointed toward the right city. And that average is running the throttle flat-out, so we can go a bit slower to conserve fuel, though we don't need to. Might just be helpful to follow the ferry and stay in their lane to make sure we get to the right place."

She goosed the engine to test the speed, and she was impressed to see the speedometer reach 60 MPH. At that speed, they'd be docking in Italy in just over three hours.

"We'll make better time than we would have by taking the ferry," Ben said, verbalizing her thoughts. "Let's shoot for dead west and just see where we land. We'll be able to aim toward a city once we see land."

She nodded, pushed the throttle fully open, and stood up behind the wheel. For a fleeting moment, as she felt the wind pushing her hair up and around her eyes, she felt like a kid again, gunning her dad's boat out on the lake.

She tried to hold on to that feeling, but it disappeared almost as soon as she acknowledged it.

CHAPTER 43

BEN

AFTER REACHING the port city of Santa Miranella, Italy, they promptly rented a small car and a paper map of Italy, as well as a small 'burner' phone, from which they called Mrs. E.

They had to leave the assault rifle behind a dumpster in an alley while they rented the car, but once they had the papers in hand, Julie drove by and Ben grabbed it. It felt odd to have a weapon like that in their compact sedan, but Ben knew he'd rather keep it with them than risk being caught empty-handed once again. They planned to leave the rifle in the car's trunk until they'd checked into their hotel.

Rome was a short trip down a highway, and they were within the city limits in about half an hour. Julie had driven the boat for about half their trip over the water, and now she was behind the wheel of the car.

Ben had never been here — Italy, Rome, or the Vatican — and he was blown away by the architecture. A city that had existed, adapted, and reinvented itself many times over the course of two-thousand years, Rome was a sight to behold to Ben, a man interested in history but never able to spend considerable time in other countries.

This trip was no different, and he found himself frustrated that their mission here was to get in, find a Catholic relic, and get out again. There would be no time for exploration, historical study, research, or any relaxation.

There would be no time for food, either. Julie had pulled into a major fast-food chain's drive-through window to grab a pile of whatever was already ready. Ben had inhaled the sandwich and wrap and washed it down with a bit of water, but the smells of the bread vendors and cafes they passed on their way through the city made him wish they had more time.

One of his life's dreams was to take a 'food tour' of the world — hitting the best restaurants in the best foodie cities on the planet. He'd always been interested in *eating* food, but only recently — after meeting his best friend, Reggie — had he been more interested in the more nuanced aspects of food, like how it was made, why it was served where it was, and the stories behind the meals.

Julie wasn't as avid a fan as food as Ben was, but he knew she was infatuated with the city for her own reasons. She'd grown up a Catholic, her father and mother devout all her young life until high school. When she'd left for college, her schooling had taken precedence over her religious life, but she'd held onto her beliefs and brought them along into her relationship with Ben.

They didn't attend church, and Julie didn't practice any overt Catholic traditions, but he knew she cared deeply for the traditions and histories of the Church.

It was surreal to be in a city that had existed for ten times as long as his entire *country* had been around. It was mind boggling, to be weaving through buildings and streets and alleys and places of business that could be fifteen years old or fifteen-hundred. They passed modern boutiques, small mom-and-pop bakeries, and ancient-looking churches and cathedrals, and alongside any of the historic sites there were plenty of modern-looking conveniences, from gas stations to malls to cellular phone stores.

Vatican City, the 'city within a city,' peered in on Ben though the rental car's windows. The smallest country in the world, the 109-acre region operates as a monarchy, yet is completely surrounded by a two-mile-long wall separating itself from the rest of Rome, Italy. Ben watched the buildings pass by on the Via de Porta Cavalleggeri, then on the Via della Stazione Vaticana, until Julie pointed at their destination.

The hotel was small, smashed between two larger buildings that loomed over it on both sides, but it had a quaint, welcoming feel. The hotelier apparently owned a few of these small buildings throughout the city and used them as short-term rentals and bed-and-breakfasts, which had been on the rise everywhere. Ben wasn't surprised to find the same deal in Rome, but he was surprised to discover that they allowed them into their room with little fuss, considering he and Julie were traveling from another country and had only Ben's ID between the two of them — no bags or extra clothes, no cameras or phones, and no other identification. Further, the desk clerk didn't give them any grief about being illegal tourists in the country. He didn't ask for passports or travel papers of any sort — money, apparently, was the only currency they needed.

Once they were checked in, Ben and Julie descended the staircase to the lobby where they found a door leading into the dregs of the building. They waited for a moment, scoping out the foot traffic. Aside from a bellhop-turned-desk-clerk, they saw only a single other employee and no guests. The employee appeared to be a cook, as he was a disheveled-looking kid with a wild crop of dark hair that fell out and around his ears and nearly onto his food-stained shirt. He barely shot them a glance as he speed-walked through the lobby and into a deeper area from which Ben could smell faint strains of some kind of pasta.

"Seems deserted," Ben said.

"Just a small hotel," Julie answered. "But that's good news."

"Yeah, but let's hope this entrance to the secret Vatican tunnel is easy to find. You think the employees know about it?"

"I doubt it," Julie said. "Archie said the tunnels predate most of the modern buildings here in Rome, and when the Vatican architects consulted on their construction, they hid the doors inside closets, cellars, and beneath staircases. None of the doors would be obvious to anyone not looking for them."

"And this one's supposed to lead to an underground tunnel, not an above-ground one. So that means we need to get access to the cellar."

"I'd guess a place like this has at least a small wine cellar. Start there?"

They found the cellar's door within a few minutes of poking around behind closed — but unlocked — doors. It was a short door, and it led to a half staircase that descended beneath the foundation of the building. Ben had to duck to enter it, but found he could almost extend to full height once he was in the cramped cellar space.

Inside the cellar, Julie found a single bulb with a pull string, but the bulb illuminated the entire room. Three walls around them were covered in racks of wine bottles, all laying on their sides and at a slight angle. There were small handwritten labels on the wooden racks beneath a few sections, but the majority of the wines were identifiable only by their own labels, and Ben couldn't see any particular order to the collection. Whites were stored with reds, ciders and ales all mixed in.

"Any ideas?" he asked.

"Maybe we take a short break? Share a bottle between us before we go?"

Ben laughed. "I'd love to, actually. We could both use a break."

"Yeah. But I think if anyone deserves a break, it's Reggie and Sarah."

"Okay, fair. So, should we canvass the area? You take the left wall, I'll take the right? Meet in the middle on the far side?"

She nodded and got to work, and Ben followed her lead. After ten minutes of searching through the entire cellar, including the short wall at the opposite end of the room, Ben shrugged. "There's nothing here."

"Well..." Julie said, poking at something. "Hang on."

Ben tried to see what it was she had found and stretched his head up and over her shoulder.

At that moment, before he could make out what it was she was looking at, Ben heard a crash and a loud yell from somewhere upstairs.

CHAPTER 44

REGGIE

THE SOLDIER CAME BACK in later that day, apparently to provide Reggie with some food. MREs, by the look of it, but Reggie didn't get a good look. He had one eye open, barely, squeezing the other shut tightly. He watched the soldier through a single slitted eyelid.

Reggie had gone back to his casket, gotten inside, and pretended to be asleep. He'd brought the bucket, now empty, with him and set it about five feet from the table, hoping the soldier would retrieve it rather than replace it with a new one. He wanted the soldier to feel safe enough to grab it without moving too close to Reggie.

Unfortunately, the soldier simply dropped the food onto the top stair as he'd done with the water.

But five minutes later the soldier returned, this time with a buddy. Another armed guard entered the room behind the first, holding an SMG that was pointed at Reggie's 'sleeping' body. The first guard descended the stairs, heading for the empty bucket.

I knew it, Reggie thought. *They only* have *one bucket.*

Best of all, neither man seemed to notice that the light in the room had dimmed.

When the soldier was closest to Reggie, he made his move.

The man turned as he knelt to grab the bucket's handle, facing away from Reggie for a brief instant. Reggie kicked the thin boards that made up the bottom side of his casket, easily breaking away the wood. He lunged up and out of the box, directly at the man, who fumbled with the bucket in one hand while trying to retrieve his weapon in his other.

Reggie kicked him in the groin, then swiftly jumped backward. He pushed the table up and onto its side, sending the casket crashing down and onto the floor.

But he now had some protection, and it was just in time.

A round of bullets pinged against the top of the table, behind which Reggie crouched. They dented the metal but didn't pierce — there was no way the tiny submachine gun would puncture from that distance — and Reggie waited.

The first man would have easily recovered by now, and would be waiting for his teammate to end his volley to attack.

That attack came, and it came fast. Reggie saw the bucket first, thrown up and over the side of the table, and he instinctively held an arm up to protect his head as the bucket fell.

... Which was exactly what the other attacker wanted. While Reggie's focused had been pulled in the direction of the flying metal bucket, the man rushed behind the table and aimed his pistol down at Reggie.

Reggie saw the man lining up the shot, but he was too close, and Reggie took advantage. He kicked out, hard, aiming for the man's knees. His left boot made contact with the man's leg and he went down.

Reggie stayed low, trying to keep the table between himself and the second gunman, but he came out from the table and twirled around on the stone floor, bringing his hand up above the man's face just as he tried to regain his balance.

The man's face turned, just in time to see Reggie's fist come crashing down.

But it wasn't Reggie's fist that he would feel. Instead, his eye immediately exploded when the lightbulb Reggie had removed from the work lamp, the tip carefully broken off on the edge of the casket, smashed into the man's face.

Blood spurted everywhere, more than Reggie would have expected. Then again, he'd never punctured a human eyeball with a razor-sharp glass lightbulb before.

The effect was immediate and profound. The Ravenshadow man imploded, collapsing in on himself as he moaned in agony. Reggie reached over the man's waist and ripped his rifle from his side, then planted two rounds into the man — one between his shoulders, and one to the back of his neck.

He didn't pause there. Reggie shifted again, this time rolling in the opposite direction. He came up and aimed, knowing from the sound of the footsteps exactly where the *second* gunman had traveled. He fired two more shots into that man's chest, sending him flying against the back wall. He was wearing body protection, so a third to the man's neck finished the job.

He ran to the man before he'd even closed his eyes in death and took the SMG from his hands. *Never hurts to have too much weaponry.*

He was about to leave when he took another glance down at the fallen mercenary. The man was wearing his bulletproof vest above his shirt. *Never hurts to have too much protection, either.*

Reggie strapped on the man's bloody vest and checked his newfound gear. An MGP-84, developed in Peru for close-quarters protection. Capable of firing Uzi rounds, it was introduced in the '90s and he'd seen more than a few of them show up while in Brazil, typically bought and sold on the cartel and black markets.

He slung the MGP over his shoulder and examined the other weapon. This one he was intimately familiar with. An IMBEL IA2, used as the primary rifle of the Brazilian Army. 60,000 of the guns had been manufactured, and plenty of illegal versions had washed up onto the shooting range he'd owned in Brazil since then.

Best of all, he'd run over 10,000 rounds through them, and he knew that a well-maintained A2 in his hands was deadly.

Game over, Garza.

Reggie stepped to the bottom of the stairs and took a last-minute inventory. Satisfied there was nothing else from the two downed guards he needed, he began scaling the stairs. They were even larger than he'd initially thought. The dimly lit room had been playing tricks on him — these stairs had to be three feet wide and two-and-a-half tall.

He jumped forward and began climbing. He needed to move quickly — the room they had kept him in might have been close to soundproof, but the heavy door was open during the skirmish. If anyone on Garza's team was in the room above, they would have surely heard the gunshots.

He planted a foot just inside the open doorway, waiting. Listening.

Hearing nothing, he crept farther out into the open space beyond the stairs. The air felt warmer, more humid. The space felt larger, too. There was light in the room, but it appeared to be moon-light, and not much at that. It was filtering down through tiny rectangular slits, barely large enough to be called windows. The room itself was round, like a citadel or castle minaret.

And, in the center of the room, laying on top of a huge stone circle, was Sarah.

CHAPTER 45

REGGIE

HER ARMS and legs were strapped down using vinyl cinch straps that been tightened over her body and hooked into rings cemented onto the stone floor.

Her head face-down on the stone pillar, was facing the opposite direction, but Reggie could tell she was in severe pain. They had stripped her clothes back from her shoulders, halfway down her back, revealing the wound from the rubber bullet.

Reggie approached, cautious of anything or anyone that might be waiting for him in the dark crevasses of the shadowy room. Thankfully, there were no corners in the room, though there were plenty of sections beneath the rectangular windows that could have hidden a person. He took care to pass through the center of the room slowly but on a spring, ready to pounce and hide behind the stone table at any moment.

But no one came. None of the Ravenshadow men or Garza popped out from a shadow, and no shots were fired. He had a feeling of uneasiness, but shook it off. *One goal at a time. One moment at a time.*

He looked down at Sarah. Her bronze back was dotted with darker splotches. Dried blood. He saw a gruesome web of dark-blue lines working their out from the central gunshot wound. It seemed as though Garza had been true to his word — the lines were veins, poisoned and radiating outward, carrying the toxins to the rest of her body.

What the hell did he do?

Reggie had to fight against the rage, against the desire to smash through everything in sight and destroy the entire place in his hunt for Garza. Sarah's life was at stake, and she needed medical attention.

"Reggie?" she whispered.

Oh, God. She's awake.

"Sarah," he said. "Sarah, just rest. Don't —"

"We have to get out of here. We have to leave. Now."

Reggie ran a hand through his hair. "Yeah, uh... about that."

"Reggie, there's no time. That man — Garza? He said... he told me —"

"Shh," Reggie said. "Just rest. I'm going to figure this out."

"No," she said, her voice pleading. He told me... he said that he knew you would —"

Suddenly the room was bathed in blinding-white light. Reggie pushed his elbow up over his eyes, then swung around. He removed his arm and tried to get his bearings, bringing the rifle up and to the ready.

He had almost turned a full circle when he heard a slow clap from the space beneath the windows to his left. He whirled around, preparing to fire on whoever it was.

"Take the shot and Sarah dies," the voice said. *Garza.* He stepped out from the shadows. "I do appreciate your willingness to test a few of my new recruits."

Reggie frowned.

"Those two men downstairs — well done, Red. You know, the best way to test a security system is to place it under pressure. Well-trained pressure, like you. Rest assured, I will be improving my security protocols based on your little MacGyver routine down there."

"What's wrong with her?" Reggie asked, throwing a thumb over his shoulder to Sarah.

"As you have seen, the poison we've given her is spreading, and it will consume her nervous system within two days. One day from now and she will lose all motor function. Hours from now, severe pain." He coughed. "Well, more pain than she'd in now."

Sarah groaned.

"You're a bastard," Reggie said. "I thought we'd come to an agreement, but I knew I couldn't trust you. That's why I didn't —"

"Tell the truth?" Garza said. "The truth that you believe the Catholic Church is the organization looking for the Book of Bones?"

"You didn't ask."

"I told you I wanted to know *everything* you know."

"Set her free and I'll tell you whatever you want to know."

"Too late for that, my friend," Garza said. "I need the Book of Bones — the missing pieces of it — and I need them *now*. You and your girlfriend are no longer of any use to me, and your other friends, that bumbling idiot Harvey Bennett and his little fling Juliette, seem to have gotten sidetracked in Rome."

Rome? he thought. *What the hell are they doing in Rome?*

"So your entire team has proven useless, once again. My client expects delivery of the Book of Bones within a day, and I expect to keep that arrangement."

Garza turned to a dark spot along the wall and nodded. A door began opening, another of the massive, hidden-hinged doors. Two Ravenshadow men stood on either side of it, now illuminated by the light gleaming in from the other side. Reggie couldn't see what was beyond it.

"I'm going to leave you with my men. They will finish what we've started here today."

Reggie sensed the presence of more men, now behind him, stepping forward and into the central chamber.

Shit.

He wanted to run, to start firing. He could take a hit or two. Maybe three, if they weren't in life-threatening places. But that would guarantee Sarah's death. He didn't have time to free her, and even if he could, he wouldn't be able to fight his way out of the chamber while carrying her.

He did the only thing he knew would give him a chance at living long enough to save her.

Reggie stepped up next to the stone pillar, placed his weapon on the floor, and raised his hands above his head.

"THE HELL WAS THAT?" he asked.

A few seconds later, he heard gunshots.

"Shit," he whispered, running toward the stairs. "Who the hell are those guys, anyway? Jules, we can't stay down here. We're sitting ducks —"

"They know we're here, Ben," Julie said, her voice calm and even. "That's *why* they're here. We don't have any time left — we *have* to find this entrance to the tunnels."

Ben listened for a moment. More gunshots, closer this time. *They're moving in.* He wondered if the men knew they were in the cellar somehow, and if Ben and Julie were in it. He wondered if they were the same men — or part of the same group — that had attacked them in Corsica.

"Ben, come here," Julie whispered.

He ran back to her side and moved his head out of the way of the light. Beneath Julie's fingers he saw a bottle of wine, covered in dust and seemingly no different from the rest of the bottles on that rack. It was full, the cork still in place on its top.

"What about it?"

"The label," Julie said, pointing to the rack it was sitting on.

He looked down as Julie brushed some dust off the bottle's label. Instead of a handwritten paper label, someone had scratched a symbol into the rack itself. It was tiny, nearly invisible, and only because of the lighting of the room did it have a small inner shadow that caused it to stand out against the rack.

"That's the symbol for the Vatican," Julie said.

She was right. He recognized a simplified version of the Vatican seal — two crossed keys with a rope hanging between them, a crown above.

"That has to mean something, right?" Ben asked.

Julie spun to the left, then to the right, whispering to herself. "We came in from that direction... this is... yeah, I think it has to be it. I'd guess the Vatican is right over there, in the direction the seal is pointing."

She reached out and pulled the wine. Ben watched as... nothing happened.

"It's stuck," Julie said, her voice growing frantic.

Ben didn't hear any more gunshots, but he knew there weren't many employees in the hotel in the first place. He only hoped that whoever was up there was safe; that the gunshots were meant as warnings.

But he had a feeling that whoever was after them wouldn't care about a few innocent lives that stood between them and their goal. He knew Garza's team wouldn't have wasted any time making that decision, but these men were somehow different. Somehow colder.

Who are they?

He didn't have time to ponder the question. Footsteps, deep and menacing, pounded around on the floor above, and he heard men's low voices calling to each other as they checked and cleared each room. They would find the cellar door in seconds, and if Ben and Julie didn't find a way out before then...

Julie tried again, this time lifting the bottle up from the front instead of trying to pull it forward. Ben heard a click, and then a deeper hiss as a cool blast of air from the floor blew dust up around them.

"What was that?" he asked.

Julie turned to face him. "We opened something." She looked around the floor, then pointed. "There!"

Ben stepped over to where she was pointing. A square, each side about two feet long, had been marked out on the floor. Ben hadn't noticed it before, and he assumed it was because of the care the craftsmen of this room had taken in laying out the floor planks. But when Julie had moved the wine bottle, air had rushed out from the cracks, pushing away dust and debris.

"It's a door," he whispered.

"We don't have time to check it out," Julie said. "I'll go first, you follow. Close it after."

He nodded, but Julie was already waiting in front of the heavy square planks. Ben heaved it open and saw a staircase, dilapidated and rotting. The wood planks on the stairs seemed decayed, but Julie didn't hesitate. She shot down the steps, the creaking and groaning of them giving Ben a bit of anxiety, but they held.

Julie disappeared into the depths of the staircase, her frame easily blacked out by the deep shadows from within. None of the cellar's single bulb's rays reached her.

Ben took a breath. *Afraid of planes, afraid of heights, and now afraid of tight spaces?* He hadn't ever realized this was a fear for him, but he didn't have time to register much beyond that. The shuffling and voices of the men up above and behind him urged him forward.

He dropped into the staircase, crouched, then turned and pulled the square door shut. He knew the soldiers would easily find the marked lines of the hatch, but he'd rather give themselves a chance at getting away.

As soon as the hatch door closed, every drop of light they'd had vanished, and Ben was plunged into complete darkness. He quickly hopped down the flight of stairs until he felt Julie's outstretched hand. He heard her rustling with something, then a bluish glow emanated from her palm.

"Here," she said, holding the cheap flip-phone up and in front of her. The stone walls around them seemed to push inward, compressing into a smaller and smaller space, but at least they could see. "It's not much, but at least we won't have to walk in the dark."

"Walk?" Ben said. "I'm jogging. No way I'm getting caught down here by those assholes. I knew we should have brought the rifle with us."

"There was no way to sneak it in while the bellhop was there," Julie said. "Let's just get across the street and into the Vatican, and we can see where we are then. I don't think it's a long trip — hopefully we're far enough ahead that we can get up and out of here before those guys get a bead on us."

"Yeah, hopefully."

He didn't want to think about what it would mean if they *didn't* get out before they were spotted.

Ben took a breath, blinked, then charged forward, allowing Julie's phone-powered flashlight to guide their way.

JULIE

THE PATH through the underground tunnel ended at another staircase. The entire path was pitch-black, save for the light from Julie's open phone, and during their run she could see small holes along the walls on both sides — mounts for torch lighting. She imagined a time in the past when relations and tensions between the Vatican and Rome were high, when these tunnels would have been manned by Swiss guards and Vatican soldiers, the routes in and out of the city lit by heavy torches.

She got a chill thinking about it. This place — Rome, The Vatican, these tunnels — was *old*. Ancient, especially compared to the country she was from. American history barely went back 200 years, and perhaps twice that if she counted the time before the Revolutionary War. Rome, by contrast, had been around from before Christ walked the earth.

It was stunning, and she felt the depth of the history and the importance of every stone beneath her feet as she ran. When they reached the staircase at the opposite end of the hallway, she paused to catch her breath. Ben was there, waiting.

The staircase rose higher than the one they'd used to enter the tunnel — it was possible this entrance would lead them to a main level instead of a basement or cellar. Instead of a square hatch in the floor, the door at the top of this staircase hung on old iron hinges and appeared to open inward.

She heard the unmistakable sound of heavy footfalls echoing through the hallway.

"They're here," she whispered.

Ben nodded. "Here goes nothing," he said. "Let's see where this tunnel ends up."

He pushed hard, and Julie heard the creaking sound of old wood and rusted iron groaning against his weight. But it gave, and the door opened. A faint splash of light spilled outward into the tunnel, but Ben moved through the open space and into the room beyond, which blocked the light. She followed behind, but Ben had stopped in the small space just beyond.

"Ben?" she asked.

"Uh..."

She stood higher on her toes and peered over his shoulder.

"I think we're..."

He took another step forward and Julie again followed, and she shut the door behind her. When she turned back around, Ben was smiling.

"It's a bathroom," he said. "We're in a doorless closet, like a nook. But this is definitely a bathroom."

Julie looked around, holding her phone up. The room they had stumbled into was, indeed, a restroom. They were standing inside a small storage nook in the corner of the room, and directly in front of ben was an old, cracked toilet. A pull string hung from the ceiling next to it. The larger room beyond was too dark to see clearly, but it appeared as though they were inside an old, unused restroom.

"Looks like they just sealed it off," Ben said. "It's dusty and dank in here. No one's using this place anytime soon."

"Those guys behind us will," Julie said, shuffling around Ben and out into the main room. "There's got to be a door out of here, right?"

She saw it before she'd finished the sentence, and in another few seconds they were standing in front of a standard-sized door. The knob was locked. Ben tried shimmying it, but the door seemed to be locked from the outside as well.

"It won't budge," Ben said. "Hold on, I think I can break —"

A tapping sound rang from the other side of the door. A nervous rattling joined in, and Julie looked at Ben.

Then she heard a sound from behind them — footsteps.

"We're out of time," she whispered. "The soldiers are here."

"And whoever's on the other side of this door is unlocking it," Ben added.

They stood, hand-in-hand, waiting for the door to open.

Footsteps fell upon the stairs behind the door in the nook. Heavy, brooding pounding from the soldiers' boots.

Julie closed her eyes.

The door opened, and the entire room was filled with brilliant light.

Ben rushed forward, pulling Julie along with him. He ran *through* the shape in the open doorway and out into the hall, and Julie nearly fell over as she stumbled out. Two shapes, each brandishing an assault rifle, swung by Ben and through the open door. Ben turned and slammed the door shut again behind them, already shouting before they'd even had a chance to see who had freed them. He heard gunfire being shared by both sides.

"Get — the door — the soldiers..." he panted. "Chasing us... lock it down and get some guards. We're —"

"Right on time," a man said. He had a thick Italian accent, but spoke with an authority and confidence that told Julie more than his words. "Although I am surprised you came with no weapons."

Julie saw the man just as he spoke. Wearing an all-black uniform, a holstered sidearm, and a grisly looking assault rifle slung over his shoulder. He had a short beard on a rounded face, but Julie could tell the man was far from pudgy. About fifty- or fifty-five years old, he wore his weight well, and she assumed that most of that weight was muscle mass.

The man was flanked by two more similarly dressed men, but both seemed at least a decade younger. Their eyes were on Julie and Ben, but she could tell they were examining the door in their peripheral vision. *Waiting.* For whatever would come out of it.

The leader casually stepped forward and placed his hand on a locking mechanism, then pushed the door closed. He locked it, then slid a bracing bar mounted onto the front of the door down into a cavity in the floor.

He reached to a walkie-talkie on his belt and spoke into it; the words clipped Italian. "Rochat, Gerber, rapporto." He waited a moment, holding a hand up to his ear as he listened to the response.

Apparently satisfied, he nodded. Julie heard no more gunshots coming from the opposite side of the wall. The battle in the tunnel had ended.

When he stepped back, Julie noticed that the door was completely camouflaged in the hallway wall. Even the molding and trim ran alongside the exterior of the door, a continuous line that split the light floral wallpaper on the top half of the wall from the dark blue paint on the bottom half.

Aside from the tiny metal lock and the brace, the door leading into the old bathroom would have been invisible.

"An old water closet, as you may have gathered."

"I thought this hotel was built in the '90s," Julie said.

"Indeed it was," the man answered, turning to face her. "But it sits atop an older structure that was repurposed. The bottom floor — specifically this room and a few others like it — have remained sealed and unchanged."

"You mean hiding secret tunnels," Ben said.

"The tunnels are not a secret," the man said, a curious expression on his face. "They are simply *off-limits* to most people."

Julie stepped forward, toward the man, and was surprised to see the two other men react in kind. She paused. "Sorry, I — we — are just lost. We can —"

The man held up a hand. She looked at each man's face, trying to understand their roles here. *Are they on the same team?*

The leader spoke into the radio once again and one of the men next to him turned and faced the hallway. Rifle drawn, waiting.

"Mr. and Mrs. Bennett — or Richardson, my apologies — I was told you would be here."

Julie frowned. She could sense Ben tensing up next to her.

"We were informed of your arrival when you entered the hotel next door. Our cameras and security monitoring systems alerted me, and we followed your movements through the building. It appears as though you have led others to our location as well?"

Julie knew it wasn't a question as much as a scolding.

"Please, follow me."

The man turned and began to walk away. Ben stiffened. "I'm not going anywhere until you tell me what the hell's going on."

The soldier next to Ben simply raised his rifle and pointed it directly at them.

Ben paused, but Julie nudged him forward.

"Fine," he said. "But I want answers."

The leader kept moving, about ten feet away from them, and he spoke over his shoulder. "It is always answers we want, Mr. Bennett, but never questions."

CHAPTER 48
BEN

BEN'S WRISTS were nearly bleeding, but he ignored the pain. They were secured to a huge oak tabletop by handcuffs that had been tightened far tighter than he would have thought necessary. The handcuffs were fastened to the table through a heavy metal ring, and he knew it would be useless to fight against them.

But that didn't mean he was happy about it.

The guy in charge had led them to some sort of waiting room near the hotel's lobby, where he had been joined by three more of the black-clad security guards, then led into a smaller chamber off of the waiting room. There he had been forced into the chair and his hands bound, then left to himself for nearly an hour.

He and Julie had been separated immediately after entering the waiting room, and he tried to see where she had been taken. The men handling him were harsh, careless, and annoyed by him. No one spoke to them, and after a few minutes of yelling and trying to get someone to answer his questions, Ben gave up.

He figured it out after about thirty minutes into his stay: he was a prisoner here.

Ben and Julie would be questioned.

His decision was now simple: he had two options.

He could lie his way out. Hope that the men would understand that he and Julie were simply lost in the hotel — they'd come in through the main entrance and found the 'secret' door, and just wanted to look around.

It was a long shot, but could he expect anything better with the second option?

He could tell the truth. Tell the men they were here to steal property from the Pope, to send a fraudulent message to an archbishop that would allow them access to an ancient, top-secret document?

He couldn't decide which of the options available to him would lead to a better result.

And worse: what decision would Julie make? If she were being questioned in a similar room, what outcome would she come to? What would she tell the men?

He was contemplating these decisions when the door swung open and the same man who'd found them in the hallway entered. His face was blank, his expression a practiced nothingness. He was a professional, and this wasn't his first time interrogating someone.

"Mr. Bennett," the man said.

"How do you know my name?"

"As I said, we saw you enter the hotel. Anyone who enters the St. Michael is watched, *closely*. In case something like this happens."

"Something like what?" Ben asked.

"How about you tell me?"

The man took a seat across from Ben at the oak table, then unfastened his collar a bit. Ben saw the gleam of a chain necklace around the man's neck, the silver glinting against the fluorescent lights. He loosened his shirt and then sat back, looking at Ben.

"I don't know what you want from us," Ben said. "You unlocked the door in the hallway, but we were just —"

"Hoping you would walk freely right into the house of the Seat of the Vatican?"

"I was going to say that we were just exploring, trying to see the hotel. The door shut, and —"

"And somehow it latched itself and was secured from the outside."

Ben sniffed, then shrugged. "We were being chased."

"By whom?"

Ben's eyes widened a bit. He tried to stop it, but it was too late.

"What is it, Mr. Bennett?"

"It was your own men, wasn't it?" Ben asked. "The guys who chased us — they were following us all along. Shot our plane down, ran us directly toward you here. You faked a gunfight in the tunnels, in that abandoned room. Why?"

"My men are loyal to the Vatican."

"Something tells me your men are loyal to you."

The man shifted in his seat, but didn't take his gaze off of Ben. "Mr. Bennett — Ben, I believe? This investigation will end one of two ways: you tell me *exactly* why you are here, and why your girl-friend is here, and we decide where to go from there. Or you do not tell me, and I keep you here until I am satisfied."

"Are you easily satisfied?"

The man didn't respond.

"Those endings sound a bit vague. What are we talking, like prison?"

The man, again, didn't respond.

"Look," Ben said, holding his wrists as high as they would go. "I don't know who the hell you are, or what you think I'm doing here. And I don't care. But I need something, and if I don't get it, people will die."

The man's eyebrow raised, and he leaned forward. "Can you be more specific?"

"No."

"Can you tell me who will die?"

"Friends."

"Their names?"

Ben frowned. "I thought you were tracking us. Knew our names and everything."

The man sighed. "Ben, this is not one of your American television shows. This is the Vatican. We know who comes and goes from our country, and we know what they want. When we do *not* know, we talk to them. We know your names because they are listed in private security databases that —"

"You hacked into government servers?"

"We have the internet, Ben. You flew here using your government-issued IDs. And you checked into the hotel using your real names. *And* those names are attached to numerous *escapades*, if I am not mistaken. We saw the two of you exploring the hotel, looking for something... and then we saw you enter the wine cellar, where you then found the entrance to a Vatican-controlled tunnel."

Ben sat back, his arms on the table now. "We need to find something here. That's it."

"What do you need to find?"

"A... souvenir. A stamp."

"A stamp. Like a postage stamp?"

Ben didn't answer.

The man chewed the inside of his lip for a moment, squinting at Ben. He pulled out his phone, tapped a few times on its screen, then set it facedown on the table.

"Mr. Bennett," he said. "My name is Roger Godiva."

"Like the chocolates?"

"Yes, like the chocolates. I am Head of Security for the Department of Papal Affairs in the Vatican. What that means to you is that I have total and final authority over any visitations within the Vatican, as long as I deem necessary. I have given my life to the Church, and to the Pope, and I do not intend for that life to be a wasted effort."

"Okay, Mr. Godiva," Ben said. "We're on the same page. *I* do not intend to get in the way of that... wonderful life."

Godiva stared at Ben for a long moment, then he stood up.

"Are we done here?" Ben asked. "I really do have somewhere to be."

He waited another few seconds before answering. Godiva then moved forward, pressing his fists against the tabletop next to his phone. He leaned down, reaching his head toward Ben. His necklace fell out of his shirt and dangled for a brief moment, the pendant on it catching Ben's eye. He pulled it back inside his shirt as he spoke.

"We are investigating a threat that was called in earlier today. An assassination attempt on the Pope, Mr. Bennett. For that reason, we must detain you and your girlfriend until further notice, but I have just been instructed to move you outside the walls of the Vatican for security reasons. These matters can be... how should I put it? Rather exhausting."

"An *assassination* attempt?" Ben asked. "What are you talking about? We've got nothing to do with —"

"Save your stories, Ben," Godiva said. "There is little time for that. You of all people should know how serious this threat is."

"And why is that?"

"Because you and I are intimately familiar with the man who warned us."

Ben's face fell.

"Archibald Quinones sent us an email earlier today, informing us of your intent."

CHAPTER 49

JULIE

"COME WITH ME."

The man's voice was blunt, clipped and to the point. Julie looked up at him, her hands shackled to the heavy table she was sitting behind, and rattled her wrists. It was the same man who had brought them to the Papal security headquarters within the hotel, but he was now alone.

She rolled her eyes up, a look of annoyance, and the man stepped forward.

"Right," he said. "I am going to release you from the table, but I will be putting the cuffs back on. My men are stationed directly outside this door, so if there is any sound of fighting, they will enter. And they will kill you. Do you understand?"

She nodded. "Where's Ben?"

"Harvey is waiting for us."

She frowned, but didn't ask any questions. The man unlocked her cuffs, removed them from the metal ring on the table, then pulled her chair out for her while he refastened the cuffs around her wrists.

"Where are we going?" she asked.

"Outside the Vatican."

"Why?"

"Harvey will fill you in. For now, please walk to the door and open it. I will be directly behind you."

She did as she was told, and she found Ben, similarly handcuffed, waiting for her on the other side of the door in the hallway. The younger soldiers who had accompanied them here an hour ago were also waiting, their guns drawn.

"Please," the man said. "That way." He pointed down the hallway and Ben and the two soldiers began walking. They were led to a doorway that led outside, and then Julie and Ben were corralled into the backseat of a tiny sedan.

"Where are we going, Godiva?"

"Get in the vehicle, Bennett." Godiva's voice was lower, nearly a grumble now. Whatever his plan was, Julie sensed he was running out of time.

As Julie got into the car and one of his soldiers slammed the door shut, she heard Godiva speak once again into his radio. "... incontreremo in Peru."

Incontreremo in Peru?

She didn't speak or understand Italian, but it sounded like Godiva had said the word *Peru*.

Julie turned to Ben, taking advantage of the few moments they had alone in the car. "He said something about Peru," she said.

"Peru? Like the country?"

She nodded. "Ben, do you think —"

"It has to be related. Whatever Garza's up to, he's involved in this... assassination attempt."

"*Assassination* attempt?"

Ben looked at her like she were crazy. "Did Godiva not question you?"

"No, he — I didn't even know that was his name. They left me in there for an hour. No one came in."

"Hmm," Ben said. "He left me alone for almost an hour. Then he came in, asking about our plans and what we were doing here."

"What did you tell him?"

"Nothing. I mean, I guess I mentioned the stamp."

"You *guess*?"

"He didn't seem to care. Or if he did, he didn't question me more about that. He just told me that we had to be moved outside the Vatican because there would be an assassination attempt on the Pope."

Julie shook her head. "But... why does he think we're involved?"

"Because he said Archie was the guy who tipped him off."

Julie's eyes widened. "*Archie.* He said Archibald Quinones called *him* and told him there was going to be —"

"Yes," Ben said. "An assassination. And somehow he thinks we're involved."

The car door opened, and one of the soldiers got in the driver's seat.

"Ben," Julie whispered. "It's a lie. We're not —"

"Silenziosa!" the soldier said as he started the small car's engine.

Ben ignored him. "I know. And I think he knows that, too. There's something else going on here, and we're going to —"

"*Stai zitto!*" the young soldier said again.

This time Ben stopped talking. The car lurched forward, and the soldier aimed it toward a narrow opening between two buildings. Julie craned her neck around and saw another car behind theirs, this one with Godiva in the front seat and his other soldier driving.

Weird, she thought. *Godiva's coming with us, wherever we're going. He must want to keep us in his sights.*

They drove for a few minutes and Julie saw the gates of the Vatican as they passed through them, once again back onto the streets of Rome. The soldier's radio squawked to life, and she heard Godiva's voice issuing orders in Italian.

She couldn't understand much, but she heard some of the street names he'd said as she saw them on the signs they passed. After fifteen minutes of driving, she saw the coast.

And then she heard the radio again, this time with a few words she recognized.

"... gli Americani... la sparizione."

She sat up straighter. While she had no knowledge of the Italian language, she *did* have a passing understanding of its Romance language cousin, Spanish. And one of the words she'd heard sounded oddly familiar to her.

Sparizione. The Spanish word it reminded her of was *desaparición.*

To disappear.

She turned to Ben once again, who was already looking at her. She held her cuffed hands up to her neck and slid her finger across it horizontally.

Ben understood the motion immediately. His face was stoic, but she could see the rage building behind his eyes.

He nodded slowly.

REGGIE WAS SURROUNDED by monitors and whirring machines, gurneys lying on their sides and stacked against a wall, and bright hospital lights.

He'd been in a hospital before, so he wasn't surprised by all that. What he *was* surprised by, however, was the fact that this particular hospital was inside an ancient temple.

Or whatever structure they'd been in. Reggie had found himself inside a wooden coffin in a basement, then escaped to a round chamber with stone walls, and was now strapped to a table in some other similarly styled chamber. Best guess, he figured, he was in the same ancient complex he and Sarah had been in, the same complex Vicente Garza was using as his hidden headquarters.

They had turned this room into a makeshift hospital, and he could see his vitals on one of the screens near his bed.

A woman entered, followed by a man. Both were wearing white lab coats, and both were holding clipboards.

"... because nearly *all* bacteria found in the human body is related to Candida somehow."

The woman shook her head. "That's patently untrue."

"It's an exaggeration, but it's close. If it's not Candida, I don't know what it is."

"We *do* know it's Candida, but we're not sure which strain. Candida albicans has been known to cause osteoporosis in certain situations, and those —"

"Those situations are obscure and exceedingly rare, and are most likely caused by something *besides* albicans reacting with it."

"Dr. Prichard, that's exactly my point. We're not looking for Candida albicans, we're looking for what the *other* yeast strain could be."

The man, Dr. Prichard, sighed. "I know. I'm just thinking out loud. These — tests, if we can even call them that — are so inconclusive I can hardly pass them off as useful data. We need more time with the primate trials and more conclusive lab results before —"

"Garza isn't going to give us that time," the woman said. "You know that. He wants this phase complete *tomorrow.*"

Reggie grunted, and both doctors turned to him.

"Oh," the woman said. "I — I didn't realize you were awake. The soldiers said you'd be sedated."

"Yeah, well, it takes a lot to sedate this guy. Where the hell am I?"

"This is the medical wing."

"In Detroit?"

The doctors looked at him strangely.

"Ah, well, it was worth a shot. Say, you think I could get the all-clear? I've got a date later with this hot lady they're keeping upstairs somewhere, and I —"

"Ms. Lindgren is safe, Mr. Red."

"Where is she?"

"Exactly where she was before. Her wound is not healing, but our orders were to keep it that way. Trust that she is safe, for the moment."

"Why am I here? What are you idiots going to do to me?"

"We're testing a drug based on the Candida albicans yeast strain, and we're hoping that it helps regenerate the growth in your skeletal structure. These initial dosages will —"

"Wait, wait. Hold on," Reggie said. "You're injecting my with *yeast*? To regenerate *what* skeletal structure are we talking about? Mine?"

The doctors looked down at him blankly; the woman working her hands over a syringe filled with a semi-opaque liquid.

"Yeah, I don't think I signed the consent form to be one of your little experiments. Did Garza send you here? Where the hell is he?"

Reggie heard a voice over a hidden speaker. *"I am right here, Gareth. In the next room over, watching your progress from a camera feed. I hope you find Drs. Prichard and Jenner accommodating. They are some of the best geneticists money can buy."*

"Well, whatever happy pills you're about to pop into me, just know that it's not going to change the fact that I'm going to kill you."

"Sarah said the same thing an hour ago, Red. Fiery one, that woman. Her body had a hard time accepting the initial dosages, but like I said — Prichard and Jenner are the best there is."

Reggie yanked hard against his bonds, smacking them into the table.

"Those straps are far stronger than you, Red, but I do enjoy watching you struggle. It reminds me how rash and naïve you are, getting yourself into these impossible situations. The ironic thing is — in about a year, after your full dosage, you might actually be strong enough to break free."

Reggie's heart raced. "So that's it, Garza? You're making a giant? Turning me into one of your insane freaks?"

"Those 'insane freaks' were volunteers, Red. Members of my team."

"How did you do it?"

"That is what my geneticists are trying to figure out. What is it the ancients were able to mix with the Candida albicans yeast to cause such rapid bone growth? They left us a few pieces of the puzzle

— the remnants of their medicine, their legends, and the Book of Bones."

"Which you need to figure out the rest of the puzzle."

Garza paused, but didn't answer the question. "My scientists have been instructed to continue testing, to continue practicing and honing their methods until they are able to provide me with an army of giants."

"You already *have* that, though. Those six grunts in Alaska."

"They are a remarkable start, I admit. But you saw them yourself. They are vulnerable. Weak in undesirable areas. Their limbs have been stretched and broken and re-healed so many times their musculature cannot keep up. Those men will be dead within a year, thought they don't know it yet. Their bodies are incapable of managing such gigantic systems."

"You're murdering them slowly."

"Men like you have such a stark view of the world, Red," Garza said. *"The reality is something more nuanced — these giants I'm making, these 'beasts,' as they will be called, aren't the first of their kind. In fact, they're not even the* biggest *of their kind. I am not killing anyone, Red, but merely restarting the beginning of an amazing, ancient race."*

"They lived here, didn't they?"

"Astute observation, Red. Yes, they built this place. Exiled from their home thousands of years ago, they came here. Built their temples and homes to match their old ones, and hid in this valley, hoping to live out their days in solitude and peace."

"Great story," Reggie said. "But I call bullshit. These giants were able to hide, build their little oasis, and were unbothered for that long? How'd they survive?"

"They didn't," Garza said. *"Their race was diluted as they bred with the local population, and word eventually got out that they were here. They tried to maintain their isolation, but —"*

Garza stopped. Reggie smiled. *Got him talking, now he's said too much.* "But what?"

There was a pause, then Garza's voice came back over the intercom. *"But nothing. I've said too much — Doctors, please resume your administration of the first dosage."*

The doctors turned back to Reggie's bed and held out their hands. Each was holding a massive syringe, each one filled with the semi-opaque fluid.

"Where's that thing going?" Reggie asked.

"Garza has instructed us to work on rebuilding the structure of your upper humorous. This first dosage will go directly into the bone, and due to the nature of the yeast molecules, we cannot risk anesthetizing them."

"Ah, wonderful. Nothing like a shot to the bone."

"Correct," Dr. Jenner said, her voice ringing through the stone room with the emotion of a robot. "It is a significantly painful operation."

Dr. Prichard chuckled. "Although it's nothing compared to the breaking."

"The... breaking?"

"Well, of course. In order for the yeast to get into the bone's bloodstream and marrow production facilities, a significant breakage in the bone's lattice structure must be present."

"A *significant breakage?*" Reggie shuddered.

"Yes, Mr. Red. A significant breakage."

CHAPTER 51

BEN

THE CAR SLOWED when it left the main highway, and Ben saw a sign that labeled the area they were entering *Punta Rossa*. High hills, covered in thick forest, met his gaze as their driver sped up again. Their vehicle was quickly consumed by the trees, and they traveled onward, ascending one of the hills toward the ocean.

Julie seemed calm, but he knew she was considering their options. *Should we attack once we're out of the vehicle? Or make our move now, while it's one against two?*

He glanced over at Julie, and she nodded at him.

Guess that settles it.

The driver pulled the car toward the side of the road to pass a bicyclist in the middle of the lane, but Ben didn't notice any other vehicles or people on the road. The sun was setting, and the heavy tree coverage bathed their surroundings in shadowy darkness.

Ben watched the soldier's eyes in the rearview mirror. The kid had to be no older than twenty-five, and he thought back to when he was that age. *I was lost, drifting around like a nomad, trying to figure out what life wanted with me.* He wondered if the kid had had any such experiences. He wondered if the kid had signed up for this —

for killing innocent civilians by driving them out to a remote area and executing them in cold blood.

He wondered, too, what it all meant: if the kid *was* involved, and knew what he was doing, then why? What purpose did it serve? *Who* did it serve? Ben knew by now that every person, regardless of race, religion, upbringing, or belief system thought they were in the right. They believed they were the heroes of their own story.

What was this kid's story, and what belief system had he bought into?

The kid met his eyes in the mirror, and Ben smiled. He figured the guy didn't speak English well enough to pick up on his vernacular. "You sure about this, buddy?"

The kid frowned, then glared at him.

"Okay, man. Your funeral."

The kid continued to ignore him, and Ben noticed they were nearing the end of a long climb up a hill. An old, small castle sat perched atop a rock outcropping, overlooking the water. In the distance, a modern communications depot and satellite array stood like a sentinel on a similar rock stand. Two juxtaposed versions of the same thing.

The car pulled off the road and onto another one-lane gravel road. The tires crunched along, and Ben saw their destination. An old, decrepit wall, pockmarked with the beatings of time and weather. It stood alone, perpendicular to the edge of the cliff. Ben knew then what the plan was.

It was crude, but simple. Two Americans, their bodies found washed ashore with bullet holes in their skulls. Authorities would blame local gang activity and ship them back to their homeland, where they'd be buried and remembered for a full length of the national news cycle.

This is it, then. Time to move.

Ben didn't hesitate. He reached up and over the driver's head, then immediately pulled back — hard. The kid's neck met the metal chain of Ben's handcuffs and he choked, spitting as he tried to keep control of the vehicle.

Julie was already in motion, however. She yanked the wheel from the kid's hands hard to the right, forcing him to apply the brakes as they rolled off the side of the road. When the car stopped, she quickly flung her door open and ran around to the driver's side.

The car behind them that was carrying Godiva and his other young soldier was still a few hundred yards behind, just now cresting the hill. She heard it accelerate, and she knew they'd spotted her.

But it was too late. She had the kid's door open and his seatbelt unbuckled in seconds, all while Ben held his hands tightly around the man's neck. The soldier was gasping for breath, and blood — either from Ben's wrists or the kid's neck — dripped onto the soldier's collar.

She waited for Ben to loosen his grip and move his hands up and then she yanked the man from the front seat. He fell to the ground, still gasping for air, and Julie kicked him hard in the belly, causing him to groan in agony and retch even harder. Then she knelt down and pulled out his sidearm.

She held it up and aimed toward the approaching vehicle. Ben and Reggie had helped train her, but she'd quickly gotten better than Ben and nearly as good as Reggie himself with small-arms weapons. It was an easy shot, but she wasn't sure how many rounds were left in the pistol, and she didn't want to take the chance of a firefight between herself and two armed men.

So she waited. The car was speeding now, heading straight for them. Ben fell out of the back of their car and landed on top of the driver, holding him down.

She aimed. Steadied her gaze. She could see the eyes of the second car's driver, the soldier from the hotel. Godiva was screaming next to him, but she ignored him.

She pulled the trigger. Twice, then a third time. The cheap windshield glass of the sedan was not bulletproof, nor did it seem to change the direction of her second two bullets. They slammed into the face of the young driver, his head falling.

The car was twenty feet from them now, and the kid's foot had fallen on the accelerator as he'd died.

She winced, preparing to try to jump out of the way, when the car veered sharply to her right. It stayed on the gravel road, kicking up dust and debris behind it, and as it passed her — barely missing her right arm — she saw Godiva's panicked face in the passenger seat.

He was screaming, but she had the feeling it was no longer in rage. He was afraid, but his fear only lasted a second.

The car shot off the cliff, sailing next to the old stone wall, and was gone.

She took a breath, then jogged to the edge. She didn't want to look, but she needed to know.

There, at the bottom of the cliffs, was the car. Totaled, completely unrecognizable. Just a mess of twisted, smoking metal lying in a heap on a huge boulder. Sea spray splashed against the wreckage, and she saw pieces of the car floating in the water, banging up against the rock.

The sedan had bounced down as it fell, and the now-faceless driver had been ejected out onto the rocks. She didn't see Godiva's body, but it seemed there was a growing pool of blackness near the wreckage, spilling out onto the surface of the boulder.

Ben was there.

"That... that was something," he said. "Nice shot."

She was shaking, and she felt his hand squeeze her shoulder. "I didn't... know. I didn't know what to do, Ben. I just... grabbed the kid's pistol and..."

"You knew exactly what to do."

"I did, but I didn't *think* about it. Like — like I've done it before."

Julie was breathing quickly now. She had never thought she was capable of killing someone like that. Near point-blank range, directly to the face. She saw the young man's eyes in her mind, his face as it existed one moment and then imploded the next.

I've done that before.

She turned to Ben.

He was looking at her, watching her.

"Ben, I — I think..."

"It's okay, Jules. We'll talk about it later. Right now we need to figure out how to get to Peru."

CHAPTER 52

BEN

FOURTEEN HOURS Later

"Archie, can you hear us?"

Ben tilted the iPad's screen up on its stand and slid it across the tray table so he and Julie could see it. They had purchased the iPad in Rome, using Ben's credit card, as well as plane tickets to Peru, a change of clothes for both of them, and a few essentials they deemed necessary for the next leg of their journey. The tickets had cost around thirty-five hundred dollars, but Ben's credit card, funded by the CSO, had a limit that only Mr. E knew — he had hesitated for only a moment before handing it over to the ticketing agent at Leonardo da Vinci International Airport, but he'd had no trouble and no fuss getting the boarding passes.

He'd had a few moments of concern once they'd safely boarded the plane and begun their takeoff. *Are we too late to save Reggie and Sarah?* he'd wondered. *Who's after us? And what do they want? Do they know we're going to Peru?*

And, most of all, the most important question of all: *are they even* in *Peru?*

They'd slept for about eight of the sixteen hours on the plane, and even though Ben's thoughts had raced over the events of the past day — their near-death experience in the small prop plane, their boat chase in the port of Corsica, and their battle with the Vatican guards — he had been able to sleep. They'd hoped that by boarding a large, international commercial airliner, their pursuers would think twice about taking down the plane. Still, a feeling of dread had washed over Ben as he saw Archie's face on the screen in front of him.

Did he betray us?

"I can hear you, Ben," Archie said. The older man's face was lined in wrinkles, his thick, black hair waving around his ears, disheveled, as if he'd just awoken from a night's sleep. *"Before we talk, please know: I believe my home computer has been hacked. I have been at the university library for the past day, trying to make sense of all of this."*

"We know," Julie said, breathing an audible sigh of relief. "We got caught in the Vatican, just after we got inside the hotel. They detained us, then told Ben that *you* called in an assassination threat."

"Oh, dear," Archie said. *"It is worse than I thought."*

"Is it?" Ben said. "We didn't even get to the part where we were taken outside the city and driven up a hill to be executed."

Archie's face fell. Ben could see that the lighting of the library the man was in was dim, set for the nighttime hours. His face seemed weathered, older somehow, the shadowy light playing tricks. *"I — I am so sorry, Harvey. I did not mean —"*

"It's okay," Ben said. "So far today, we remain *un*executed. And as far as near-death experiences go, that wasn't even the worst one of the day."

They filled their teammate in on the events leading up to their capture, as well as what they had learned.

"We believe the man working security in the Vatican hotel, Roger Godiva, is not exactly who he says he is."

"Without a doubt," Archie said. *"He must be involved in whatever faction is trying to overthrow the power structure in Rome. The same faction that kidnapped a colleague of mine yesterday."*

"A faction?"

"*Another* kidnapping?" Julie asked.

"*Yes,*" Archie said. "*She is a brilliant professor, and she has written numerous papers on the Church and its many secret orders and factions. And when I say faction, I meant like a fraternal order or some other organization. Godiva is listed in my database as a devout Catholic, born and raised in Rome. A member of the Society of Jesus, which is how he knew my name.*"

"He's a Jesuit too, then?" Julie asked.

"*Yes, it appears so. But remember — the Jesuit order is a large, international organization. We are many, and we are not always on the same page. I can easily believe that there is a group of Jesuits out there hoping to harm the current Pope, upset at his liberal tendencies and hoping to overthrow the system.*"

"They would go so far as to *assassinate* the guy?"

"*It has happened before. Pope John VIII was clubbed to death, and a few were strangled. Pope Clement I was thrown into the sea with an anchor around his neck.*"

"Wow," Ben said. "People get *really* worked up about religion."

"*Indeed. There have been at least twenty popes who were murdered. Remember the first pope, Saint Peter?*"

"Crucified upside-down, if I remember my Sunday school lessons correctly."

"*Yes. And Pope John Paul II was shot and severely wounded in 1981, right in St. Peter's Square. So, yes, I believe there are plenty out there who intend to harm our Pope, including some within my own order.*"

"Do you know Roger Godiva?"

"*I do not, but he has played a hand that will now help us track down the other members of his faction, whoever they are.*"

"He had four soldiers with him," Julie said. "Two of them stayed in the tunnels and fought off... whoever *else* was after us. And the other two..."

Her voice fell, and Ben reached out and grabbed her hand. The wounds on their wrists where they had been handcuffed lined up, a single row of red, blistered skin. "One is in critical condition, but he'll never be able to talk right again. The other one faced the same fate as Godiva."

"I see," Archie said. *"So there are at least two factions we are dealing with. The soldiers in the tunnels, likely the same group who brought your plane down in the Mediterranean. And the guards from the Vatican, who are almost certainly a group within the Catholic Church itself."*

"The Catholic group might be the group that wants the Book of Bones," Julie said.

Ben picked up the thread. "Which means the *other* group *also* wants the book, or they just don't want the Catholics to have it."

"Yes, that is my understanding as well. And if that theory is correct, Vicente Garza is working under the employ of the Catholics — the group within the Vatican working to overthrow their own Pope. It could also be that Garza is working for another sect within the Church; we simply do not have enough information to know at this point."

"Is there any way to find out who they are?" Julie asked.

Ben shifted in his seat. "Yes," he said. "Archie, when I was in the room, getting interrogated by Godiva, his necklace fell out of his shirt. There was a pendant on it with some sort of snake wrapped around it. That pendant had some symbols on it, too. It was something I feel like I've seen before, but I couldn't quite place it."

"Can you describe it?"

"Actually, I can probably draw it from memory." Ben reached down to the seat back pocket in front of him and took out a pencil, then reached over to Julie's tray table and grabbed a napkin.

"It was like an oval. Or an egg. And inside of it was that... that seeing eye thing that's on our money. And wings, maybe?" Ben scribbled on the napkin, and Julie watched over his shoulder while Archie waited on-screen. "And two pillars, leaning toward one another, but not quite touching. Like they're holding something up; just a round dot."

He leaned back, then held up the napkin for Archie to see.

On the iPad's screen, Ben watched as Archie's face melted into a ghostly shade of white.

"You recognize it?" Ben asked.

"I do. The elements of it, individually, are instantly recognizable, though I've never seen them together. But I know, without a doubt, what they all represent."

"What's that?" Julie asked.

"Each of those symbols — the all-seeing eye, the pillars, the shape they're making together, and the square measure behind it — the upside-down triangle.

"Those symbols are some of the most iconic symbols of the society of Freemasons."

CHAPTER 53

VICTORIA

THE ROOM WAS ROUND, made of stone. Nothing but a single, round pillar stood in the middle of it. It sat on a raised dais, also made of stone. The entire space was about the size of a small amphitheater, perhaps two- or three-hundred feet from one side to the other. The ceiling stretched far above the line of light, and Victoria could see the shadowy lines of stone supports running up to the center of it all.

Victoria Reyes shook away grogginess from her eyes. *Have I been asleep?* She remembered driving to the airport, the car pulling off to an unmarked hangar near the main entrance, and then...

Nothing.

She'd woken up a few minutes ago, told to walk through a door, and then she'd found herself inside this room.

Are we still at the airport then?

Her mind pulled her back to the moment, her senses returning quickly and sharpening. She took in the space, admired its architecture. She'd never seen anything like it. For one, it seemed to have been carved from one massive block of stone, a mountain-sized sculpture. Second, the proportions were off — she'd seen someone enter from a door across from her, and this door was disproportionately tall. The pillar at the center, whatever it was used for, seemed large as well. Too tall to use as a table, too short to be a stand for something, and its diameter was easily fifteen feet across.

"Do you know where you are?" she heard a voice ask.

She shook her head.

"Please speak up for the council, Ms. Reyes."

She flicked her eyes left and right. If there were others in the room besides the man who'd addressed her, she couldn't see them.

"I do not," she said.

"Are you sure?"

She sighed. "A temple? A sacrificial tomb? A preparation chamber for your secret Mason rituals?"

There was a slight chuckle from behind her, then a quick covering cough.

"The Freemasons have always performed rituals as a way to remind ourselves of our history and ancestry. We —"

"I'm a professor, and a published researcher on the intricacies of ancient cults," she said. "I do not need a lecture about who the Freemasons are."

"Very well, Ms. Reyes," the man said. "In that case, you should know that having you, a woman, in this chamber at all is a rare occurrence."

"Well," Victoria said. "Assuming this isn't some bi-annual wives event for your chapter, then yes, this is a remarkable occurrence."

"We are not a 'chapter,' in the traditional sense —"

"*But* it's not unheard of," Victoria said. "Throughout history, your ranks have debated the number of women who have claimed involvement in the organization. Elizabeth Aldworth, for example, wore the regalia in public after she was admitted into her father's lodge.

"And Salome Anderson hid in her uncle's lodge room, learned

your secrets, and was admitted in order to swear her to secrecy. And —"

She stopped herself, realizing that now *she* was the one lecturing.

There was a pause, and then a man stepped out of the shadows to her left. She didn't recognize him, but he wore an apron, the traditional lodge apron she'd seen many times. This one had the mason's compass and letter "G," which stood for geometry, but it also featured the upside-down angel-winged logo she'd seen on the website while talking to Mark, just before her abduction.

"My colleague was correct. You *are* a special mind, Ms. Reyes. I must apologize for our barbaric form of requesting your help, but —"

"You're asking for my *help*? By kidnapping me, taking me here, and — where the hell *are* we, anyway?"

"You are standing in the temple of my ancestors. *Our* ancestors." The man lifted an arm up, and she saw seven more men, each wearing the same lodge apron, step out of the shadows. They were surrounding her, pressing in on her.

She felt threatened once again. "Wh — what is this? Am I some sort of sacrifice?"

There was a heavy silence for a few seconds, and Victoria worried her heart would beat so loud the temple would come down around them.

Then... laughter. The man stepped closer to her, smiling. His eyes were kind, yet serious. Blond hair, grayish skin. She couldn't tell if he was closer to thirty or sixty, so she guessed somewhere in the middle. "Ms. Reyes," the man said. "We are the Guild Rite, an ancient sect similar to the Masons, but with a few key differences."

"You're Dieter Luthig?" she asked.

"I... am not. But your detective work is nearly as impressive as your intellect. Ms. Reyes, the Guild Rite predates most Rites by an order of magnitude. In fact, we claim our roots extend to before the time of Noah."

"Noah... that's antediluvian history. Basically unreliable."

"Good point," the man said. "But consider: what was the *reason* for Noah's existence?"

"Biblically speaking?" Victoria asked. "To save the world."

"Correct. How?"

"God tasked him with saving the human and animal races while God stamped out wickedness in the world." She fell into her lecturing mode once again as she recited text from the Book of Genesis, chapter 6: "*'Now the earth was corrupt in God's sight and was full of violence. God saw how corrupt the earth had become, for all the people on earth had corrupted their ways. So God said to Noah, "I am going to put an end to all people, for the earth is filled with violence because of them. I am surely going to destroy both them and the earth."'*"

"Yes, and he did this by causing a worldwide flood. One that appears in every civilization's origin story. An account which is, I would argue, *quite* reliable."

"Fine, I'll concede that," Victoria said. "But what does that *mean*? Just because you guys predated Noah means you're more important than *real* Freemasonry?"

"No, it just means that our mission, like Noah's, is as far-reaching as human history itself. Our mission is one that lasts generations rather than lifetimes, millennia rather than centuries."

"You're about as cryptic as the brother you sent to kidnap me."

"Again, we are terribly sorry for the method that was chosen to seek your compliance. But trust me, our battle is nearing its peak, and we truly do wish for your help."

"How? What is it you need help with?"

"Ms. Reyes," the man said. "Since the time of Noah, long before and long after, we have been at war. King David warred, as did his son Solomon, where the first Masonic rituals were birthed. His friend, Hiram, was also at war."

"Men have always been at war," Victoria said.

"Listen to your words, Ms. Reyes," the man said. "You *know* the answer to the question that you seek."

"And what question do you *think* I am seeking?"

"You want to know who, exactly, we are at war with."

"THIS ALIGNS *with what Victoria told me,"* Archie said. *"She was able to call me back, just before she was apprehended in her office. She left the phone on, and the man who took her — whom I do not believe wishes to harm her — did not take it from her. I was able to hear small snippets of their conversation."*

"You don't think he'll harm her?" Julie asked. She looked at the screen, then out the plane's window. They were cruising at around thirty-thousand feet, and all she could see was a sea of white. She knew they were over water anyway, so if she were able to see through the clouds her view would be of nothing but a sea of blue.

"I do not — he said something about 'protecting' her, which could be a lie, but I somehow believe this man thinks he and Ms. Reyes are on the same side of things. That they need her for her mind and knowledge of their shared history."

"Well, we can't take the chance that he's lying," Ben said. He pressed a thumb and finger against the bridge of his nose. "After we find Garza, get Reggie and Sarah back, and stop whatever this 'faction' is doing, we're going to get Victoria Reyes back as well."

Onscreen, Archie nodded. *"I am proud of your commitment and your desire to right these wrongs, Harvey. But I do fear we are severely outnumbered and outmatched."*

"Never stopped me before," Ben said.

"Indeed, it has not. But again, this is something that is beyond our expertise. Even if we had Reggie and Sarah fighting with us, I do not think this is a group to trifle with."

"There will be no *trifling*," Ben said.

"You have a plan, then?" Julie asked. "Once we're in Peru, what are you going to do?"

Ben shrugged. "Find someone to hit."

"We may be able to get close to them, but I still fear they will be well-protected. If Reggie and Sarah were taken to Peru by Garza, we have his team to deal with. But if Victoria Reyes was also *taken there by her captors, we may have an entirely different army to contend with."*

"How do we know he's taking her there, too?"

"She seemed surprised when the man told her they had been following her work. Specifically a paper she published years ago, but I could not hear the title. But I heard a word — one I recognized — that led me to this conclusion. She said 'Chachapoyas' more than once in their conversation."

"What's a Chachapoyas?" Ben asked.

"Not what, *but* who. *The Chachapoyas are a tribe of South American people who had resisted Incan power for as long as anyone could remember. Up until the Spanish Conquest, they existed in an isolated valley also simply called Chachapoyas — mostly because we have never been able to pinpoint exactly where it is."*

"So we're going to a secret valley hidden in Peru that no one's found for hundreds of years?"

"I haves narrowed it down to a two-hundred square mile radius, and I believe I can narrow the search zone further. The Chachapoyas were builders, and they will have erected structures in their valley. My old university has LIDAR-generated 3D maps of the entire

Amazonian Basin, including areas surrounding it in Peru, Columbia, and Venezuela.

"If that is where Garza is taking your friends, that is what we will find."

"'We?'" Julie asked. "But Archie, you're —"

"Old?" the man onscreen grinned, the lines running through his face and forehead deepening. *"I am old, but I seem to remember a jaunt through the Amazon with your group, and I made it out alive then."*

"Archie, we *all* nearly died in that jungle."

"But we did not, and I am here to laugh about it. Harvey, Juliette — you make an exceptional team. But every team, no matter how exceptional, needs a wise old sage. You never know when you will need to stop 'hitting people' and begin thinking through the problem a different way."

"Touche, old man," Ben said, smiling. "Happy to have an extra set of brains on board, especially since I rarely can rely on my own."

"Perfect. I will go now. I must prepare for my portion of this journey, and I have more research I would like to do. I believe we have the pieces now, friends. The puzzle is still quite blurry, but it is coming into focus more and more. I am confident and optimistic."

Julie wasn't sure she felt as optimistic, but she was happy to borrow Archibald's. The man had helped them through more than one terrible situation, and they had come out victorious. He was an asset to their team, no matter his age.

THE NEXT TIME Reggie woke up, he was cold.

Still strapped to a table, this one made of stone, but somehow the stone felt colder on his back than the metal hospital table had.

He was sweating, but his back seemed frozen. He groaned, feeling a wave of nausea swimming through his insides.

"You okay?"

A meek voice, coming from somewhere behind him. Or... near him. He couldn't tell — the room was nearly pitch-black, and he was lying on his back in the center of it. He squeezed his eyes closed, then opened them again.

"Who — who's there?"

"It's me..."

The voice was faint, nearly a whisper, but it was right behind him.

"Sarah?"

He tried to move, to get up, but he found his feet were once again strapped down. One hand was free, and he used this hand to wipe his eyes. His other was outstretched and secured above his head. A headache seared through his skull as the nausea passed, but he shook both feelings away and tried to focus.

"Yeah."

"Sarah, it's me. Reggie. I — I was in... it was like..."

"A hospital. Just a room."

"Yeah. Yeah, that's exactly what it was. Two weird scientist doctors were in there. They —"

"They gave you a dose of *Candida albicans* bonded with a liquid acetaminophen coating, to help with the administration."

"Wha — what does that mean?"

"It means they gave you a shot of some weird crap that's based on yeast."

"Yeah, I heard them say that. They did that to you, too?"

She didn't respond, but he felt her nodding. He was confused at first, then he tried to move his hand.

"They stuck us on that rock thing in the center of the room," Sarah said. "On our backs."

He was about to respond when he realized what she was implying. "Oh, my God. Sarah, your back. Are you okay? You got shot, and then —"

"I'm okay," she said. "For now. It hurts, but it's a dull throbbing. Those doctors patched me up a bit when Garza was done torturing me. It's been getting better every hour."

"Yet something tells me our *situation* is not getting any better."

She sniffed. "Well, at least we're together."

Reggie chuckled, but found that he was strapped down so tightly even his lungs had a hard time moving. He hated to imagine what Sarah was feeling.

"Yeah, I guess there's that. Die together, right?"

"I wasn't planning on dying today," Sarah said.

"Well, fine. I guess we can wait until tomorrow."

Sarah let out a single breathy laugh, then fell silent. A minute later, Reggie heard her voice again. "Hey, Red?"

Reggie's eyes immediately tinged with the sharp pang of tears. Sarah had begun calling him Red, as it seemed awkward for her to call him Gareth and there was no easy way to shorten Reggie. It was endearing when she said it, unlike anyone in the past who had called him by his last name. "Y — yeah?" He choked on the word.

"I just wanted to tell you that, uh, no matter what happens, I —"

One of the massive stone doors pressed open to Reggie's left, and Sarah cut herself off. Reggie sucked in a quick breath of air.

"Good evening, you two," a man's voice said. Bright floodlights flicked on at the side of the room, and Reggie squinted as his eyes adjusted.

Garza.

"The *Hawk* himself," Reggie said. "Coming back to his lair to watch over his victims. You're like a Batman villain, you know that? No brains, one really cool trick you use over and over, and absolutely no exit strategy."

"Is that so?"

"And if we're lucky," Reggie continued, "you'll tell us all about your plans. Just in time for Sarah to save the day."

"If you're lucky."

Reggie swallowed. He felt his confidence wavering.

"But," Garza said. "I don't think you *are* lucky, Red. I think you're an idiot. A callous, rash, idiot, and I think *you've* got one trick, but it's not even 'really cool.' It's your ability to fight — to use your hands and feet in ways the human body was never designed to. You're scrappy, able to see an opening where your challenger cannot."

Reggie forced a laugh. "Ah, is that it, then? You strap down my arms and legs so I can't fight you? So it's a bit more of an even competition?"

Garza walked across the room and stepped up onto the elevated platform that held their round stone platform. He leaned in over Reggie's face. "Close, Mr. Red. *Very* close."

Reggie worked on some saliva, preparing to spit.

"But I have absolutely no interest in fighting you. This isn't a comic book, Red. I have plans, and I have people waiting on me. I told your friends that — that my benefactors are waiting, and they are not going to take 'no' for an answer, nor will they allow me to mess with their timeline.

"Your friends know that — I told them that myself. Yet they are not here. They are *nowhere near here,* as far as I can tell. So do you know what that means?"

"They had to catch up on their favorite television show?"

"It means that we are almost out of time, and I am going to move on with my plans *without* the *Book of Bones.* A minor setback for me, but, I suspect, a *major loss* for you."

"Nah," Reggie said. "I never liked that damn book. Lot of people died because of it."

"Indeed," Garza said. "Red, have you analyzed your situation? The way I trained you?"

Reggie felt his heart drop. *What the hell is he talking about?* He had just woken up, spoken with Sarah, but he wasn't able to see well in the dim light.

He didn't want to give Garza the pleasure of victory, but Reggie couldn't help looking around. He took in his surroundings — recognized the chamber he was in, saw Garza standing over him, the high, dark ceiling far above his head. He felt Sarah next to him, lying nearby but not speaking. He felt...

His arm.

He tried shaking it, moving his wrist, but it was tightly bound to the stone slab. Yet it was still... different. He felt warmth, a gently beating heart.

Sarah.

His wrist was bound to Sarah's, and both of their arms were outstretched over their heads. They were laying on the slab of stone, head-to-head, facing upwards, but both of their right arms were outstretched, tied together and secured to the slab.

"What the hell?"

But that wasn't all he noticed. He looked up, straight above his head. A shiny, glistening object stared down at him. Long and flat, the sheer edge of it sparkled in the bright floodlights. Almost like...

"Oh, shit," he whispered. He felt Sarah catching her breath over and over, starting to cry silently as she realized their predicament.

"Red," Garza said. "I have been working on a project here that will pay unfathomable dividends. You have seen the beginnings of that project, but — as I said before — it is far from finished. Those giants, the soldiers I have tested my research on, are still in a beta phase, if you will. Strong musculature, but their bone structures are extremely weak. They break down. Useful for a while, but over time..."

"Your doctors... they injected me with what's inside them. That yeast stuff."

"Correct. It's related to *Candida albicans,* but it's slightly different. Faster growing, it is able to survive inside the human body. We discovered it here, inside these walls. Dormant for centuries, we were able to activate it and use it for live applications. It is what we believe helped these people, the original inhabitants of this place, to grow to remarkable sizes. It causes rapid bone growth in mammals, though as I said, it is far from perfect."

Rapid bone growth. Reggie shuddered. *A significant breakage in the bone's lattice structure must be present...* "A significant breakage..."

"Yes, Mr. Red. In order for us to adhere the yeast cells directly to your skeletal structure, we must cause a breakage. The skin and muscles have no trouble growing back together, and the bones, bolstered by the yeast, will harden and expand from both sides."

Reggie looked up. The menacing blade hanging above him looked back.

"We *aren't* barbarians here, however," Garza said. "'Breakage' just means the yeast needs direct access to the marrow production facilities of the bones. It can be a clean break, but it does need to break."

"You tied us to a guillotine," Reggie said, his breathing rapid. His voice was frantic, his eyes darting back and forth. "You're going to *cut our hands off*. Both of us."

Sarah's sobs grew in volume.

"Yes," Garza said. "That is the plan. I need the *Book of Bones* in order to understand *exactly* how this ancient yeast works, but as I said — I will not wait forever. If your friends do not arrive with the book in hand in exactly..." he paused to look at his watch. "Forty-seven minutes, this blade will fall. My doctors have assured me that you will survive the significant loss of blood, and they will most likely be able to reattach your hands. After that, we can begin with the second phase of turning you both into one of my giants.

Garza turned to leave, but then turned around once again just before exiting. "But I had them prepare some adrenaline as well, which they will administer immediately after, to make sure you are awake for as long as possible."

"YOU KNOW, THAT'S TRUE," Victoria said. "I *do* want to know who you think you're at war with."

"And the answer to that question lies in the actual *question* you are asking."

She sighed, wishing that for once something in her career could be easy. She may have the unique ability to put pieces of history together in a way that made sense and created a compelling tapestry, but that didn't mean it *came* easily to her. She often slaved in front of her computer for the perfect link, the missing piece that existed somewhere in the world.

But today — or tonight, whatever time it was — she was tired. She was tired of putting things together, and this little test this Masonic cult was putting her through to determine her worth was beyond cryptic. She needed more information. She needed more *pieces*. Her tapestry involved what most people knew of the Freemasons — they were a men's fraternity founded in the 1700s in London, but many claimed their history extended long before that. They existed as a brotherhood that worked toward mutual benefits in their countries and communities by donating their money, effort, and time.

These men, obviously, were less like a Freemasonry lodge and more like a ring of spies, working toward a goal that was yet to be revealed.

They wanted her help, but they hadn't yet told her how. *What am I supposed to do? How am I supposed to help them?* They told her they were at war, but they hadn't yet told her whom they were fighting. Knowing a bit of biblical history wasn't enough — the Bible was a tome of historic and anomalous information, filled with stories and legends and characters and —

She shook her head. *Is that it?*

She thought about the characters they'd been discussing. Hiram Abiff, or Hiram I of Tyre. The king who was friends with another king — Solomon, for whom he'd built the temple. Solomon, the son of Hiram's other friend, King David, the famous biblical man who'd toppled Goliath.

Goliath.

She thought about what she knew of the ancient warrior. A "giant" from Philistine, fighting against the Israelites, who was defeated by young David's stone. The Dead Sea Scrolls manuscripts and the Septuagint described the man as 'four cubits and a span,' which would have placed him at six feet nine inches tall.

She then thought about the previous verses in Genesis. She spoke them aloud: *"When human beings began to increase in number on the earth and daughters were born to them, the sons of God saw that the daughters of humans were beautiful, and they married any of them they chose. Then the Lord said, 'My Spirit will not contend with humans forever, for they are mortal; their days will be a hundred and twenty years.'"*

"The war we have been fighting ever since, Ms. Reyes."

She walked toward the dais, stepped up the round altar there, and leaned against it. "You're fighting... the people of Goliath? Canaan?"

"In a sense, sure. But their ancestors, the Nephilim. The Anakim, their descendants, as well as the people of Gath, the Raphaim."

"The biblical giants."

"*'The sons of God and the daughters of men.'*"

Victoria's body went rigid. *Sons of God, and the daughters of men.*

She thought back to her conversation with Archibald Quinones, the professor from Brazil. He was concerned about his friends who had been kidnapped and taken somewhere, all in a ploy for their captors to find Plato's lost book, *Hermocrates,* or the *Book of Bones.*

In the histories of Atlantis, Poseidon, a god, had borne children with a woman named Cleito, a human woman. Scriptures stated that angels always appeared to humans as men, and in Genesis, as well as in other apocryphal texts, some of these angels bore children with human women, creating the...

"Benei Elohim," she whispered.

"Yes," the man said. He was now standing in front of her, near the altar. "Benei Ha'Elohim — Sons of God."

She wasn't fluent in Greek or Hebrew, but she knew this term. "It means 'child or grandchild,' or..."

"Go on," the man said.

"A member of a guild."

"Correct."

"And *Elohim,*" she said. "A common word, often used as a name for God. But it literally means 'powerful ones.' *Benei Elohim* means 'Guild of Powerful Ones.'"

"Yes," the man said, stepping even closer now. "The Guild Rite — the Guild of Powerful Ones..."

"The Nephilim. The 'sons of God, daughters of men' who were the bane of God's existence in pre-flood times. The reason he wanted to wipe the earth clean of all humans."

"But he didn't, did he?"

"He didn't. Genesis 6:4: '*The Nephilim were on the earth in those days—and also afterward—when the sons of God went to the daughters of humans and had children by them. They were the heroes of old, men of renown.'*

"They were still around *after* the flood. Exiled to the lands beyond biblical accounts. David fought Goliath, a descendant of these same people. Solomon fought them as well, and his temple — the place believed to have been the resting place of the Ark of the Covenant — was built for this purpose."

Victoria's mind raced. Her tapestry was being extended, patched, reworked, and redesigned. It was as if years of research fell into place simultaneously. Her beliefs, goals, and dreams came to mind, and she felt as though she'd advanced forward a decade.

"You are here because you believe these people — the Nephilim — are still here."

"We *know* they are still here," the man said. "This group — the Guild Rite — has existed for millennia, hunted by our enemies, chastised by governments and populations as a radical cult. But we have never intended to hurt or harm any of them, but to bring truth — *ultimate* truth — to light."

"A lofty goal," Victoria said. "But your grunt told me you're trying to build a New World Order."

"No," the man said. "But he isn't technically wrong. What we are trying to do is reinstate the New World Order that was *supposed* to already exist. The order that God himself passed down to us in his own words, in his own book. *'The Sons of God and the Daughters of Men'* are the people he placed in charge of his world. *'The Nephilim were on the earth in those days — and all afterward — when the sons of God went to the daughters of humans and had children by them. They were the heroes of old, men of renown.'"*

"You think the Nephilim are supposed to *run the world?*" Victoria asked.

"No, they were never supposed run the world. But they lost out to the *true* power that is running the world. We want to end that, just as the Nephilim did in their time. We exist to destroy the Catholic Church."

CHAPTER 57

BEN

THEIR PLANE HAD LANDED in Manaus, Brazil, where Ben and Julie had met up with Archibald Quinones. They hadn't seen each other in over a year, but to Ben it had felt as if no time had passed. Quinones had just as much gray working its way through his otherwise jet-black hair, his face had only a few more distinct wrinkles, and his sense of humor was still intact.

They'd embraced, updated each other with a few quick tidbits about their lives, and then boarded a smaller plane headed to Peru. Archie had identified a few options for airstrips, one of which was within walking distance of the valley he felt was the most likely candidate for the home of the Chachapoyas, but, he'd explained, it was a 'cash only' situation.

The airstrip was owned by a farmer who had some ties to both the US government *and* the Peruvian drug cartels, but Archie had gotten the man's approval that he worked for money, not loyalty. If they needed a 'quick drop,' as he'd described it, he was the only man in Peru who could guarantee their safety and his own silence.

Plus, Archie said, the man was going to throw in some 'goodies.'

And for the cash they were able to front, those 'goodies' ended up being all manner of weapons — grenades, Peruvian knockoff AK-

47s, and pistols — as well as some communications equipment. Archie passed each of them a walkie-talkie with a solar charger, and he and Ben lifted a massive block of wires and hard plastic casing that looked like a generator into their vehicle. Archie said it was a 'remote relay communications array,' the sort of thing soldiers in the field used to communicate with their base. They would set it up essentially in reverse, to scan the area for any signals, at which point the radio would home in on the band and broadcast the feed to their handheld radios.

Placed in the middle of a search area, the apparatus would allow a team to broaden their radius by a factor of five while remaining within radio contact.

It would also allow them to remain in contact with the *other* Jeep in their party. Archibald had called in a few favors and drummed up some support in Ben's and Julie's favor, and the second Jeep was parked and waiting when they landed, four Peruvian Army soldiers ready for orders loaded within.

The weaponry was passed to their rented Jeeps in three separate black duffel bags, and within fifteen minutes of landing in Peru, Ben and Julie found themselves driving through South American cartel-controlled land with no passports and a hatch full of illegally obtained weapons, another Jeep full of guns-for-hire trailing behind.

Whatever it takes, he told himself. *We have to find Reggie and Sarah.*

And in the same thought, he added the name of Victoria Reyes, the professor who had recently been kidnapped as well. *If she's here, we'll find her. If she's not... we'll still find her.*

Ben was adamant that they would accomplish their goal, but that was where his confidence ended. He had *no idea* how they were going to pull this off. They were being chased by at least one upset faction, that faction — a segment within the Catholic Church — had already proven that they were willing to kill them.

If they ran into Garza's well-trained private security force as well, Ben wasn't sure they'd make it out alive.

He looked over at Julie, in the passenger seat. She seemed calm, but her face was lined with a tension only someone close enough to her could see. It reminded him of when they'd met, driving cross-country as they tried to stay ahead of mysterious virus that was spreading around the midwestern United States. Her face then and now was tight, eyes peering straight ahead, her mind no doubt churning.

"You okay?" he asked.

She glanced over. "Huh? Oh, yeah. Just thinking through our options."

"Options?" Ben asked. "Not sure we have any."

"Right — it was a short thought." she smiled. "We're going to get them back."

"I hope so. But Rome was a bust. A complete failure. They were onto us before we even *got* there. And we don't have the *Book of Bones*, or anything else that might help."

"We can figure things out as we go," she said. "Isn't that your motto?"

"Well... sorta. But it sounds way less confident coming from you."

Archie spoke from the back seat. "We will prevail, Ben. We have tracked them this far. And I have seen you — *both* of you — in action. I would rather be with no one else."

Ben smiled in the rearview mirror. "Thanks, Archie. But I'd rather be with Reggie and Sarah, for what it's worth. No offense."

Archie laughed. "Fine. If we are being honest, I would much rather be with a team of Navy SEALs."

"Their strategy is no different than mine. Rush in, take advantage of the element of surprise, and make a lot of noise."

"That's... *exactly* what their strategy is," Julie said.

"Whatever. Where did you say this place is?" Ben asked.

"I was told it will be unmistakable if you know what you are looking for. The abandoned site is about twenty miles off the road, accessible only by finding a pathway hidden to all but the person looking for it. Wide enough for a truck, bound on both sides by massive boulders."

"Okay, so two big rocks. Like bowling balls?"

"Like pillars," Archie said. "Towering over the pathway and pushing up against the jungle around them, as if they were not originally from this area."

CHAPTER 58

VICTORIA

VICTORIA REYES LOOKED AROUND FRANTICALLY. She tried to keep her breathing under control, her eyes from flickering back and forth in a way that might cause them to secure her. For now, she was free — untied and able to move around. There were eight men, eight Guild Rite members, surrounding her in this strange room, but so far she hadn't seen a weapon.

Can I fight my way out? As soon as she thought it, another voice inside her head began arguing. *With what? And you're a professor — you study this stuff, not actively perform it.*

These men were serious — whatever they believed, they thought she could help them. And their leader had made a case that she wouldn't be harmed if she agreed to solve their problem.

She made her decision, placing her hand back on the circular stone table. "What do you need from me?"

"We need to find the Nephilim. The race of men who existed before and after the flood, the ones exiled to a new land time and time again."

"Why?"

"We need to prove that they exist," the man said. "Only by bringing them back into the fold of civilization, by showing the world what the Church has tried to keep hidden, can we begin to make reparations."

"Make reparations? You're talking about parading a group of people — assuming they exist — in front of the world? To what end?"

"'Reparations' simply means we believe these people are owed some of what the Church has spent over the centuries in trying to find them. Their pain, their torture, was *directly* caused by the seat of power in Christianity. To prove to the world that they exist brings the Church to its knees."

"And puts *you* in power instead?"

The man smiled. "All long roads are paved a foot at a time, Ms. Reyes."

"Some roads never do get paved."

"Fair point. But rest assured, this is not some project the eight of us — the leaders of this Rite — have cooked up over the past few days. This is a generational project. A dream that has existed long before any of us were here."

"Okay, got it. I help you find these people, then... what? You just let me go?"

"Precisely."

"Sorry if I'm a bit skeptical. If you recall, one of your men literally kidnapped me at gunpoint. *After* I got a threat from some guy named Dieter Luthig."

The man's gray skin seemed to ebb and stretch over his features, as if he was working through something internally and was trying to hide it. "Yes, Dieter. You are good with puzzles, Ms. Reyes?"

"You know I am."

"In that case, consider all of this a puzzle. Everything you think you do not know, you may know. And everything you think you *do* know, you may not."

She shook her head, frustrated. "These riddles are starting to get on my nerves."

"Well, now you understand our own frustration. This process is akin to an ancient, massive riddle. One that we have been trying to solve our entire lives."

"Where do we start?"

The man lifted his arm, palm up. "Right here, Ms. Reyes. This is a temple, built by the descendants of the Nephilim."

She looked around again. Saw the vaulted ceiling, the stonework, simple yet elegant. "This? It's — not what I would have expected."

"Nothing about this is what anyone has expected," the man said. "And yet... here we are."

"How do you know? I mean, about this place?"

"Do you know where we are, Ms. Reyes?"

She looked down at her feet. She was still wearing the flats she'd had on in her office. Her black slacks, lightly wrinkled, her blouse. Also wrinkled, with the faint smell of sweat mixed with perfume. She looked back up. "You drugged me?"

"We did what we must. We have been running out of time, and we needed your help."

"Where did you take me?"

"Peru."

She began to speak, then closed her mouth. "... How?"

"You were out for sixteen hours. A drug cocktail that leaves little residue, so you should not have to concern yourself with any detrimental side effects."

"Thank you for your concern. Where in Peru?"

"That is a bit harder to explain."

"Try." She stepped forward a bit, some of her confidence returning. She had no illusions about her gaining the upper hand, but if this was truly a negotiation — her knowledge and expertise for her freedom — she needed to start negotiating. "Where are we?"

"We are in a valley called the Chachapoyas. Are you familiar with —"

"The light-skinned tribe that some claim are of European

descent." And then, as if her mind had been working on a different problem at the same, her thoughts conjured up her discussion with whoever had kidnapped her earlier.

"We talked about this in the car," she said. "The Chachapoyas — my paper. *The Spanish in South America: Conquest or Inquest?*"

"Yes."

"And we're *in* South America?"

"As I said, Peru."

"Which means you *found* the Chachapoyas?"

"We found *this*," the man said. "The temple, the surrounding buildings. The only remnants of the Chachapoyas. As you postulated in your paper, the Chachapoyas tribe was eventually swallowed up by the Inca. Weakened by the Spanish conquistadors, they were overrun and became a part of the Incan empire that itself had been decimated by the Spanish. Over time, the tribal separations blended together, all but destroying any identifiable traits in the Chachapoyas."

"Light skin," she said.

"Correct. And, we assume, their charge died out with them."

"Their charge?"

"Their *purpose*. The reason they were removed from their homeland and sent to South America."

"To protect the Nephilim?" Victoria asked.

The man nodded. "That is what we think. The descendants of the Nephilim, after many generations of breeding with other races, were exiled to South America. The Chacapoyas came with them, to protect their secret and their location. Descended from the Phoenicians, we believe they came here long before the expansion of the Roman Empire and the Catholic Church. Together, the Nephilim and the Chachapoyas were a secret kept by the one true power at the time."

"The Catholic Church."

Again, a nod. A second man stepped forward. "Ms. Reyes," the man said. "We need your help to find these descendants. The truth of what they are will set the world free. Do you see that?"

"I — I don't know what I see. I think you're all crazy, but I have to admit..." she paused, unsure of how she'd feel admitting that something so *controversial* made so much sense. "I have to admit that what you're telling me checks out."

The men in front of her both pursed their lips, their heads bowing. She had affirmed their theory, and it seemed she was now part of their team.

"Except for one thing," she added. "If you found the Chachapoyas' valley — this place — but no *people*, and certainly no Nephilim... then how do you know they're still alive? And why wouldn't they be here?"

"Well, Ms. Reyes, one of those questions we can answer. The other — that's why you're here."

"Got it. You need me to figure out where these people went. But the other question: how do you know they're still alive?"

The leader of the masonic cult motioned toward another man along the wall, and this man stepped forward, holding a tiny leather book. He made a point of opening it slowly, carefully, savoring every second the attention in the room was focused on him. Victoria was about to protest when he looked up at her, his eyes obscured behind glasses that caught the light and reflected it back at her.

"Ms. Reyes," he said, his accent slightly French, "my name is Agent Etienne Sharpe of Interpol, and I am a member of the Guild Rite. I came across this journal in Egypt, owned by the late Minister of Antiquities, a woman who was simultaneously ahead of and behind her time."

He cleared his throat and ceremoniously flipped the journal open to a marked page.

"Ms. Reyes," he continued. "Have you heard of the *Book of Bones*?"

CHAPTER 59

BEN

"THERE!"

Ben heard Julie yell at exactly the same time he saw the turnoff. The pillars, two tall, cylindrical stones that had been partially buried in the ground, stretched upward and toward each other, creating a natural doorway. They had been overgrown with heavy vines and were nearly obscured by trees and foliage, but just like Archie said, they were unmistakable since they knew what to look for.

Ben pulled the Jeep off the road, slowing a bit as the second followed behind him, and then turned his eyes back toward the road. The pathway was wide, but it too was overgrown and brush hid the numerous bumps and potholes underneath. He quickly realized they would have to slow down, and frustratingly he dropped their speed to barely faster than a crawl.

It's taking too long, he thought. He knew that the closer they got to their destination, the longer it would seem to take. *Please be there,* he willed. *Please be the right place.*

"See anything yet?" Archie asked from the back seat.

Ben shook his head, but Julie responded. "Nothing. Dense forest, though. We could be driving through an ancient neighborhood right now and we would never know. I can't see more than five feet into the forest."

"We will know," Archie said. "We will not be able to miss it."

"How are you so sure?" Ben asked. "I thought this place had been hidden for centuries?"

In the rearview mirror, Ben caught Archie's wry grin. "It *has* been hidden for centuries, in a sense. Many locals do not know that the land is the region of the Chachapoyas, or that the peoples of the same name called this place home. To them, this valley is simply filled with more of the same ancient buildings, structures, and dwellings — too many to count, and the vast majority of them were Inca. The Peruvian government has neither the money nor the time to refurbish them and affirm their safety."

"So they sit out here and get covered by the forest," Julie said.

"Exactly. It is a problem in Brazil and Venezuela, and in Mexico with the Mayan ruins. A vast, thickly forested land filled with ancient treasures that no one knows about."

"So this place is like that?"

"Sort of," Archie said. "It is certainly not on any lists for high-priority tourism renovations, and we intend to keep it that way."

"We?"

"The Jesuit Order. We, through a set of serendipitous inheritances about three-hundred years ago, came into ownership of this valley. The local Jesuits vowed to keep the valley pristine and untouched, though they had no idea it was the home of the Chachapoyas.

"Although, now that I think of it, it makes sense."

"What? That the Chachapoyas lived here, or that the Jesuits control the land?"

"Both. There was a young Jesuit in this region in the 1500s named Blas Valera. He was an intelligent priest and spoke a few languages, most notably Quechuan because of his parents — a Spanish conquistador and an Inca princess — which helped him win favor with the Spanish. He became a renowned expert on linguistics and the history of this area, until his surprising and sudden death in 1597."

"Why was it surprising?"

"Because some say he was attempting to alert the Pope about the *real* reason the Spanish were conquering South America. The authorities found out and had him killed."

"What was this 'real reason?'" Ben asked, turning the Jeep sharply around a bend and straightening it back out again.

"No one knows," Archie said. "But there were whispers that it was not about gold or riches at all, but something... more important."

"Important like a hidden tribe of people in a Peruvian valley?" Julie asked.

"Perhaps. That is my take, at least," Archie said. "And Blas had a brother — a man named Jeronimo — who had been told that his older brother Blas had *not* actually perished in Spain."

"So that was a lie?"

"No one knows. But Jeronimo walked into this valley in 1601 with a team of Jesuits, trying to search for their long-lost brother."

"Let me guess," Ben said. "They never came out."

Archie's expression in the rearview mirror confirmed Ben's suspicion.

REGGIE

REGGIE AND SARAH tried maneuvering around on the stone slab, seeing if there was any give in their bindings. Unfortunately, even with their left arms freed, there was no way they could slide sideways. Any inches they could gain toward one of them would only pull the other the opposite direction.

"Reggie?" Sarah said. "Are we going to die here?"

He stopped moving. *How much time has passed?* It had to be at least half an hour. More? Garza had told them they had forty-seven minutes before the blade above them fell. Forty-seven minutes for Julie and Ben to get here, with the Book of Bones, or they'd both lose their hand.

But Garza had told them the doctors he had on payroll would be able to reattach the hands — that they needed a 'clean break' for the yeast to insert themselves into the latticework bone structure.

"No," he said. "Garza told us we'd be in pain. But I don't think he'll kill us."

He wanted to add, *yet*, but he knew it wouldn't helpful.

"Why is he doing this?"

"Garza?" Reggie thought a moment, trying to figure out the

right words. "Vicente Garza was a career soldier, fast-tracked to success. A born leader, good strategist, all that."

"What happened to him?"

"He... tired of the 'new way' of doing things."

"What's that?"

"Well, the military is all about efficiency. It used soldiers to fight battles when humans were the cheapest commodity around, then tanks and planes when vehicles became affordable to produce and money wasn't an issue. Now, it's all about tech. Intelligence-gathering, espionage, cryptography, even fighting itself — it's all been outsourced to computers and machines.

"It's the next phase of the military industrial complex, and Garza hates it. He's all about the *human* element — creating the best-trained, most efficient battle force that doesn't malfunction, can adapt on the fly, and is easily replaceable."

"His private army," Sarah said.

"Exactly. It's a breeding ground for people just like him — men who want to be part of something bigger, but also part of something *special*. They think they're above the law, and frankly, where they operate, there usually *isn't* a law. It's a private security force, but it's unlike any that has ever existed."

"And now he's creating giants."

Reggie chuckled. "Yeah, that. I didn't want to believe it when I saw them, but... I don't understand it, but — you're an anthropologist, is this stuff even possible?"

Sarah sighed. "Honestly? Yeah. Everything he's told us about them checks out, at least from a high-level point of view. The yeast being able to turn its environment into a sort of growth hormone, the breaking and re-setting of bones causing faster, larger growth, all that. That part is out of my area of expertise, but from a *historic* perspective..."

"You saying giants roamed the Earth?"

"Yeah, kinda. I mean, we don't have any fossilized remains, but that's easy to explain away. It would be *more* unbelievable if we *did* have some, considering how unlikely it is that any given skeleton will become fossilized over time.

"But consider the world religions, ancient histories, and almost every civilization's myths and legends. Giants were here before we were. They weren't the *fee-fi-fo-fum* 'stomp on the tiny people' variety, but they were, basically, what we saw in Alaska: larger-than-life men."

The door to Reggie's left began to slide open, and one of the doctors walked in. It was the woman — Dr. Jenner — who had treated him in the other room. She entered, hustling toward them, and the door slid shut behind her.

Before she'd reached the dais and the raised platform, Reggie called out to her. "I'd say the yeast is settling in nicely, doc. Just need to get this hand chopped off. You think I'd be able to get a prescription for codeine or something when we're done?"

The doctor looked down at Reggie and forced a half-smile. "I need to ensure the placement of the blade will sever the joints without stressing the body." Her words were stilted and robotic, as if she were talking to herself.

"I really appreciate that," Reggie said. "We'd hate to be in stress when you *cut our damn hands off!*"

He spat the words, hoping to get the woman riled up. It worked, at least partially. She got closer. "You think you are my first patients?" she asked. "You think I am going to be affected by your petty pleas? This is my *job*, and I take it quite seriously. Do you even understand how impor —"

Reggie reached out with his free hand and snagged the woman's lab coat. He yanked it as hard as he could and the much smaller woman flew toward the stone table. As she fell, Reggie reached his arm up and around her neck, latched his hand onto her chin, and spun her around.

She lay on her back, frozen in place and unable to move beneath

Reggie's monstrous forearm, which was squeezing the soft tissue under her neck. He had a handful of her now-disheveled hair in his fist.

Backup hair, he called it. Any time a combatant had long hair, he liked to get a handful of it ready in case they wriggled free. A quick snap of his wrist would bring the person's head right back into his control.

The doctor whimpered. "I — I can't..."

"Shhh," Reggie said. "I don't think this is a good time for us to be getting to know each other. You've got two options. Do *exactly* what I say right now, or I break your —"

"Please!" she screamed. "I don't know anything! I'm just —"

Reggie roared, lifting his bicep from the woman's neck and *throwing* her outward at the same time. She rose to her feet and had almost gained her balance when her head snapped backward with an insane force, chunks of hair ripping out of her skull. She fell back into the same place she had been in before, and this time Reggie kept his bicep flexed.

"*Do you think I was joking?*" Reggie screamed. "*Is this a* game *to you?*" He breathed in a few times, trying to calm his rage. "This — this woman has been tortured, abused, and terrified she is going to *lose* her *hand.* Because of you. So *do not* tempt me again. Your worthless life is *absolutely nothing* to me right now. Got it?"

The woman nodded quickly.

"Great. I figured we'd be on the same page. Now, back to doing exactly what I say: that walkie on your hip. Under your lab coat. Right side, right hand. No funny business. Take it out, put it on the stone next to my left side."

She did. "It won't — it's only meant for close-range —"

"Shut it." Reggie continued. "Dr. Lindgren is going to be freed. By you. These straps are tie-downs, with quick-release latches. Reach out with your right hand and —"

"I can't do that," the woman said, sobbing. "I'll get —"

"You'll get killed if you *don't*," Reggie said. "How's that sound?"

The woman hesitated.

"Do it."

The door slid open again.

"*Now.*"

Still, the woman balked. Reggie caught a glimpse of the two people who had just entered. It was Vicente Garza and Dr. Prichard. They were whispering about something, but Reggie saw them stop and tense up when they caught sight of their colleague in Reggie's grasp.

"Dammit," Reggie whispered. "You made me do this."

He took a deep breath, then twisted his forearm upward as hard as he could, taking the woman's head with it. Then he smashed it back down against the side of the stone table. The doctor's neck cracked and popped twice, and her skull smacked against the platform with a sickening thud. She fell limp to the dais, a crumpled heap of hair and blood.

Without stopping, Reggie grabbed the radio and pulled it up to his lips. "Ben! Julie! If you can hear me, we're in a... stone temple of some sort. Round, like a big stone circus tent. We only have about fifteen minutes left! Garza's here, with —"

The gunshot cracked through the air, reverberating forever around the room, but Reggie's call for help was cut short by the radio exploding into a million pieces, the bullet's impact a direct hit.

He looked over to Garza, who was shaking his head.

"Red," he said. "That was a *severe* mistake."

"SO THIS WOMAN told you she had the journal of her great-grandfather, a Nazi scientist working on experiments he claimed were inspired by *Atlanteans?*"

Victoria's voice barely hid her skepticism. In all her years as a professor, she'd never come across something so... out of left field.

"That is exactly what I am saying," Agent Sharpe said. He stepped closer to her, his white apron dancing in the shadowy light. "Sigmund Rascher was a well-known —"

"I've heard of him," she said. "Please, continue."

"Right. So his great-*granddaughter* found his journal, which includes snippets of *The Book of Bones* in it — Plato's *Hermocrates* — and *that* story claims that the people who became the Chachapoyas came to South America with the descendants of the Nephilim."

The three men in front of her nodded.

"And *that* is the 'proof' you have that they're still here?"

"Well," the leader of the Guild Rite said. "Not exactly. The —"

Sharpe interrupted. "From what we can gather, the *Book of Bones* describes the *method* that was used to create these giants."

"I thought the Nephilim were *divine* beings? The offspring of *sons of God, daughters of men?*"

"Well, yes, but... like in most biblical historical allegory, there is a *scientific* explanation for most *divine* results."

Victoria thought about this and couldn't argue. In her classes, she often took a biblical story and compared it to a secular, or worldly, one. The similarities were often nothing short of uncanny, and she would end the lesson 'proving' that the biblical myth wasn't a myth at all but simply a certain peoples' written understanding of events that had transpired.

Noah's flood, for example, was often viewed as a biblical 'myth' by her students, intended to coach its readers against hubris and corruption, but she pointed out that the story was actually corroborated by the recorded histories of worldwide civilizations, all scattered so far from one another that communication would have been impossible.

"Okay," she said. "So you think the Nephilim were one such myth? A race of giants, birthed by the unity of god and man?"

"Of *angels* and man," the second man said. "Numerous places in the Bible expound on this truth, and I know you've read the Apocrypha and Dead Sea Scroll references as well."

She had, in fact, read them.

"And you must look no further than the Greek mythological heroes — Jason, Achilles, Heracles, or Hercules, Poseidon — to see more of the truth. Poseidon, a *god*, lay with Cleito, *a human woman*, who gave birth to five sets of twins. Heracles was the product of Zeus, a *god*, and Alcmene, a *human*. These were all heroes who were born of human women and descendants of the Nephilim or the Titans, the second generation after."

Victoria pulled at a strand of hair. "Okay, okay. I get it — it's compelling, but I would need to see more. Still, how does that answer my question: where are they now? How do you know they still exist?"

"We found a bone," the leader said.

"A... bone."

"A femur. Just outside, in the jungle. It was buried about a foot deep, but it was in reasonable condition."

"Reasonable condition?" she asked. "Then how can you know —"

"It was in *impeccable* condition, considering there was hardly any of it left."

"I don't understand."

"Well, we had a doctor perform an analysis on it. It was nearly disintegrated, broken in over a hundred locations, and it was deteriorating quickly. But for its age, the doctor said it was in immaculate shape."

"So how old is this femur?"

"It's gone now — it essentially evaporated, as if it had been made of ice. Our doctor told us it was one of the most remarkable things he had ever seen, like it were eating itself from the inside out. But he estimated that the femur had been in the ground for fewer than fifty years."

Victoria scoffed. "That's impossible. A human femur *completely* disappeared in fewer than *fifty years?*"

"That is not even the most incredible part," the man said.

"Do tell."

"The bone shards we recovered were found to have signs of osteoporosis and a lack of necessary calcium."

"And that means what?"

"It means that someone was subjecting these bones to radiation therapy — shooting radiation into the bones to stunt the growth of cancerous tumors."

So the bones couldn't *have been old,* she thought. "So the bones were not ancient in any way."

The leader of the Guild Rite shrugged. "That is what the doctor believed. And that answers your previous question. The reason the bones of these people — the descendants of the race of giants, the Nephilim — are no longer around is that their skeletal structure is somehow different from ours. They are strong, huge, tall, like the legends say, but they are simultaneously weak, their bones brittle and quick to fail, and therefore any fossil record we would hope to have of them has been lost to time."

"Okay, fine. You're looking for giants, and you can't find them because they don't stick around after they die. That's not uncommon — only a small fragment of a percent of what's lived on Earth leaves a trace in the fossil record. But I *still* don't understand why you think these guys are supposed to be *here*. In Peru. In the Chachapoyas region."

When she said that, the third man — Etienne Sharpe of Interpol — began to speak again. "Well, Sigmund Rascher, who claimed to have had access to a full account of Plato's *Book of Bones*, wrote that the ancient Atlanteans eventually sailed 'to the islands and continents of the Atlantic, landing in and settling the lands beyond the Pillars of Hercules.' Plato wrote that these people, after having their world destroyed by the Great Flood, reached out to distant civilizations in order to rebuild and repair their race."

"What does that have to do with the Nephilim and Chachapoyas?"

"He wrote that the Atlanteans 'took up their ancient charge,' meaning they set off to find a new land, a new place to protect their ancient secretes. Plato wrote that they 'imposed their own exile, seeking new treasures to enhance their old.'"

"So they came here," Victoria said.

"Yes, precisely."

"But the femur you found," she said. "You said it was no more than fifty years old."

The man nodded.

"And the radiation therapy to stall the growth of tumors: It means someone *else* is here, and they're trying to figure out how to make these giants again. They're literally *growing* them."

CHAPTER 62

JULIE

"BEN! *Jul — hear me, we're — some sort.*"

Julie heard the words flying out from her radio and she whipped it up to her ear. She turned up the volume. "It's Reggie," she said.

Ben nodded back at her, his head cocked sideways as he listened to the feed on his own walkie-talkie.

"*Round — big stone circus — only — fifteen minutes — Garza's —*"

"Garza's here," Julie said. "This is the right place. Ben, *we're here.*"

Ben drove along silently. He sped up, but the severe potholes prevented them from moving rapidly.

"He said 'fifteen minutes.' What does that mean?"

Archie spoke from the back seat. "Best case, there is fifteen minutes left before Garza does something terrible. Worst case..."

"They're in trouble," Julie said. "Ben, can we make it?"

"We have to," he said. "We *have* to."

"What about 'big stone circus...'?" Julie asked. "Circus tent?"

"That would be my guess," Archie said. "Perhaps it is where he is being held?"

"Sounds like the kind of place you can't miss," Ben said. "That's what we're looking for, got it? Eyes up, guns ready. I'm not going to screw around with Garza. You see him, you shoot."

Julie nodded, and Ben caught Archie's eyes in the mirror. He had a grave expression on his face, but he too nodded.

VICTORIA SAW a fourth man enter the lit area, stepping out of the shadows and jogging toward the group of three men in front of her. He whispered something to the leader.

"Now?"

The man nodded.

"I see."

The leader turned to Victoria. "Ms. Reyes," he said. "It appears there has been a... complication. Our work will continue, but we need to attend to something. Do you feel comfortable here?"

"Not at all," she said.

He smiled. "Not what I meant, but do I have your permission to *leave* you here? To work? I can have my men bring in whatever you need so that you may help us. Our first order of business is to understand this place. This temple."

She frowned. *Whatever's going on has them pretty worked up.* "You'll just... *leave* me here?"

The man seemed to contemplate this from a new perspective, then his eyes widened and his face lit up. "Ah, I see. You feel that by staying here alone, you will somehow be able to *escape*."

"Something like that, yeah," Victoria said. "I mean, you did kidnap me. It's sort of a built-in natural response. Get kidnapped, try to get free."

"Of course. Well, I expect you *will* explore. But you know where we are. You also, therefore, know where we are, *regionally*. The dangers that await you there far —"

"— outweigh the ones in here," she quipped. "Yeah, I've seen those movies."

"In that case, know that there are four Guild Rite members just outside the doors, armed and expecting you to escape. They have been informed that if any such thing is to happen, they have my permission to shoot on site."

"Got it." Victoria said. *Now that sounds more like an expected kidnapper move.*

The men, without fanfare, turned to leave.

She wanted to know what they were doing, what they had been informed of. But she also had some ideas...

The things the man had told her about the Guild Rite, the ancient races of men, the history of the Freemasons and their ongoing war with the Church... all of it was beginning to take shape, at least loosely, into a connected set of patches.

And she wanted to add those patches to her quilt.

She walked over to the dais, stepped onto it, and kneeled in front of the round pillar. It was like a table, about chest-high, but there was no protruding edge on top. It would uncomfortable to sit there on a chair, as there was nowhere for legs to go.

She examined the stone face of the pillar, finding that there were nearly invisible lines pockmarking the facade. Faint, worn, and nearly smooth. But the lines weren't accidental. She noticed they were ordered in some way, as if...

Hieroglyphics.

She couldn't see the images clearly, but by rubbing a hand over them she felt some of their characteristics. Where Egyptian glyphs were often blocky, with hard angles, these felt more like Chinese text, the lines curved and some parts rounded. And while she had no working knowledge of the language, she knew enough to know it wasn't Chinese text.

So what is it?

She thought through the different civilizations that had used hieroglyphics. *Egyptians, of course. But also in the Henan province in China, Harappa, Pakistan...*

No. Something closer to here. South America? She remembered the Olmecs' language in ancient Mexico, the 'Epi-Olmec,' but these symbols were more advanced.

Something closer to... where the creators of this place came from.

There was an article she'd read long ago about the history of communication, specifically through writing. Most scholars believed that the first 'true' writing system had been developed in ancient Sumeria, or present-day Iraq.

The Guild Rite had given her an alternative view of history, but this writing style could fit that alternate view perfectly. She examined it more.

The pillars of Solomon's temple. Jachin and Boaz. Victoria's mind raced with the possibilities, narrowing them down to the one that made most sense. *Solomon's temple, built by Hiram Abiff, had a porch which had two pillars named Jachin and Boaz.*

She recalled the verse immediately: *1 Kings, chapter 7: 'And he set up the pillars in the porch of the temple: and he set up the right pillar, and called the name thereof Jachin: and he set up the left pillar, and called the name thereof Boaz.'*

And it was less than a week ago when she had taught this lesson to her class, talking about the Masonic text called the Cooke Manuscript... *and that he would write in the two pillars all the science, and crafts, that all they had found, and so he did...*

The two pillars were the pillars of Solomon's temple. Built by one of the most famous Masons in history, and upon those pillars he wrote *all the science, and crafts, that all they had found...*

Her mouth dropped.

All the science, and crafts...

In *Antiquities of the Jews*, a text written by a Roman Jewish historian in the time shortly after Christ's life, Josephus wrote that Seth, the third son of Adam and Eve, was given the heavenly wisdom — the seven sciences of Freemasonry — and that his descendants build the pillars of the sons of Seth, which were two pillars depicting that knowledge and the secrets of the sciences. Cain, his older brother, was also given this knowledge, but it led to corruption and the drive for power.

The same Seth who appears as the foil to Cain, the son of Adam who murdered his brother Abel.

The same Seth who fathered generations of descendants that eventually led to Noah.

And the same Seth whose children built the pillars based on Adam's prediction that the world would eventually be flooded, killing all humans.

It's all connected, she thought. *Everything — the tapestry. The quilt of history. It's all one, massively complex quilt.*

CHAPTER 64

BEN

THE NEXT BEND emptied the Jeeps into a long, narrow clearing. Ben sped up, taking advantage of the relatively flat, open area, then slowed again when he realized what lay in front of them.

"That's it," Julie said. "It has to be."

A squat, stone building sat near the edge of the trees to their right, and Ben saw that it was a long, rectangular structure. The roof was stone, and he could see a doorway that stretched nearly to the roof on the end pointing toward them.

Directly in front of them but farther away, a larger, round building stretched nearly to the tops of the trees, which bent in toward the roof of the domed structure. Both buildings were weathered brown, dusty, and seemed to have been hewn from single stones. From here, Ben couldn't see any patchwork of masonry or stonework. No lines crisscrossed the structures' walls.

Looks like a big stone circus tent, he thought.

Beyond that, stretching up and over the scene, was a massive, perfectly triangular peak with a rounded top. It loomed upward like a stone titan, guarding its temple and valley.

But his attention was quickly pulled to the *left* of his vision, where he noticed movement in the forest.

"There," he said, throwing the Jeep into park. Julie followed his gaze, then put a hand over her mouth.

"It's them," she said.

"Get the weapons," Ben said, holding a hand out. Before he'd finished the sentence, Archie had placed one of the pistols into it.

"What's the plan?"

"How long do we have?"

"Ten, maybe twelve minutes," Julie said. "But that's a best guess."

The other Jeep pulled up next to theirs, and Ben looked over at the short, wide Peruvian soldier in the passenger seat. He pointed two fingers at his eyes, and then one at the men, who had now broken through the trees and were walking away from them in the distance. Ben nodded.

"They haven't seen us yet," he said. "But the Jeeps will tell them we're here, and if we try to back out we risk them hearing us. I want to be in the woods when they figure it out, ready to ambush."

"Got it," Archie said. Ben had a fleeting moment of despair when he realized the man he was planning a gunfight with was old enough to be his grandfather, but he shook the feeling away. *He's been through much worse. He'll be fine.*

Still, he made a mental note to try to put himself between any gunmen and Archie's body.

They piled out of the Jeeps, crept behind them, and checked their weapons. Each of the soldiers had a rifle and a sidearm, and each carried two grenades. Ben and Archie carried the same rifles, while Julie had one fitted with a distance scope. If they needed to adapt their plan and got captured or stuck out in the open, Ben hoped Julie could get off a clean shot while still hiding in the trees.

They split up into two groups, Ben, Archie, and two soldiers heading to the left, and the other two Peruvian Army men and Julie heading right. The plan was simple — head through the trees around the narrow clearing until they were sure there were no more hidden guards, then open fire on the men walking toward the large round building.

Ben told them they would only fire when they were near the first building, to maintain a triangular shape as their two flanks fired on the enemy. Any closer and the enemy soldiers could be directly between them, the two teams risking the exchanging of friendly fire.

It took only five minutes walking through the forest to get even with the first building, and Ben held up a hand for his team to stop. They were about equidistant from the front of the stone building and their Jeeps, a good place to set up an offensive without being too far from their escape route. Ben wished he'd thought to turn the Jeeps around, but he knew it would have risked being spotted or heard.

"Okay," he whispered, holding his walkie-talkie up with his free hand. "Those dudes are coming back this way — obviously a patrol. When they get to the opposite edge of the smaller building, we take them out. Julie fires first, got it. Then our marksman. If they're not both down after that, we open fire. But let's not waste ammunition — we don't know how many more are inside."

He looked around, then pressed the button on his radio once again. "... Over."

He heard a quick succession of clicks, the sound of his teammates confirming the order, and a sense of pride welled up inside him. *I'm actually running a military battle,* he thought.

Then his heart sank, and the pride was almost immediately replaced with anxiety. *I'm actually running a* military *battle. I'm a park ranger. I barely even know how to use this —*

"There!"

Ben heard the man shouting and pointing toward their Jeeps, then the two men were joined by two more soldiers who had appeared from the side of the round building. The four began racing up the middle of the narrow clearing, their boots pounding.

"Change of plans," Ben said. "Julie, take your shot *now.*"

The gunshot rang out and echoed off the exterior walls of the buildings, but Ben didn't see anyone fall.

Dammit.

"*Ben,*" the voice through his radio said. "*She missed. We need to —*"

Ben started shooting, wildly at first as he got a feel for the rifle, then with a bit more precision. The Peruvians joined in with a zealous, rapid pace, and he saw two of the men in the field fall.

The other two had realized what was happening and had stopped, falling to the one knee, and were now hiding behind the longer rectangular building.

"Julie, Archie," Ben said. "Take your soldiers around the back of that building. I'll run around to that side, too, but do not take the shot unless they're firing at you. We can't risk hitting each other."

"*Got it.*"

The men took turns popping their heads out from the side of the building, but neither fired on them as they moved through the forest. Ben assumed that meant they still hadn't figured out their location. He wanted to take that as a small victory, but he knew better. *No plan survives first contact with the enemy*, he reminded himself. *And we don't even know if this is* all *the enemy.*

He was almost certain these men were guards on patrol outside, or just taking a break. But that meant there would be more of them.

Julie reached the rear of the building before Ben, as his radio crackled to life while he was still jogging over. "*Ben,*" she said. "*I'm here.*"

He looked up and took in the situation. Both men hiding behind the building were facing his direction — if he fired on them, they'd see him. The building was also farther from him than from Julie. She had a clear, open shot, and it was as close to a can't-miss situation as they would get.

"Take the shot," he said, keeping his voice down in case the volume on Julie's radio was still turned up.

Within seconds it was over. Ben saw the men fall after four gunshots — Julie and one of the soldiers, or Archie, had aimed and fired, and all had hit their marks.

Ben waited, holding his breath. *Do the others know we're here? Will they come out?* He took a step into the clearing, heading toward the dead soldiers' bodies. The others followed behind, everyone careful to watch their surroundings as they moved.

He looked toward the strange, round building. It looked like a miniature observatory that had sunken into the ground, with a slightly flattened top. Again, the architecture was strange. Nothing like the Incan designs he'd seen before with their tight-fitting stones and layered structures. This was something that reminded him of the Anasazi and their carved-stone buildings.

And yet... it was *big*. It seemed off, as if this temple or meeting place had been designed for taller, wider people. He saw a vertical, rectangular indentation along the rounded wall — a door? It was tall, its top reaching nearly to the start of the roof, but it too seemed as though it had been made from one massive brick of stone.

And as he examined it, as Julie and Archie and their other teammates walked into the clearing and joined him, the door began to slide open.

"Move in!" Ben yelled. "We don't have time to explore — get inside and keep your eyes up!"

CHAPTER 65

REGGIE

"DOCTOR PRICHARD, please prepare your medications for the immediate treatment of the bone lattice."

Prichard's mouth dropped. "But — but the preparation will take an hour, at least. I need to run the analysis on the yeast to ensure —"

"Skip the analysis, Prichard," Garza said. "I'm no longer interested in ensuring this is a properly controlled trial."

Reggie swallowed. Both his eyes were bloodshot, rims of dark purplish bruises around the soft skin. Garza hadn't spoken another word to him, simply raising his pistol over his head and smashing it down between his eyes. The blow had decimated Reggie's nose, blackened both his eyes, and left his mouth full of blood, which he'd been trying to clear every few seconds.

Spitting it out caused him severe pain, however, and swallowing it made it feel like he would choke.

"But Mr. Garza, I strongly advise that the testing continue as —"

"Your advice is duly noted, doctor. Thank you. Now kindly *do your job*. The one *I* hired you to do. Do you understand?"

Dr. Prichard nodded.

Garza had kicked Dr. Jenner's lifeless body out of the way before he'd struck Reggie, and he could see her shadowy shape slumped into the edge of the rounded room.

Please come, Ben, he thought. *For Sarah.*

"How long?" Garza asked.

Prichard didn't answer at first, instead checking mental calculations by tracing a finger around in the air in front of his face. "If I... there could be..."

"Well?"

"Sir, we would be ready to go now, potentially. One, two minutes tops — we have medication leftover from —"

"Do it."

Garza turned on a heel and exited the chamber, while Dr. Prichard walked the other direction — apparently the direction of the small hospital-like room they'd been in previously.

Reggie groaned.

If you're coming, Ben, now would be a great *time.*

CHAPTER 66

BEN

BEN BLINKED A FEW TIMES, his eyes taking an unnaturally long time to adjust to the dim light.

Julie was there, next to him. He sensed the others as well, Archie and the Peruvian soldiers.

But he also noticed another person, a woman, kneeling at the foot of a massive stone altar.

"Hey!" Ben shouted.

The woman turned around, her eyes wide.

"Where are they?"

"Who?" she asked. "The weird Freemason guys? They left."

THE SOUND FELL out from a PA speaker hidden somewhere along the side of the room.

Fifteen seconds.

Fourteen seconds.

Thirteen —

Reggie tried to tune it out. It was torture, and he knew Garza was doing it on purpose. The voice, a computer-generated woman's voice, carried no emotion or remorse.

Sarah was silent as they listened to the sound of the ticking clock.

Come on, Ben, he thought. *Now's the time for a big entrance.*

Ten seconds.

Nine seconds.

It wasn't going to happen. Reggie knew that even if Ben were in the area, somehow fighting his way in, he wouldn't be able to make it to them before the blade fell.

He gripped Sarah's wrist. He wanted desperately to reach her to hold her, but they were stuck. Bound to the surface of this stone altar, bound to the fate Garza had laid out for them.

Shit.

He tried to think of something.

There's always *a plan. There's always* something *we can do. Think, Red.*

All his training had led him to this. To fight, to adapt, to —

He stopped.

Five seconds.

Four seconds.

He squeezed his eyes shut, ignoring the pain and surge of liquid that pumped down his nose. *No,* he thought. *There's got to be a* better *way.*

His training was there, waiting for him.

When a 'perfect' plan seems impossible, a 'good enough' plan takes its place.

The perfect plan was to escape. His hands and Sarah's hands intact.

The perfect plan was to get out, free and alive.

The perfect plan was to kill Garza.

The perfect plan is impossible. But maybe we can keep some of those elements in the 'good enough' version.

Namely, he wanted to kill Garza.

Two seconds.

But for now, he focused on just getting out.

"Hey Sarah?"

"Yeah?'

"Bend your legs. Unlock your knees."

One second.

CHAPTER 68

BEN

BEN WAS THROWN off for a moment, but he stepped into the room and continued barraging her with questions. "No, the two people who — Reggie and Sarah. Dr. Lindgren. Gareth Red."

The woman's mouth dropped open. "Archie?"

She was looking over Ben's head, and Archibald Quinones stepped forward. "Victoria?"

"What the hell's going on?" Ben asked.

Victoria ran over, stopping in front of the group. The Peruvians moved to get ready for an attack, but Julie waved them down. "You — you must be Harvey. And Juliette. I'm Victoria Reyes."

Ben nodded slowly. "What is this place? And where are our friends?"

"This place is a temple," Victoria said. "And that —" she pointed to the big, round rock in the center of the room. "Is a *pillar*."

"Why is that important?"

"Because I think I just figured it all out. And I think I know how to find your friends."

Ben waited.

"Because there's another pillar."

VICTORIA STARED AT THE LARGE, thick man in front of her. He wasn't ripped, but he wasn't fat, either. Brownish hair, brown eyes, and tanned skin, he looked like he was a construction worker who'd come in from outside to take a quick break.

Harvey Bennett, she thought. He held himself well — handsome in a very unassuming sort of way, like a guy confident about his own abilities, but lacked the knowledge that the opposite sex might find him attractive.

A woman stood next to him — Juliette Richardson — and behind them was Archibald Quinones, flanked by some armed men who looked to be locals.

She reached out a hand. "I — I'm Victoria," she said again. "Reyes. Professor of —"

"Sorry," he said. "I hate to cut this short, but I've got some friends who *really* might want some help right now. You said there's another pillar? What does that mean?"

"Right," she said, dropping her hand. "I, uh, came here — I was kidnapped — and I think I might know where your friends are."

"Tell me."

"It's... not really that simple."

Harvey Bennett stepped toward her. He seemed to grow larger as he got closer. She involuntarily took a step backward. "What do you know?"

She shook her head, then pushed a strand of hair out of her eyes. *Where do I start?* "Harvey, the guys who took me, the Guild Rite, they —"

"The *Guild* Rite?"

"It — it's a Freemason thing, hard to explain."

Ben stiffened. "Masons tried to kill us in Rome."

Victoria bit her lip. "Yeah, same group. They... brought me here to help them."

"They *kidnapped* you."

"True. But I think they can help us. They might be —"

"They tried to kill us. What is a pillar?"

Victoria swallowed, then turned around and pointed at the circular stone table. "This is a pillar. It's got writing on it. A language I can't read — it predates ancient Egyptian."

"This is older than Egypt?"

She shook her head. "No, I don't believe it is. But whoever put it here knew the language." She paused. "Anyway, there's *another* one. A pillar. Just like this one."

"How do you know?" Juliette asked.

"Well, it's a long story. But I can explain it, I promise. You said your friends are in trouble, correct? That means we have little time to talk through it. Do you trust me?"

"No," Harvey said. "But we don't really have a better option. You think this other pillar is close?"

"Yes," she said. "It has to be. We just need to get out of —"

One of the massive doors slid open, and Harvey and his team turned to see a man walking in. He was in a hurry, his white apron bouncing as he steamed ahead.

"What fresh hell is this?" she heard Harvey say under his breath.

He reached for his weapon, and Victoria only then noticed that their entire team was loaded down in weaponry, including grenades.

The man continued toward them, and Victoria saw his face once he stepped into the light. "Agent —"

"Etienne Sharpe?" Juliette asked. "What the hell are *you* doing here?"

He stopped, his hands falling to his sides. He looked at Victoria, then flicked his eyes to Harvey and the rest of his team. His mouth moved, but no sound came out.

Before he could speak, Harvey Bennett walked forward, reached toward Agent Sharpe, then swung a right-hook across the man's face.

Victoria gasped. The soldiers with them, Peruvian, most likely, raised their weapons. The Guild Rite men behind Sharpe stopped short.

"That's for Egypt, you son of a —"

"Ben," Archie said. "Stop."

Harvey Bennett stopped, turned around, and seemed to recompose himself. He sniffed, rubbed his knuckles, and walked back over to Victoria and Juliette.

Sharpe stumbled backward, holding his chin. He tried to stand upright, but Harvey loomed over him still.

"What's the plan, then, Archie?" Harvey said, his voice a growl, his eyes not moving from Sharpe's face.

"Wait," Sharpe said. "Please. Wait."

Victoria watched the exchange. Harvey seething, Etienne cowering.

"I — I wanted to warn you," Sharpe said, casting a glance over his shoulder. "My — the men here. The Guild Rite, our group. I overhead that you were coming."

"And?" Harvey asked.

"And they think you're here with the other group. The ones funded by the Catholic Church. That you want to bring them *The Book of Bones*."

"That's... not entirely untrue," Juliette said. "But what does that mean for us? Where are they now?"

"They're outside," Sharpe said. "Waiting for the rest of us, and waiting for you to get corralled inside here. And they're going to kill you."

Harvey looked over at Victoria. "These 'Guild Rite' folks. They need you to find this other group?"

"Yeah. Sort of."

"And they can't do it without you?"

Victoria felt her heart sink. *Are they going to kill me?* She shook her head. "No, apparently they can't."

"Okay then," Harvey said, turning to his own team. "Let's get behind this pillar thing. Victoria's with us. She stays alive at all costs. She's the key to finding Reggie and Sarah, got it?"

Nods all around.

"Sharpe, you're either with us or you're dead. Decide now."

Agent Sharpe's head fell, but he didn't hesitate. He walked next to Archie to the far side of the stone pillar, then turned back to face the doors.

Victoria watched as the two massive doors in the room began to open again, and the team in front of her spread out a bit. Their guns rose, pointing toward the doors.

"Sharpe," Harvey said. "What kind of power are these guys packing?"

Sharped looked over at Harvey and was about to respond when the floodlight in the room shut off. Another second passed, and Victoria heard a *pop*.

Her eyes were blistered by light, and she screamed. Pain seared into her head, and she fell sideways, blinded.

Gunfire blasted into the room next, the battering sound of automatic rifles ripping around the stone chamber and echoing into a cacophony.

CHAPTER 70

BEN

BEN WAS BLIND. The flashbang grenade the Guild Rite men had thrown into the room had caused him to backpedal and knock over Archie, where the two of them fell into a heap on the floor. The motion might have saved their lives, as Ben then heard the telltale whizzing sounds of rapid-fire rounds shooting over their heads.

He held a hand over Archie's chest, waiting until his eyes adjusted. He knew it would take more than a minute to fully recover, but it would be only a matter of seconds before he'd be able to see enough to mount a counterattack.

He only hoped the Guild Rite wasn't already in the room and rushing their location behind the pillar.

"Jules!" he shouted.

She responded, telling Ben she was okay and almost able to see.

Thoughts crashed into Ben's mind as he tried to make sense of what was happening. Agent Sharpe was here, in the flesh. That meant he had been playing them in Egypt — either pretending to be part of Interpol, or, more likely, an actual high-ranking Interpol officer who *also* was a member of this secret fraternity.

But why had he switched sides? Sharpe had told them that when he'd discovered Harvey Bennett and his friends were here in Peru, he felt compelled to warn them. Did that mean the man would only condone the brutal killing of innocent civilians if he didn't personally know them?

But these were questions for another time — Ben needed to stay alive, and that meant he needed to focus on the enemy he could see. *Barely see*, he thought.

He heard footsteps — boots approaching from his right. He turned and fired an awkward spray of rounds in the general direction and was surprised to hear the sound of a man falling to the ground.

His vision slowly returned, and he rolled toward the edge of the pillar where two of the Peruvian soldiers were posted, their guns aiming around the cylinder and toward the two doors. Ben couldn't see around them, so he wasn't sure if there were any men approaching from that side.

He got his answer a second later, when one soldier fell, a gunshot wound in his chest. He was still alive, and Ben knew he was wearing body armor, so he dragged him backwards and behind the pillar.

"You'll be okay," he said. The man — barely twenty-five, from the looks of his wide-eyed, young face — stared up at Ben as he clutched his chest and tried to breathe. Ben wished he knew more Spanish than how to ask for a beer and where the restroom was. "I — I don't even know your name," he said instead.

Ben felt a sudden feeling of anxious dread, as if a car were slowly being released onto his chest. He had approved Archie's hiring of these men, but he hadn't even taken the time to get to know them. He'd asked them to fight — potentially to give their lives — for him, for a cause Ben hadn't even explained to them.

I need to do better, he thought. *I need to do more.*

He patted the soldier's shoulder and nodded. The kid nodded in return.

Ben extended his legs a bit so his head was barely above the top of the pillar. There still was no light in the room, but the weapons were still firing, lighting up the areas directly around the muzzles of the rifles. It was clear to Ben that these men — the Guild Rite — were not trained soldiers. They were sporadic, spread out in a haphazard way, and they'd clearly overestimated their element of surprise.

Especially since they don't remember that we've got these, Ben said to himself as he reached down and grabbed a hand grenade from the wounded soldier. He pulled the pin, waited a few seconds, then heaved it up and over his head toward the door closest to him.

He had spotted at least three muzzle flashes from that direction, so he figured there was a group of Guild Rite men over there. The grenade sailed through the air and in a brief pause between bursts of gunfire, he heard the explosive hit the stone floor and roll.

He had no idea where it ended up until it detonated. The blast lit up the entire room and sent four Guild Rite members flying in opposite directions, one of them landing behind the pillar itself, where Archie fired a round into the man's head with his pistol.

The force of the explosion in the tight space blew chunks of stone and debris over the dais and pillar, but the pillar itself remained firmly in place, protecting Ben and his team.

He hadn't intended to cause a cave-in, but that was exactly what happened. He heard a deep rumbling sound, then poked his head up once more and looked in the direction of the blast. It was still dark in the room, but a flashlight had been turned on and dropped, its beam pointing toward the door. He saw chunks of stone falling from the ceiling and doorframe, and one massive rock fell and completely covered one of the fallen Guild Rite men.

"We have a problem," Ben said. He had felt the ground shake, both when the grenade first exploded *and* a few seconds later. "It's unstable here. That grenade caused a bit of a shakeup."

"Well, I'd rather die fighting these assholes than die underneath a pile of rubble," Julie said.

"Same here," Archie said.

For a moment the gunfire ceased, but Ben knew the men were just reloading, checking their weapons, and using the flashlight's dim light as an opportunity to regroup.

"Here's the plan," Ben said. "Julie, grab another one of those grenades."

JULIE HAD NEVER THROWN a grenade in her life. She hadn't planned to, but then again she also hadn't planned on having to postpone her wedding three separate times because she and the man she loved continued to find themselves under attack.

Thankfully, throwing a grenade was about as simple as it seemed. She'd pulled the pin, 'cooked' it for a few seconds, then tossed it gently toward the same door Ben had thrown his.

The plan was simple, and it had worked flawlessly: by throwing another grenade toward the door that was about to collapse, the team pushed the Guild Rite men toward the *other* door. They were able to keep them pinned down as they ran from behind the pillar toward the decimated stone opening, chunks of ceiling and pieces of floor breaking off and creating a terrible obstacle course the entire way.

There were two Peruvian soldiers remaining in the fight, as Archie and the third man had carried the fourth soldier between them as they made their escape. Those two soldiers had proven to be extremely effective, each of them taking down two Guild Rite men as they ran.

Julie and Ben had made it to the opening in the side of the temple first, but the rest of the team was right behind. Julie and her fiancé laid down covering fire as the rest of them escaped into the waning sunlight. They'd made it out alive, but the enemy was still only a hundred feet away.

Worse, Garza was still out there with Reggie and Sarah.

"What now?" Julie shouted. They were once again in the clearing, this time with an injured Peruvian soldier and two additional team members.

"We get to the Jeeps," Ben said. "I don't see any other vehicles here, but I wouldn't be surprised if they've got some. Those Jeeps are our best bet."

They were already moving as fast as they could, keeping close to the tree line, where they could duck and hide when the Guild Rite members eventually emerged from the temple and caught sight of them. Julie ran next to the second, longer building and stepped over the two fallen Guild Rite soldiers who had been guarding that space earlier.

They made it all the way to the Jeeps, and were getting everyone loaded inside, when the Guild Rite men began firing at them. They were too far away for accuracy, but Julie heard at least one bullet pinging off the frame of their vehicle.

"Victoria," Ben shouted, revving the engine before Julie had even gotten inside. "You said the second pillar is around here somewhere?"

"I think," she said. "I mean, it *has* to be."

"Why does it have to be?"

"The one in the temple, the one we hid behind? It's a replica — an homage — to the pillars that led into Solomon's Temple."

"Which is?"

"A temple, built for King Solomon, by one of the first Freemasons."

Julie didn't understand why that was important, either, but they didn't have time for an explanation. "So I'm assuming this *replica* will have a counterpart, since there were two pillars in Solomon's original."

"Exactly."

Ben turned the Jeep onto the dirt road that led out of the clearing and back out to the main road. Julie, Ben, one of the Peruvian soldiers, and Victoria drove in this one while Archie, Etienne Sharpe, and the three other Peruvians, including the one who had been injured, rode in the Jeep behind them. They were broadcasting their conversation through the Jeep's stereo using the in-car microphone and the communications rig in the back.

"Any idea how to find the other pillar?" Ben asked.

"Well, the pillars were originally built to guard the entrance to Solomon's temple, so they stood on either side of it. If the one we were just at is one pillar, and we know the distance between both pillars — the radius of a circle, if you will — the second pillar will be somewhere along the circumference of that imaginary circle."

"I don't math," Ben said. "Jules?"

Julie closed her eyes and pictured a circle, the first pillar at its center. The second pillar, then would have to be somewhere along the border of that circle. But... "We need to know the distance between them."

"Right," Victoria said. "I have an idea about that. You guys have a phone with cell service?"

Julie nodded, reaching into her pocket. Archie had given them both replacement smartphones, as both of theirs were somewhere at the bottom of the Mediterranean Sea by now. They'd set up their SIM cards to use Mr. E's communication access point, which was a global satellite array owned by his company, giving them crystal-clear connection to the internet around the world, as long as they had a line-of-sight view with at least two of the satellites.

Victoria wasted no time, pulling open a search engine and typing in a few words. "Okay," she said. "I'm reading that King Solomon's temple was oriented east to west. That means the pillars were in a north-south line. And this, from the Book of Jeremiah, chapter fifty-two: *'And concerning the pillars, the height of one pillar was eighteen cubits.'"*

"And a cubit is…"

"A measurement used in the Bible. Which puts the height of the pillars at about…" she typed more. "Twenty-seven feet tall."

"But how far apart were they?" Julie asked.

"Well, it looks like the measurements aren't exact, but they might get us close. Seems like most experts say the pillars were three times taller than the distance between them, which would make them about nine feet apart."

"How does that help us?" Ben asked. "I didn't see another giant circus tent-shaped temple nine feet away, if I recall." He pulled the Jeep around a tight bend, and Julie could tell he was getting frustrated. They were moving at a crawl, and they were no closer to tracking down the whereabouts of Reggie and Sarah.

Even worse, if it had truly been a countdown they'd heard Reggie mention during the radio transmission, that countdown had already reached zero…

"We need a multiplier," Victoria said. "We have the numbers, but we need to know what scale the pillars are supposed to represent."

"Thirty-three," Julie blurted.

Ben and Victoria glanced at her.

"It's one of the most famous Masonic numbers. All kinds of symbolism involved with it, right?"

"That's right," Victoria nodded, her eyes lighting up. "It's the highest order attained in Scottish Rite Freemasonry, for one." She took a breath, as if realizing something, then straightened her back and continued. "Christian numerologists revere the number — the word *Elohim* appears in the book of Genesis 33 times, and 33 is the age Jesus Christ was crucified and died."

"Don't forget about the Temple of Solomon," Archie said. *"It stood for thirty-three years before it was sacked."*

Victoria nodded. "Yeah, I think it's as good a place to start as any.

So that means the distance between the pillars is thirty-three times larger here than at the original temple. That's 297... what?"

"What?"

"What unit?" Victoria asked. "Cubits? Miles?"

Julie bit her lip. She had no idea where to go from here.

Archie's voice crackled from the Jeep's speaker system, routed through their walkie-talkie communications array. *"Ben, take a left at the road we came in on."*

Ben nodded, and Julie confirmed. "Archie, you know where to go?"

"I think. And it is 'stadions' — the measurement you are looking for."

Victoria began running some calculations on Julie's phone. Ben shouted over the noise of the engine. "Archie, how do you know?"

"Because I am looking at a map of the region," he replied. *"And this valley, the Valley of the Chachapoyas, is about fifty miles long, end-to-end. It curves in a half-circle around that peak behind us."*

Victoria spoke from the passenger seat. "'A biblical stadion is 183 meters, or 600 feet.' So 297 multiplied by 600 feet gives us 178,200 feet between the pillars. Which is..."

"33.75 miles," Archie said. *"And if you position the temple we just visited on the map and trace a straight line that is 33.75 miles long in a north-south direction from it, you end up in the valley again on the opposite side of the mountain."*

Ben reached the main road and turned left. Julie smiled, even knowing that the fate of their friends might already be out of their hands.

It was hope — only a small amount, but it was hope nonetheless.

CHAPTER 72

BEN

THE ROAD that led toward the eastern side of the Chachapoyas Valley was rugged; potholes dug into the tires of the Jeep and tested its suspension. Ben, however, was not about to slow down. They were close. He knew it.

The farm road was paved, but so much growth and gravel covered it that the only clear way to tell they were still on it was for Ben to follow the gap in the trees, pointing the Jeep toward the break and hoping there were no deathly large holes for a tire to get hung up on.

He wondered how the young kid, the Peruvian man in the backseat of the rear Jeep, was faring. The soldier had proven tough so far, but Ben knew a bumpy ride *away* from civilization and the nearest hospital was not going to help with his injuries. He hoped that Reggie — if they found him — might be able to patch him up a bit.

"Ben," Julie said from the backseat. "We've got company."

He hadn't heard it before, but now the sound was unmistakable. "A *chopper*? Are you serious?" he shouted.

The dark-green heli had been hovering just beyond sight of the road, but it drifted toward them, creeping up menacingly over the treetops. Worse, he saw the sleek-black mounted gun turret hanging beneath the chopper's nose.

"Army?" Ben asked.

"I doubt it," Archie said. *"It looks like a hack job. Black market thing. Very common in this area, but the fact that it still flies means it has been well kept. I would guess those Masons have some very deep pockets."*

"Well, they *did* infiltrate the Vatican," Julie said.

"And that gun's about to infiltrate our faces," Ben added. Everyone in the car turned to look at him. "What? Sorry. First thing that came to mind."

"The angle's wrong for an attack here," Victoria said. "It will have to back up and hit us from the road, but the road's too twisty. And it can't hit us from directly above — the trees are too tall."

"So that means we're safe?" Ben asked.

"No," she said. "That just means they're waiting for us to lead them directly to the other temple. Where there will probably be another clearing."

"... where it will *then* be able to hit us."

"Yeah," she said. "Something like that."

"Can we take potshots at it?" Julie asked.

"You can try to get one through an opening," Ben said. "But its hull will withstand any of our rounds, and the windshield will be bulletproof."

"So we wait and just lead them to the temple," Julie said. "And I'm sure Garza's going to be waiting for us there, too."

"Garza?" Victoria asked.

"Yeah," Ben said. "Asshole. Vicente Garza, but people call him The Hawk. Not sure why, but it has to do with his military background somehow. He runs a paramilitary security group called Ravenshadow."

"Vicente Garza is the man who took your friends?" she asked.

Ben nodded. "And..."

He cut himself off. He met Julie's eyes in the mirror, but couldn't tell if she was concerned for their current situation or thinking about her past. Still, he didn't finish the sentence as he had originally imagined it. While it would have been true, there were too many people listening in — Archie, Victoria, and Etienne, not to mention the Peruvian men. They all didn't need to know Julie's history. It was her story to tell, not his.

She'll come to it in time. She'll realize, and I'll be there for her.

He cleared his throat, feigning a cough. "We — we've just got a bit of a history with him, that's all."

Victoria looked out her window. "I see," she breathed. "I want you to know that I will do whatever it takes to get your friends back."

Ben nodded. "Thank you. That means a lot to me."

"*Whatever* it takes."

CHAPTER 73

BEN

THE CLEARING APPEARED BEFORE THEM, and the second temple complex came into view next. It looked like a mirror-image of the last; the long, rectangular building sat just off the side of the larger, rounded temple. The circus tent-shaped roof loomed over the smaller building, but it was dwarfed by the mountainous cliffs that jutted upward and into the sky.

"There it is," Victoria said. "Archie — you were right."

"Nonsense," the older man's voice sang out through the Jeep's speakers. *"I just happened to be thinking along the right lines first. You would have gotten there within seconds."*

Ben shook his head and smiled. *Academics.* They were a weird mix of pure competitive envy and selfless humility, all wrapped up in an insecure package.

"And we have company again," Archie added.

"I hear it," Ben said, flicking a glance up through the Jeep's open top, trying to pinpoint where the chopper was.

"No, not the chopper," Archie said.

"Ben!" Julie shouted. "Look!"

The temple doors were opening in the distance. Ben squinted, leaning in. The building appeared to be the exact same layout as the first one they'd been in, but Ben saw movement through the two now-open doorways. Men — soldiers — were running out of them. They ducked as they exited, then lifted their weapons, which appeared to be subcompact assault rifles. They took a moment to gain their bearings, then began running toward the Jeeps.

"This isn't good," Victoria said. Her voice was merely a whisper.

"It's okay — there's only a few of them, and I think we've got the firepower to —"

Ben stopped talking. Slammed on the brakes. The Jeep behind them swerved to miss them, then came to a dusty halt next to them.

"What the —"

"Holy mother of God," Julie whispered.

"This... is incredible," Archie said.

Ben saw the men running toward them, saw their hands moving to bring the rifles up to their eyes to take aim, and he knew the truth in that moment.

Those aren't subcompacts. They're not Uzis or assault rifles. Those are full-size machine guns.

And they are absolutely minuscule *in their hands.*

"Wha — what the hell am I looking at?" Ben asked. To him, it seemed that five *extremely large men* — men almost twice the height of himself — were bearing down on him.

Victoria's breathing was loud enough that Ben could hear it over everything. "Those, I believe, are the Nephilim."

JULIE DIDN'T KNOW if she should trust her eyes or if her mind was playing a trick on her. Men — *giants* — had emerged from the two open doors in the temple. Five of them, each carrying a rifle that looked like a miniaturized toy version in their hands. They ran, their feet pounding over the earth, toward the Jeeps.

The giants were still a hundred yards away, but their weapons — full-sized machine guns that should not have been light enough for men to carry — could easily stretch that distance. As if knowing this, and assuming their advantage, they stopped in the middle of the field and kneeled.

"They're getting ready to fire!" Ben shouted, revving the Jeep once again. He put it in gear and released the clutch, slamming the vehicle forward just as the rounds began ripping through the air. The two men on the outsides of the line of giants had reached their destination first and were now sending 50-caliber bullets their direction.

Ben looked over at the second Jeep, driven by one of the Peruvian men, just as one of the soldiers in the backseat glanced back at him. Ben was about to shout an order over the close-range radio — head back to the trees and get out of the Jeeps — when the man's head simply vanished, a tiny cloud of red dispersed in its place.

Etienne Sharpe screamed.

Ben panicked.

He yanked the wheel the opposite direction, causing him and the rest of his passengers to sail sideways until their belts stopped them mid-flight, and he pulled the Jeep harder to the left. The trees were closer on this side, and — more importantly — by moving away from the other Jeep they might be able to split the giants' fire.

He was right, but it didn't matter. There were still three of the five giants firing at them, and two of them were even walking closer as they drove. The trees were twenty yards out.

Then ten.

And then one of the Jeep's tires blew out. The Jeep careened to the right, and Ben tried to pull it back and decelerate, but they were moving too fast. The vehicle bounced, landing directly on top of a small boulder. Ben's teeth clamped down, removing a small piece of his tongue with it.

His mouth was immediately filled with blood, and his vision doubled. The jolt had shaken them all, and he heard Julie groan from the back seat.

He smashed the gas pedal once again, but the car was high-centered. The rear tire, the only one left that hadn't been shot or mounted atop a rock, flinging dust and rocks up as it dug into the soft mud of the valley floor, but it couldn't find enough purchase to launch the heavy Jeep off the rock.

The gunshots continued, and Ben didn't need to turn around to know that the two giants who were walking toward them had halved their distance by now. Another gunshot took out the second back tire, and then another pinged into the back hatch panel.

"Time to go," he shouted, holding his mouth with one hand as he unbuckled his seatbelt with the other. The words slurred, coming out sounding like he was drunk. Victoria and Julie were already moving to unlatch theirs, but the soldier next to Julie hopped up and over the side of the Jeep and crouched beneath the side of the car.

The gunfire from the giant men picked up in intensity, and Ben winced, waiting for one of the massive rounds to remove an equally massive section of his body — or, like the poor man in the other Jeep — his entire head.

"Move!" he shouted. Then: "move to the woods and get behind a tree," Ben said. His voice was low, and he could barely understand his own words. Blood was gushing out around his hand, but the pain had become a dull throb.

They ran together, Ben jumping over another boulder half-sunk into the forest floor, Julie and Victoria weaving left and right around fallen tree trunks that had slid past the edge of the rainforest. The smell of the dense, rich fauna hit Ben's nose and replaced the taste of blood.

He wasn't sure who he was yelling at — no one else needed his instructions. The forest, their only hope at finding cover, was directly in front of them, merely feet away. No one needed to remind him of the literal *monsters* chasing them, and the monster-sized weaponry they were chasing them with.

Three bursted rounds from a machine gun. Three basketball-sized explosions in the dirt next to his feet.

He was only a few feet from the trees when he realized that the 50-cal rounds they were firing wouldn't have any trouble at all smashing through the foliage.

They were sitting ducks.

And they were going to die.

He looked over at Julie as he hurdled the last boulder and was about to enter the woods. Her eyes met his, and they shared a silent sentence between them.

No way out of this.

He nodded.

"I love you."

"I love —"

Julie's body disappeared.

One moment she was there. The next she had ceased to exist.

Ben stood, shellshocked. He tried forming words, a scream, a tear, anything. Nothing. His body seemed to be locked in place.

Unbelieving.

"J — Jules?"

He heard Victoria's voice. Distant. Far away.

The soldier, in the corner of his eye. Saw the man lift his weapon, aiming at him.

No.

Aiming *next* to him.

The weapon bounced slowly in the soldier's hands as he fought back. Ben didn't hear any of it. The rounds flew out of the barrel of the rifle in a surreal, silent volley of fire.

Julie! He couldn't hear his own voice. Had he even yelled? Was it all in his head? *Is this* all *in my head?*

He turned around, slower than he would have liked, but his body was unresponsive. It took an eternity.

He saw the giants walking toward them, firing blasts of high-powered rounds into the world around him.

He saw the Jeep, on fire.

What was left of it. *What the hell?* It was still perched on the rock, all four tires still intact, but two of them flat. The top half of the Jeep's frame, including the seas, steering wheel, doors, and windows were all gone. Smoke billowed out from underneath the vehicle.

"Ben!"

He heard the voice, pounding through his skull. *Or was it just the gunfire?* It was like a song, trance music, pounding out the beat of the bass and kick drum.

"Ben!" the voice again. "Come on!"

Victoria was at his side, and the soldier poked out and around the tree again and fired a few shots, protecting them all.

Covering fire.

Ben didn't look back, but he hoped that meant he had a few extra seconds to get to cover.

He reached the trees, fully enclosed the relative safety of the foliage — at least for a moment. But his own safety was the last thing on his mind.

"Ju — Julie?" he looked around. His head darted back and forth. "Julie!"

"Right there," Victoria said, pointing. He followed her finger. Down, aiming toward a pile of massive leaves that sprung up and outward from a huge bush.

And there, just at the base of the bush, was Julie.

He ran over, his ears still ringing. She was in a heap; her legs curled back underneath her backside, her arms splayed out sideways. But her eyes were open, and she was mouthing words he couldn't hear. There was a gash on her forehead, and her eye looked bruised.

He crouched beside her. "Julie! Are — are you okay?"

"I'm fine," she said. "Hit this big, squishy tree on the way in."

"On the —" he didn't understand, then it came to him. *The Jeep. The explosion.* Julie had been right in front of the Jeep when the giants had hit it, and she must have been thrown into the forest.

"It's actually kind of nice," she said. "But damn if the ride wasn't scary as hell."

He reached down and began to feel around her arms and shoulders, trying to determine whether she had any broken bones. She swatted his hand away. "I'm fine," she said. She pulled herself up, using Ben's outstretched arm as a support.

He paused, taking a breath. The gunshots had slowed. *Did the other guys make it out?* he wondered. *Did Archie get them to safety?*

"You okay?" Julie asked. "You look like you bit half your tongue off."

Ben shrugged. "Maybe a tiny little piece of it. But it hurts like hell. Probably worse than yours."

"I'll call the *wam*bulance," Julie said.

"Mr. Bennett," the soldier said, breaking into Ben's attention. He whirled around and looked at the man still guarding the entrance to the trees.

"What's up?" Ben asked. But he followed the man's gaze and saw *exactly* what was up.

The giants — the five men, larger than life, carrying their larger-than-life weapons, were heading directly into the forest.

The forest on the *opposite* side of the road, where the other Jeep was parked.

The giants had changed their strategy. They'd decided to regroup and send in their entire force, rooting out Archie's team.

The first giant in the line raised his machine gun and started to fire. The rounds blasted out from the tip of his gun, shredding the foliage at the edge of the forest as the man moved.

The second in line followed suit.

"They're too far away to fight back," Victoria said.

The third and fourth giant lifted their weapons as they drew near to the tree line. Ben held his breath. *Please, Archie, tell me you're no longer there. Tell me you moved deeper into the woods.*

He spotted movement. One of the Peruvian men, moving into position.

No.

The man was close — too close.

He saw more movement in the trees. This time two men.

Archie and Sharpe.

They didn't appear to be armed, and they didn't seem to know that *all five* giants were nearing their position.

Move, Archie.

Ben wanted to get the message to him. His walkie-talkie was within range, but he didn't want to risk alerting the enemy to their exact location.

Archie and Sharpe stayed put.

The five giants were now all firing, their rounds cutting the forest down as if they were a lawnmower moving through tiny wisps of grass. Only a few seconds before they would find the first soldier, then Archie and Sharpe.

Only a few seconds until...

The chattering sound of another machine gun, this one twice the speed, reached the clearing. Then the sound of rotor wash, the beating of the massive flying machine betraying its position.

Ben caught sight of the helicopter just as it fell beneath the tree line and into the open valley.

The Masons are here.

THE CHOPPER SAILED into the clearing, its front-mounted gun hot as it sprayed 50-caliber rounds into every square foot of space between it and the giants. It flew forward, impervious to the giants who had abruptly tried to change their target.

The first and second giant were ripped in half. One man's arm fell to the ground, the machine gun falling with it, while the other half of him fell to the side. The second man imploded in on himself, his intestines spilling to the ground moments before the rest of his body followed suit.

Julie's mouth hung open.

I'm watching a battle between a helicopter and giant-sized men welding 50-caliber machine guns, she thought. *I don't think I would have imagined this in my wildest dreams.*

"Come on!" Ben yelled.

Julie took off running, wiping at the open gash on her forehead as she lunged over a felled tree. Ben was fast, but he was big, and she caught up to him in the clearing and ran next to him. Victoria and the soldier were close behind.

There was no communication. No explanation of what Ben's

plan was. She didn't need one. She knew him well enough: someone was in trouble, and he was going to try to help.

Those things didn't always go as planned. But from the day she'd met him, the day she'd stumbled upon Harvey Bennett sitting cooped-up in a corner in a Yellowstone ranger cafeteria, his hair a mess and his eyes bloodshot, she'd known that he was the sort of person who rushed *toward* danger when innocent people were involved, not *away* from it.

He'd tried to save his ranger friend, Carlos Rivera, from falling into a gaping wound in the earth after a devastating thermonuclear explosion. He'd tried to save his own brother and father after a brutal grizzly attack in his youth.

And he'd tried to save her...

Julie stopped.

What is happening?

She was suddenly somewhere else. She'd been transported to... *where?*

She knew this place. She'd been here before.

"Jules!"

Ben's voice echoed in the gymnasium. *That's where I am,* she realized. *A gym. In... Philly.*

"Julie! What are you doing?"

His voice was booming, raging right next to her —

She jolted back into the present. The forest, the humidity, the clearing.

The ricocheting of bullets as they were denied purchase in the chopper's side, the helicopter's own return fire ripping downward and decimating the ground and anything that was in its way.

What the hell was that? she wondered. It was as if her mind had just conjured up a scene from a memory — a movie, almost — that it wanted her to see again. But she wasn't sure if it was *her* memory or someone else's.

They reached the trees on the opposite side of the road where the battle was taking place. Only now it wasn't much of a battle. The giants — and she was sure that's what they were now that she could see them close up — were focused solely on the chopper and its strafing fire as it passed repeatedly above them.

She saw Archie and Sharpe, both firing with their own minuscule-looking weapons at the beasts and the chopper alike.

And she saw something else. In her peripheral vision, as she dodged what appeared to be a giant leg and foot, severed at the knee, and entered the forested cover where the rest of her team was, she saw the temple in the distance.

Men were pouring out of it. Normal, human-sized men.

Ravenshadow.

Julie saw their black outfits, their trained postures and organized lines and knew immediately that she was seeing the bulk of Vicente Garza's forces, now deployed to clean up the mess in the clearing.

They were all carrying assault rifles as well, and they were already firing up at the chopper.

Whatever the chopper's plan was, it was about to get significantly more difficult.

Another second passed, and she changed her mind: a *second* helicopter, a carbon copy of the first, flew over the burnt-out hull of their Jeep and into the clearing, its mounted gun already winding up and firing at the oncoming army of men. Bodies flew upward and out, pieces of weaponry and armor and men exploding and disappearing into nothingness behind walls of dirt and earth.

On the road, mere feet from where she was crouching in the forest, she saw more men — the much smaller army of Guild Rite men — driving toward them.

The problem was that they were driving a *tank.* Men hung off the side of the tank and were piled on top of it like ants on a floating stick. They were dressed like the soldiers they'd come across at the other temple, but wearing white aprons. They too were firing assault rifles, aiming at the giants and the Ravenshadow army.

It was, in a word, appalling. She'd never seen anything like it. The giants, the Ravenshadow men, the tank full of white apron-wearing soldiers.

"Julie," Victoria said. "We're moving to the temple. If Reggie and Sarah are here somewhere, that's where they'll be."

Julie stood up, careful to ensure she was still out of sight of the tank and its men, and followed Victoria and the others. The injured Peruvian was lying on the ground, but two of his fellow soldiers picked him up and carried him between them.

"Stay in the woods," Ben shouted. "We'll be hard to see in here, and both sides are a bit preoccupied now, so I don't think they'll send anyone in looking for us."

The team began their journey — the majority of their short trip would be behind tree cover; it was the last few-hundred feet, from the edge of the rainforest to the temple, that would be wide open.

Julie took a deep breath and plunged ahead.

CHAPTER 76
VICTORIA

VICTORIA'S KNEES were cut and scraped, but she could barely feel it. Their journey through the forest — about a half-mile trip total — was uneventful.

She couldn't say the same about the battle that was waging out in the valley, however. The five giants had been cut down to two, but then *four* more showed up from somewhere beyond the temple where the valley met the cliffs.

There was no way to know how many there were, but Victoria hoped that the nine they'd seen so far was it.

Nine giants.

Nine Nephilim.

She still couldn't believe the Guild Rite had been correct — that these giants were, in fact, Nephilim.

She recalled the verse from the book of Numbers: *"The land that we have gone through as spies is a land that devours its inhabitants; and all the people that we saw in it are of great size. There we saw the Nephilim... and to ourselves we seemed like grasshoppers, and so we seemed to them."*

The Israelites had gone to Canaan to scout the territory and found it to be inhabited by the descendants of Anak, who came from the Nephilim.

She also recalled the other accounts throughout history of giants walking the earth, fighting with men and gods alike, and the stories that came from it.

And here they are, alive. Fighting.

She shook her head in disbelief, but she pushed the thoughts out of her head. There was more to think about now.

Much more.

The battle had slowed, each side entrenching itself and waiting for the opposing forces to drive forward. One chopper had been shot down by a giant, and the other had taken cover hovering over the trees where the Guild Rite was camped.

It had been fifteen minutes since they'd started their trek through the woods, and now they had reached their exit point.

"Okay," Ben said. "On me. You guys —" he pointed to the soldiers — "cover us. We'll run, then turn and cover you."

The injured man nodded, trying to lift his weapon, but Ben stopped him. "You need to stay here. We'll set you up against a rock or tree, but if you go in there, if you try to run they clip you or anything, you might not come back."

He waited for the recognition of understanding, but none came. Archie turned to the young man, still bleeding from a chest wound, and started speaking. The kid's face fell, but he nodded. "Okay," he said.

Sharpe stepped forward. "I'll stay with him."

Ben stared at him. Victoria knew the look. He didn't trust the Interpol agent, but she also knew he didn't have a choice. "Okay," he said. "Keep him alive. He dies, you die."

Sharpe nodded.

If it were up to her, she'd have made the same decision. *I'd rather keep the untrustworthy party as far away from me as I can.*

"On my count," Ben said. "Ready?"

Nods all around.

He counted off one and two, then shouted 'three' a bit louder, crashing out of the forest a moment later. Victoria pumped her sore legs, trying to stay to the right of Ben's large frame. Julie and Archie were right there with him.

A few of the soldiers from Ravenshadow turned and began firing at them, but the Peruvian soldiers hidden in the trees returned the volley of gunfire, driving the Ravenshadow men back into their cover. A burst of chopper fire earned both sides' attention, and the battle resumed.

They reached the open doors of the temple and Ben peered into it.

"It's dark," he said, "but I don't think anyone's there." Victoria saw him palm a round object as he stepped into the temple. *A grenade?*

Victoria followed Julie inside. Dark, damp air, and a musty smell greeted them, tinged with something else. *Metal? Chemicals?* The space appeared to be exactly the same as the temple as the one at the other end of the valley that she'd been in with the Guild Rite.

The walls were rounded, the ceiling vaulted. Hardly any light broke through the doorways that led into the room, but it was enough to see that there were no other nooks or recessed areas to hide in. They were alone.

Until she saw the pillar. There, in the center of the room, on top of the same rounded pillar on its low, wide dais, were two people — a man and a woman. They were stretched and tied down, one of each of their hands tied together above their heads.

Reggie and Sarah.

But it wasn't the two people she was focusing on. Instead, her gaze was pulled upward to a giant steel sheet. It glistened in the light, the silvery and yellowish tone reflecting the sunlight and bouncing it another direction. It was mounted between two guides, both of which hung from a suspended beam that had been erected across the top of the room.

It was brutal, but she knew it had been built for efficiency. She was looking at a modernized version of a guillotine.

Ben stepped forward. "Reggie!"

A voice caught her attention. It came from the *other* doorway, across the temple from them. "I would think twice about approaching the dais, Harvey."

She felt her blood run cold.

Ben froze, and she saw Julie grab his arm. Archie, too, stepped behind Ben.

This can't be happening. I never thought —

"Garza," Ben growled. "What have you done?"

Vicente Garza's heels clapped at the stone floor as he approached them. Sauntering nonchalantly.

"Take a step and I drop the blade. Fire at me and my team drops the blade. It's a simple request, Harvey. We finish this here, but on my terms."

Ben brooded, but none of them moved.

"Have you enjoyed my creation?" he asked. "It was a joint effort, but I trust my benefactors will care little with what I do with the giants after our project is complete."

"They're an abomination," Ben said.

"They're a *masterpiece.* Unfinished, for sure, but *can't you see?* God's hand is in this work! He created these men to *rule!* The only thing missing then — what I provide now — is a leader powerful enough to keep them focused."

"You — killed them."

"No, I gave them a purpose. They worked for me. They knew the risks, and they knew the rewards. Sure, they will probably not last a year, but think of the work that we have completed by then. Future models will not suffer from the osteoporosis and tumors, and —"

He stopped.

Leaned forward a bit, then squinted as he tried to see better in the dark room.

He turned his head to the side, as if not believing what he was seeing.

Finally, he spoke. "Victoria?"

She felt her heart sink. She didn't want to believe it. She'd heard the name, heard the way they spoke of him.

And then she'd seen him and still thought it might be a lie, an act.

But no. He was here.

She stepped up next to Ben and Julie. Hoped she could borrow some of the couples' strength just by being near them.

She took a breath, blinked, then uttered the words she hadn't thought she'd ever say again.

"Hello, Dad."

DAD? What was going on? This woman — Victoria Reyes — was the *daughter* of Vicente "The Hawk" Garza?

And why didn't she say anything?

"Victoria," Garza said. "What the hell are you doing here?"

"I — was kidnapped. By the Guild Rite."

"Guild Rite," he said, chewing on the words. "Is that the group of masons attacking my soldiers outside?"

She nodded. "They're not really masons, but they have ties to them. They're against the Catholic Church. Against the people you're working for."

"I'm *working* for myself, Vic. But they have invested heavily in seeing this project through, and I intend to keep my promises."

He flicked his eyes to Julie. "And I *do* keep my promises, isn't that right, Ms. Richardson?"

Julie didn't respond, but Ben tensed up. "What are you doing here, Garza? With them?"

Garza smiled and shook his head. "Don't you get it? Harvey, my goal was simple: find the *Book of Bones*. Do you happen to have it with you?"

Ben clenched his fist, his white-knuckled grip wanting to reach up and smash through Garza's face. But Garza was smart — smarter than him, at least. And he was good. He might be a formidable opponent against Reggie, but against Ben... well, he didn't like his chances. The man might be older by at least a decade, but he was still in top shape.

Plus, Garza had stopped in the center of the room, about halfway between them and the pillar where Reggie and Sarah were strapped down. Ben couldn't see the details, but it appeared as though their arms had been bound together beneath the massive blade. *A gruesome threat,* Ben thought.

But he had no idea how he could get to Garza before he did whatever he would have to do to drop the blade. Ben couldn't see any button or control surface on Garza's person, but that didn't mean the switch wasn't a tiny, nearly invisible object. And Garza had said that he could have his team drop the blade as well — did that mean they had cameras in here? Were there more soldiers watching in on them now?

"Let them go."

"I asked you a question," Garza said.

"You know the answer to that question. Of course we don't have it. The closest we got was Rome, to the Vatican, but — we failed."

"You didn't find the book there?"

"We failed because there *is* no book."

"That's a lie."

"It's not," Ben said, his voice even. "The Book of Bones, the Dialog of Hermocrates — it's a *myth*. A legend purported by Plato's followers to earn him more recognition. It was a scare tactic, and —"

"That's a lie, because I have the *Book of Bones* back in Philadelphia, on my desk."

Ben swallowed. "Whatever you have, it's not the —"

"It *is*, Ben. Don't you see? This is a game, all of it. My success, the success of my benefactors, my enemies. We're all *maneuvering* around each other, trying to gain purchase, to gain control. *This —*"

he raised his arm and swung it around the temple's interior once — "this is *control*."

"You control nothing, asshole."

"Careful with your choice of words, Harvey." Garza looked over to where Reggie and Sarah were bound to the table. "You saw my army out there. My Ravenshadow forces against a couple choppers and about fifteen men? How do you think that will end?"

"No, you're wrong, Harvey. I *do* have control. Finally, and very soon I will have even more of it. That's what this was all about — the *Book of Bones*, that's *how* I created these people. Break the bone, reset it after injecting the area with a strain of yeast, and then let it grow. Do it again, and again. Add targeted radiation to the affected areas to slow and stunt the growth, and eventually you have a giant.

"The human form is truly remarkable. Able to withstand an *agonizing* amount of adaptation and paid. Skin and muscles regrow, stretch, and eventually move to fit their new skeletal host, with — I'll admit — a *few* minor deformations."

Ben thought about the giants he'd seen in the valley. Their faces seemed sunken, their eyes too small for their heads, their foreheads stretched tightly.

"You already have the *Book of Bones*?" Ben asked. "Then why make us find it for you?"

"Ben," Garza said. "Like I said. This is a *game*. It's being played on an Earth-sized chessboard, and I didn't know exactly who my enemy was."

Ben squeezed his eyes shut as he realized the truth, but it was Archie who spoke up. "We were your pawns. The disposable chess pieces on your board."

"Precisely," Garza said. "By having you find the *Book of Bones*, it drew out the enemy. I was safe to create, to experiment, to grow my army here. But eventually they — this Guild Rite group — found me. You helped a bit with that."

"Etienne Sharpe. He had pieces of Plato's book in the journal he took from us."

"Yes," Garza said. "He was likely the one who led them all here."

Garza took a few steps toward them, now reaching into a pocket and taking out a small, remote control-looking apparatus. *So it is a little button*, Ben thought.

"I don't need to explain what this is, do I? Press it, real quick, that blade falls. Your friends will lose their hands. I was going to use them, to begin the process of creating a couple more members of my *larger* team, if you will, but then... I changed my mind."

"Why?"

"They were going to be my first *breeding pair*. All this talk, all this history about the Nephilim, the 'giants of old,' they were all *men*. Nowhere is there any writing about giant *women*. But there had to be, right? How else would they have populated their world?

"But then I heard that *you* were here, Ben. I heard you brought the whole group, too. Julie, Archibald Quinones, whom I have not had the pleasure of meeting. And, of course, my own daughter."

CHAPTER 78

BEN

VICTORIA SPAT AT HIS FEET.

"How long has it been, Vic? Ten years? Fifteen?"

"You're dead to me."

"I was all you ever had!" Garza shouted.

Victoria sniffed. Ben could sense that the woman was on the edge, on the brink. He wanted to help her somehow, but he knew the risk. He knew what was really at stake. *She'll be fine,* he told himself.

"I loved you!" he continued. "And you, what? Threw it all away for an academic degree?"

"I threw it away when you decided you cared about your own personal gain more than your daughter. Your only family. You're a monster," she said. "You've always been one."

"You know nothing of who I am."

There was a pause, and Ben took that opportunity to get back on track. "So, Garza? What is it? What do you want from us? You've got your book, you've got your little science experiment. What's it going to take for you to let them go? Me?"

Garza laughed. "Ben, you *truly are* naïve. I wondered about you in Philadelphia, and again in The Bahamas. But then I realized: your naivety is *why* you are driven into things like this. You don't *know* the risks, so you rush in headstrong and fearless."

"Get to the point, Garza. Me for them?"

"No, no. That's just it. The thing about *control* is there's no reason for any *negotiation*. I hold the cards, Harvey. And I intend to play my hand to the very end."

Ben realized just then that the fighting outside had come to an end. *Not good.* It meant that one of the sides had prevailed. Either was bad for him, as both sides were against him.

A few soldiers appeared in the doorway Garza had come through. *Ravenshadow.* Another handful approached the temple from Ben's doorway. They were still holding their weapons, and Ben caught sight of two giants, their faces and bodies a mangled mess of blood, walking toward the temple.

They were now trapped inside the temple with Garza, his private army surrounding them.

"Harvey," Garza said. "I wanted you *here*. I waited for you. I put my experiment with your friends on hold so you could *enjoy* this with me. Please, if you would direct your attention to —"

Ben rushed forward, aiming for Garza. Garza's eyes had flicked sideways toward the pillar, and Ben took the only opportunity he thought he had. A second more and the Ravenshadow forces would be inside.

Garza didn't see the attack coming until it was too late, but he was able to turn to the side so as not to take the blow head-on. Ben nailed him in the hip, and the two went down.

He heard Julie yell from behind him. "Get to the sides!" she shouted. "Away from the doors! Go around, then toward the pillar."

Garza landed a hard blow to Ben's side, and Ben let out a gasp. He loosened his grip on Garza's shirt, and the two men wrapped up in a wrestling match. Ben tried lancing out with his fists, but Garza's training was able to easily parlay the attacks to his own advantage.

One such punch Ben tried to land left his arm outstretched, and Garza immediately smashed his elbow through Ben's forearm. Ben cried out in pain as the bone inside snapped, and he felt his body instinctively move to the defensive.

He rolled off Garza, holding his wounded arm.

Garza kicked him, hard, in the stomach. Ben felt the air escaping his lungs. His vision started to fade.

Before he could fall to the stone floor, he started to hear the gunshots. The Ravenshadow men were in the room, firing at his team.

And before he could get his bearings, Garza ripped upward on a handful of his hair, pulling Ben's head back. He screamed in fury and pain, but he couldn't control his own body as he stood, propelled upward by Garza's force.

When he was fully standing, Garza hit him again, right in the spleen, with a tight, sharp pointed fist. Ben winced and his body collapsed, but Garza was still holding his hair.

Suddenly Vicente Garza's face was next to Ben's ear. His breath was hot and ragged, but he was not breathing more heavily than he had been before. The skirmish had no effect on the man whatsoever.

"Harvey," he said. "I think you are done making mistakes. I think you are *finally* ready to experience what it feels like to be *out of control.*"

He whipped Ben around and pointed his face at the pillar in the center of the room. Ben saw his team against the wall on the side of the temple. They hadn't made it to the pillar yet. Their arms were up, the soldiers who'd rushed in quickly subduing them.

"Are you ready, Harvey?" Garza asked. "Are you ready to watch your friends suffer for *your* stupidity?"

Garza lifted the tiny one-button device and held it out in front of him.

He waited two seconds, then pressed the button.

Reggie and Sarah screamed, and Ben thought he heard the sounds of Julie and Archie shouting something as well.

Ben heard a deep *thunk* as the blade fell from its harness and began its descent toward the altar.

CHAPTER 79
REGGIE

REGGIE SCREAMED, but his own voice was drowned out by the *clunk* sound of the guillotine's blade-release latch. It lifted from its enclosure, dropping the heavy, steel blade.

He had been silent during Garza's and Ben's interaction. Waiting, listening. He wanted to fight, but he knew there was little he could do from here.

They'd gotten lucky before. He and Sarah had listened as the terrifying countdown clock had hit '*one second.*' He'd waited for the inevitable fall of the blade, but none came. In fact, *nothing* came. They'd waited, shaking, unable to do anything at all but contemplate their own fate.

At the time, Reggie had just assumed it was a final method of torture. A way Garza could exert his power over them. Make them wait until the countdown hits *one*, anticipating the blade's fall. And then... nothing. It would happen later, at a time they'd least expect it.

But nothing had happened. They'd remained bound to the stone table, their wrists tied together. For hours they wondered when it would happen.

And then Ben and Julie ran into the room. Archie was there too, he'd heard. He couldn't see any of them, but he knew there was a newcomer, a woman named Victoria.

And then Garza, and then the soldiers and the gunshots. Ben and Garza were fighting, and then Garza won.

And then he pressed the button.

Reggie looked up as the blade began to fall, and he knew what he had to do.

Reggie tried bending his knees, using whatever small amount of give he had in the straps. It was enough.

He launched himself *toward* Sarah, toward the space where the descending blade would land. He felt like a slow-motion Superman, one hand straight above his head as he flew. He pushed himself toward the opposite side of the table, Sarah's wrist moving with him.

Her wrist moved away from the blade as Reggie's moved toward it.

The blade was a foot above him now. His face was right there, right in front of it as it fell. He saw his own reflection in the blade's polished steel, a falling mirror showing himself his own terror.

It brushed past his face, mere inches from his nose.

And continued falling, *right through his right arm.*

He screamed, but there was no pain. Not at first.

The blade severed his upper arm, a few inches below his shoulder. There was blood, but less than he would have thought. *Maybe that comes later. Maybe it's so clean there won't be any.*

He'd never thought about it before.

The blade stopped with a sharp *click* and a louder scraping sound as it impacted the stone slab beneath his arm. For a moment, everything fell silent. He heard nothing else but the sound of his own heartbeat.

He dared a glance up, a glance at the blade that was now separating him and Sarah. His face was a mix of confusion and surprise, his eyes registering shock. *Is that what this is?* he thought. *Am I in shock?*

He looked at his arm. The blade's sinister mirror reflected what he was hoping not to see: the place where his arm should have been was a circle of red, a large white dot in the center.

And then there was blood. *Lots* of it. It poured out from his shoulder-circle and pooled next to his face, on his face. A disgusting amount of it. Deep crimson. He could smell it, then he could taste it.

There was screaming. *Sarah?* But she sounded far away.

And then, the ultimate realization: Garza was standing over him now, close enough to grab with his free hand. *My only hand.*

And finally he realized:

My upper body is no longer strapped down.

He pulled himself up, out of the blood and gore of his own wound, and roared out of pure adrenaline.

Garza's eyes widened, but Reggie had already begun reaching for the man's face. He aimed for one of those wide eyes. Grabbed one with a finger, dug in pulling the man's head toward his face.

Garza screamed in pain, but Reggie kept pulling. Garza's head smacked against the stone table, sideways, one of his eyes pushed sideways as Reggie's forefinger dug into it.

And then, *pop.* Reggie removed his finger from the man's eye, taking whatever he could hold on to with it.

And then Reggie collapsed.

"GET OUT!" Julie yelled, aiming her words at Ben. "Go! Now!"

The others were already on their way. Archie had grabbed Reggie and was hauling him out the doorway. He'd cut the straps binding his feet and had lifted him in a fireman's carry over his shoulder.

Victoria and Julie had gone for Sarah, who was screaming and frantic but otherwise fine. She had a gunshot wound between her shoulder blades, but it seemed to be healing well and was currently bandaged.

Ben had started toward Garza, but Julie interrupted his movement with her yell. He seemed confused at first, but a few gunshots from the Ravenshadow soldiers snapped him back to life.

He turned and ran, quickly moving out of the center of the room. The soldiers fired back, but Julie was already tracking their movements. She fired three quick bursts, and the two on Ben's tail fell. Another burst and one more soldier fell.

Their luck would turn — these were well-trained mercenaries, and if it weren't for the surprised attack on their leader at the center of the room, and the obvious chaos that ensued, they might all be dead by now. So Julie needed to get them all out of the temple and back to the forest.

The doorway was twenty paces away, and Archie and Reggie were already almost there. She ran along as well, holding Sarah on one shoulder and firing her weapon with the other. They would make it to the door a few seconds behind Ben, who was halfway there already.

But then the doorway's light was blocked. Julie frowned, trying to make sense of what had happened. It was as if a massive stone had been rolled in front of the opening, blocking out the light.

And then that stone moved.

A giant. His body was bleeding, his face a distorted mess of flesh. He stepped through the doorway and into the temple, right in front of Archie and Reggie.

Oh, no.

The giant lifted his weapon and pointed it down at the pair. Julie wanted to fight him off, but there three soldiers moving to her right that she was tracking in her peripheral vision, waiting for a clear shot.

The giant's weapon raised slightly, and Julie winced, knowing what was coming next. Archie lifted his own weapon, but too slowly.

The giant fired.

Archie fell, Reggie landing on top of him.

And then the giant reared back, his head up. He stumbled backward, then out of the temple.

The Peruvians.

Julie saw a man run past the doorway, behind the giant, firing up at it as he did. The giant's attention was pulled in the other direction, however, from where there were more rounds being fired at it. The giant fell to one knee, but began firing his machine gun toward the trees.

Julie saw Ben scoop up Reggie, then help Archie to his feet. The older man was bleeding, but Julie wasn't sure if it was a bullet wound or something related to his fall. She didn't care, at the moment. They were almost at the doorway, and she intended to get them all through it safely.

Outside, the giant wavered and hit the ground, now on both knees. He tried looking over his shoulder at the first Peruvian soldier, but was suddenly thrown down onto his face with the blast of an explosion.

Grenade, Julie thought. *A perfect shot.*

The giant's body heaved and lurched, then fell still. Bullets still impacted the man's body, but he never got up.

They were at the doorway now, and Julie and Victoria, carrying Sarah, stumbled through it after Ben and Reggie. Archie was close behind her, and then they were outside.

The sounds immediately shifted, now thin, distant *tapping* sounds from the rifles instead of heavy, dull thuds. They would chase them, but at least they had a chance at getting away. Julie had only seen ten men, and at least three of those she'd shot. The Peruvian soldiers were now behind them, firing into the temple as the Ravenshadow troops tried to escape. The situation had turned to their favor — it was much easier keeping the enemies inside the temple.

Ben reached the edge of the forest and set Reggie down on the ground. He turned to Julie. "We've got a problem," he said.

Julie helped Victoria get Sarah to her feet, but by this time she was almost able to walk on her own. She quickly checked her bandage and then turned to where Ben was pointing.

Where the injured young Peruvian soldier had been with Agent Etienne Sharpe, there was now no one. The depressed spot in the foliage where they'd laid the man was still there, a slight indentation in the leaves in the shape of a man's body.

"Where are they?" Ben asked.

"I have no idea," Julie said, trying to catch her breath. "But we can't worry about that now. We have to get —"

"Hey!" Julie heard a man's voice, far off in the distance, shouting. Then she heard an engine running at a high speed. She turned to look.

It was the Jeep. Plowing toward them from the middle of the valley, driven by Sharpe.

"Well, I didn't expect that," Ben said.

Etienne waved, then shouted again. "Let's go!" he said. "Hurry!"

Julie helped Sarah to her feet, holding her arm as they once again exited the forest. Ben and Reggie shuffled forward, and Archie waited next to them. The Jeep swung around hard, revealing the driver's side to them, the temple and mountain behind it. Ben wasted no time, and they got everyone aboard in a few seconds. Ben and Julie had to ride on the side rails, but they held on to the upper frame of the Jeep as Sharpe accelerated away.

A few bullets landed around them, smacking into trees and heavy leaves, but the soldiers were still cowering inside the temple, effectively being held off by the Peruvians, who were now hunkered down in the same natural trench the Ravenshadow men had used against the Guild Rite forces.

"Where's the kid?" Ben yelled down at Sharpe. "He's injured — you can't just leave him —"

"He's fine," Sharpe yelled back. "He's waiting for the rest of his friends to get back far enough."

"To what?"

The Peruvian soldiers in the valley stood up, and Julie watched as they backpedaled away from the temple even more, allowing the Ravenshadow soldiers to sneak out of the temple a few steps. They lined the walls outside the temple, and a few began running toward the smaller rectangular building.

As they ran, Julie heard a deafening *boom*. She whipped her head around, trying to see the source of the blast. Her eyes were on the temple, waiting for Garza or a giant to emerge with some sort of massive new weapon they hadn't seen before, but instead she saw something else entirely.

The temple doorway the soldiers had emerged from *exploded* in a fury of fire and dirt. Stones and bodies flew outward, then fell to the ground.

Julie turned again and finally saw it. *The tank.*

"I told you," Sharpe said. "He was just waiting for his comrades to get out of the way."

Julie smiled. *He's in the tank.*

Sharpe continued, aiming the Jeep across the vast expanse of the valley toward the road they'd come in on. "He said he was too injured to drive anything, but that he might be able to figure out how to shoot the tank. We got him in and situated. I'd say he did all right."

"Yeah," Ben shouted. "I'd say he did just fine."

BEN

THE RIDE back to civilization took longer than Julie would have expected, but part of the problem was that she, Ben, and one of the soldiers had to ride outside the Jeep, hanging on with an arm clamped over a bar. After half an hour of driving like this, they stopped at the first sign of civilization they could find: a corner store with a single gas pump.

The owner was working when they arrived, and the Peruvian soldiers developed a rapport with the man until he was persuaded to let them borrow his own vehicle.

They put the injured man in the back of that truck and the men followed behind the Jeep until they reached the town of Chachapoyas where they pulled off and headed a different direction. In the small city, Agent Etienne Sharpe was able to find a private flight using his Interpol credentials, and the team — now seven in total — split again. Reggie and Sarah, aided by a doctor they'd called on the way to town, were driven to a regional hospital where they could be examined and patched up as much as possible.

Ben had wanted to go with them, but Julie had talked him out of it. She wasn't sure what Sharpe and Archie might add to their discussion, and they needed to get a handle on the situation and prepare a report for Mr. and Mrs. E. Besides, Julie said, Reggie was sedated, and he probably would be for at least a day. Sarah Lindgren promised she would call when he was feeling better.

So Ben had reluctantly climbed aboard the large twin prop aircraft, bound for Lima. Due to the heavier load and the smaller plane, the flight would take about three hours.

Worse, it was loud inside, and the noise-canceling headphones they were given did little to block out the wash of the propellors. However, they each had a built-in microphone they could use to communicate during the flight.

So while it was impossible to sleep during the trip, the head-phones gave them time to catch up, to exchange pieces of their stories, and helped Ben craft a narrative for what had happened over the last few days.

"Sharpe," he said, his voice still tight and focused, not wanting to let his guard down around the man. "How long have you been part of the Guild Rite?"

Sharped looked up, thinking. "It's been a long time. I started right out of school. I was interested in the Freemasons, and somehow ended up finding my way to a Guild Rite meeting. Never really thought about it much until the initiation."

"It was different than you expected?"

"It was... real. Rather than some weird fraternity-style tradition, the Guild Rite *vetted* me. Interviewed me. Asked my about my beliefs and somehow knew the answers already. It wasn't hard at all, just... different. I think *they* were looking for *me*. My new role at Interpol was absolutely a factor."

"You did them favors?"

"I was part of their group. Yes. But it was never like the mafia or anything that — I liked them. And they were really interested in the things I was: history, politics, world religion. And they knew *so much*. It was like each of them was a library of world history, only not from the perspectives we have all heard before."

"'History books are written by the victors?'" Ben asked. "Or something like that?"

"Exactly. These men were able to back up their claims, too — that the world was under the authority of the Catholic Church and its offspring political systems, and that it had been for centuries. That the Bible and so many other ancient texts had been written as *histories*, not just as allegorical devices."

"So you were on the same page?"

"I was, but... I never really thought they would take it this far. I came with them here because I truly believed in their cause — that they were on to something enormous. It would change history."

"It definitely will," Archie said.

"But then... after you showed up..." he looked at Victoria. "I realized what they had done. They crossed the line."

"You didn't know about the plane crash?" Julie asked. "That they tried to kill us in Corsica?"

"No," Sharpe said, his head down. "Nor did I expect that they were so far up as the Vatican. We are a *very* secretive organization. Unlike the Masons which is an organization *with* secrets, we exist *because* of secrets. Truths, hidden from its own membership, even members hidden from one another."

"Dealing with something this profound, I'm sure it made sense at the time."

"Of course," Sharpe said. "But I *never* intended to hurt anyone. They gave me a gun — I have been trained to use them, after all — but they expected me to use it on *you*."

"Well," Ben said. "We truly appreciate you *not* using it on us."

Sharpe smiled, but Ben could tell he was still feeling awful about the entire thing.

"And you lost friends today, I'm assuming."

Sharpe nodded. "Though nothing can justify what they were trying to do."

"No, perhaps not. But that's all in the past. We need to focus on moving forward."

"Your organization is still alive, yes?" Victoria said.

"I — I suppose," Sharpe said. "We were rumored to have more than 10,000 members. Stretching back to antiquity, past Solomon's temple and Hiram Abiff and past Euclid himself. Back to the original Nephilim."

"Bene Elohim," Victoria said. "The powerful ones."

"Exactly. Like many translations, time and language has distorted some true meanings."

"Dieter Luthig," Victoria said. "Is he your leader? Someone with power?"

Sharpe looked confused, then his eyes focused. "No," he said. "The Guild Rite likes to hide truths in plain sight."

Victoria looked away, out the window, then turned back to Sharpe. "*Dieter Luthig. The Guild Rite.*"

Sharpe smiled. He nodded once.

"It's an anagram. And the rest of his website is probably written in code as well."

"Just like the original writers of the biblical knowledge of the Nephilim and who they were. They wanted the truth, and they wanted it in plain sight. But they wanted to protect it as well."

"That's why Plato's third dialog was written," Victoria said. "He stopped working on *Critias* mid-sentence because he discovered the truth. Something so compelling that he *had* to finish *Hermocrates.* He couldn't *not* write it."

"And he chose to protect it as well," Sharpe said. "That is why it has been so difficult to find. We think there is only one remaining copy."

"Garza's copy, wherever that is," Ben added.

"Yes. But there are more — many more."

"They're just hiding in plain sight," Victoria said. "Encoded in some way, disguised as something else."

"The original message of the Atlanteans, the descendants of the Nephilim, and encoded by the Guild Rite."

Ben shook his head. It was all too much. He believed it — he had no reason *not* to believe it — but this was all out of his element. He wanted to just read it in a book, have it all presented to him in an easy-to-digest way.

But that wasn't going to be possible — they would solve this together, putting the pieces together until it made sense enough to know what to do next.

He pulled his shirt down from his neck a bit to get more comfortable, then turned back to the discussion. He knew what the answer was, but he didn't want to admit it to himself.

Unfortunately, when he looked back into the plane, Julie caught his gaze. She raised an eyebrow, and he knew what he was going to say.

"We're alive now, thankfully. We got away, but we still have a *major* problem."

He turned to Victoria expecting her face to be showing something other than agreement, but she was nodding along.

"We need to find Garza."

CHAPTER 82
BEN

TWO DAYS Later

Ben sat up straighter, something in the back of his mind pushing forward, begging for attention.

The cabin's work crews had gone home for the day, and he and Julie were watching a rerun of a show they'd seen a few times before. They had flown directly to Alaska after their trip to Peru, and were home for the first time in a week. Mr. and Mrs. E had been working on the report the team had filed — mostly just a collection of anecdotes and opinions mixed in with the factual information. They wanted to keep a record of their interactions, both for their own protection as well as for future opportunities.

Victoria Reyes was staying at the cabin temporarily, working through her own issues. She ate meals with the group, but mostly stayed to herself. She had been writing almost nonstop since they'd arrived, informing Ben that she wanted to record her thoughts before the shock of it all wore off. They gave her the space she needed, understanding what it was she was going through.

Julie was curled up on the couch, her head tucked onto Ben's shoulder and her feet crunched up beneath her. They watched the show, but Ben knew neither of them was really into it.

A commercial began playing, and Ben muted the television. Julie pulled her head up slowly, yawned, then looked at Ben. "Everything okay?"

"I was just thinking," he said.

"Oh, no," she said, laughing.

"No, no, it's good. I think."

"I told you not to think," Julie said. "It gives you a headache."

Ben rolled his eyes. "It's about the Temple of Solomon."

"*That's* what you're thinking about? Not me? I thought when you were quiet like that you were *always* thinking about me."

Ben chuckled. "Is that so? Well, I'd say it's about 80-20."

"Eighty percent thinking about me?"

Ben paused, considering it for a long second. "Uh, yeah. Sure."

She socked him on the shoulder. "Okay, smart guy. What about the Temple of Solomon?"

"Well, I think we missed something. I know we weren't there for sightseeing, but remember Egypt? The Great Sphinx, and the —"

"The Hall of Records," Julie said, interrupting him. "You're thinking it's the Temple of Solomon?"

"Yeah, I am. The original temple was sacked by Nebuchadnezzar, and then —"

"Look at you, getting all 'history professor' on me," Julie said, taking the opportunity during the commercial break to sip at her glass of wine.

"I read Victoria's report," Ben said. He shrugged. "Bet you didn't know I could read."

Julie snorted as she laughed, and a bit of wine dribbled down her chin, which made her laugh even more. Ben joined in, and then he grabbed her chin and kissed her.

"Wh — what are you doing?" Julie asked. "I'm covered in wine."

"Never thought you looked more beautiful," Ben said.

"Give me a break. My hair's wet from the shower, and I'm wearing sweatpants. *Sweatpants*, Ben."

"Yeah, they make your butt look great, too." Ben reached out and grabbed her hand. "You know what? Never mind about the Temple of Solomon stuff. I lied."

"You haven't figured something out?"

"Oh, I figured something out about it, but it can wait. I lied about *how much* I was thinking about it."

Julie's eyes narrowed.

"I was *mostly* thinking about you. About us."

One of her eyebrows raised back up. "Go on."

"We're not going to stop. The CSO. It's sort of taken on a life of its own, and I... well, I guess there's never going to be a *perfect* time, so..."

"What are you saying, Ben?"

"Well, I was thinking. No matter what happens, I want to be with you. We've tried making that official, twice —"

"Three times."

"Right, three times now. And I'm tired of having bad guys and almost getting killed preventing us from tying the knot."

"Oh, really? You're not a fan of saltwater crocodiles and attack helicopters?"

"I could do without those for a while."

"I'm listening."

"Jules, why don't we just *do* it. Invite our close friends, family, whoever. No frills, no destination wedding, none of that. Just you and me, and a... whatever the guy... the preacher man —"

"He's called an *officiator*, Ben."

"Right. One of those guys. Is that — okay? I mean, I want you to have the ultimate wedding, with princess castles and really fancy flowers, and all the expensive tableware, and —"

"Ben, I love it."

"You do?" he asked.

"Of course I do. I never wanted any of that other stuff. It's all extra. And do I seem like a princess to you?"

He laughed. "I guess not. Anyway, I thought maybe we could just do it here. At the cabin. If... that's okay with you."

"I love that idea."

Julie crawled over the couch to Ben and inserted her head right onto his shoulder, where it had been before. "I just want to be *married*."

"Why? So you can take all my money?"

"Yeah, Ben. That's it. So I can take all your money."

"Good. Jokes on you, I don't have any."

She brought his head down to hers and kissed him, then through pursed lips mumbled the words, "shut up."

EPILOGUE

THREE WEEKS **Later**

"Hey, brother — how you feeling?" Ben asked as he entered the room. Reggie was in the new CSO wing attached to the cabin, and his personal bedroom had been converted into a makeshift hospital. After surgery in Peru and Anchorage, Mr. E had flown out three medical professionals to assist with Reggie's recovery.

The two doctors and nurse, as well as Dr. Sarah Lindgren, looked up. They were taking turns checking spots on Reggie's body for nerve function, and the nurse was observing an IV drip nearby. Reggie couldn't move his head that far around, but Ben saw his eyes widen.

"Ben? That you?"

"Yep."

"Man, I never thought I'd see you again. I figured you ditched me. You know, remember how you left me in a jungle and then they chopped my arm off?"

Ben's mouth opened. "I — I didn't... Reggie, I can't ever tell you how sorry —"

Reggie started laughing, the swells rising in volume until he was nearly choking. One of the doctors, unamused, put a hand on Reggie's chest to calm him down.

"Oh man," Reggie said. "You should see your face right now! Ha!"

"That's... really not funny," Ben said.

"I have to agree with Ben on this one," Sarah said. "And you have to stop getting yourself worked up like that. You'll injure yourself."

"My *arm* got chopped off. I'm not dying."

"Well, that's good news," Ben said. "They — think you're going to be fine?"

"*More* than fine." Reggie used his left hand to pick up the right side of his sheet, showing off a firmly bandaged shoulder. Ben could see it wiggling beneath the gauze pad. "The little nubby in here is almost cleaned up, and it's healing fine. They'll be able to fit me for a prosthetic in a few days, and then I become *bionic*.

"Ben — you gotta see some of these arms they're making now. They can have built-in weapons. *Weapons*, Ben."

The doctor and the nurse turned and gave Ben a look of exasperation. "He'll be fitted for a *standard* prosthetic, Mr. Bennett, and then we can see about including myoelectrics and running sensors to test if targeted muscle reinnervation is needed, and then —"

"It's gonna be *cool*, Ben," Reggie said. "Watch. I'll be shooting lasers from my fingers in a month. Garza was right — it was a clean cut."

Sarah's head fell, and she turned away slightly. Ben caught it and turned to her. "You doing okay?" He placed a hand on her shoulder.

Sarah placed her hand on Ben's and nodded, wiping away a tear. "Yeah. The bullet wound is totally healed. No negative reactions with the... whatever it was they were poisoning me with. I think because Garza wanted us as an experiment later, he made sure the doctors kept the area from getting infected."

"Good to hear. Again, I cannot tell you how —"

"Ben, please," she said, sniffing. "We're *alive* because of you guys."

"Yeah," Reggie said. "Who knew there were *two* of those stupid, weird temple thingies."

"I guess," Ben said. "Still, I wish could have known."

"Julie mentioned you have some other thoughts? About the Temple of Solomon?"

Ben nodded. "I do. But that can wait. I've got another mission for you."

Reggie's slid his head sideways, wincing a bit at the movement. "Yeah?"

"Yeah."

"Something cool? You figure out where Garza is?"

Ben shook his head. "Still working on that."

"What's the mission? I can get these docs off my back, if you're worried about that."

"I'm not worried about that, buddy," Ben said. "And actually, you won't need your arm for it."

"I'm intrigued."

"Yes, Ben," Dr. Lindgren said. "Are you sure it's a good idea to get him back in the field so soon?"

"What?" Ben asked, mock surprise on his face. "I never told you what it was I want him to do!" He paused, then walked closer to Reggie's bed. The doctor and the nurse shifted away from the bed. He'd already cleared it with them, and he thought he caught a smile on the nurse's face as he moved away.

"It's going to be harder than anything you've ever done," Ben continued. "And... I'm not sure you'll be able to pull it off. It involves a serious amount of work on your part, work that I'm not sure you've ever done before."

"I can do it," Reggie said. "Just tell me."

"Okay," Ben sighed. "Gareth Red, I need a best man."

AFTERWORD

If you liked this book (or even if you hated it...) write a review or rate it. You might not think it makes a difference, but it does.

Besides *actual* currency (money), the currency of today's writing world is *reviews*. Reviews, good or bad, tell other people that an author is worth reading.

As an "indie" author, I need all the help I can get. I'm hoping that since you made it this far into my book, you have some sort of opinion on it.

Would you mind sharing that opinion? It only takes a second.

Nick Thacker

READY FOR MORE?

Get your copy of The Cain Conspiracy today!

BOOKS BY NICK THACKER

Jake Parker Thrillers

Containment (Book 1)

The Patriot (Book 2)

False Allegiance (Book 3)

Six Assassins Thrillers

Primary Target (Book 1)

Subtle Target (Book 2)

Unstable Target (Book 3)

Captive Target (Book 4)

Vendetta Target (Book 5)

Final Target (Book 6)

Mason Dixon Thrillers

Mark for Blood (Book 1)

Death Mark (Book 2)

Mark My Words (Book 3)

Harvey Bennett Mysteries

The Enigma Strain (Book 1)

The Amazon Code (Book 2)

The Ice Chasm (Book 3)

The Jefferson Legacy (Book 4)

The Paradise Key (Book 5)

The Atlantis Artifact (Book 6)

The Book of Bones (Book 7)

The Cain Conspiracy (Book 8)

The Mendel Paradox (Book 9)

The Minoan Manifest (Book 10)

The Napoleon Job (Book 11)

The Embers of Siwa (Book 12)

Harvey Bennett Mysteries - Books 1-3

Harvey Bennett Mysteries - Books 4-6

Harvey Bennett Mysteries - Books 7-9

Jo Bennett Mysteries

Temple of the Snake (written with David Berens)

Tomb of the Queen (written with Kristi Belcamino)

Harvey Bennett Prequels

The Icarus Effect (written with MP MacDougall)

The Severed Pines (written with Jim Heskett)

The Lethal Bones (written with Jim Heskett)

Gareth Red Thrillers

Seeing Red

Chasing Red (written with Kevin Ikenberry)

The Lucid

The Lucid: Episode One (written with Kevin Tumlinson)

The Lucid: Episode Two (written with Kevin Tumlinson)

The Lucid: Episode Three (written with Kevin Tumlinson

Standalone Thrillers

The Atlantis Stone

The Depths

Relics: A Post-Apocalyptic Technothriller

Killer Thrillers (3-Book Box Set)

Short Stories

I, Sergeant

Instinct

The Gray Picture of Dorian

Uncanny Divide (written with Kevin Tumlinson and Will Flora)

ABOUT THE AUTHOR

Nick Thacker is a thriller author from Texas who lives in Colorado and Hawaii, because Colorado has mountains, microbreweries, and fantastic weather, and Hawaii also has mountains, microbreweries, and fantastic weather. In his free time, he enjoys reading in a hammock on the beach, skiing, drinking whiskey, and hanging out with his beautiful wife, tortoise, two dogs, and two daughters.

In addition to his fiction work, Nick is the founder and lead of Sonata & Scribe, the only music studio focused on producing "soundtracks" for books and series. Find out more at SonataAndScribe.com.

For more information, visit Nick online:
www.NickThacker.com
nick@nickthacker.com

facebook.com/AuthorNickThacker
twitter.com/NickThacker